CHOCOLATE JUNGLE

A Sedona Chi Mystery

A Sedona Chi Mystery

CHOCOLATE JUNGLE

A GRIPPING CHASE FROM THE WILDS OF THE YUCATAN
JUNGLE TO THE STUNNING RED BUTTES OF SEDONA

PAUL JOHNSON

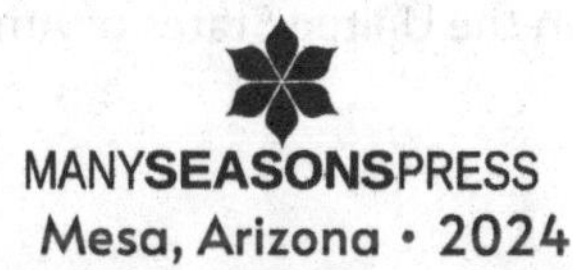

MANY**SEASONS**PRESS
Mesa, Arizona • 2024

FIRST EDITION

Chocolate Jungle; A Sedona Chi Mystery
A gripping chase from the wilds of the Yucatan
Jungle to the stunning red buttes of Sedona

Series: A Sedona Chi Mystery - Book 3

Copyright © 2024 Paul Johnson

MANYSEASONSPRESS

Published by Many Seasons Press
an Imprint of Multimedia Publishing Project
123 N. Centennial Way, Suite 105
Mesa, Arizona 85201
480-939-9689 | ManySeasonsPress.com

Book designed by Yolie Hernandez
(AZBookDesigner@icloud.com)

Paperback ISBN: 978-1-956203-54-7
eBook ISBN: 978-1-956203-55-4

Library of Congress Control Number: 2024940297

Cover picture of Chocolate cup, A.D. 600–800 - Late Classic - Maya
Ceramic with polychrome slip
h. 17.6 cm., diam. 17.9 cm. (6 15/16 x 7 1/16 in.)
Princeton University Art Museum. Museum purchase,
Fowler McCormick, Class of 1921, Fund 2002-9
Image courtesy of the Princeton University Art Museum.

Printed in the United States of America.

Contents

PROLOGUE
The Red Queen

IN 1994, A YOUNG ARCHEOLOGIST DOING REPAIR WORK AT *PALENQUE,* a Mayan ruin in Chiapas, near the Guatemalan border, spied a crack in the stone stairway of Temple XIII. Temple XIII was minor compared to the elaborately decorated Temple of Inscriptions next to it, where *Pakal* the Great's burial chamber had been discovered five decades earlier.

The crack opened into a narrow passageway that led to a sealed door. Outside the door were signs that Mayan priests had performed elaborate death rituals, including the remains of skeletons. *Pakal* the Great himself had likely overseen the sacrifice of a young woman and man to serve the person inside on their journey to the underworld. Jewelry made of precious jade, obsidian ear spools, weaving spindles, and figurine whistles were placed around the couple for their use.

Suspecting a fragile burial chamber beyond the sealed door, the archeologist made a small opening above it and shined a lamp on the long-lost scene. The chamber was tiny. The light revealed steps leading to a room occupied by a sarcophagus covered in red cinnabar. It was a spectacular find; Maya used cinnabar as a preservative in royal burials. Whoever was entombed in the temple was a king or queen.

Later, once inside, a drinking vessel was found by the archeologist on the first step leading into the burial chamber. Simple in design, the vessel was six inches tall, had no handle, and had a rounded bottom. The vessel, or cup, was decorated with two rings of geometric patterns, and carved around the lip was an indecipherable Mayan inscription. The archeologist carefully set it aside in her rush to reach the sarcophagus.

It took a hydraulic lift to raise the lid of the sarcophagus. A red-stained skeleton, a woman, was lying on her back, her bones permeated with red cinnabar. She was Queen *Tz'aakb'u*, the wife of *Pakal* the Great. She had died in 672 AD, eleven years before her celebrated husband. Jade beads formed a headband around her skull. Maya priests had covered her torso with a golden vest, adorned with more jade and obsidian spools. A mosaic of greenish blue malachite formed a death mask. To the archeologist, the Queen's expression seemed tired, as if she were bored by the tedious proceedings that accompanied her internment.

In 2021, a new exhibit opened at the *Museo de Sitio de Palenque*. Museum officials had dedicated Room Three to the funerary practices of the ancient Maya. The Red Queen and the offerings left to her were displayed along with artifacts from her burial chamber.

The drinking vessel with the strange inscription was included in the exhibit, sitting in a glass case behind the Queen.

PALENQUE

GABOR COCOM WAS A GUARDIAN OF HIS PEOPLE'S PAST. HE TOOK immense pride in living up to the traditional meanings of his Mayan name. Though small in stature, he embraced being the *brave man who listens carefully*. Earlier, Gabor had been in a cantina keeping his drunken cousins from making fools of themselves. With pesos in their pockets from their excavation jobs raping their shared heritage, they had been in the cantina for hours drinking cheap *balché*. It was there he overheard plans to steal the Red Queen's cacao vessel. The royal vessel from which she ceremonially drank the sacred chocolate.

A team of Guatemalans, drug dealing scum from the south, Gabor had no doubt, had been sitting at the next table, running their mouths like his foolish cousins. Gabor listened. They planned to steal the vessel that very night and take it to their wretched country. They had easily bribed the afterhours guards. True, the Mayan civilization was as much Guatemalan history as his own, but *Palenque* was not in Guatemala. *Uxmal*, another ruined Mayan city, farther to the north, was his ancestral home, not *Palenque*, but it was all his ancestral land, long before there was a Mexico or a Guatemala.

Gabor knew better than to go to the *policía*, and it was too late to notify federal officials. They had never done anything for the Maya anyway. He had to be brave – *Gabor*, God's brave one.

With so little time, Gabor chose to act.

It might work, he thought, as he drove his old Toyota truck to Palenque National Park. He would beat the Guatemalans to their prize. The big one, their leader, his name was Gomez, still had half a bottle of dark rum on his table. Gabor would tell the guards he was one of the thieves. *He* would steal the Red Queen's sacred vessel. Tomorrow, he could turn it over to the INAH, the National Institute of Anthropology.

He parked on the opposite side of a row of wide, low-growing ceiba trees near *Palenque's* empty parking lot. From behind his seat, he found a worn sisal bag he had used to carry avocados. He crept along the edge of the lot, staying in the shadows, until he was across from the guard station. There were only two cars, one had to belong to the guard – probably the beat-up Sentra. The second car bothered Gabor; it was a newer, expensive Ford Explorer. Maybe there was a guard at the museum as well – of course, there would be – but how could he afford such an expensive vehicle?

Gabor surprised the station guard. The man had been standing outside the red roofed building smoking, watching the parking lot. He was likely expecting the Guatemalans to arrive in trucks or vans. And not just one man.

"Are you with the Guatemalans?"

"Sí," Gabor said. The less he said the fewer his chances of making a mistake.

"Well... the code?" the guard grunted.

Gabor had not thought of this possibility. He had believed the difficult part would be breaking into the museum. He thought hard...what would the stupid ones at the bar use? "The Red Queen," he guessed. The guard eyed him suspiciously. "The Red Queen's vessel," Gabor added quickly.

"They should not have hired a peasant to do their work," the guard scoffed. "There is an official waiting for you at the museum entrance. He will not go in with you, but he will give you access. Just make sure you remember the code this time."

"*Sí. Gracias.*"

Gabor ran down the winding path, through the trees, to the *Museo de Sitio de Palenque*. If the big Guatemalan, Gomez, drank his rum as fast as his cousins drank their *balché*, he and his men could be arriving soon. Gabor needed to have the vessel and be gone as soon as possible.

Being let into the museum was a break. He had planned on smashing a door or window, doing the same to the case with the Queen's vessel, and running back to his truck. If an official could get him in, hopefully he could also disable any security measures. But an "official" also meant this was a conspiracy.

Gabor thought of turning around. He had not thought this through like he should have. *The guard and an official* – once Gabor had the vessel, who could he trust? Maybe the cooperating official was with the INAH? Then he heard the wind and the sounds of the jungle. Scattered farther in the National Park were the temples and palaces of his ancestors. He could feel their presence. Even the Red Queen would be with him. A howler monkey sounded, and Gabor took the animal's urging as a sign. He needed to see this through; the Maya of the past were relying on him.

There...in the shadows...a man the front of the museum, waving him forward. Gabor approached him cautiously. He was dressed sharply, wearing a dark suit, even at this late hour. Gabor couldn't tell if it was black or blue. A fedora was pulled low over his eyes.

"*Está abierto,*" he whispered, walking off without saying more.

Already open, Gabor thought. Why hadn't the man just gotten the vessel himself?

Gabor stepped into the museum entryway. The lighting was spotty, not like the times he had visited when they were open. Dull, emergency lights over the doorways made it so he could see, but little more. He looked at the white boxes below the lights, wondering if he was being filmed; something else he hadn't thought of. Staring up, he tripped over something solid on the floor. *Oh Dios mío!*...another man, this one face down. Gabor crossed himself, seeing the blow to the back of his head. He didn't need to feel a corpse to know it was dead.

Gabor raced through the halls to where he knew the Red Queen's vessel was on display. That case was open too! Grabbing the vessel, he retraced his steps, expecting alarms to begin sounding and the *policía* to be waiting for him outside. They weren't. Even the guard at the station was gone, though his Sentra was still in the lot.

He was running around the trees to his truck when he saw their lights. They hadn't seen him, and he quickly ducked out of sight. Two vans, the dome light lit in the lead vehicle. Inside he could see the big man from the bar, Gomez, pointing at a map, yelling at the smaller man driving. They drove to the entry station, and Gomez and his driver got out, looking for the guard.

Gabor didn't see if the men found the guard. He was in his truck speeding away toward town. From there, he had no idea what he was going to do or where he would go. He needed to find somewhere safe, he needed to return to his Mayan roots. But right now, getting away was all he could think about. The Red Queen's vessel rolled in the sisal bag on his passenger seat.

CHICHÉN ITZA

THE SERPENT SLITHERED DOWN THE STEPS, HIGHLIGHTED BY THE setting Yucatan sun. Kukulkan Bonifacio Balthazar gazed to the top of the temple bearing his name. *K'uk'ulkan* was the plumed Snake God of the Maya.

Kuul, as he was known to his friends, listened as a Mexican tourist explained to his children that the trick of light streaming down the temple was *Quetzalcoatl*, the Aztec winged serpent god. From his father's stories and lessons, Kuul knew that his namesake and the Mayan civilization were much older than the tourist's Aztecs. His ancestors had founded *their* empire over a thousand years earlier. By the time the Spanish arrived and pushed the Aztecs from *Tenochtitlán*, modern day Mexico City, Mayan cities were mostly abandoned.

The spring equinox at *Chichén Itzá* was a special time in the Mayan calendar. The ancient architects had faced *K'uk'ulkan* Temple so that evening light, only on that day, lit the edges of the north stairs. The shimmering streak of light ended at a stone statue of a serpent's head. Thousands of people from all over the world came to observe the spectacle.

But Kuul was there for a different reason; his ancestors had directed him in a vision. They had asked that he visit his homeland and his People, to pay his respects and to learn.

Kuul was only part Maya. A native of Arizona, he was also Yaqui and Prussian, thanks to a grizzled mercenary who had fought for Maximillian. Back home in Sedona, he played at being Navajo for tips, and even then, only when tourists' insensitivities toward Native cultures justified the deception. But it was Maya, his father's people, he most identified with. Though he was much taller than the Maya gathered around him, he had the same round face, the same thick neck and chest, and the spirited, kind, black eyes that always seemed to be watching and listening.

Kuul's friend, Skip Rhodes, had joined him on his journey. Rhodes had brought his on-again-off-again girlfriend, Lilac Williams. He had yet to experience a visit from his ancestors. His spirit wasn't ready. His demons haunted his dreams, and exorcising those had to come first. Three months earlier, a crazed man extorting one of Skip's tour guests had unleashed those demons. The man's grandson had nearly killed Williams. While Kuul had saved her, Rhodes had hunted her attacker.

It was Williams, ex-Tucson police officer and private investigator, now yoga instructor and firearms trainer, with her long swimmer's body, auburn red hair, and take-no-prisoners attitude, who kept his friend grounded – for now.

Rhodes had slowly changed over the three years Kuul had known him. At first, he had been a sullen loner. Now, the burly American with the powerful shoulders, shaggy hair, and fraying Tewa sandals, was kicking a ball in the field with Mayan kids.

Kuul had also invited Toni Wathetewa to accompany him. Toni was a Yavapai woman from Arizona with a keen mind and sharper tongue. The Yavapai were a small tribe living in the valley south of Sedona. She had been the first woman elected to their tribal council. Her People claimed she was a seer, like her grandmother.

Kuul and his friends were sitting amongst the crowd, waiting, and watching the Mayan pyramid.

"We align our doors to the east, to welcome the beginning of the day," Toni said. Kuul's hook for getting her to come had been the similarities between Mayan beliefs and the stories told by her People. Archeoastronomy was just one connection. "But building a seventy-five-foot temple and precisely aligning it to an event that happens once a year is extreme."

Kuul had been educating his guests since their arrival. "*K'uk'ulkan*, the king, had a lot to prove. His real name was *Topiltzin*, but he adopted a local god as his namesake. It was a smart move. He was Toltec, not Maya, and had invaded their lands from Mexico. He won and set up his throne here at *Chichén*. That was at the end of the Mayan Classic Period, when Mayan cities were already declining due to drought, overpopulation, depletion of resources, and intercity warfare."

"Drought and an invading army sound familiar," Toni said, thinking of her own People's history.

"But *Topiltzin* was remembered by the Maya as a just political leader and good steward of their world. Of course, it was his own ruling Toltec nobles that memorialized him here at *Chichén*," Kuul wirily added. "The same men who most likely oversaw construction of the pyramid."

"You don't fight a war without ruffling feathers," Skip said, suspecting a darker side to the story.

"Maya murals in the Temple of the Warriors agree with you," Kuul said, pointing to a smaller, flat-top pyramid surrounded by columns with a *Chacmool* altar atop. The *Chacmool* looked innocent enough, a statue of a man reclining with his knees bent, holding a square plate in his lap. "That's where *Topiltzin's* priests cut out the hearts of conquered Mayan kings as a sacrifice to their feathered serpent."

"So, are you Maya or Toltec?" Skip asked.

"The Mayan people have a complicated history from that point on. The two cultures blended over time."

"Like the Yavapai and the Dilzhé'é Apache," Toni added.

Kuul nodded, "The Maya beliefs and customs remained dominant though. After *Topiltzin* returned home, things gradually reverted, but not completely. But to answer your question, I am Maya."

The light show at the temple mesmerized Lilac Williams. As the snake slithered down from the top of the temple, the crowd began waving their hands above their heads, like they were at a Ricky Martin concert. Locals were chanting in a language that she guessed was Yucatecan. Clapping, caramel-faced children with jet-black hair, the little girls braided, and the boys cut in short bangs, were sitting on their parents' solid shoulders. The women's beautiful huipil dresses with intricate, handstitched patterns were swaying back and forth.

"This is probably more attention than even old *Topiltzin* dreamed of?"

"It would be exactly what he'd counted on," Kuul answered. "Mayan kings were more than just royalty. They were the centers of what we would call religious cults today. They demanded the worship of their subjects. Without that they were powerless."

"So, the light appearing as a snake was a trick to impress and control the masses?" Skip said. He had learned to be jaded when it came to dictatorial leaders.

"An amazing, precisely calculated architectural and astronomical *trick*," Lilac said. "Not exactly a propaganda flyer scattered on the ground." Skip waved a mock white flag in defeat. He hadn't meant calling the light show a trick to be an insult. He actually saw it as a clever application of advanced technology.

"There would have been heart sacrifices as well, and some of these cute kids would have been tossed in the sacred cenote to appease the underworld gods," Kuul said.

"Cenote? That's like Montezuma Well, right?" Toni questioned.

Montezuma Well was a spring-fed sinkhole in central Arizona where Yavapai believed their people to have climbed from the old world to the new world.

"Pretty much. They're local watering holes, usually a spring where the limestone collapsed above. In the Yucatan, they're the only reliable water sources. The Maya saw the one here as an entry-way to the underworld, not unlike the Hopi sipapu or your origin story."

"So, Mayan gods weren't particularly benevolent - throwing children in a hole," Lilac said.

Kuul and Toni answered together, "Neither is yours."

"The kings would take care of the families of the sacrificed," Kuul added. "Dying for the people was considered an honor."

"May I never be so honored," Skip said.

The light show was ending, and the crowd began leaving, helped along by friendly park staff in red shirts ushering them toward the exit. Kids kept trying to do an end run around the laughing staff, who kept waving them back to their smiling parents. Everyone was happy and buoyed by the experience they had shared. It was a Mayan celebration of their cultural ingenuity.

"We'll return tomorrow morning when it's cooler," Kuul said. "We can take our time visiting the older sections of *Chichén Itzá*. They are purer Maya, none of the Toltec influence."

"It's margarita time, then," Skip said, enthusiastically. "It's hot down here." Their drinks last night had been cold and cheap. After being in the sun for the past few hours, he was looking forward to a second round.

"And real corn tamales with guacamole," Kuul said, grinning. "Maya were the first to cultivate maize, and they gave the world avocadoes."

The next morning, walking to the park, Kuul asked, "How did you sleep, Kemo?" They were on their way to *Chichén's* back entrance. Lilac and Toni were ahead at a sidewalk market.

"The room has two beds," Skip answered. Sleeping wasn't what he was asking about. Lilac had been on the cool side since the episode in Arizona when Kuul had saved her...and he hadn't.

"She's still making up her mind, brother. Whether you are a part of her journey or not."

Lilac was studying an elaborately carved mask and Toni the embroidery work on a white huipil blouse. The female vendor was smiling but shaking her head *No*, holding up four fingers. Lilac hesitated, then held up one of her own.

"*Señora, mi* husband – he take *treinta días* making this. He harvested the wood and I handmade the dyes," the woman said, eyeing Skip as he got closer. She was hoping the woman's man would help with the sale. American men liked to show off with their money.

"Oh, it's very beautiful and I can see the fine craftmanship, it's just more than I want to spend, *señora*."

"*Cúanto es?*" Skip asked, coming up beside Lilac.

"She's asking one-forty, I'm at one hundred. "Dollars, not pesos. It's lovely but..." The woman offered the mask to Skip to inspect, but Kuul took it instead.

"It's *Chahk*, the Rain God. Number two in our pantheon. This is the work of a traditional artisan, Lilac. Better than what we saw yesterday inside the park. See the serpent wound around the ornate head dressing and jaguar markings on the collar. The face shows a duality of being. One side is human flesh, the other a skull, representing life and the underworld. Aside from the symbology, just the detail of the carving is remarkable."

"*Gracias, señor*," the woman said, beaming at Kuul. She could see the Mayan politeness and gentility in his eyes.

"*Por nada. Chahk* ensures not only successful harvests...but also fertility," he said, grinning at his two star-crossed friends.

"Thanks," Lilac said. "Where was he ten years ago?" Her clock was ticking, and she knew it. That was one of the things that gnawed at her about her attraction to Prince Charming. She had a tough time picturing him as a father.

"I'll take the blouse - *as marked*," Toni interrupted, handing the woman a fistful of pesos.

"And *Chahk*?" the woman asked, smiling at Lilac, while glancing at her companion.

"*Sí*," Skip said, fishing in his vest pocket for his money clip. "Lilac, it's yours if you want it, otherwise, I've got an empty wall in my cabin."

"Your cabin can use the decoration...any decoration," she said, handing the woman seven twenties.

Kuul, after snapping a picture of the woman, Lilac, and the fertility God, led them to *Chichén Itzá*. Their hotel, the Villas Arqueologicas, was a short walk from the secondary entrance which led directly to the older section of *Chichén*. Avoiding the main entrance meant avoiding the busloads of day trippers from Cancún and the men dressed as Mayan lords hawking pictures of their shaking a rattle in your face - not that they didn't deserve a buck or two from the ancestors of white colonialists.

Two lefts inside the smaller gate and they were at the bottom of a wide, stone staircase. The Caracol Observatory, an ancient viewing station with a domed top, loomed before them.

"This is 'Old *Chichén*.'" Kuul said. "The structures here are classic *Puuc* style, predating and uncorrupted by the Toltecs - mostly. Before there was a need to scare the people with the grotesque imagery on the Temple of Warriors. Before the sacrificial *Chacmool* altar."

"It looks like the Lowell Observatory in Flagstaff, only larger with a grander approach," Toni said. "I can almost picture telescopes sprouting from those windows slits."

"It's been compared to a layered wedding cake sitting on top of its box," Kuul said. "The Maya aligned markings on the platforms with marks on the doors and windows to track the planets. They charted their rising and setting, and positions throughout the year. They were most focused on Venus."

"Venus," Lilac, the part-time yoga instructor, said. "The planet associated with the feminine. It rules how you express passion and view beauty."

"Like the Navajo idea of *hózhó*," Toni added. "To us, a spiritual connection exists between all material things. The stars are a part of our world, a part of us. The same with mother earth, mountains, water...and that family of iguanas over there in the sun."

"From their sky tracking, the Maya knew a Venus year equaled five-hundred-eighty-four days. They also knew that five of those years equaled eight Earth years," Kuul said. "They were fascinated with the cyclical nature of time. They associated those cycles with ideas of how things end and are reborn - crops, people, and civilizations. It took decades for archeologists to grasp the sophistication of their calendars, and that was only after realizing they were even calendars. There was no Mayan Rosetta Stone; the Spanish burned all their books and codices, except for the few found in sealed burial chambers. To the missionaries, Mayan writings were heretical teachings. And without them, decoding Maya hieroglyphics was nearly impossible."

"Venus, the morning and evening star," Lilac mused. "It releases a force that creates harmony in life and unifies the opposites," she said, eyeing Skip.

Kuul smiled, knowing the yoga instructor was into his story – if not his friend.

"Every eighth year, if you drew a straight line from that window centered in the dome, down the middle of the stairway, and extended it to the horizon, it would point to Venus at its northernmost point."

"They knew their sky," Skip said.

Astrology was big business in Sedona, and it wouldn't hurt him to learn a little 'mystic' mumbo-jumbo. He could sprinkle in bits during his history and geology tours. The serious star and vortex trips, he could leave to his assistant, Sapphire Sky. She was developing a line of New Age Cosmic tours. He should pick up a book or two for her at the visitor center. "Did they leave a record of their charts anywhere other than in their codices?"

"Not exactly – but serpents, turtles, and even peccary constellations are depicted on the walls of the Nunnery," Kuul said, pointing to a smaller group of structures to their right. "The Spanish thought the buildings looked like a convent, hence the name."

"Peccaries? As in javelinas back home?" Lilac asked.

"Like Spike, Zula's pig," Skip added. Zula Ballsy, his salty landlady, owned the cabin he rented in Sedona; it was part of her Sands Retreat and Lodge. Spike was her spoiled pet javelina.

"Javelinas get around, especially that one," Kuul laughed. "They're endemic to Central and South America. The peccary and turtle are both central to the Mayan origin story. Temple mural artists depicted the Maize God as having been reborn from their backs. Each night the Maya saw both creatures in the sky as groupings of stars, same as we see Gemini and Orion."

"Let's not tell Spike," Skip said. "His head's big enough."

COW POSES AT CATHEDRAL

SAPPHIRE SKY WAS TAKING MARRIED LOS ALAMOS SCIENTISTS on an afternoon, Sedona Chi New-Age Spiritualist hike in Sedona, Arizona. Zula Ballsy had come along to keep her company.

Sedona Chi Tours was run by Skip Rhodes, her boss and - *well, what else was he* - father-figure, mentor, friend, boyfriend? Sky, as her friends called her, still wasn't sure what she wanted. The latter wasn't likely with the *older* Lilac Williams in the picture. In the meantime, she was happy being a tour guide, especially in a mystical place like Sedona. The scientists had picked a pretty landscape to visit, or as they put it, investigate an alternative explanation to the connectivity of the universe.

"Spike! Leave their bags alone!" Zula yelled, shooing him away. "I apologize for the pig. Must be food in your backpacks?"

"Just leftover crackers," Jean Bergermeier said. "They're in a baggie."

Jean was a fellow at the laboratory and a specialist in the computational approach to evolutionary biology. Her husband, Gene, was working on a model of the interplay between charged particles from geomagnetic storms and the earth's magnetic field. Eggheads, Zula thought.

"Bet they're bacon flavored. That pig loves bacon."

"Interesting, and, yes, they are," Gene said. He grinned at his wife, "Good thing he's a peccary and not a *sus scrofa* or he could have been sniffing a distant cousin."

Jean found her husband's obscure joke hilarious. Zula winced at the woman's squeaky laugh which sounded like a dog toy was caught in the back of her throat. No doubt that went over well in the lab. And what the hell was a *sus scrofa*?

"Let's keep climbing," Sky said. She had heard enough about solar winds, ionospheric disturbances, and how Gene didn't give a rat's ass about their effects on Elon Musk's SpaceX rocket. Apparently, Musk had snubbed him on a consulting bill.

They were hiking the Rector Connector trail off Courthouse Butte Loop. The trail went up and over the saddle of red rock separating Courthouse from Bell Rock, so named because it was shaped like an enormous church bell. Near the top of the bell was one of Sedona's famous vortexes, where the energy from the earth's core breached its crust, curing every ailment from arthritis to athlete's foot..

"How far to the vortex?" Jean asked.

"Two moon beams and a Gene Roddenberry warp year," Gene quipped, a squeaky rubber ferret erupting in his wife's gullet.

"We won't be going that far," Sky said, chuckling. "We'll stop below it, but well within the magical quarter mile of its energy center. Bell Rock, by the way, is the most popular place in town to get airlifted from," she said, parroting what she'd heard Skip tell every tour he'd taken on this trail. "The effects will be the same, but it will be a whole lot safer."

"Just keep at least one foot on the ground. Don't want anyone levitating away," Zula joked. She glanced at Jean - nothing.

"There's a shelf of rock up ahead with magnificent views. We can do our morning yoga there," Sky said, making a face at Zula. If there was a bear, the old girl would poke it.

Gene said, "As a scientist, especially with my specialty of study, I know there isn't anything uniquely different about a

Sedona vortex. The disturbance in the magnetic readings left in the lava from tectonic movement simply is not varied enough from the earth's magnetic field to exhibit any physiological anomalies. Of course, with a true vortex, the energy weakens with each successive outward wave. So theoretically, distance would matter. However, it is beautiful here. I notice a sensory effect from that."

"You have to accept that it's not a disturbance of physical energy but spiritual energy," Sky countered. "The resonance, if you're open to it, happens because that energy is similar to the energy locked inside your inner being. That's why people have heightened psychic powers here if their chakras are aligned. Even those whose aren't, sometimes feel a tingling of their skin or a vibration in their feet."

Gene still looked unconvinced.

"Look at Spike, that pig's feeling it," Zula said. Spike was standing on a shelf forty feet above them. He was pawing the ground, his nose in the air pointed at Bell Rock.

Sky laughed, "He's saving our spot."

Sky had introduced Zula to yoga. For the past few months, after their morning coffee and tea, they had been meeting in front of Zula's Lodge and progressing through an escalating series of stretches. Zula was in her seventies and a bit skeptical at first, preferring a "healthy shot of Jack" in her coffee to "get things moving." She claimed to have done enough bending and stretching in her Vegas showgirl days to last a lifetime. And that didn't include her and Shirley getting chased by 'ole blue eyes' and that silky talking Italian *Amore* singer around their Vegas suites. She had to be limber back then.

Two weeks of cow and cobra poses had oiled Zula's old joints and muscles. They were just neglected, not dead. She had worked her way up to the one-legged pigeon pose which required extra flexibility and a squirt of WD40 in her Nescafé. Sky was a good yogini too, patient and encouraging, except when Lilac Williams joined them from time to time. Those routines always evolved into a contest with Zula playing referee.

By the time they reached Spike, the javelina was in a modified thunderbolt pose - nose still in the air, sitting on his haunches, back as straight as possible for a peccary. He was watching two other budding yoga practitioners. They were an odd pair to say the least – Steel Calves Kempdinger and Big Bob Baker

Steel Calves Kempdinger was the head of the Sedona Westerners, a local hiking group. A retired Phys-Ed teacher from Nebraska that coddled no babies, her approach to training was to punish the trainee. With her leading the march, Sedona's fittest hikers wore out a pair of Magellans every two months. She was holding Big Bob's ankles to the ground, yelling at him to get his ass off the red rocks.

Zula whispered to Sky, "I've seen them around town together. Holding hands."

Kempdinger was screaming at Big Bob, "*THRUST YOUR PELVIS – PUSH!* No one said the Seta Bandha Sarvangasana was easy!"

Big Bob was doing his best, but his inability to say no to a free Corona at the VFW was working against him. As was the twenty-four-pack quaking around his belly. His knees were bent, his feet and shoulders pressed flat on the ground, his arms spread like the Vesuvius Man. Both hips were six inches off the rock, straining to push his pelvis higher.

"Damnit, Steel Calves," he said, puffing hard. "This is a lot more fun on a Posturepedic."

"Give the libido a rest, Bob," Kempdinger said, without a hint of embarrassment after seeing Zula and Sky. "We've got company. But you're still going to work on the Dolphin Plank. We can use it later."

"Thank God! Going down is better," Bob said, collapsing just as the Bergermeiers followed Sky and Zula onto the ledge.

Gene did a quick analysis of the situation and said, "You were dead right about the view, but it looks like the javelina was beaten to the spot. Maybe there's somewhere else?"

"We'll use that next ledge," Sky said, pointing Zula to a higher point on the opposite side of the trail.

"Best to let Big Bob buckle his pants in privacy," the show-girl joked. "HEY, YOU TWO ROCK SCIENTISTS WATCH OUT FOR SNAKES!" she yelled, walking after the Bergermeiers who were already moving. Spike was leading the way, his concentration broken.

Sky stayed back, smiling coyly at Kempdinger. It had been months since she'd last seen her and Big Bob. That had been at Zula's monthly Tequila Moon party, a BYOB affair she threw for locals and guests staying at her lodge. Baker had lost weight - Steel Calves' doing, no doubt. The big man was sweating a bucket and wiping his forehead with his shirt tail, his pants hanging dangerously low. Steel Calves swatted his hand and thrust her bandana toward him.

Sky laughed, "Aren't you looking comfy together. I didn't know you had paired up. Sorry for the interruption."

"He had to loosen his belt for the yoga," Kempdinger said.

Sky grinned slyly, "They certainly restrict blood flow to the lower extremities."

"Just teaching Bob some basic poses for his back. He's carrying too much weight for our longer hikes," Kempdinger said affectionately, patting Big Bob's Buddha belly.

She doubted Steel Calves was training him for *hiking*. "With your help, I'm sure he will be able to fully participate. Try slowing down the pelvic presses, he'll last longer."

Big Bob smiled sheepishly, "We're dating."

Sky winked. "Well, see you both later. If they weren't custom-ers, I'd stay and teach you the Cat-Cow stretch. That one is useful... on a Posturepedic." She brought both hands together over her head, her fingertips pointing toward the blue Sedona sky. "The divine light in me honors the divine light in you. Thank you for sharing your practice," she said, bowing and slowly lowering her hands to her heart center.

"Back at you, Sky," Big Bob said. Kempdinger rolled her eyes.

She climbed the path to join Zula and the Bergermeiers from New Mexico. The older woman had them midway through their warm-up stretches. The scientists' boots and hats were sitting on a rock, their vests with infinity symbols folded neatly on top.

Sky chose to not break their rhythm, so she sat on the far side of the ledge, peering down into the valley. From high above, the Village of Oak Creek spread below her but was still close enough to see everyday life happening in the small town – jeeps gassing at the Circle K, a red-vested worker at Ace Hardware loading two-by-fours in a handyman's truck, dogs being walked back in the neighborhood, and tourists making illegal turns into the art market to buy hummingbird whirligigs and crystals.

Sedona had become a mecca for the New Age elite - the *wealthy* New Age elite. With her double-jointedness and belief in alien abduction, she had fit right into this goofy town. Two years ago, she had arrived carrying a heavy load of emotional baggage and unknowingly working for a con-artist preacher. Skip had been the one to pull her out of trouble, with an assist from the precious lady pushing the scientists. *How they had changed her life...*

Sky filled her lungs with fresh air. The shrouded vestige of last night's full moon was still visible. This was one of her favorite spots to stargaze; a bottle of Bordeaux, weed, and quiet – what more could a girl ask for? Out here there was no ambient light or noise like at Zula's Sands Lodge, where she lived. Out here she was alone with the stars and planets.

Maybe she could upsell the Bergermeiers on an Age of Aquarius after-dark tour. They were both fit, a night hike would be easy. They hadn't so much as taken a deep breath climbing up the trail. No problem following Zula's yoga routine either. Jean was in the middle of a Revolved-Half-Moon pose, pointing to the sky while her other arm was held parallel to the ground. She was balancing on one leg, her other leg stretched back behind her. Gene was standing on his hands, leaning against a wall of red rock, doing push-ups.

Such a good match, Sky thought. One of them had to be a Libra like her, the sign dominated by Venus. *Love, luck, the cosmic roulette of romantic chance* - the bond between men and women arose from the planet's female energy. And Venus people find pleasure in older partners. She had met Skip when Venus was in conjunction with Saturn, which certainly fit their relationship. Saturn was a slow and sluggish planet.

Sky stared at the blue space below the moon. She knew Venus was there somewhere. The 'Morning Star,' her star, was keeping watch. It was waiting for her - love, luck, romance.

"Earth to Sky," Zula said from behind, breaking her thoughts. "You here or somewhere else? Doctor Quantum and Doctor Squeaky decided to hike the rest of Courthouse Loop. They wanted time alone and said to meet them back at the parking lot. We called, but you didn't hear us. Honey, what were you thinking about?"

"Venus and Saturn."

POTUS GAS

"THESE DAMN GUT CRAMPS ARE WORSE THAN PISSING WITH gonorrhea," the President of the United States groaned. He was sitting on the toilet in his private suite at Walter Reed Medical Center.

He should know, thought the Secretary of Health and Human Services, who was standing in the doorway. If the fat slug would stop ordering double cheeseburgers from the cafeteria, it would at least smell better.

"Hand me my phone. I want to call the First Lady. Where the hell is she, Stinker?"

The Secretary grimaced at his nickname. He had run against the President in the primaries and the man had unveiled the moniker during their first debate. His legion of bellicose fans had picked it up and peppered him with it until he had dropped out after South Carolina. It wasn't his fault his name was Orville Stinckner.

"I'll call her," the Secretary said, pulling his own phone from his pocket.

He wasn't about to touch anything POTUS had been fingering. God knew where he'd been keeping it. The only pocket in his hospital gown was beneath the presidential seal sewn on his chest - where he insisted on keeping a small pump spray of tanning color.

"Never mind, Stinker," POTUS moaned, squirting diarrhea into the bowl. "God damnit, all over my ass again. Call that Mexican nurse instead, they're good cleaners. You would think those Kochs could make a better toilet."

"I think you mean the Kohlers."

"Stinker, what have I told you about arguing with me?"

"Yes, Mr. President."

Orville Stinckner had never wanted to be in politics. To his regret, he had let the Grand Ole Party talk him into running. This is what came of donating all that money over the years. Of course, that's what any self-respecting owner of a pharmaceutical company would do - buy your way to the table. He'd been perfectly happy running his family-owned business. They had made a fortune on diet pills in the nineties, and they were coming back. The fen-phen class action suits were almost all settled. Good thing too because the prescription pain-killer business was getting pretty litigious.

By the time of the palmetto state's primary, he'd been ready to call it quits. POTUS's under-the-table investment in his company had closed the deal. He had thought being the HHS Secretary would put him in a position to ward off the press vultures. Opiates, opiates, opiates - no one made people pop them like Skittles. The boys at CNN liked nothing better than a good exposé about a politically connected drug company. It wasn't really any of their business what he sold. This was America.

"I've got a job for you, Stinker."

"Yes, Mr. President."

A large woman with hairy arms, uncomfortably squeezed into a blue nurse's scrub, came into the room. "Maria is too small to lift you," she said, approaching POTUS.

"Damnit, not Helga! Stinker, I told you to get the Mexican one. Helga here was an Olympic weightlifter for Belarus. The clean and jerk is all she knows."

The nurse's badge read 'Mary.' "You know I'm from Michigan and the only one here that can get you onto your bed, roll you over, and clean up your mess. God knows, I did not sign up to be your momma. Clean *a jerk*, that's what this is."

"And you probably voted mail-in," POTUS sneered as she wrapped her arms under his armpits.

"Don't they have a dietician at the White House?" she shot back.

With the Secretary's reluctant help, they managed to waddle the President onto his hospital bed. True to her promise, Mary rolled him over, wiped his ass, and dusted him all over with baby powder.

"Getting back top side is your problem, but you might want to let things air out a bit," Nurse Mary said and walked out.

"Stinker!" Stinckner snapped to attention. "Get me a couple of pillows for under my chin."

One for each, Stinckner thought.

POTUS laid out his orders while lying on his mountain of a belly with his butt exposed. He had been in secret consultation with his good friend Hector Colon, President of the Republic of Guatemala. Hector claimed to have discovered an ancient cacao recipe for weight loss. It was a miracle drug and rumored to allow one to eat all the tamales one wanted and still shed pounds like a Mexican drug dealer in federal prison.

His "good friend," Stinckner thought. Hector Colon had headed the notorious *Kabilies*, the special forces unit of the *Ejercito Nacional de Guatemala*, Guatemala's Army, before the prosecutions. He had escaped jail by stoking a wave of populist antipathy toward the neighboring Mexico and its drug cartels. That ended in his occupying the Presidential Palace. Colon, of course, was amassing a private fortune cooperating with the same cartels.

"Hector, who is a beautiful man, the most beautiful man in that country, reports that a long dead queen etched the chocolate recipe on a vessel she owned. She was unable to process calories same as me and Hector. He has sent an elite team of his Palace

Guard to acquire the recipe. I could use a storm trooper group like those boys…if not for those constitutionalists in the Senate…Stinker, when I'm out of here, remind me to reorganize the Secret Service."

"Where is this vessel?" Stinckner asked hesitantly, suspecting trouble.

"Stinker."

"I know, Mr. President. No arguing."

POTUS nodded. "That's the rub. It's in a shit-hole Mexican museum at an Indian ruin called…Par…Par-K. That's it, Parque. Like a floor."

"That means park in Spanish, sir. Perhaps Hector means Palenque, a major Mayan site in Mexico, near the Guatemalan border?"

"The fucking name doesn't matter, Stinker. Hector says the vessel is actually theirs. Those Indians came from Guatemala and whatever they had should belong to his country, not Mexico. And I agree. Mexicans have the Aztecs, you know. Too many Indians screw a place up, anyway. Just look at Arizona. Christ, they can't even dig a little open pit in the Grand Canyon for uranium without Pocahontas calling for their scalps."

"Yes, Mr. President."

"Now, Stinker, this is top secret, okay? Since I'm laid up here, I need you to run point. I've told Hector to pass everything through you. I'd prefer to be personally involved…but…plausible deniability and all, you understand. Just keep me informed. I need that weight loss recipe, Stinker. That nurse, I hate to admit it, but she's right… and I like chocolate. You manage this for me, Stinker, and I'll make sure your company gets dibs on the formula."

And you will also get fat annual dividend checks, the Secretary of HHS thought.

The House of Turtles

"**U**XMAL **WAS MORE IMPORTANT IN THE CLASSIC MAYA PERIOD** than *Chichén Itzá*. These ruins are truer Maya, not as much Toltec influence," Kuul explained.

When they left *Chichén*, their next stop had been Campeche, a quiet, colonial city on the Gulf of Mexico, situated on the opposite side of the Yucatan Peninsula from touristy Cancún. Kuul had picked a small hotel, near the town's sleepy plaza. It was the proximity of *Uxmal* that had drawn Kuul to Campeche. The sleepy ruins had once been the apogee of Mayan culture and power.

They had spent their first morning at *Edzna*, another Maya site to the east, allied with the powerhouse *Chichén Itzá*. At *Kabah*, another, smaller ruin ninety miles north, they had broken into the sack lunches made by their hotel. Sitting in a field by themselves, they had shared their cold tamales and beans with the hundreds of *Chahk* images, the Mayan god of rain, thunder, and lightning, staring down at them from the famous Palace of Masks. From there, they drove to *Óoxmáal*.

"*Óoxmáal* is the Mayan name for *Uxmal*. That means 'three times built' or 'three harvests,' we aren't sure which. According to legend, *Uxmal's* Temple of the Magician was built by a dwarf on a single night. He later became king. Dwarfs were revered in the Mayan world for their magical powers."

"The Crows have a dwarf hero called Greasy Spirit; the Cheyenne and Arapahoe tell of a race of fierce cannibal dwarfs they defeated in battle long ago," Toni Wathetewa noted, realizing the similarities in their mythical stories.

"I've read the Aztec kept them in a human zoo," Lilac said.

Kuul pointed to different sections of the Magician's pyramid, "It's actually five temples, each one built on top of its predecessor. But we can only see the last two."

The tall pyramid with its distinctive rounded edges and narrow central stairway dominated the entrance to the ruined city. Images of the Mayan rain god, *Chahk*, lined both sides of the steps. The two exposed temples stood on its top, high overhead, above the steeply rising stairs. "As worshippers and victims climbed the steps to face the sacrificial altar, they were ceremonially ascending to their gods."

"It's not busy here like *Chichén*. Or noisy. The wind could be the People's voices," Toni said.

"Neither Campeche nor Merida further north are beach resorts, no tiki huts or swim up bars. No tour buses or cruise excursions from Cancun," Kuul answered. "The visitors here come to do a deeper dive into our history – not to party, which is why most vacationers come to Mexico."

"Their loss," Skip said. "These ruins rival what I've seen in Greece and Cambodia. More expressive."

"The art is phenomenal," Lilac said.

"*Uxmal*, *Kabah*, *Edzná*, and *Chichén* all have characteristic *Puuc* architecture: fancy friezes, columns, and detailed, stone latticework. *Uxmal* is the largest and oldest. The *Xiu*, an elite family, ruled here from the city's founding around 500 BCE up until the Toltecs, our friends who conquered *Chichén*, chased them away as well. According to Spanish journals, Maya were still living here when they arrived. That is two thousand years of occupation."

They strolled through the park, listening to Kuul's stories, staring in wonder at the various structures. Skip couldn't resist and tossed a stone through the elevated ring in the ballcourt. They stopped on a raised platform with a statue of two conjoined jaguars. A series of wide steps led from the platform up a terraced hill to the Palace of Governors overlooking the entire *Uxmal* complex.

"The jaguars are believed to be an altar used for rituals," Kuul said. "Use your imagination," he said to Skip, stopping the question he saw his friend getting ready to ask. Kuul pointed to the Palace. "Let's go up there. We'll be able to see the entire city."

A graveled plaza wrapped around the front and sides of the Palace, which consisted of three separate buildings connected by vaulted archways. Eleven doorways led to fourteen unornamented rooms, which had once been brightly painted and elaborately furnished. There was no mistaking the importance of the royal residences. On the same hill, set to the right on a lower terrace, was the Temple of the Turtles, with its carefully carved namesakes.

"The stone faces with the hooked noses?" Skip asked, pointing to the corners of the Palace.

"Early archeologists believed they were depictions of *Chahk*, the rain god, like those at *Kabah*. Some now think they are representations of ancient mountains. See the flowers above, that look to be eyes? They are actually Venus glyphs. These buildings were celestial paradises on earth for the kings and queens who lived here."

"They look like masks," Lilac said. "Scary masks."

"Who knows for sure?" Kuul said.

Toni was studying the small temple below with turtle icons sculpted in its stone cornice, "The same symbols were on the Nunnery at *Chichén* too. The Maize God was born from a turtle's back, right? That has to be an important building."

Kuul smiled. His lessons were taking root.

"There's forty-five minutes before closing, and I still want to climb that Magician pyramid," Skip said. From their vantage point, he could see the two temples and the top of the stairs past a grove of ceiba trees.

"No climbing that big boy, Kemo. Not allowed. You can climb the Great Pyramid behind us, but not the Magician.

Toni had wandered away from the palace to the edge of the plaza, captivated by the ancient site spread below. There were large public buildings like the pyramids and palace, but also smaller structures scattered amongst trees and buried in the woods. Remnants of stone roads crisscrossed the ground like in a modern town. The land around undulated like a Scottish golf course; it was obvious that more of *Uxmal* remained to be excavated.

There were no stairs leading to the lower terraces from this end of the Palace, just a crumbling stone wall. At the bottom, a grassy area, the width of a football field, extended to another, shorter wall. The building with the turtles sat at the edge overlooking the ballcourt, a wide, open alley of grass. Stone rings, the ones Skip had played with, were attached to the sidewalls of the playing field. Past the ballcourt, a grassy corridor led to the Nunnery, a quadrangle of ornately decorated buildings flanked by the Pyramid of the Magician.

Toni saw a guide leading his group past the pyramid and back to the parking lot. "We're the last ones here," she whispered to herself, awed by the breadth of the civilization that had once existed here. She could feel the People's presence.

A throat cleared behind her and she also felt the presence of the man she was with.

She turned to Kuul, "Thank you for bringing me here." Toni closed her eyes. "I can hear their sounds; it is noisy. Mothers are chasing and calling their children, men are doing the things men do, there is a game being played. I can see the shamans on the top of the temple performing a nightly ceremony and the royal families milling around this plaza."

Toni's visions always cast a spell over Kuul. The misty, far-off look in her deep brown eyes touched him deeply. She was the oracle of her People, her seeings were prophetic. But here, in his ancestral home...in this moment...he was more attracted by the woman and her spirit. His heart was captivated by the soft skin covering her proud, intelligent eyes, her noble forehead, the warmth of her words and what they meant to him.

"Their lives would have been much like the Puebloans at Chaco Canyon or Mesa Verde, only on a grander scale. These People, their accomplishments, their blood – they are in you." Toni said, opening her eyes.

For a second, fresh from her vision, her sight still clouded, the Mayan face studying hers was that of a priestly king – proud and protective of his kingdom. She blinked and it was Kuul. The same gentle look he always wore, only there was something deeper, more personal. She took his hand and kissed him. "Thank you."

Skip and Lilac had been standing behind the royal couple, quietly enjoying the view and Toni's descriptive vision. She had brought the empty scene to life. Skip had often had the same sense of déjà vu, heard the same cries from the past at Montezuma Castle in Arizona, the ancient cliff ruin of the Sinagua People. His visions were never so serene – fire, battle shouts of warriors, screams of the dying – he had never seen the children or their mothers. Nor had he witnessed the...

"*On the lower terrace,*" Lilac said, elbowing him and interrupting his thoughts, "That's a head rising above that wall past the Temple of Turtles! There's something wrong with him!"

"A Mayan head," Kuul answered, seeing a man pull himself up onto the grassy area below them and collapse. Seconds passed... he struggled, raising himself, looking over his shoulder toward the ballcourt. Straining, he finally stood and limped toward the temple, disappearing inside.

"Was that blood?" Lilac asked, alarmed. The front of the man's serape had been dark red, and there was a stain where he'd fallen. He had been holding his stomach, his other hand dragging a coarse sisal bag the size of a backpack.

"That's what it looked like," Kuul said.

Skip was already climbing down the stone wall from the palace plaza. Kuul joined him, and they jumped to the grassy field, running toward the temple. Lilac started to follow, but Toni stopped her, "Let's take the stairs!"

Toni and Lilac raced across the front of the Governor's Palace and back down the stone stairs. A hard left at the twin jaguars and they were running across the lower terrace, thirty feet below the plaza where they had been standing. The Temple of Turtles was past the end of the wall, thirty yards ahead. The boys were nowhere in sight, nor was the man they had seen.

"They must be in the temple," Lilac said, glancing at Toni who was racing beside her step-by-step.

Toni nodded, "the middle door."

There were three doorways in the structure, the middle the largest. Below the roofline, was a cornice with stone turtle carvings. Entering, they could see through the temple. Framed in a window opening on the far side, past the ballcourt, was the Nunnery, the late afternoon sun spotlighting its intricate stone latticework. To their right and left, melting into shadow, was a maze of rooms extending through both wings of the temple.

"Kuul!" Toni called.

"In here!" he yelled from their right. "He's dying!" From the hollow sound of his voice, they were several rooms away.

"He's dying," Kuul repeated as they entered the second room. The man's eyes were closed, his breathing shallow. His dangling hand still grasped the sisal bag.

The roof was partially gone, and rays of light, filtered by dust motes, were shining on the man he held. The touching scene looked like Michelangelo's pieta in St. Peter's. Kuul was on his knees, cradling the man's body in his lap, holding his head with his hand. The man's right arm listlessly fell to the ground.

"We ran in the first doorway, through four rooms, and found him lying here. He was conscious at first," Skip said.

"We need to get him back to the visitor center. Our phones are no good from here." Lilac said.

The man's breathing quickened into short rasps, and he regained consciousness. His expression was painful but clear. His eyes began darting around the room. His wild gaze settled on Kuul, and he reached for him with his free hand. He tried pulling Kuul toward him but gave up, muttering in a language none of them understood. Kuul's confused look must have told him he didn't understand. Again, the man tried pulling Kuul down, more urgently this time, still attempting to speak. His voice was fading. The big man lowered his ear to the man's mouth.

Whispering, the man said, "I am Gabor Cocom, a...brave man... who...listens." Each word was a fight.

Kuul didn't know what to say, "I am Kulkulkan Balthazar."

Gabor's eyes widened at the name of his Mayan god. His instincts had been right to return to his ancestral home, *Uxmal*. The gods had found him.

Gabor spoke softly, coughing at the effort, and shoved his avocado bag with the Red Queen's vessel into Kuul's hand, "Bless me... great serpent...of...the sky. Protect..."

The man gulped for air and fell back into Kuul's lap. His breathing slowed, then stopped. His eyes were still open, locked onto his god.

Skip knelt and pressed the man's neck below his jaw, checking for a heartbeat. There was none, and he gently closed his eyes. He looked at his friend and shook his head.

A voice from outside broke the silence in the chamber. *"SEÑOR! SEÑOR AMERICANO...HEY AMIGO!"*

HOUSE OF IGUANAS

HERNANDO GOMEZ WAS NOT A HAPPY MAN. HE HAD BEEN traipsing around the hot, buggy jungles of Mexico for two weeks. Gomez was a big man, and the heavy cotton tactical pants made him perspire uncontrollably - the *comisario* should have given them lightweight *pantalones*. The jungle rot was not just in his feet. Even his neatly clipped mustache was dripping sweat. And his bald head beaded like a waxed windshield after a summer rain. At least the tees he and his men were wearing were lighter, though white would have been a better choice than black. Climbing up and down these old ruins was killing him.

Capitán Gomez had been given one set of orders after another. His bosses were loco, as was the team they had stuck him with. His second in command, Chuuy Salamandor, was an idiot. Trusting him with a gun was an act of foolishness. The man couldn't weigh more than sixty kilos; Hernando's fourteen-year-old son had more hair on his chin. Unfortunately, Chuuy was his brother-in-law, his wife's younger brother. Lupe had probably dropped him on his head as a *niño*.

Gomez was sick too. Chuuy had talked him into sharing a bottle of tequila and tasteless tamales last night - it wasn't really a bottle, it was a plastic jug - with a brown, gooey worm in the bottom. Real tequila did not have worms; mezcal had worms. That should have been his second clue, the first having been the dirty container. And it was an earthworm, not a grub. At home in Guatemala City, he would have been drinking a mojito at El Portalito, his favorite bar, with a hot bowl of spiced turkey soup. Rum, that was a man's drink, not this cactus piss water Chuuy bought from an old man along the road.

But duty had to come first if he wanted to make *Capitán Primero* in the Presidential Guard. Only last year, he had been hand-selected to oversee protection for the female American Vice President's visit. If the woman had not insisted on visiting a barrio where a mangy street dog had bitten her, he would have already made it. With a promotion, his wife would stop harping about his time away from home, his neglect of their eight boys, none of whom looked like him, and her limited budget for food. This Mexican operation was his redemption, *Coronel* Mancoros had told him.

Well, redemption was still waiting, and he had missed acquiring the Mayan drinking vessel at *Palenque* by minutes. President Colon was hopping mad, and Mancoros was pouring the shit downhill. Not to mention the bad tequila and mosquitoes the size of toucans.

When Chuuy had reported that First Soldier Pérez had fought with the Mayan thief, his hopes had peaked. But the mulatto had pulled a machete after Pérez had stabbed him, and Pérez had run away like a pig. He had, however, watched him climb the hill and run into the building...followed by two American *touristas*.

"*Sargento* Salamandor, you must train your men better," he had yelled at Chuuy. "That mulatto had the vessel we seek."

"*Sí*, Hernando. Why do we want a cup, again?"

Gomez's head and stomach were too embroiled to bark at his simple brother-in-law. He just shook his head in disgust. Chuuy lowered his, scraping the grass with his black boot. But Hernando had also wondered, why all the trouble over an old vessel. He had not been entrusted with the reason. *Presidente* Colon could easily buy a similar artifact on Guatemala's illegal antiquities market.

"In front of the men it is *Capitán*, Chuuy - *Capitán*. And the vessel is important to our *Presidente* and the Guatemalan people - that's enough for an imbecile such as you."

"*Sí, Capitán Segundo*," Chuuy said, grinning, hoping the formality of his present title would show respect for his testy brother-in-law.

With the unexpected appearance of the Americans, Gomez realized this business had become more complicated. They now had the Mayan vessel. Were they even tourists? If *Presidente* Colon had tasked *Coronel* Mancoros and the *Ejercito Nacional* with finding it, wasn't it possible other services were after it as well? Could it really be that important? The tourists could be from the *gringo* Central Intelligentsia Agency, trained agents also on the vessel's trail. He needed to be careful, or he would find himself again patrolling the tough gang-controlled streets of Guatemala City.

"*SEÑOR! SEÑOR AMERICANO...HEY AMIGO...YOUR WOMEN SON MUY BONITAS*," Gomez called out, adding an indirect threat against the two women he had seen run into the turtle house. He wasn't sure about the one with dark hair, but the red head with the long stride and hiking boots had looked American.

Gomez had led his men through the ballcourt and had Chuuy station them on the stone wall below the temple with the *tortugas*. There was no immediate answer from inside. He glanced over at his brother-in-law. The idiot was trying to extricate his rifle from a stack of rocks. *Madre de dios!* Why had he poked the barrel of his Kalashnikov in there? He checked the rest of his men, counting – *uno, dos, tres, quattro*...Shit!

"*Sargento* Salamandor, where are Pérez and Morales?"

Chuuy yanked his gun butt, dislodging the pile of stones. He slid with the rocks to the bottom of the wall. The gun went off, and a shower of bullets narrowly missed the nearest soldier. The man screamed, threw his gun to the ground, leapt from his perch, and ran behind the narrow trunk of a ceiba tree.

"They were spooked by the stone masks of *Chahk* and the carved skulls, *Capitán*," Chuuy said, dusting himself off and acting like nothing had happened. He motioned to the soldier to retake his position, but the man didn't move. "I left them as lookouts near the park entrance. They are simple country soldiers from Santiago Atitlan; they claimed this place is haunted. It is *muí* spooky, *Capitán*."

The soldier Chuuy had shot at was sitting on the ground, his back against the tree. The man had lit a cigarillo, Gomez could see the gray smoke and smell the pleasant, toasted aroma. *Madre María*, he wished he had a good, black Cuban cigar right now. It was like leading five silly children against a team of Venezuelan commandos. With the errant shot, there would be no diplomatic resolution with the Americans in the Temple of *Tortugas*.

"Locked and loaded," Chuuy gamely said, climbing back up the wall, responding to his commander's glare.

Gomez rubbed his temples. His brother-in-law had been watching too many American movies at the *Cinépolis Portales*. The battle fatigues and his automatic *carbina* had elevated his courage, which was typically on par with a rabbit lost in a panther den.

"*Sargento*, send that coward behind the tree to get Peréz and Morales. I want all three of them here. We may need them - even if it is just to show our strength in numbers."

Chuuy scurried back down the wall and ran to the tree. Gomez watched as the soldier argued before throwing his cigar away and stalking off. He would be lucky if the three didn't leave the park, let alone come up as reinforcements.

Maybe he could still convince the Americans to talk. They had no way of knowing the uselessness of his scattered squad.

"*SEÑOR*, THAT LITTLE SHOT *ES UN POCO ACCIDENTE*. THE MULATTO HE STEAL FROM US. CAN WE TALK, *AMIGO*," Gomez called up to the temple, hoping those inside would mistake them for local bandits. Better if they underestimate him.

Skip reacted quickly to the shooting and ran to the central corridor of the temple. He was surveying the threat and situation from the window opening, in no hurry to answer before seeing what they were up against. Lilac had followed him.

"I count five, one ran back through the ballcourt. The big one behind that rock," Skip said, pointing, "seems to be in charge. He's the one talking."

"What a corny accent. Like Ben Stiller playing an East L.A. gangster."

"More Pacino in Scarface. Go get Kuul and Toni. We don't want to get trapped in a room with no exit."

"He won't want to leave the dead man."

"Guess again," Kuul said from behind, coming through the doorway with Toni from the interior chamber. "I suppose you have a plan, Kemo?"

Skip shrugged.

"How about running the other way, back toward the Palace of Governors?" Toni suggested. She knew the option of retreating would never occur to Skip. And Kuul would follow him.

"Then what? No, we've got some time...if they were going to charge in here, they'd have already done it, and they wouldn't have announced their presence."

Skip shouted through the opening, "HE DIDN'T HAVE ANYTHING! *AMIGO*, YOUR SHOT WOULD HAVE BEEN HEARD IN THE VISITOR CENTER." Maybe he could sow a seed that help might be coming. He doubted it, they were a long way inside the Mayan ruins. A distant shot would sound like any number of noises in the jungle.

"I HALF *HOMBRES* BACK THERE!" the big man yelled back, sticking his head out from behind the rock. "*AMIGO*, WEE JUS WAN THE MAYAN TRINKET! IT SEEM WEE HALF A MEXICAN...*CÓMO SE DICES*...STANDOFF."

"I don't think they're Mexican nationals," Lilac said. "That shot was from a 39mm AK. Rules out any local thugs."

"Maybe, but whoever he is, he knows about Gabor Cocom's treasure," Kuul said.

"Those tactical pants and black shirts spell military," Skip said. "That means they have *some* level of discipline and training to go along with the firepower."

"Why don't we just give it to them?" Toni said, stating the obvious. *Was she the only one thinking logically?*

Kuul had Cocom's sisal bag tied to his belt. "Because I promised a brave man that listens," he said, using Gabor's own words, "He died protecting it. I will keep it safe. When he spoke to me, he said it was a valuable vessel, a part of our heritage, and to not let it fall into the wrong hands. He warned me he was being chased. I think our '*amigos*' out there qualify as the wrong hands."

Skip knew his friend. He'd had the same thought as Toni - give it to them. But Kuul's glare and set jaw quickly settled the question. "Okay, we're not turning whatever it is over. Any other ideas?"

Kuul thought for a moment, "We go out the back, same way Toni and Lilac came in. But instead of retreating to the palace, we go left along the temple where they can't see us. Once we reach the edge of the hill, we scramble down the last wall. Then we run like hell around the ballcourt. The main path out of here isn't far from there. Worst case, we can hide in the House of Iguanas and make a stand if we have to...but..."

"Uh-huh." Skip knew what he was thinking.

"We need a distraction, though. You keep talking to your *amigo*, while Toni, Lilac, and I make our break. They will eventually see us and give chase, but hopefully we will have gotten far enough away. Once he follows, you should be able to flank them and escape the other way."

"You forgot they have guns, Eisenhower. What's to keep them from shooting him - or us?" Lilac questioned. She didn't like splitting up but wasn't seeing a better option.

"Like Kemo said. If they were willing to go that far, they would have attacked us by now. I think they want to avoid the trouble dead tourists would cause with the Mexican authorities."

"That would be troubling," Toni said, sarcastically.

"Well, at least it's a plan," Skip said.

"HEY, *AMIGO*!" Skip yelled through the opening, nodding at Kuul to get going.

Lilac hesitated, "Stay safe, and I had better see you back at the car. Do *not* play hero."

Kuul, Toni, and Lilac slipped out the back and crept along the wall of the Temple of the Turtles. It was no more than a hundred feet to the corner. After that, they would be running in the open. The plan was to stay far enough back on the terraced hill so that their attackers couldn't see them - as long as Skip kept them occupied.

"YOU CAN DROP THE BAD ACCENT," Skip called to the man.

"OH, *AMIGO*, YOU GOT ME. LET US NOT PLAY MORE GAMES. JUST PUT THE TRINKET IN THE WINDOW WHERE I CAN SEE IT, AND LEAVE. WE DO NOT NEED TO FIGHT OVER SUCH A SIMPLE THING, DO WE? IT IS SUCH A LOVELY DAY."

Kuul and the girls were at the far corner of the temple, listening, waiting for their chance.

Gomez motioned his men to reposition themselves closer to the center of the temple. Having the men spread along its entire length left too many gaps. With only Chuuy and three other men, he wanted to concentrate the force he had. If the gringos complied, one of them would have to leave his safe spot to get the vessel. That would not be him – maybe he would send Chuuy – no, his wife would not be happy if he did not bring her little brother back.

After shouting to the man outside, Skip moved unnoticed through the inner chambers of the temple to its far end. He planned on calling him next from there - opposite the end where Kuul and the girls were. With any luck, once the man realized the cup was not forthcoming, he would send his men toward his voice. That would be Kuul's opportunity to cross the open field.

"WE WILL NOT WAIT MUCH LONGER!" the man yelled, the patience draining from his voice.

Gomez had been hoping to see the ancient vessel placed on the stone sill. He doubted these people were trained agents, but he could not be sure. The one he was negotiating with was smart; scared tourists would have already given him what he wanted. And if they were not tourists, they might be armed. This really was a standoff. He was not about to send his untested men into the no-man's-land between the top of their wall and the temple. Maybe if his reinforcements arrived, but he wasn't counting on them. They were probably smoking cigarillos at the van and joking about him behind his back.

Skip slowly counted to ten before answering, "I'M AFRAID WE HAVE TO KEEP THE...TRINKET...*AMIGO*."

Gomez's head snapped right. The Americano had moved. He motioned to Chuuy to reposition the men. They scrambled down the wall and ran along its base until Chuuy sent them back up. Gomez stayed put. With the men poised just below the lip, he signaled Chuuy to send them over. There was no choice now. To get the vessel, they would have to take it.

Kuul peered around the corner of the temple and saw what was happening. So far so good. Skip had drawn the men away. "Now," he whispered.

Toni and Lilac raced across the open field, aiming for the deep shade of a large ceiba tree at the corner of the hill. Kuul was right behind them, trying to keep up. Past the tree's exposed roots, another crumbling, stone wall dropped to the next grassy terrace.

Kuul glanced over his shoulder twice – no one was pursuing. Their plan had worked. He knew enough about his friend's background, what Skip Rhodes was capable of and who he had been, to not worry about his being caught. He was more worried about the fallout from what Skip, even unarmed, could do to their attackers. He was a good man to cover their rear but extremely dangerous to those threatening them.

Skip calmly watched the big man position his men for an assault but waited. As they clumsily began stumbling up the wall, he raced back through the rooms to the central corridor, slipping out the back doorway. Sprinting across the backside of the temple, he entered the open field. Kuul and the girls had reached a big tree and were disappearing down another wall.

Chuuy and his men topped the wall, the soldiers nervously glancing at each other, pointing their automatic weapons at the temple. He motioned them forward with his pistol, *"Vamonos, compadres!"* Entering the building, they worked their way, chamber by chamber, to the opening in the center.

Chuuy stuck his head out and yelled at Hernando, *"Capitán, está vacío! The gringo se ha ido!"*

Gone, Gomez cursed, motioning for Chuuy to move through the other half of the temple. *Madre de dios*, why did he need to tell him that. He swept the field to his left. *There!* The Americano had tricked him; he was running into the shade of a ceiba tree – alone.

"SARGENTO SALAMANDOR, HE IS ESCAPING FROM THE OTHER END, TOWARD THE BALLCOURT!" Gomez yelled. He heard a muffled response from Chuuy from inside the temple.

Gomez climbed down from his perch in the stones, slipping and falling the last two feet. He jogged parallel to the base of the wall, the end of which was where the American should be appearing. The jungle rot between his testicles and thighs made running out of the question. *Where were the other Americanos? Could they still be inside? No, they must have left sooner out the back of the temple like the gringo.* Gomez hoped he was guessing right about their escape route. Then he saw the gringo run from out behind the wall, heading for the backside of the ballcourt. He raised his weapon but decided against firing – not until he was closer and had found them all. He slowed, looking up the hill, expecting to see Chuuy and his men running across the field. *Nada. Madre de dios.*

Skip saw the man aim his gun, fortunately it wasn't an AK like they had heard earlier, and then decide against firing. It was a long shot for a pistol. Ahead he saw Kuul, trailing Lilac and Toni. They were at the far end of the ballcourt, heading toward another structure. What had Kuul called it...the House of the Iguanas? Kuul looked back, and Skip waved at him to keep running.

"I'LL MEET YOU AT THE PARKING LOT!" he shouted. Kuul nodded.

Gomez was standing alone, cursing at Chuuy. The idiot and his men had backtracked through the turtle temple and were outside of where they had originally entered. Chuuy was scanning the park in the opposite direction; his men sitting on the top of the wall in front of the temple. Gomez shook his head in disgust, unholstered his gun again, and fired a shot into the rocks beside them. The men jumped and cowered below the wall thinking they were under attack. At least Chuuy stood his ground, finally seeing his *Capitán.* "*Vamonos,*" Gomez heard him yell to the men to no effect.

Lilac rounded the corner of the House of the Iguanas. A dozen scaly, beautifully colored iguanas were lounging in the sun on its warm stone steps. The largest, six feet long, nose-to-tail, raised its iridescent, lime-green head and lazily followed her movements. The House of Iguanas was smaller than the Temple of Turtles. Crowning the front façade was an intricately carved frieze, eleven thick columns rose from its base, behind which a deep porch disappeared into the shadows. She couldn't see any openings leading inside, but they were heading for the pathway anyway. She stopped to catch her breath, letting Toni, then Kuul, pull up beside her.

"Skip?" she anxiously asked.

"He's behind us," Kuul said, hands on his hips, gasping for air.

Toni was scanning the area left to right. The pathway out of the park was just ahead, between the huge Temple of the Magician on their right and the block-sized Nunnery to their left. She was searching for another way out than through the narrow passageway. If they ran between the two imposing structures, it was all or nothing.

She was about to yell at the others to move when three soldiers appeared on the path. They were in no hurry, joshing and pushing each other, like boys on a playground. One of them was smoking, and they were passing a bottle between them. The man smoking saw her, threw down his cigar, and pointed toward them.

"Guys, we have a problem."

Lilac and Kuul followed her stare.

Skip ran up behind them, looking back for the men he knew would be following them, "We've got a little time, but not much."

"Try again...*spymaster*, you're right at home, aren't you?" Lilac said, pointing at the soldiers ahead, giving him a cold glare. They had a lot to talk about on this trip, but not now.

"They'll be on us before we can get past the Magician's Temple," Skip said. Their predicament wasn't good, but it wasn't hopeless. He had been in tighter spots. "There are only three of them. They don't look particularly tough...maybe a little drunk," he said, noting the one holding a nearly empty bottle. "We either fight them here in the open or on the porch among the columns. There's no other choice. We can't go back; we'd run into the others."

"Columns," Lilac decided. "It worked for Cary Grant and Audrey Hepburn in *Charade*. They might be drunk, but they're still armed. We'll at least have the columns to protect us. Let's go before they –"

The soldiers suddenly stopped, staring into the vaulted arch of the Nunnery. Lilac couldn't see what was capturing their attention, but whatever they saw scared them...two of the soldiers screamed and started running toward the Magician's Temple. The remaining soldier stood riveted to his spot, trying to get his Berretta out of his holster. His panic kept him from opening the flap.

"*Demonios Mayas!*" he screeched, tripping over his feet as he stumbled backwards.

Pouring out of the Nunnery, fanning in all directions, roared a spiked-back army of iguanas. The head iguana, with spines as tall as bowie knives, charged the panicked soldier. The iguana snorted, opening its jaws. The bloody pink lining in its mouth made it all the more menacing. Fifty of its lieutenants joined the chase. Even the big sucker Lilac had seen lounging on the steps, joined in the melee. The soldier was in full retreat and jumped a yellow rope in front of the Temple of the Magician, catching his foot on the first step and landing flat on his back. Ten snapping iguanas leapt on top of him. His two *campañeros* were already twenty steps above him. One of them had managed to extricate his weapon and was aimlessly firing at the advancing reptiles as he fell. He emptied his gun and instead of taking the time to load another clip, threw it at the iguana leader, missing it by a mile. Clawing reptiles had circled the other soldier and were ripping his pants to shreds.

"NOW'S OUR CHANCE!" Toni yelled, running around the side of the temple instead of through the iguana army. The grassy field behind the Magician led toward the parking lot and visitors center.

Across the field, they jumped over a wooden barrier onto a pathway that led them through the dense jungle. Monkeys were howling at them overhead while they dodged overhanging palm fronds the size of bedsheets. Skip took the lead, planning to bowl into any more soldiers coming their way.

At the end of the path, the gate from the visitor center and parking area was closed. They didn't see any staff or security present and ran into the nearly empty lot. Only their rental car and a white cargo van remained; the unmarked van with two empty Oaxaca Blanco rum bottles by the back wheels undoubtedly belonging to their attackers.

Kuul, Toni, and Lilac ran straight for their car. Skip veered off to the van.

Kuul began ransacking his pockets for the key fob. "Skip has the key!" he shouted.

"Get in!" Toni yelled from the passenger side, unlocking the door, jangling the keys at him.

Kuul punched the brake and start button, slipped the transmission into Drive, and stomped on the gas, fishtailing to his friend.

Skip had been busy at the cargo van...the tires on the left side were partially deflated and they could hear air hissing. For good measure, he had popped the hood and yanked out a hose, which he threw on the ground.

"*VAMONOS*, BROTHER!" Kuul yelled.

Lilac swung the back door open and Skip dove into the seat, pulling the door shut a second before three loud thuds sounded against the metal, echoed by gun blasts. As Kuul peeled away, they peeked out the back window. The big man who had led the attack was waving his pistol, screaming at one of his soldiers.

What none of them had seen was the Persian woman who had stampeded the iguanas. She had followed them to the lot and was hiding beside the visitor center...*still in disbelief*. Her Sig P226 with titanium suppressor was drawn, and she had been ready to take out the Guatemalan if the man he was aiming at had not gotten safely into his vehicle.

ARRIVAL OF THE CHINESE

CAMPECHE SITS ON THE OPPOSITE SIDE OF THE YUCATAN Peninsula from Cancun and Cozumel with their hordes of rowdy vacationers. Traditional Mexican hues of yellows, purples, and reds cover the stucco walls of the historic district's colonial era buildings, now boutique hotels, restaurants, artisan shops, and tequila tasting rooms with modern interiors. Wooden balconies spilling with gardenias and thick oak doors open onto cobblestoned streets. Warm southern breezes from The Gulf of Mexico, two blocks away, mix the smell of fresh catch with spices and flowers.

Lilac and Toni were sitting at a table outside the Hotel Misión in Old Town. It was the day after their adventure at *Uxmal*. The street was pedestrian only and filled with seating. Lilac was devouring the best huevos rancheros in the world. Fried egg, potatoes, and squash salsa filled the warm, handmade tortilla covered in a perfectly blended habanero pepper sauce. Toni was sipping her second cup of unsweetened Mayan coffee with chocolate and cinnamon. Later in the afternoon, waiters would add spiced Rum liqueur to the same drink.

"This is amazing," Lilac said between bites, scooping leftover chili sauce onto her beans.

"Let's hope you still think so this afternoon."

"What? It's not street food. Probably safer here than in Uptown Sedona."

"Different inspection standards in Mexico. How do you eat like that and stay so fit?" Toni chuckled. "One blue corn taco and I see it on my hips."

"Yoga and running," Lilac answered, wiping a trail of green sauce from her lip to chin.

Toni stirred her coffee. She was near the bottom of the cup, where the strong cocoa had settled. It tasted bitter at first but had a sweet aftertaste. Their Mayan waiter, sporting a white guayabera shirt and black dress slacks, appeared from inside the cantina, sitting another cup on the table and refilling Lilac's water glass for the fifth time. They were in no hurry. The boys had gone to an early appointment with the *Policía Federales*. Given what they had reported the day before, they might be a while.

"So, you and Skip?" Toni asked, treading carefully. Kuul had been surprised when Lilac had agreed to come on this trip.

He had told Toni about the incident at the Grand Canyon. Lilac had chased a man along the rim, fought with him, and been shoved over the edge. Fortunately, she had caught herself on an old telephone pole, where Kuul had later rescued her – while Skip, believing she had died, had chased her attacker. Something had changed between them that night; she had been upset and left the next day. Why, Kuul wasn't sure, unless it was because his friend hadn't been the one to stop and save her. All he had gotten from Skip was that she had later questioned, *"Who he was."* She had not liked his answer.

Lilac drained half the glass of water, studying Toni's impassive face. It was impossible to tell what she was thinking...or what she'd been told. Laconic with words and in expression would be one way to describe her. They were friends, but not close friends.

"How goes it with Kuul?"

Fair enough, Toni thought. "Slow. I haven't decided if I am meant to be part of his 'journey.' He is honest, kind, and deserving of trust, a good man, just too easy-going. He is still searching for his place."

Kuul's journey. Many women had taken that ride. Lilac had been surprised when Toni had showed up with him at one of Zula's Tequila Moon parties. They seemed polar opposites - Toni was dedicated to her people and serious, Kuul more a floater. Her coming to Mexico had been even more surprising. Toni wasn't the type to undertake any journey lightly. *If she wasn't sure, what was she doing here?* The thought had no sooner crossed her mind than Lilac realized she should be asking herself the same question.

"Skip and I are working through some issues. Maybe we'll get through them and maybe we won't. He's loyal as a Labrador, even caring when he thinks of it...but *trusting*? There is a line he draws and anything past that he's not sharing – and there is a lot on the other side of that line."

"Men have secrets. Sometimes we do not want to know them. Sometimes we should not. His is a good heart, but it is shrouded in dark clouds. He will always live his life according to his own rules."

Toni had hit the nail on the head. That night at the Grand Canyon, Skip had shared enough about his past to scare her. He admitted to having been an assassin for a government agency more secretive than the CIA. He had sworn that life was over. But he hadn't been willing to share any specifics about what he had done or who he had been before, not even his true name. He had said none of it mattered now. Lilac had not been willing to accept those blanks.

When she'd pushed, he had admitted to being in love – he had said, "once" not *before*. That ended when the woman abandoned him in the middle of the night. He claimed that the woman was dead now, killed by her own people. But could she ever be sure? There was so much he refused to tell her.

Lilac stared past Toni, beyond the next street, out to the *malecón* where couples were walking hand-in-hand. She could smell the salt air and see simple fishing boats out in the bay; men casting nets to catch what would be on these tables tonight. Men who would go home at the end of the day to a loving wife and adoring children. It was such a long way from where she imagined she and Skip could ever be.

Lost in her thoughts, the scuffling of chairs brought her back to the real world. A hand rested on her shoulder, affectionately massaging the soft spot beside her neck.

"It's peaceful here, isn't it?" Skip, the man without a name said, pulling up a stool. "How was breakfast?"

Lilac sighed and he released her neck. "Excellent. You should try something." Lilac motioned to the waiter who was already heading their way with two menus.

Skip waved him off. "Kuul and I already ate."

"You won't believe what the Federales told us," Kuul said.

"What happened?" Toni asked.

"Not what we expected. They think the men at *Uxmal* were part of a gang, possibly even the Jalisco Cartel, which is moving into Cancun. Cocom had probably crossed them somehow. We might as well have been talking about a dead coyote alongside a road. I wouldn't even bet they will inform his family – they didn't write down his name."

"They weren't very concerned about another drug killing," Skip added.

"Or, I guess, with American tourists being attacked," Lilac said.

Skip shrugged and motioned to the waiter. The aroma from Toni's cup had changed his mind. "The lieutenant said we were unfortunate to have been caught in the middle, but it has happened before. They didn't seem motivated to investigate further."

"Apparently, they're used to it," Kuul said. "We filled out a report, gave descriptions, and let them know where we're staying. And that was the end of it."

The *Federales* reaction had not surprised Skip. Life was cheap in poorer parts of the world. He'd seen the same thing, counted on it even, in more places than he cared to remember. The waiter arrived and Skip pointed to Toni's cup, *"Uno más por favor."*

Kuul had been studying the menu, breakfast had been a donut and glass of pomegranate juice in the hotel lobby. *"Señor,* how are the shark tacos?"

"Fresco. Bueno," the waiter said. "They are babies, *más* tender."

"You know sharks are endangered, right?" Toni chided Kuul.

"So are Mayans," the waiter answered, still smiling.

"I can vouch for the *Huevos,"* Lilac said.

"You sold me. The tacos, *por favor."* The waiter nodded and again disappeared into the restaurant.

"So, a gang of thugs wearing paramilitary clothing and carrying automatic weapons didn't bother them. Makes you wonder how cozy they are with the cartels," Toni said. "What did they say about the Mayan artifact?"

Kuul glanced at Skip before answering.

"Nothing. I didn't tell them about it. I was not comfortable giving it to them. If the vessel is what Gabor Cocom said it is, I didn't trust them not to sell it. We're taking it to Merida and turning it over to the Mexican archeological authorities there. They are responsible for the care of Mayan antiquities. It will be safe with them."

After Kuul's shark feast, they wandered through the quaint colonial streets inside Campeche's old walls. Rivaling Havana and Cartagena, the Spanish had built the port city to ship the newly discovered region's natural resources to their home country. They had climbed the thick, stone walls, exploring the bastions and turrets used to keep pirates out, and gazed across the red rooftops of the old town. At the canary yellow *El Palacio* Museum they posed with full-sized cutouts of the romanticized, swashbuckling thieves – Henry Morgan, Abraham Blauvelt, and Diego the Mulatto. Skip was particularly interested in the story of Sir Francis Drake, a man sanctioned by his government but considered a demon by everyone else. *Cut from the same cloth*, Lilac thought.

Across the central plaza from the museum stood the sixteenth century *Catedral de Nuestra Señora de la Purísima Concepción*. The simple beauty of its two bell towers, the white stucco shining against the blue sky, starkly contrasted with the golden entrance and red doors. With the cathedral's erection and the religious paintings inside, the Spanish had proclaimed a new spiritual identity for their conquest, replacing the two-millennium old beliefs of the Maya.

From the church, Kuul led them outside the old city walls through the *Puerta de Tierra*, the original gate to the city. They casually strolled to the Mercado Campeche, enjoying the street life along the way. The labyrinth of vendors in postage-stamp-sized stalls were selling everything from freshly butchered cuts of meat to secondhand soccer shirts in the claustrophobically narrow aisles. The mix of odors was overwhelming in the humid, tropical air.

"This afternoon heat is unbearable," Lilac said, dodging a vendor pressing a headless chicken toward her. "The hot air from these noisy fans only make it worse."

"Not a dry heat like back home," Kuul joked.

"Not your typical guidebook spot either. That place next to the stall with baby dresses is selling skinned pig heads and rocky mountain oysters," Toni said, pointing. "Locals shop here."

Lilac was looking for anyplace that might have a cold cerveza when she saw a group of men who definitely weren't local. "Not those guys in business suits, by the corn-husked tamales," she said. "They look Asian, but it's hard to tell with their dark sunglasses. And I don't think they're tourists.."

Skip had already noticed them. There were five, definitely Asian. They had also been in the plaza and followed them to the cathedral. He'd guessed Korean at first because of their lighter skin but had settled on Northern Chinese because of their rounder faces and shorter noses. They were *all* tall, which was unusual unless they were part of a select team. The tallest one had been watching him. There was a bulge in his jacket...same size, same spot for a shoulder holster.

Skip began walking toward them, returning the man's stare. "I think I'll say hello,"

The man with the jacket smirked, turned, and led the other men through the back of the tamale stand, disappearing into a maze of stalls selling I Love Mexico shoulder bags, knock-off designer jeans, and three-for-the-price-of-one t-shirts. By the time Skip waded through the next section of stalls with string hammocks and embroidered pillowcases, they were gone.

"Anyone you know?" Lilac said, catching up to him.

"In sleepy Campeche? Not likely." They were a type he knew though – he had been one himself.

OLD LADY WHITE STONE

AS THE SUN SET, KUUL AND TONI MADE THEIR WAY TO CAMPECHE'S central square, *Plaza de la Independencia*. Skip and Lilac were off exploring an old Spanish fort on the outskirts of the city. They planned to meet for drinks later at Casa Vieja del Rio, a restaurant overlooking the square.

After dark, the plaza became the old town's living room. In front of the brightly illuminated bell towers of the cathedral, vendors set up carts selling tortillas and tacos. The colonnaded buildings surrounding the square – their colorful exteriors so vibrant in sunlight, had mellowed into cool pastels. Laughing couples packed a gazebo in the center of the plaza, dancing to music drifting across cobblestoned streets.

The *paseo nocturno* had begun; young lovers strolled hand-in-hand, parents watched their children play in the soft grass and run along brick paths, elderly *Campechanos* lounged in lawn chairs, enjoying the cool night air. With her arm through Kuul's, Toni and he had done their own *paseo*, finding an empty park bench in a quiet corner to take in the show. Hips touching, watching life, they sat happy and anonymous among people who looked like them and who they understood. This was a simple place with simple rules. The complexities of the modern world were far away..

"It is wonderfully peaceful here, isn't it? Uncorrupted," Toni said.

"This park was the center of a Mayan village, pre-conquest. I doubt these people are much different than the Maya who lived here then. They're celebrating the end of the day, together, the way they have for hundreds of years."

Toni turned Kuul's face to hers, studying his eyes. "Your spirit has been here before; you believe you belong to them." He smiled and his soft Mayan face glowed.

"I feel I'm home."

Toni kissed his cheek. The salt from a tear met her lips. They sat in silence, Kuul's long legs stretching straight as he relaxed against the back of the bench. Toni nestled closer against his side and his arm held her tighter.

"You think Skip and Lilac will find us?" she asked, not wanting to break the spell but hoping to understand where his mind had gone.

"It would be okay if they don't."

Toni watched as he slipped back into his own thoughts. He had been sent elsewhere by the innocent laughter of children, an old man singing a soulful song, and the tangy ocean air mixed with the floral scent of frangipani. His hand absently caressed her shoulder, gently brushing her long hair behind her ear. Goosebumps rose on her arm.

Since he was a boy, Kuul had wanted to visit his ancestral home but had never made the time. His feelings had always been mixed. His father had been Maya, forced to leave in the early eighties. As a young, progressive, Indigenous man, he had been active in land reform politics, working with Francisco Luna Kan, the first Maya elected governor of the state...the first Mayan political head since the Spanish conquest. Their methods had been non-violent protest against the Mexican government's caste-based exploitation of native peoples. Despite the election, his father's footing changed with the emergence of the Zapatista National Liberation Front, the EZLN, in neighboring Chiapas. For them, violence became the new norm of resistance. His father had been bountied and chose to relocate to Northern Mexico, eventually making his way to Nogales where he met Ania Balthazar, Kuul's part Yaqui mother.

His father had settled into a quiet agrarian life, never revisiting his troubled times or his home in Mexico. Never had the proud rebel expressed any disappointment in his big son who, thanks to his wife's German genes, towered over him and outweighed him by "half a lamb." Not a word of rebuke when Kuul had become a plumber for rich Norte Americanos nor when he had pretended to be Navajo. On the day he died, the old man had kissed him and merely said, *"Look at yourself in our mirror to see who you truly are."* It was an old Mayan saying. His father's 'mirror' was his Mayan homeland.

"They all look like me. Shorter, but otherwise like me," Kuul finally said, straightening in his seat, smiling wanly at Toni. "Back home, I am taken for Navajo...Hopi...Apache...even Yavapai. Never has anyone ever seen me as Maya."

"Back home, you are Kuul. Same person you are here – at least to me."

"Until this trip, I never actually thought of the Maya still being here, not in my heart anyway - in my head I knew they were, but not in my heart. I thought of them as kings and warriors, living in temples, growing maize, holding bloody contests in their ballcourts, and studying the cycles of time and the stars. I thought of them as conquered people subsumed by the Spanish then Mexican cultures, not as people who have persevered and still maintain their identity. I can see the pride in them I saw in my father."

Toni stood, pulling her favorite Mayan man off the bench. "Let's walk. I would like to see inside the church at night. Immaculate conception – only the devout Spanish would believe a woman would endure the pain of childbirth without first enjoying herself."

Kuul accepted the lighter mood and laughed, "Yavapai women are much more demanding."

Holding hands, they strolled through the park. The moon had risen, and the sky was an inky, navy blue. They could hear the dancers at the pavilion, but the parents with young children had left. The street vendors had also packed up. The cathedral's huge red doors were open, inviting all in who wanted to thank God for another day and to pray for tomorrow.

It was dark beneath the canopy of limbs. The last streetlamp was out, and lights from the bell towers barely penetrated the thick trees. Partly concealed by shadows were two Asian men standing next to the walkway.

"You see them? They were at the market," Toni whispered as they got closer.

Kuul nodded, "Yes. Keep walking. There will be people at the cathedral."

Two more men were standing in the street by an empty vendor's stand. The man who seemed to be their leader was sitting on the stairs leading to the cathedral...watching them approach. A plume of golden smoke, colored by the church's lights, curled above a cigarette he held between two fingers. Toni glanced back, sensing the men in the park and by the stall were following them.

"Just keep walking," Kuul whispered.

The man on the stairs stood, raising his cigarette to his mouth. He inhaled deeply and slowly blew smoke in the air. He had changed since their afternoon encounter. Same jacket, but he now wore dark jeans and caramel-colored loafers, with a black tee instead of a white dress shirt and tie. Kuul couldn't tell if the holster was in place, but assumed he was still carrying a weapon. Ominously, Beijing Bond's mirrored aviator glasses were aimed at Toni.

"Keep walking," Kuul repeated.

Not what her grandmother would do, Toni thought. She would never have ignored such a challenge. She let go of Kuul's hand

and faced the man. His henchmen stopped pretending and began moving quickly toward their boss. The Chinese man removed his glasses, motioning his men to back off.

"You're following us," Toni said.

The Chinese man smiled, purposely tucking his aviators into his jacket pocket, and adjusting the sleeves. The bulge of the gun holster was obvious. "This is a small town. The places to visit are limited."

"What do you want?" Kuul asked.

"You should be very careful with what you have," the man said, dropping his cigarette on the ground, crushing it with his shoe. "It is easy to lose things in Mexico...even people. Kidnappings are common here."

"Thanks for the warning. We're just here to visit the cathedral."

The man grinned as if they were playing a game. "You are a believer then, a Christian? You have faith in resurrection, in things being recovered."

"No more so than your ancestors, who, unlike mine, didn't cross the land bridge to Alaska and populate the Americas." Kuul detected a moment of confusion at his obscure reference to their ethnicities. "We probably share a genetic marker."

"Someday soon we will control them both," the man said, catching on.

Toni had heard enough macho man chit-chat and nudged Kuul, "I still want to see the cathedral."

The Chinese stepped aside and turned toward the church, gesturing like a waiter ushering diners to their table. "Make sure you visit the reliquaries. There is a *vessel* depicting the burial of Jesus Christ. It is said to hold great power...unless it has been stolen by someone with evil intentions."

Kuul didn't budge, despite Toni's tug. "They have an urn here, not a vessel...and it's safe where it is." He didn't like the man's threats, no matter how cleverly they were delivered or how obvious the point.

The two men locked eyes, both of them standing their ground, fighting a cold, deadly war in their heads. Toni had given up trying to move Kuul – they couldn't win this battle, he had to know that.

The Chinese finally spoke, "Don't test my patience...Indian." He extracted his glasses and began cleaning them with a cloth. "Talk to your man," he said sharply to Toni, then walked away.

By the time Kuul and Toni reached the cathedral doors, the Chinese team had disappeared into the park.

"Land bridge to Alaska?" Toni hissed.

Kuul shrugged, "It's what popped into my head."

The worn and unfinished facade of the church reminded Toni of the Alamo, its scalloped roofline recalling the Texas mission. The old, double red doors would be easy to breach. Not a place to be making their last stand. But at the moment, it was their closest sanctuary.

Inside, wooden pews filled the cavernous nave. Side chapels with paintings of saints and glass-encased statuary lined the walls. Toni didn't see an urn or vessel, but there was a sign saying the Chapel of *Jesús Nazareno* was *cerrado*, closed. The cathedral was empty except for two old women praying, a priest straightening the high altar, two tourists at the door checking their cell phones...and Our Lady of the Immaculate Conception above the altar.

"What do you think she would say?" Toni asked, nodding at the figurine of a dark-haired woman wearing a crown. Even in a church dedicated to her, a man had top billing – Jesus was above, looking down, signifying he was in charge.

"Nothing just happens...beware of strange men," Kuul quipped.

Toni frowned. "Jokes aside…"

"It's clear they want the Mayan vessel. We'll stay in here a while to make sure they've left."

Kuul watched the priest smooth a white cloth he had placed over the communion table. Communion – the blood and flesh of Jesus – symbolism not much different than what Mayan priests performed on their sacrificial Chacmool and jaguar altars. But this priest was not Maya or Mexican. He was white, yet the spiritual leader of this religious community, assuming a divine connection and ability to intercede with supernatural forces on their behalf. To do that, he prayed to his Christian God in his holy church. Did he even acknowledge that prayer ceremonies had been happening in the Americas long before Christianity, long before cathedrals? Chants and dances for good hunts, rain, health - weren't they prayers? Weren't they religions that bound pre-contact civilizations? Kuul's people's belief in higher powers had been interwoven with their daily lives for millennia.

His own beliefs were not complicated. They were not tied to the litany of Mayan gods and goddesses. Rather, he believed that everything in nature possessed a spirituality, not just christened humans. Everything had a divine force of existence, a sacredness born from the simple act of being. Ancient Maya referred to the force as *K'uh*. Like *hózhó* in Navajo, *K'uh* meant all things, the stars, the animals, the plants, and the earth were connected. They were all to be equally respected.

Toni's thoughts had been mirroring Kuul's. She was fascinated by the church's iconography and creamy statues of the virgin Mary. "Yavapai have our own *woman* that we pray to. *Old Lady White Stone* was a healer god. She sowed all the healing plants that grow around us, back home. She taught us how to cultivate nature to sustain our bodies and use her to treat our sicknesses."

"And your *Lofty Wanderer, Skara K'a mca.*"

Kuul knew Toni believed in the legend of the Lofty Wanderer. He who ordered the chaos of an early, unruly world, not unlike the white man's God. European missionaries had appropriated the stories of the Old Lady and the Wanderer, melding them with their own doctrines, to appeal to her People's pre-existing beliefs. The Mayan creation stories in the *Popol Vul* and *Chilam Bilam,* recorded in the time of Spanish colonialism by an ingratiating Jaguar priest, were similarly tainted. The *Popol Vul* credited *Huracán,* a major Mayan god, as being the "giver of life" and "heart of heaven and earth." Some Mayan sects saw him as the ultimate creator.

"It is hard to know what our ancestors originally believed," Kuul said.

"I believe in our stories," Toni answered. "Yes, they are hazy. And some have been reimagined. But the cores of personal spirituality, the sacredness of the earth, and their being gifts from the Great Spirit is what I know and trust – you do too." Kuul nodded, but Toni wasn't sure if he agreed or was just giving in.

"Let's see if the Buddhists are still outside," he said.

The Chinese were nowhere to be seen, so they took a chance, strolling back through the emptied park. Only one pair of lovers remained, intertwined on a bench, wrapped in their own emotions and dreams, not caring about one more native man and woman sharing the intimacy of the warm night.

Kuul spotted a horse and buggy in the street. The driver, straw hat in hand, was beckoning them over, "A ride along the promenade *Señor*? The moon is shining on the gulf and your woman is exceptionally beautiful."

Kuul smiled at Toni, "*Sí.*"

CANNON FIRE

"**S**O, KUUL TAKES TONI TO A ROMANTIC DINNER AND SQUARE, and you bring me to a fort," Lilac chastised, gazing across the quaint fishermen's harbor. She and Skip were atop the old walls of Fort San Miguel, three miles from the historic center of Campeche. The traditional white and blue boats were resting listlessly in the calm, late afternoon water.

"It was built to protect the city from the English, who had already taken Belize," Skip said, looking down at the dry moat at the base of the walls, ignoring her sarcasm. "The Fort of San Miguel was constructed in 1792 and now serves as Campeche's *Museo de Arqueología*," he read from a signboard.

They had already toured the lower rooms housing small, funerary figurines from the island of Jaina, and death masks uncovered at *Calakmul*, another ancient Mayan city. Skip had read every line in the glass cases and exhibits while Lilac had done a slow burn the entire time – lover boy was putting off the inevitable.

"This trip was to be about how we move forward...if we move forward. About your past and if that's who you still are," Lilac said. She was done with listening about forts and masks. "We can't just keep pushing all that back. Ignoring the gorilla won't make it go away."

The dull stone fort had turned deep gold in color. As pretty as the late afternoon was, she wasn't going to let him forget his

60

promise. Months earlier, in an emotionally charged moment – she'd nearly died – he'd admitted he wasn't who he pretended to be. He had worked for a special agency of the government and done awful things. Things he had become unable to justify in his mind. Burnout and the death of another foreign agent, an agent he'd been in love with, had led him to walk away. Whether his walking into her life was a good thing or bad thing, Lilac was still trying to decide.

"I know we need to talk," he said.

Skip watched the last fishing boat come into the harbor with their day's catch and dock alongside an old pier. Two men in white chef's uniforms were waiting. The bay was calm, the sun casting a yellow streak across the silvery water. He turned and stepped toward Lilac, uncertain, not sure how she would react. The little he had shared had torn a rift between them that he wasn't sure could be repaired.. He knew he needed her; he had realized that at the rim of the Grand Canyon.

Lilac stepped back into a turret of the fort, barely big enough for both of them, her eyes on his, begging him to follow her. He had no way out if he did. Would he come to her, or would he stay outside, afraid of being trapped?

Skip ducked under the low doorway, turning sideways to fit through the tight opening. She was standing in front of a slit in the stone intended for a rifle. A soft halo of golden light surrounded her red hair and cast her face in shadow. She didn't move – *was she afraid? Had he confused her that badly?*

"How do we move forward?" he asked, using her words. She was his height, her questioning eyes level with his. "We just do," he said, taking her in his arms.

There was no wistful tilting of her face to his like in the movies. His hands dropped to her waist, and he pulled her against him. Before their lips met, he whispered, "I need you. You keep me from being who I was." They kissed over and over, letting their lips make promises neither was sure they could keep. They were together now, and in this moment that was enough.

"I have always loved you," Lilac breathed. "The rest, the future...we can figure out."

"Lilac, I –"

His head cocked away from her...like a dog that had picked up a scent. His stare, riveted on her seconds before, shot out the door. He pushed her back, instinctively shielding her body with his.

The motion outside had been something he sensed more than saw. His sixth sense, the alarm he had learned to trust most, rang a bell in his head. *There... in his periphery*...across from the turret, on the top step of the nearest stairway...*a woman*...fluid movement...*a body he knew*.

The woman glanced at him, their eyes meeting, and his heart leapt. The flawless olive skin he'd found comfort in years ago, the impenetrable, dark brown eyes that had lied to him – she stared back with a pained expression. Skip froze, unable to move or breathe. Then she disappeared down the stairs.

"Who is she?" Lilac said, bumping into him as he abruptly stopped.

"Daria...my God...Daria Ahmadi," Skip stammered, gaping at where she had been. "I thought she was dead."

Daria's mission and world had been turned upside down when she saw him at *Uxmal*. She had been told by her MOIS commander that he was dead. But lying to their agents was standard procedure for the Ministry of Intelligence Services for the Republic of Iran.

It had been seven years since she had seen him. Singapore – two weeks off their country's grids – alone...at first hating each other, then, inexplicably, falling in love. They had fooled themselves.

Seven years ago, she had been the leader of the MOIS team sent to find and dispatch him after his escape from Tehran. They had chased him to Bangkok, and, if not for a timely knock at his door, her shot through his open window would not have missed. In Hong Kong, they had almost gotten him again, but he had slipped away with the help of a local informant. There had been hell to pay then. The Supreme Commander had called her team back, but instead, she had continued on her own, continuing their cat and mouse game across Southeast Asia, before it ended in Singapore, where he had surprised her.

He had lured her to a killing room he kept in the back of a dingy shop in Chinatown. She had watched him eat at a hawker stand and followed him through a maze of alleys until he had disappeared on a quiet lane. She had entered the alley, pistol drawn, but woke up hours later in her bra and panties chained to bed springs, the metal eating into her flesh.

He was there sitting on a wooden stool...waiting. He told her in a cold, monotone voice that he planned to eliminate her after getting whatever information she gave up. From the look in his dead eyes, Daria knew he had killed before.

"We can make this easy or hard," he had said. "That's up to you."

A shriveled Chinese woman had entered the room depositing a tea set. She poured two cups and then left. He sipped from his, smiled, held the other steaming cup above the soft flesh of her inner thigh and poured slowly. When she didn't scream, but rather spit at him, he had seemed impressed not angry.

The interrogation had lasted two days, during which there had been no further physical torture, just endless questioning at irregular intervals each day and night. The burning tea had been a warning; her understanding that he could do other things, more painful things, was enough. Fear was as much a part of their trade as death.

By the third day, they reached a sort of détente. He had unchained her, leaving her free to move about and use the bucket in the corner of the room. By day five, she knew he had given up breaking her without resorting to crueler measures, measures which he did not seem to relish. The interrogation turned into conversation. He began talking about their lives as agents and the "insanity" of what they did. Saying that was not who they were. At first, she thought it was part of a 'good cop' routine. But as the days passed, she realized he was deeply conflicted – conflicted about her, conflicted about the things he had done, conflicted about how this was supposed to end.

Intimacy eventually formed between them. Their lives weren't all that different, both dictated by duty. In their talks, he had told her that their kind did not murder or torture out of passion. Passion, they set aside, stored in a deep part of themselves; passion was dangerous. Daria found she no longer hated him...she understood him.

At the end of a week, their talks ended. He came in the morning.

'We have to end this,' he said, raising the pistol held in his hand.

The barrel of his gun shook, and wetness clouded his eyes. *She* had broken *him*. Daria stepped toward him, and he lowered his hand. Another tenuous step and she took his pistol from him. He shook his head in resignation. Daria touched his face, wiping away a tear as she put the gun back in his holster.

The next two weeks they barely left the room. The Chinese woman brought them what they needed. It was only moments after Daria had put his gun back that he had taken her, and she him. From then on, the room became their sanctuary. Nothing existed past the walls, no duty, no countries, no violent pasts, no training. Just passion. They knew their safety was only temporary and didn't care. They talked about who they had been. Daria had been recruited by

MOIS as a girl from Khorramabad in western Iran. She was Shiite Muslim and her family and home had been destroyed during the Iran-Iraq War. She had been angry and had never known anything else...until now...in this room.

He was sleeping when she left him. She could still feel her tears burning her cheeks. He was so peaceful, so helpless lying there, expecting her to be next to him when he awoke. The night before they had pledged their love and their allegiances to each other, over their states. They had made promises and had meticulously planned their disappearances. They would spend forever together, however long that might be. He had held her, swearing on his life to keep her safe and happy, telling her how she had saved him, how she had delivered him from certain hell. She had known it could not be, but not him. *They* wouldn't allow it.

Now, here he was, in Mexico, back again. Back from the dead. Back in her life...holding another woman and somehow involved in her assignment. When their eyes had briefly locked, she had seen the flare of recognition and the flood of buried emotions. She wondered what hers had shown him.

If not for her intervention, the Guatemalans might have killed him and that red head. He was lucky MOIS had been in charge and not the Islamic Revolutionary Guards Corps, who would have assassinated him and his friends to get what they were after. That she had not, meant there would be repercussions if the President of Iran discovered what she had done. Her decision, she realized, might cost her everything she held dear.

"STAY HERE," Skip barked, running toward the stairs.

Screw that, Lilac thought. Two flights of stairs rose to the top of the fort from opposite sides of a lower courtyard. She would let him follow whomever he'd seen, and she would take the other set.

If the woman he was chasing doubled back, she'd be there to cut her off.

Skip reached the courtyard just in time to see Daria exit the fort through an archway onto a drawbridge and disappear again. She was heading for the parking lot, where he guessed she either had a car or someone waiting. Glancing over his shoulder, he didn't see Lilac – for once she had listened to him.

Daria had not gone to the parking lot. She was fast, but he was faster. She hid below the drawbridge, in the dry moat, under a pair of stone arches shaped like an old aqueduct. She heard his heavy feet overhead, pounding across the wooden planks. He never slowed down, and, as she had guessed, discarded any idea that she might have climbed down the shaky, workers' staircase at the end of the bridge. He would pursue her all the way to the parking lot, even farther when he found she wasn't there. Her heart had screamed to stop and let him catch her, but now wasn't the time, not with the other woman.

Lilac reached the courtyard, but they were both gone. The gift shops and small museum rooms looked empty except for a clerk she could see through a window. The woman's head was down, and she was shuffling papers on a counter, readying to close for the day. Lilac passed through the arched exit, half expecting to see Skip coming back across the drawbridge. He wasn't and she stopped midway, scanning the moat – *no one*. But there was a small stairway on the far side of the bridge.

Daria heard a lighter set of feet stop overhead. Within seconds, the shaky stairs she had climbed down began to creak. She slid deeper into the shadows. *The red-headed woman.* She was tall, a head taller than herself. A ponytail reached her shorts, the hem folded to show off her tanned, finely muscled legs. *Western women were so vain – let them wear a burka for a week.* The woman was alert, peering through the dark arch, down the grassy moat.

They must have run toward the parking lot, Lilac thought. Or, if they were running fast enough, they had rounded the corner of the moat to the other side of the fort. She was deciding what to do when a pistol pressed against her back. *Where was lunkhead when she needed him!*

"Do not move and do not yell for him," Daria whispered.

"Who are you and what are you after?"

"A little conversation between two girls…that is all."

"But not a friendly one."

"It will be as friendly as you make it," Daria answered. "Did the dead man give you the Mayan formula at *Uxmal*? Is that why you are here?" After stampeding the iguanas, she searched the temple and found Gabor Cocom.

Lilac's mind was racing. Should she engage her, stall for time in hope that Skip came back soon, or fight? All the man had given them was an old cup. The police had not cared, but the gang at *Uxmal* and Chinese in town had. And now this woman with her noticeable Mideast accent. Keeping her hands up, she slowly started to turn.

"Don't," Daria said, jamming her gun deeper into the woman's kidney. "Whatever he gave you, I want."

"All he gave us was a worthless old cup."

Daria's training told her she was telling the truth, even though a *cup* was not what she had been sent to find. A gun in the woman's back didn't scare her either. She needed to be careful with this one. Being cool in this situation implied training, and she was with him, suggesting she could be dangerous in her own right.

"How do you know him?" Daria asked.

"He died, I didn't."

"Not the dead man, the man you're with. What has he told you? What name is he using? Who sent you?"

This was Lilac's worst fear. She'd been afraid of Skip's past life resurfacing. That it would was inevitable, but she had expected it to come from within him. It was his nightmares and his screams in the middle of the night that she expected to battle. That old life was forever a part of him. He had admitted that, even warned her, telling her she shouldn't trust him. Was that what was happening here? Was this why they'd come to Mexico? Was he working again?

"Did he tell you who I am?" Daria asked, frustrated that the woman wasn't answering.

Lilac detected more than just business in her questions – *Skip's name...had he mentioned her*. The answers were personal for her. Skip had told her about another agent, a woman who had changed him, a woman he'd been prepared to give everything up for...before she had left him. But he had claimed she was dead – *the same thing he had said about this woman earlier*. Lilac was putting the pieces together when they heard Skip run back onto the drawbridge.

"He came back for you. I will shoot you both if you yell," Daria whispered. The red head wisely stayed quiet. His footsteps faded away, and Daria guessed he had gone back into the fort. "Start walking down the moat, do not look back," she said, shoving the woman forward.

The woman started moving, and Daria quickly reclimbed the shaky stairs. From the drawbridge, she stared at the woman below. The red head had stopped and was staring back. For a moment they studied each other. Daria finally broke their gaze and left. She wasn't going to get her answers here, not now.

Lilac took her time climbing out of the moat. She had no intention of chasing the woman, not before having a long talk with Skip. When she entered the courtyard, he was coming down the stairs from the top of the fort.

"Who is she?" Lilac asked.

"I don't know."

"You called her Daria Ahmadi. You know her. She asked about you. Don't lie!"

"What did she say?"

"She asked why we are here and what we have found...about a Mayan formula. Is she why we're here, is that damn cup why we're here?"

"Lilac...not now–"

"Who is she? Last chance."

He sighed, "Lilac, it was a long time ago. She was the woman I told you about, the one woman I loved... I thought...I thought she was dead. I was *told* she was dead. Believe me, I don't know what's going on here anymore than you."

Skip was just now beginning to process seeing her. *Daria was alive.* Alive and close. She hadn't been assassinated by her own people as his agency had reported. All the doubts, questions, suspicions, and emotions he had buried for seven years were bursting over him. His heart was pounding. The aching, empty hole he had lived with filled with...*relief.* The part of him that had died that morning in Singapore was suddenly resurrected.

"The *one* woman you loved," Lilac said, repeating his words. She could read his face like a book.

10

Patriotic Duty

"**G**OD DAMNIT, STINKER! THERE ARE BUGS ALL OVER THIS place," POTUS yelled. "Where is Walter Reed? Get him on the phone. What the hell kind of hospital is he running here? You're my medical director, can't you do something, go check their HEPA filters."

"Secretary of the Department of Health and Human Services, Mr. President." The man thought all two million federal employees were his personal servants. "I can call the Director of Homeland and order a sweep?"

"What? No damnit, not that kind of bug. The kind that can kill me!"

"I don't see any Mr. President. Walter Reed excels at pest control."

"GERMS, Stinker! GERMS!! I can smell them, Stinker. Now get on the damn phone and call Reed!"

"Walter Reed died, sir, quite some time ago."

"Probably from one his IVs," POTUS moaned. "God damn germs, Stinker. They are all over this line. They've let that Mexican nurse fiddle with it. Tamales under her fingernails, Stinker. I could smell them. Pork, Stinker, nothing more dangerous than poorly prepared pork."

"Pork, sir?"

"I want you to start an investigation of whoever it is that

makes pork. I shouldn't have to tell you this, Stinker. It's your god-damn job to keep me protected."

"Yes, Mr. President, I'll assign an undersecretary to it. And Walter Reed, sir, he discovered yellow fever was caused by mos-quitoes, which allowed us to finish the Panama Canal. The field of biomedicine owes him." For all Orville Stinckner's faults, he was a student of pharmacology and biomedicine.

"Yellow fever! That's fucking great! I have a serious bowel infection and they bring me to a place teeming with yellow fever. I would never have given that canal back, Stinker, fuck the Panamanians. Find out if Noriega is still jailed here, we'll hook him up to one of these fever infected IVs. Make the call, Stinker, make the damn call!"

"Noriega or Walter Reed?"

POTUS eyed his secretary. He could never read the man, whether he was loyal or another smart-ass, back-stabbing son-of-a-bitch. He had the man by his balls after he'd taken his bribe, but that could be reason enough to sabotage his recovery. He was too close to the Vice President, that wimpy, Bible-quoting, presbyterian from Ohio. He didn't even have the cajones to call himself an evan-gelical, it didn't play well with the unions.

"Stinker, what have you heard from Hector about the cocoa from the park?"

"His people haven't yet acquired the cacao recipe from *Palenque*, sir. They're covering all the bases though, trying to locate some coprolites from the Queen. President Colon said they could be dried, distilled, and smoked like a fine cigar. He said they have discovered Mayan hieroglyphics in her tomb recording huge cer-emonial feasts that were actually for the purpose of *losing* weight."

Stinckner smiled smugly, knowing POTUS was clueless that coprolites were human feces; his well-documented germaphobia would have set off another tantrum. *Coprolites* – when Colon had mentioned them on a secure video link, he had wanted to laugh in his face. *El Presidente* was a bigger moron than POTUS. Stinckner found the image of the two Presidents smoking what would likely be the excrement of a Mexican worker hilarious.

"What are you grinning about, Stinker? Royal tobacco would go well with chocolate. Let's mix those polites with the chocolate too, double down. Think big, Stinker! That's your problem, you never see the big picture. Let's get your chemists thinking outside the box on this. A good smoke and candy bar that melts fat would make us both tons of money. An exclusive dessert at my clubs."

"President Colon is causing a problem, though, Mr. President." Stinckner used his words carefully to avoid any blame. He knew how explosive POTUS's reaction was going to be. The man was already salivating thinking about chocolate bars; Stinckner didn't need another Presidential shower.

"I don't like problems, Stinky."

"It's Stinker, sir."

"Don't fuck with me, Orville."

"The Presidential Guard unit sent to acquire the asset, ran into a group of American tourists who had stumbled onto the thief who stole the vessel containing the chocolate recipe. The Guatemalans were unable to take it from them and allowed them to escape. Colon says not to worry, they have found them and have them under surveillance, biding their time until a more successful acquisition can be accomplished."

Stinckner watched POTUS turn red in the face, which took on a pinky coral tint with his orange tanning lotion. He backed farther out of range. POTUS's free hand shot forward, punching the air emphatically. Spittle sprayed from his mouth as he yelled, and Stinckner heard grisly farting sounds, "Americans! God damnit! Stinker, don't they want to help their President, don't they understand their patriotic duty! Stinker, I want you to go down there personally, appeal to them, explain how badly I need this chocolate. Appeal to their patriotism, Stinker."

"I'll take care of it, Mr. President."

Orville Stinckner wasn't about to go to any jungle, especially one in Mexico. He hated the food, the people, and the steamy climate, not to mention the snakes and scorpions he knew would be waiting for him. Besides, he suspected the American tourists might not be tourists. He didn't believe in coincidences, and their beating Colon's men to the Red Queen's vessel had to be a planned operation, a well-financed operation. He could see the handwriting of Bathsheba Cosmetics all over this. They had been a thorn in his company's side for years, stealing every formula they could get their greedy hands on. And this Mayan recipe was the pharmaceutical industry's holy grail. If the Americans were one of their teams, they would be far more dangerous and craftier than the Guatemalans. It also meant the value of the vessel was known outside the Presidents tight circle. There would be more complications, more players, if he didn't act fast.

This could not be an official government operation, not if Stinckner wanted to maintain control. Too many forms and bureaucrats, too much oversight. The do-gooders at HHS would offer it for free at every clinic from D.C. to L.A. They would call it a miracle for public health services. No, he had another operative in mind, an industrial mercenary he'd employed on-and-off to spy on his competitors and to do whatever needed to be done.

"I'll take care of it, Mr. President," Stinckner repeated, outlining his plan to POTUS.

"Now you're learning how to run a country, Stinker. Fuck the deep state." POTUS grinned.

And how to manage a narcissistic idiot, Orville Stinckner thought.

11

Sedona Chi

ZULA DIDN'T LIKE THEIR LOOKS, SO SHE MIXED THE SANGRIA WITH Mogen David instead of blackberry brandy. She was a good and quick judge of character. But they were customers at her Lazy SOB Bar and Grill, and that, at the very least, entitled them to more than a watered-down cabernet.

The SOB was named after Sonny O'Bryan, the foreman of a ranching operation that was long gone, but not forgotten. Zula had bought the dilapidated ranch house twenty years ago. Her retirement plan. By that time, the old place had already gone through several iterations of rebranding as a lodge and wooded retreat. None had been successful. The previous owners had added to the collection of bunkhouses and cabins that surrounded an open field in front of the main lodge. The lodge itself had a handful of guest rooms and the SOB was just past a small lobby. Zula's private residence was on the second floor.

Other than an old barn and couple of sheds, the only other structure on her property was Sonny's old cabin, remotely located a half-mile away and accessed by a sandy path that led beside Oak Creek. That was Skip's, who had been renting it since showing up on her doorstep four years ago. He had been holding her handwritten card advertising its availability to anyone that "didn't piss the management off." So far, he hadn't.

Zula couldn't say the same about the yahoos sitting at the

table closest to the bar. They were a group of four, three men and a woman – the woman with the yellowy eyes being the most outspoken. She was built like an aging female ninja warrior, her pockmarked skin the result of too many anabolic cocktails. When they entered, she had told each of the men, in her deep baritone voice, which seat to sit in, positioning herself where she could see both the bar and door. Zula had pegged her as a hard drinker, bourbon, and splash of soda type. It had been a surprise when she ordered Sangria for the table. The two men with buzz cuts frowned, *more the malt liquor type*, but they chose to stay on the boss's good side. The third guy ordered vodka and Seven Up.

They were not guests of the lodge – another reason for the Mogen David. She'd overheard them talking about their fancy rooms at the Wiley Coyote Resort and Spa, fifteen miles around the sprawling, table-topped, Airport Mesa. Not that she wanted them staying at what she considered more her home than a hotel.

"No brandy, huh?" Mustang Timmy smiled.

Mustang was an SOB regular and local fixture at Zula's monthly Tequila Moon parties. Once a month, she hosted, by invite, a gathering of friends, people she cared to hoist a Don Julio with. It was supposed to be BYOB, but she'd gotten used to supplementing that with her own liquor as the nights wore on. Mustang was a colorful, spry octogenarian with a wandering eye for the ladies. Tonight's paramour, Agnes Speer, a volunteer librarian, was sitting on the stool beside him. Last week it had been her sister, Gladys. Mustang wasn't known to spend much time in his stable.

"Just be happy she gave you the Centenario and not the Cuervo," Agnes said. She was new to the west, and, under Mustang's tutelage, working her way through popular tequila brands. She needed to stay busy with something when not stacking books.

Sitting on either side of Mustang and Agnes were Big Bob Baker and Steel Calves Kempdinger. Big Bob was keeping an eye on his buddy as he was known to wobble atop his stool. He'd suggested a table, but Mustang was having none of it.

"What's wrong with them?" Steel Calves asked Zula, who had handed the pitcher of Sangria to Sky. "I like the way that woman seems to be in charge of the men, dishing it out instead of taking their male baloney."

"Thought you were fond of tubed meat, baby," Big Bob snickered, elbowing Mustang. Steel Calves leaned over the bar and mouthed, "just you wait." Big Bob winced. God knew what screwy position she would torture him with later.

"Woman's intuition," Zula answered. "Sky said those bozos checked her out head to toe as she took their order. The woman did the same. And those hiking clothes they're wearing, they look like costumes on those jokers. They have *City* written all over them. I doubt they know a pine nut from a brass ball. Kempdinger, that woman's bossy, which is different than being in charge."

"Different than you, honey," Big Bob said, hoping to redeem himself.

All four regulars swiveled in their stools to check out the four strangers. Big Bob swung the wrong way, spinning into Mustang, sending the Korean vet on a 360 turn. Zula had oiled the bearings again. Mustang's knee bumped Agnes, who in turn bumped Steel Calves, and they all swiveled in countering circles as if caught in a vortex.

Meanwhile, at the strangers' table, Sky was filling three glasses with sangria. The woman seemed friendly enough and her companions harmless, despite the two with buzz cuts ogling the tops of her boobs as she poured their drinks. She sat the vodka and seven in front of the third man, who was better looking and blond, with more life to his eyes. He at least smiled and said "Thanks."

"How'd you find us?" Sky asked the woman. Guests not staying at Zula's lodge had usually been hiking at Red Rock State Park. She doubted they had come from the trails, though. Their boots looked new and didn't have a speck of Sedona's red dust. "The SOB's not exactly on the tourist map."

The woman held up a Sedona Chi brochure and smiled, "Spiritual Essence of the Red Rocks," she read. "I like the artwork. Yours?"

Blue sky with billowing clouds filled the top third of the brochure. Zodiac signs revolved around a yellow sun with sunglasses, and stars with rainbow faces gazed down on a green earth. Unicorns munched on flowers and spewed lemonade into the cups of children playing in a field. Bell Rock rose from the center, a tree of life sprouting from its crest. A guru in a white robe sat at its base, his arms and legs crossed, reading a book titled *Sedona Chi, Tours from $199*.

"On-line graphics," Sky chuckled. "My boss isn't much on advertising but gave me the green light to market my own tours. I might have gotten a little carried away."

The woman shrugged. "It caught my attention. Johanna Mosby."

"Sapphire Sky." The woman held out her hand and they shook. Her palm was oily to the touch; Sky chalked it up to moisture from the sweating glass.

She looked expectantly at the man with the pretty blond hair. He had been sipping his vodka and checking emails on his phone.

"Jerry Mosby...Johanna's...smaller brother." He glanced at Johanna and laughed.

"More relatives?" Sky asked, nodding toward the other two. They were picking at the fruit in the bottom of their glasses. Neither seemed interested in the conversation.

"Employees," Johanna said. "We were at a convention in Phoenix and decided to take a few extra days. Kind of a mini retreat."

"We call them Lloyd and Roid," Jerry joked.

"Whatever," Roid said. He had been the primary ogler.

The two fruit-enthralled buzz cuts didn't appear to be the convention-going type to Sky. They looked more World Wrestling Federation – the Brooklyn Butchers. But who was she to judge? Her own arrival in Sedona hadn't been with the purest of intentions. It had taken Skip to set her straight.

"We offer corporate rates, if you're interested in a group tour?"

"Triple A too," Zula said loudly, eavesdropping. She was rooting for Sky, hoping the girl would stick around. A little extra money in her pocket wouldn't hurt. Scrape off the tourist trappings and Sedona could be a pretty boring, lonely place for young people.

Sky grinned and rolled her eyes. Zula was leaning over the bar, stopping Mustang from spinning off his stool. Big Bob, Steel Calves, and Agnes were also watching. All like they were sitting in the loge of the Sedona Performing Arts Center following a live performance.

"She packs a good power lunch," Steel Calves added. "Protein and electrolytes, that's what you need out here."

Sky turned back to the table, laughing, "We're big on local color here. Never a dull moment."

Johanna Mosby grinned and sipped her sangria. "You have a fan club. So, is the $199 per person or for a group?" she said, licking her lips. She wiped a drop of red juice from the rim of her glass and stuck her finger in her mouth; the action suggestive enough to make Sky uneasy.

Jerry smirked and poured more Seven Up into his glass.

"Per person, but we knock off twenty percent for groups of four or more, and the corporate discount is another ten percent. The wine and cheese packages are a little more but optional."

"Beer possible?" asked Roid.

"Anything's possible," she said, without thinking.

Roid chuckled. Johanna glared at him, and he went back to thumb wrestling with Lloyd. They had finished the fruit.

She probably wasn't the easiest boss, which was understandable for a woman leading a bunch of men. But there was a black aura around her. That didn't mean she was a bad person, but it did suggest her true self was hiding.

"It's four hours, the hike is over moderate terrain," Sky said formally, half-hoping Johanna wouldn't book a tour. "The focus is on New Age mysticism, and we stop for yoga. We discuss the astronomical, religious, cultural, and artistic knowledge of the ancient people who were here and how their beliefs translate to us today. It's a new tour and I'm working on how to incorporate their theories with modern business practices. I'm not quite there yet, so it might not be what you're looking for."

"Too bad Kuul's not back from Mexico," Agnes added. "He's exploring how Mayan cosmology, especially their calendars and their star tracking, compares to our Sedona mystics and Toni's ancestral beliefs."

"Hopefully, they're exploring more than that," Zula quipped, interrupting the talkative librarian. Once Agnes got wound up, there was no–

"I'm reading up on ancient philosophies during my down times at the library," Agnes continued. "Hours of free time when the weather's good, at least in the stacks. People are getting outside, not reading as much. Even my sister Gladys has taken to walking in the mornings and working more in her garden. My late Mr. Speer, God rest his soul, a saint that man was, taught her everything he knew about gardening. He was a master gardener. Even Gladys says she misses how he used to spread her ground and plant his seeds. She's tried to teach Mustang the same thing, but he claims it's too hard on his knees. Gladys would let Mr. Speer get down and–"

Big Bob interrupted with a loud cough to keep Agnes from further exploring her husband and sister's relationship. "Sky knows her yoga. She's double-jointed and does a trick with a nickel you gotta see to believe."

"Well, if she's that talented," Jerry Mosby said.

Johanna cut him off. "Sky, if Sedona Chi has an opening day after tomorrow, let's go ahead and book it...for four," she said, looking around the table, expecting no objections.

"I'll bring the nickel," Jerry laughed.

# HIEROGLYPHICS

THE COUPLES REUNITED UNDER THE PORTICO OF THE CASA VIEJA del Rio restaurant, both with stories to tell. Kuul recounted his and Toni's meeting the same group of Chinese they had seen at the market. Skip's only questions had been to ask which Chinese man did the speaking and how the others arranged themselves. Lilac told them about the woman at the old fort, leaving out that Daria Ahmadi was Iranian and an old acquaintance. From her furtive glances and Skip's silence, Kuul knew there was more to her tale. His friend made no eye contact with any of them.

Lilac had just finished when the bolo-tied *maître de* stepped outside and said a table was ready.

"*Quattro, por favor,*" Skip said.

The *maître de* nodded and led them upstairs, past a long bar and out the French door to a round table on a balcony overlooking the *Plaza de la Independencia.* He placed four menus on the heavy Spanish-styled table. "Your waiter, Fabio, will be with you shortly."

"*Gracias,* just drinks," Lilac said.

The man bowed and said, "Fabio," and then left.

"Pretty good English," Skip commented. "Let's hope Fabio is wearing his hair net."

"Fabio is an old Mayan name, it means 'bean farmer,'" Kuul said. "Cruise ships are stopping in Progresso, north of here, and there's a new English-Spanish school here in Old Town. Our hotel manager said they are also teaching English in the schools now. Most *Campechanos* speak Maya of course, not Spanish, but they know both. English, though, means a decent job in tourism."

The view from the balcony was magical. Dimly lit wall sconces on the colonnaded buildings wove a web of shadows and mystery over the cobblestoned streets. Limbs of ceiba trees swaying in the gentle breeze added motion and suspense. Past the plaza, beneath the first stars in the black sky, a lone couple strolled between lampposts along the Malecon.

"It's like watching a film noir movie from a mezzanine," Lilac said. The gentle view seemed oddly foreboding, as if their days had not been worrisome enough. She could not forget the woman at the fort. "All that's missing is a femme fatale," she said, glancing at Skip.

"I think our plan to split up tomorrow is good, but I'm not sure about you two spending an extra day here," Kuul said, thinking of their safety *and* their relationship. "We still don't know who Gabor Cocom was or where the artifact came from. We've been stalked by two groups and a woman, who Lilac thinks is Middle Eastern. All armed, all wanting the Mayan vessel. They could show up again and not be so patient. Maybe Toni and I forego our trip to the small ruins outside Progresso? Maybe we stay together and see about getting an earlier flight home instead?"

Skip shook his head, "Visiting those ruins is the most important part of this trip for you. They are where your father said your ancestors lived. It's only one extra day, our flight home is booked for the day after tomorrow."

"A lot can happen in a day...a lot can happen in a few minutes at an old fort," Lilac said. As much as she'd like another crack at Daria Ahmadi, she agreed with Kuul, staying longer was risky.

"Toni?" Kuul asked.

Two hours earlier and Toni would have voted to leave. But now she wasn't sure. Not after hearing Kuul talk about his life and his religion. Not after hearing the respect in his voice for the people here and how they looked like him. She was forming a deeper, more informed opinion of who he was. And she liked this new Kuul, the introspective, culturally attached Kuul. Visiting his family's ancestral home would reveal even more of his character. She found herself looking forward to more time alone with him.

"There is no guarantee we could even get an earlier flight. Merida International isn't exactly LAX," she said, thinking. "Kuul plans on giving the vessel to the museum in Merida. Once that is done, this should be over."

"*El Gran Museo del Mundo Maya de Mérida*," Kuul added.

"I'm not so sure we shouldn't just give that damn cup to the police and be done with it," Skip said. "Whatever's happening here is more than we bargained for; this was supposed to be a vacation. Those Chinese goons upped the ante." He was still hoping to avoid sharing that the Iranians were now also involved. "They are professionals. They're after something more than a Pre-Columbian artifact. Take my word for it. All of you see that, right?"

"NO," Kuul said forcefully, stiffening at the suggestion of giving up Cocom's treasure. "Kemo, we have an obligation to keep the vessel safe and return it to where it belongs. I expect you to agree."

Skip respected and trusted his Mayan friend more than any man he had known. Kuul had been there whenever he needed him. They had been through rough scrapes before and came out okay. If not for Kuul, Skip's inner demons would have already forced him to leave Sedona, costing him this new, better life, the friends he was learning to care for...and Lilac. He owed him.

"What do you think?" Skip asked Lilac, knowing she didn't want to stay...not after the fort.

She surprised him.

"I think...I think we take the chance. Toni's right, we can't get out of here tomorrow anyway. It's late, and in the morning, we would still have to get to Merida's airport, which is two hours away. There are only two flights back to the States and we'll have missed the first. Even if we can get on the later one, Kuul would have already handed over the cup. I vote we stick with our plan, let Toni and Kuul go to Merida, complete his journey, and we'll stay here and lay low - *we'll have time to talk*."

Skip was considering bringing up the Iranian connection, which was a piece the others didn't have, when Fabio arrived.

"Welcome to Campeche," the short, bald, older Mayan man beamed. "Have you had a chance to examine our drink menu? We have special tequilas, Caribbean rums, anything you want *señors*, wine, cerveza, sangria, juice, daquiris, anything. Our mixologist, Babajide, was trained in Mexico City."

Skip decided to hold off on the Iranians. He hadn't actually seen a team. Kuul and Toni had already made up their minds to stay and Daria Ahmadi was a rabbit hole he didn't care to go down. He would end up there later with Lilac, but not now. A few margaritas, overlooking a peaceful old town, didn't seem a bad deal at the moment. "Margarita, Fabio, with Don Julio and prickly pear syrup," he ordered, leaning back into the soft leather-backed seat.

"My apologies, *señor*, we only have melon or strawberries,"

"Guess you'll have to settle," Lilac said.

"Excuse me, my name is Catherwood Stephens. I was at the table just inside and heard the big man talking about his Mayan ancestry. I'm here studying hieroglyphics for the Smithsonian Libraries and Archives Department."

The man was standing in the French doors beside their table. Lilac had just taken her first sip of Captain Jack rum and coke. She had a vague recollection of seeing him inside, sitting in the corner by himself. The eclectic décor of the dining room had been more interesting, especially the artwork hung haphazardly on lavender walls. Everything from Spanish religious paintings to cartoonish imitations of Picasso and El Greco. Even the floor was a wavy Salvador Dalí pattern of black and white tile.

Stephens didn't match her preconceived picture of a Smithsonian librarian. More like an urban version of Indiana Jones, with a groomed crust of ruggedness around the edges. Ankle high hiking boots and a pen light and paint brush in his pocket spoke to his authenticity as a field researcher. His tall, slim frame was perfect in proportion to the narrow doorway where he stood. Lilac saw a brown fedora left on his table, *well mannered* – a contrast to the tour guide sitting next to her in his crumpled Panama hat.

"Smithsonian," Kuul said, impressed and curious.

"On contract," Stephens smiled. "I've been here a month, not heading back until June when the heat and mosquitos get to be too much. How long y'all here for?"

Skip identified the accent as a west Texas drawl that the man kept in check within his scholarly circles but let loose around pretty women. What kind of archeologist couldn't handle the heat?

Lilac smiled at Skip, "We fly home to Arizona day after tomorrow. Why don't you pull up a chair."

"I would like to hear what you're working on," Toni said.

Kuul grabbed a chair from the next table, sliding it between Lilac and Skip, who had been keeping his distance. He moved his own closer to Toni, who slid hers against his.

"Thanks, don't mind if I do," Stephens said, sitting down and shuffling his seat closer to the red head, who seemed much friendlier than the man sitting next to her, who had been picking him apart with his eyes and hadn't said a word.

After musical chairs, Skip was sitting alone on the other side of the round table.

"I'm Lilac Williams, by the way. Kuul Balthazar and Toni Wathetewa." She ignored introducing Skip, which was awkward, but she didn't care. His hackles were up and there were a few hairs she hadn't pulled yet. "What got you into Mayan writing?"

"You're Maya, right?" Stephens asked Kuul. "You have the short forehead and broad face, but your height indicates that's not all...Native American, Southwest? I'm not prying, just professionally interested. I'm an ethnological linguist, not an archeologist as most presume."

"And you look Apache," he said to Toni.

"Yavapai."

"Hit the nail on the head with me," Kuul said. "Part Maya, part Yaqui."

Skip did not like the man. First, he had been eavesdropping on them, and now, he insulted Toni – no Yavapai wanted to be mistaken for Apache. There was a long history there. "You didn't answer the question – what got you into Mayan glyphs."

Stephens smiled nervously and nodded. "Oh yes, well, I did graduate work in England and studied the famous Maudslay photographs and casts at the British Museum. In the late nineteenth century, Maudslay made papier mache molds of the characters on the steps of *Palenque's* Castle C. He took them back to England, and the museum made the plaster casts. They are what led to my specializing in Mayan hieroglyphics. At Palenque, they have installed an actual replica of the steps with the glyphs. That's why I'm here – good enough?"

"You'll do," Lilac said, casting a sideways scowl at Skip. "Why place a replica of the real thing at the original site?"

"The detail of the original characters had worn," Kuul answered for Stephens. "We tend to criticize the early European and American adventurers for their clumsy excavations and looting of artifacts, but in some cases, it saved the record of past civilizations."

"Without Alfred Maudslay, we wouldn't know as much about Pakal the Great, one of the major Mayan kings during the Classical Period," Stephens said. "The hieroglyphics on the steps tell the story of his dynasty. Unlike other Mayan rulers, he was not born a king. His mother and grandmother ruled like kings, however. Because of their influence, he became king himself. The writings immortalize his mother as the First Mother who created Mayan people and all of their gods."

"She must have been busy with all that creating. And since Pakal was her descendent, he of course proclaimed himself a god," Skip said, breaking in. "It's the same old story – a would-be tyrant says he's ordained by the gods. Which gives him the justification to do whatever he wants. Archeologists always seem to gloss over the part where these characters make everyone else's lives hell."

"Like I said, I'm not an archeologist, I'm a linguist. Social analysis is the job of historians," Stephens corrected. "Pakal did have to get the approval of his priests, though."

"The priests who cut out hearts and sacrificed children?"

"At least we have a record of their history," Lilac said, ending their pissing match. They could pull out the measuring tape later. "In the American Southwest, the Ancestral Puebloans, the Hohokam, the Sinagua, they didn't leave any writings. What you're studying is fascinating, Catherwood. Maybe you'll find your way to Arizona to study those civilizations."

"My friends call me Wood. Mesa Verde's been on my shortlist."

"I know the park pretty well. I could show you around," Lilac said, continuing to torture Skip. *The woman at the fort; two can play at this game.* "There are no hieroglyphics, but there are petroglyphs. They have a nice lodge where you can stay."

Lilac, you're playing with fire, Toni thought. Skip Rhodes wasn't a man to toy with. She had been watching him. Jealousy was okay, but his expression had turned dark. He was looking toward the bar for Fabio. More alcohol would only fuel his anger.

Stephens sipped his beer, thinking. "What are you four doing tomorrow? If you don't already have plans, I've chartered a local ship captain to take me into the Biosphere of the Petenes. I dabble in ethnobotany as well. The trip goes into the mangroves to a remote cenote...if you're interested."

"We're heading to Merida in the morning," Toni quickly answered, hoping Lilac would decline too. *Smithsonian Linguist Missing in Jungle, American Tour Guide Under Suspicion* was not a headline she wanted to see.

"But we're not," Lilac said, elbowing Skip. "We were talking about taking it easy tomorrow. Getting out of town on a boat would be just the thing."

WILD FLAMINGOS

KUUL AND TONI LEFT CAMPECHE EARLY THE NEXT MORNING AND drove to Merida, leaving their friends to go on the boat with Catherwood Stephens. The Smithsonian linguist had offered to drive Lilac and Skip to the airport the next day. They were walking along Merida's busy Montejo Avenue, an upscale boulevard once lined with elegant mansions guarded by ornate iron fences. Now it was the hub of the city's tourist sector, sitting just north of the historic quarter.

"Was it a mistake separating?" Kuul asked. "I felt they needed time alone."

We need time alone, Toni thought. She doubted Lilac's plan was to spend the day with Skip, and she really didn't care to be around for the ensuing fireworks. She was looking forward to the time away with Kuul. He had begun to open up in Campeche. It's what she had hoped for, to learn more about him as a man, not as a sidekick. There was a depth to him she wanted to explore. They had their own schedule, a ten o'clock appointment with a docent of the museum in Merida, and then an excursion to *Xcambo*, which promised to reveal a lot about Kuul's true self.

"No. But your *Kemo* will deserve what he gets. Lilac will make sure of it."

A wide stairway rose from the sidewalk to a large courtyard and the museum entrance, not unlike the steps of a pyramid leading to a ceremonial plaza and temple. A monolithic sign with the name *El Gran Museo del Mundo Maya* etched in glass was a modern interpretation of a stone stella from the Mayan world. Architects had designed a five-story, mirrored building wrapped in green metal bands. The upper floors, supported by sturdy columns, cantilevered over the sunken entrance,.

"It looks like a present with ribbon," Toni said. "It is very evocative."

"The architecture reminds us of our cultural heritage. The same message Mary Colter sent with her Grand Canyon buildings, Hopi House and Desert View Watchtower. The Maya saw the universe as having three parts, sky, earth, and underworld. In the earth's center, they imagined a huge ceiba tree that connected all three. In their cosmology, the tree was a symbol of cosmic stability and our planet's fertility. Its limbs held up the sky and its roots extended into the underworld. This design does the same. The building is the body of the ceiba growing from the underworld, the green bands are the limbs. See the clouds mirrored in the glass."

"Or maybe a huge spider web that has trapped a spaceship," Toni said, still trying to come to terms with the unusual design.

"The docent is giving us a private tour. Afterward, we hand over the vessel to her or the director, whichever we're more comfortable with," Kuul said. "I want to show you wild flamingos this afternoon and visit *Xcambo*, my ancestors' home. They are two hours north of here, on the coast."

"Long day, but the one you came for."

"A good day."

The elderly docent with pageboy white hair and pink Christian Dior eyeglasses perched atop her head was waiting for them in the lobby, holding a placard with Kukulkan Bonifacio Balthazar written in black marker. Her bright eyes twinkled with amusement. "Three different guests have asked about your unusual name," she laughed. "All locals who know the legend of *Kulkulkan*. That boy over there staring at us wanted to see if you had fangs and feathers. I said just teeth and hair, but he wasn't convinced."

Kuul waved at the youngster who quickly scuttled off to join his parents who were checking a bag. Toni read the docent's badge, "Margaret Donovan. That's an unusual name for a docent at a Mexican museum. I guessed you would be local."

Margaret Donovan chuckled, "I get that a lot. I consider myself local, though. We retired here ten years ago. Merida has a sizable expat community, most living in the old colonial center. I was a volunteer interpreter at Big Bend National Park before transplanting here. When we first visited *El Gran*, that's what we call the museum, I was struck by the similarities between the Maya and Native cultures in the southwest."

"I look forward to your tour," Toni said. "I've found the similarities fascinating as well."

"Mr. Balthazar said he had Mayan ancestry..."

"Just Kuul, like C-O-O-L."

"Cool, Madge will do for me," the docent said, grinning at her wordplay. She turned back to Toni, studying her face, "But you don't, do you?"

"Yavapai, central Arizona," Toni answered. "White archeologists say we were Patayan people who migrated from the Colorado River basin sometime between twelve and thirteen hundred. Our People believe we rose from a hole connecting the underworld with the world where we live today."

"Interesting, having worked in West Texas I'm more familiar with the Apache and Comanche, and to a lesser extent, the Navajo - the Pecos culture before them." Madge turned to Kuul, "Is there anything in particular you want me to cover?"

"We've visited *Chichén, Uxmal*, and *Edzna*. We're going to *Xcambo* later today, but we're open. You can just show us whatever you would normally."

"Sounds good. You'll enjoy *Xcambo*, it's more off the beaten path and won't be as crowded. The cruise ships are not docked in Progresso today, so you should have it to yourselves."

For the next hour, Docent Donovan led them through the history of the Maya. Kuul had explained his connection with *Xcambo*, so she focused more on the Ancestral Mayan exhibits, starting with a statue of *Kukulkan*, where Toni posed Kuul for a picture with his namesake. She also stopped at a figure of the Mayan corn god, *Hun Nal Yeh* from *Mayapan*, a late post-classic site and capital of the despised Itza people who had conquered *Chichén*. *Hun Nal Yeh* was near a *Chac Mool* lazily resting atop an acrylic pyramid, waiting for its next sacrificial victim.

After spending fifteen minutes pondering an entire room of hieroglyphically annotated calendars, they passed a pedestal holding a brown, rounded object, the size of a baseball, though not as rounded. Its top was open, and the bottom was flattened.

"It looks like a ribbed gourd. There are markings around the rim," Toni said, peering closer into the case.

"This is a clay vessel for drinking chocolate," Madge said. "Many Maya had one, but this one is special. The inscription, which you noticed, attributes it to *Tzakal*, lord of *Acanceh*. Same idea as the coffee cups we find in modern gift shops that say Andy or Betty. The inscription also says it is for drinking cacao from a specific area, made in a specific way. Chocolate was a polymorphic to ancient Maya, a cross between a divinity and a sacred plant. Most royals, like *Tzakal*, had a ceremonial vessel."

"A recipe," Toni speculated, looking at Kuul, remembering the etched inscription. The Mayan artifact was in Kuul's backpack, stored in a locker off the lobby. She had the tiny key in her pocket.

"Not exactly, not this one," Madge said. "But there have been other vessels found with what you might call recipes – so much of this, so much of that, cooked for this long. Most just recorded the region where the cacao originated and how or when it was to be consumed...at a ceremony, after a battle. But because the inscribed places don't correspond directly with an area today, they're very difficult to track."

"Unfortunately," Madge continued, "one of the most famous inscribed vessels was found in *Palenque* and displayed in their museum. That vessel belonged to Queen *Tz'aakb'u,* who was the wife of *Pakal* the Great, the greatest ruler in Mayan history. She's been dubbed the Red Queen because her remains were still covered in cinnabar when the archeologists discovered her tomb."

"Unfortunately?" Kuul asked.

"Well, it *was* at *Palenque*...the vessel was stolen just last week. It was secured in the exhibit dedicated to the Queen. It's a huge scandal. The National Institute of Anthropology, INAH, was working in her tomb, and there are rumors someone from that team was involved. One member was found dead in the lobby. The museum officials are even being investigated. *Palenque* is not as tightly guarded as here, but still, you couldn't just snatch and run, there would have had to be more planning and more people involved."

"Why didn't you give them the queen's vessel?" Toni asked. Kuul had left the museum with the Mayan artifact in his backpack. They were an hour outside Merida on Highway 176, heading to *Xcambo.* "That has to be what it is. Cocom was involved in the theft."

"He wasn't, he died protecting it. What if someone at the INAH is involved? Docent Donavan would have given it to her director and the museum would have turned the vessel over to them – preserving national artifacts is under their purview. Having the vessel in our possession makes us suspect *numero uno.* Do you know any good lawyers down here, I don't?"

"This was supposed to be a vacation."

"Not any longer."

"If you're not giving it to the museum or the INAH, and you don't trust the police, who exactly do you plan on turning it over to? We leave tomorrow, you can't take it out of the country."

Toni's question hung in the air, unanswered. An hour passed; they had not seen another vehicle for twenty minutes. Kuul still hadn't said what he planned to do with the Red Queen's vessel. She suspected it was because he didn't see a good option. No doubt, he was hoping for his ancestors at *Xcambo* to give them directions.

Kuul turned off Highway 176, and they passed a small town called Dezmul. A dilapidated, wooden stand that Toni guessed sold fruit was the only 'structure' at the intersection. In the near distance, two bell towers, much smaller and more rustic than those at Campeche, rose above cinder block homes with tar paper roofs. The road became two cracked concrete lanes separated by a faded yellow stripe. The landscape was marshy. Brackish water pooled just off the pavement, past low stands of scrub and mangroves.

Toni lost track of the miles; they all looked the same. Finally, they passed a sandy side road with a bent metal sign that said *Z.A. Xcambu*. "Wasn't that our turn?" Toni asked. If Kuul's plan was for his ancestors to show him the way, he wasn't following directions.

"Flamingos," he answered, by way of explanation.

She didn't bother him again. His mood had changed, the aura of his past was claiming him. He had been silent since leaving Dezmul. He had turned off the air conditioning and rolled down the window. Steamy, tropical heat had replaced the tempered, humidity-controlled atmosphere of their rental car. The land smelled alive, a mixture of mold, dirt, and decaying plants, scented with sweet flowers.

The thick vegetation and black pools of water finally gave way to what at first appeared to be a big pond. The pond quickly became a farm-sized lagoon, an inland estuary of the gulf still miles away.

The water was shallow, just covering the feet of hundreds of gangly, pink birds. Sandy islands freckled the surface with dozens of flamingos standing wing-to-wing searching for food.

Kuul parked near a drainage channel running under the road, which was on an isthmus of land splitting the lagoon. With the crack of their doors, birds flew away on both sides, heading southwest, their giant wings as impressive as the condors that flew over the Grand Canyon. They were less graceful but much more colorful, Toni thought.

Kuul pointed, "Where they are heading...they're flying over *Xcambo*. They stay here because they are the spirits of ancient Maya. Look how many they are." Toni wrapped an arm around his waist and stared into the sky. More of the pink spirits arose and flew toward his ancestral home. "In my dream, when my ancestors spoke to me, they showed me this spot. My vision was from the air, as if I was a bird flying over the city. People were gathered in plazas, priests were atop a temple pointing at the sky, at me, at *K'uk'ulkan*, their winged serpent god."

"How did you know it was here, *Xcambo*?"

"It wasn't hard to find. I could smell salt evaporating from stone tanks and feel the breeze from the gulf. Pale pink feathers with black tips appeared from my hands as I flew."

"We will honor your vision...perhaps your people will still be there."

14

Biosphere of the Petenes

"**T**HE BIRDS ARE AMAZING," LILAC MARVELED. "WITHIN A MILE, we've seen kingfishers, cormorants, storks, herons, and a flock of pink flamingos."

Wood Stephens had taken her by boat to the Biosphere of the Petenes, a coastal wetland near Celestún, north of Campeche. Skip, in a bad mood, had refused to go, making it a challenge to her to stay as well. One which she didn't accept. She had told him to do what he wanted – "Go look up your old girlfriend."

The first part of the trip was through open water along the coast. Steamy jungle walled off the interior. The captain had turned inland through a small opening that Lilac had mistaken for a river. There were no rivers in the Petenes or in the Yucatan for that matter. The overgrown alleyway of water was just one entrance to a thousand square mile biosphere of mangrove forest. A sign in Spanish, with a cartoon sea turtle and a smiling, green crocodile, admonished those who enter to protect the fragile ecosystem.

"Actually, a group of flamingos is called a flamboyance, not a flock like a group of most other avian," Stephens said. "Pretty accurate, huh? This is also one of the few ecosystems where you can find both crocodiles and alligators. Two types of crocs are here, the American and the Moreletii. The Moreletii are a bit smaller and darker, so they can hide in this brackish water. Adults are extremely aggressive and can easily overpower a human. But most attacks are defensive rather than predatory," Stephens said, watching her read the sign.

"Their motive doesn't matter much if you're on the receiving end."

"Pathology can usually determine which from the consumptive remains," Wood said, grinning.

"And you're taking me swimming?"

"At that spot, the water is clearer because of an underground spring, it's been filtered by limestone substratum. Our toothy friends don't like the freshwater as much...the captain can see them coming and he has a rifle."

"Uh-huh," Lilac said, dubiously.

"Moreletii are an important part of a healthy ecosystem, nature's garbage disposal system. Their digestive system is immune to most bacteria. Anything that's dead or dying out here, they usually eat before other fauna who are more susceptible to infection and disease. They also patrol chokepoints in the passageways, preventing outside invasive species from wreaking havoc with the ecology."

Lilac decided to keep her feet and hands inside the boat, at least until they got to this swimming hole. The "speedboat" Stephens had told them about last night had ended up being a twelve-foot skiff that displaced no more than a foot of water. Twice, along the coast before entering the biosphere, she had thought they were about to be swamped. Thankfully, the skipper had proven himself, tacking into the cresting swales. He had even spread a tarp across four poles as protection against the harsh sun.

The waterway they were following passed through mangrove islands with mossy roots, muddy flats, and grassy marshes. Each hosting collections of crabs, mackerel, snook, hogfish, and bird rookeries. Stephens identified and lectured on all of them. Only once did the captain correct him, though he winced several more times at what Lilac guessed were further inaccuracies.

Stephens had asked her about *Uxmal* on their way out. She had given him an edited version of their being attacked, saying it was a "gang of thieves," leaving out the man who had died and his giving them the cup. He hadn't seemed surprised, and she wondered if he had overhead more from his dinner table than he let on.

"So, it sounds like you got more than you bargained for? Let's hope anyone we meet here is more friendly."

"Not what we were expecting. The sites here have been so peaceful and the people so nice; they have gone out of their way to be helpful. Of course, that might be due to Kuul...his being Mayan."

"Same here, even though I've been kicking around their sacred ruins. What did the gang want? Money? Poverty is ubiquitous here. Just look at their small towns. There are more Mayan sites lost in these tidelands, smaller fishing and salt gathering villages. The jungle and mangroves take over everything given enough time. It's always been a tough life here."

Lilac glanced at the captain, wondering what he thought of their conversation. Clearly, he wasn't wealthy and was forced to live off the largess of judgmental tourists. He had to smile, show them an enjoyable time, pocket their paltry tips, and quietly listen to their shit.

Lilac considered bringing Wood into the loop. Working for the Smithsonian, his connections could be useful. He would know if the Mayan artifact was valuable, perhaps even have contacts who could take it off their hands. "We might have stumbled onto something at *Uxmal*," she said cautiously.

"Lots to stumble over in these ruins. You have to be careful with your footing. Even the restored sections can be treacherous. I've slipped a few times myself."

This man was as clueless as Skip. Ruins, scientific names of birds, crocodile characteristics, barrier island ecosystems, and underground aquifers were all he knew. Typical cocooned scientist.

"I didn't mean we fell. We found an old cup hidden in one of the temples."

"Hmmm – probably an earthquake or the wall finally deteriorated. Happens all the time. Rocks shift, and you find something that wasn't there the day before. These sites, at best, are only thirty to forty percent excavated. Let me take a look when we get back – it's probably a minor find, but nothing particularly special."

"We don't have it any longer. Kuul is turning it over to a museum in Merida this morning."

"Problem solved then."

The captain steered the skiff into a narrow channel. The water there had less silt and was noticeably deeper. Roots from mangrove trees no longer disappeared into brown, primordial ooze. A half dozen twisting turns later, the water became clear, allowing them to see all the way to the bottom. Bright colored fish swam in the lazy current. Ahead, the channel opened into a room sized, turquoise pond. Worn, waterlogged stairs led into the water from an ageless wooden dock.

"It's beautiful," Lilac gasped.

"The captain said there are larger, more developed springs to swim in, but he brought us to a private spot he knows. He made the right choice," Stephens said, enthusiastically patting the man's back.

"*Bueno Capitán – no cocodrilo?*" Lilac asked, snapping her arms and hands together mimicking a bite. The man shook his head and beamed. She could see the pride in his face; he had been swimming here since he was a kid.

"Nothing here to hurt you," Wood said, peeling off his nylon pants, revealing a pair of cut-offs. "Yahoo," he shouted, diving in. He surfaced after gliding to the center of the pool, brushed his slick brown hair behind his ears, and with his light blue eyes invited Lilac to join him.

His broad shoulders and sculpted biceps weren't bad to look at either. *When in Rome*, Lilac thought, pulling her tee-shirt over her head.

"That caretaker looks old enough to have been a priest here," Toni said. Kuul had driven down a rutted track and parked in a dirt lot. The old man, who had been hacking overgrowth a quarter mile back, had pointed the way with his machete. Apparently, he was also the parking attendant and ticket taker because he met them at the entrance.

The man spoke Maya to Kuul, questioning his understanding with his yellowed eyes. He removed his straw hat, wiping his scalp and face with a bandana pulled from the back pocket of his worn jeans. The skin on the back of his hands was wrinkled and his knuckles were swollen from what Toni guessed was severe arthritis from a lifetime of hard work.

"You don't speak *t'aan*, our language?" he asked when Kuul didn't answer.

"No...Norte Americanos, Inglés."

The man nodded and studied Kuul's face before speaking. "A king lived here, a jeweled, death mask was covering his face when he was found," he said, pointing with his hat toward a temple across a grassy plaza. The plaza was minor compared to what they had seen in *Chichén* and *Uxmal*, less than two hundred feet long by a quarter of that wide. "With big men like you, I wonder...I asked if you had returned."

The old man had been working in the sun too long, Toni thought. "What is your name?"

"The elders considered the calendar the day I was born and named me Cadmael, it means War Chief." Toni smiled, that explained the machete. "There is also a Temple of the Virgin here, but only those with faith can see her when she chooses. I have faith and visit her every Wednesday after work," Cadmael said, a twinkle in his clear, dark eyes. The deep crevices in his weathered face looked ready to crack.

What was it with Mayan men? Devilishly charming and innocent at the same time. "Maybe you should put your hat back on."

"For three hundred pesos, I can guide you through the site. I am from Dezmul."

"I've been to *Xcambo* before," Kuul answered, not mentioning his vision. Cadmael might be a chief and wise from his years here, but he also was a talker – spreading rumors about a crazy Arizonan would be in his nature. "If we have questions, will you be here or back on the road?"

"It has gotten hot, even the stones take a siesta," he said, gesturing toward a white plastic chair in the shade of a palm tree. "If I'm there, pay for parking when you leave."

Xcambo's main ruins formed a tight site. The grassy plaza was bounded by a stepped temple behind them, another temple with dual peaks ahead, and shorter, stone structures along both sides. Both temples were truncated, flat on top, neither higher than twenty-five feet. Behind the low structure to their right was a maze of broken, limestone foundations.

Kuul led Toni to the middle of the small field. He raised his eyes to the sky, closing them against the bright sun. Spreading his arms, he swayed back and forth as if he were flying, reliving his vision.

"This plaza was the heart of the city. It's where the priests and kings spent their days, it's from here they watched me fly overhead. There was a ceremony happening where we're standing. The royal families appeared from thatch-roof structures sitting atop the terraced temples. The priests wore feathered headdresses and animal masks, and body plates decorated with shells; they were dancing to honor the god *Kukulkan*. On a platform...*there*," Kuul said, pointing and opening his eyes. "Were musicians with copper bells, shell rattles, animal skinned drums, trumpeters with conch shells, and flutists with reed whistles. Hundreds of people surrounded them, chanting and mimicking the dances. A line of women brought trays of salted fish and fruit from thatched huts just outside the plaza."

Kuul wrapped Toni in his arms, his wide shoulders bracketing hers, his hands holding hers at her waist. They were both picturing the ancient scene. Kuul's description had brought it to life. Toni saw herself in the Mayan crowd, watching him circle overhead. He swooped and dove above his People, bringing them to a fever-pitch. The priests on the temple drove them on, shouting prayers and mimicking their god's movements. *Kukulkan* had singled her out and was watching her dance. She had never thought of Kuul as a man who sought the admiration of other people. Yet here he was, respected by his tribe and receiving their tribute. She rested her cheek against his neck, her hot breath raising goosebumps on his skin. She whispered his name – "Kukulkan Bonifacio Balthazar...*Kukulkan*."

Time seemed to stand still as they stood together in the plaza. She sensed Kuul was caught between the past and his ancestors and this world. She sensed his life was changing in this moment. He was finding his place, his People.

Finally, he spoke. "You know we skipped breakfast. This Maya is starving."

Toni sighed...*men and their stomachs...Kukulkan* had flown away. "Well, don't expect this Yavapai to bring her feathered deity a plate of grouper and bananas."

"The seaside town of Progresso isn't far, maybe dinner by the beach before heading back to Merida?"

"Sounds idyllic," Toni said, turning in his arms and kissing his surprised lips. "A quiet evening alone with a Mayan god sounds perfect."

15

Tehran Interruptus

"GOD, YOU'RE SO DAMN INFURIATING! I'M HERE NOW, AREN'T I?" Lilac half shouted, opening the balcony doors to their room. Everyone in old town Campeche *should* hear what a jerk he was being.

Stephens had dropped her off at the hotel an hour earlier. She had headed straight to their room; no sense putting off what was sure to be an unpleasant reunion. Only Skip was gone. Fifteen minutes later, the door had opened while she was taking a shower. She called out and got an unintelligible grunt in return...but it was him. She finished, took her time brushing her hair, considered yelling at him to leave, but instead walked out of the bathroom wearing only a towel...a small towel. When he just sat there staring at his shoes, she dropped the towel and dressed in front of him – then started packing. Ten minutes and just as many sharp exchanges later, he had sarcastically asked how her day had gone.

"ALL day! You were gone all day!" Skip angrily repeated for the fifth time.

"Wood invited you, same as me," she said, staring out at a couple sitting at a table in the street.

The man was without a hat, his wisps of long, white hair tied at the nape of his neck with a leather thong decorated with beads. Liver spots covered his tanned arms. The woman, sitting close to him, not across the table, had frizzy, salt-and-pepper hair spread over her shoulders and hanging down her back. A headband covered in tie-dye fabric kept it off her face. They had probably met fifty years ago at an anti-war protest, Lilac guessed. Adorable how they were eating from each other's plates, occasionally forking a bite for the other. *So comfortable together, like one person.*

"Did you find her?" she asked, turning back to him. *No*, but he had tried. His guilty expression answered her question.

Skip knew he couldn't win this argument. He had spent his day wandering the streets, cafes, and hotels searching for Daria Ahmadi. Twice he thought he had spotted her a block or less ahead. Running to catch up, he had nearly fallen into steps cut into the sidewalks from the sunken roadways. At hotels he waited, hoping to see her coming down a stairway or find her standing at a bar.

"Lilac...it's complicated. What would you do if I disappeared, you were told by those you trusted that I was dead, and then you saw me years later? I don't have a choice. You would do the same."

Lilac's concern wasn't his finding Daria, it was about what would happen when he did. Had he even thought that far ahead? He was right of course, which frustrated her even more. She *would* do the same, she would search hell and high water until she found him. She understood he needed answers, even if she was scared of where they would lead him.

Seven years ago, Daria had changed Skip's world. It had already been a world that was crumbling. He had become his agency's most experienced and efficient operative. An efficiency they viewed as a justified return on their investment. More of his jobs were wet and in risky, dangerous places. His trainers had taken a raw kid and molded him into a killer. Over time, he'd grown sick of their secrets and suspicious of their reasons for eliminating his targets. Daria and her team had been two days behind him after he fled Tehran, a promising reformer dead in his wake.

He had led the Iranians on a transcontinental chase, toying with them until they tired of the contest. All, that is, except for Daria. She had doggedly continued their dance alone. Only after he had seen the fire of life and commitment in her eyes, and the same vitality that had left his, did he understand he couldn't end it the way he had planned. After endless days of talking, he had decided the girl from Khorramabad, who had been recruited the same as a dumb kid from the Midwest, had more of a right to live. There was still hope in her; in him there was nothing.

When she hadn't killed him, but loved him, the weariness, his hopelessness, had slowly gone away. He hadn't cared that she could easily end her mission any given night after he fell asleep. Weeks passed and she didn't. That wasn't to be their ending, maybe they could find something else. She had made him believe so...then she left his life as suddenly as she had entered it. Leaving him to stumble back into his old world, scarred by rejection. Four years passed without a word, then the agency informed him she'd been killed by her own people. Burnt out and suicidally reckless, he had cracked and badly botched his next assignment. The agency had not used him since. Eventually, he glued the shattered pieces together and made a new life, never truly expecting it to last – expecting his demons to never let him go.

And then he met Lilac and his world changed again.

He'd given her bits of his past, but only vague comments about Daria, about having been in love once. In his mind, she hadn't had a need to know. What difference had it made – Daria was dead?

But it made all the difference now. How much dare he share, should he share? A giddy sense of anticipation had accompanied his search the entire day. His gut had flip-flopped every time he thought he'd glimpsed her dark hair or lithe movement. Was it love he felt or a sense of unfinished business – closure before moving on?

From the balcony doors, Lilac asked again, "Did you find her?"

He took a deep breath and admitted he had looked for her. "No. I haven't lied to you, Lilac. I told you there had been a woman, that we had been...close...that she was dead. All of that was true."

"But yet, here she is." Lilac was crying inside, trying not to show it, the hurt threatening to overwhelm her. "Do you think she's after you or the Mayan vessel?" She didn't give a damn about the cup but letting him see her pain was not going to happen. And she didn't want his sympathy either.

Skip screamed at himself; he could see the hurt in her eyes. She didn't deserve any of this. She deserved a medal for saving him, and he loved her for it, more deeply than he had ever loved Daria. With Daria it had been emotion intertwined with disenchantment about his life. The idea that the future could be different, that it was still possible to leave the evil things they had done behind. Did he still love her, had he ever loved her? Was that what was driving him to find her? He needed to answer that question for all three of them.

"The cup," he simply said.

"You would think a secret agent would be a better liar. You still love her."

"Lilac..."

"I know, it's *complicated*. Well, let me uncomplicate it." She grabbed her suitcase and began gathering the last of her clothes from the Spanish styled armoire.

"Stay," Skip pleaded. "It's one more night. We're heading to Merida and home tomorrow." She continued tossing her things into the case. "At least tell me where you're going?"

"Wood said his room has two beds," she answered, stuffing a sexy set of undies and strapless bra into a mesh bag.

"Not when we don't know what's happening here. I can sleep on the floor."

God, he was *an ass* – she'd just met Stephens. Why would she jump in bed with a man she had just met, look where that had gotten her now.

"So, hooking up with Wood is okay as long as I wait until after you figure things out? You're such an idiot. The hotel has vacancies. I reserved another room. Catherwood is picking us up at 8:00 tomorrow morning. Meet us in the lobby...unless you're attending to *other* business," she said, carrying her suitcase into the hallway.

"Have you had dinner?" Skip lamely asked.

"Seriously? Eight in the morning, with or without you. I don't really care which," she said and slammed the door.

Skip sat on the bed, confused and hungry.

Bar Stool Mountain

FIVE STREET TACOS AND THREE MODELOS WITH TEQUILA SHOTS later, balanced atop a bar stool in a cantina next door, Skip was less hungry but still confused - *Catherwood Stephens*. He had called Lilac three times, each time getting her message and muttering, "Hey, it's me." Obviously, not who she wanted to hear from.

After the fourth attempt, Harry the bartender – there seemed to be a Harry's Bar every place he had been – had commiserated, "Maybe she's not in, mate." Harry was an Aussie from Melbourne; his girl had dumped him for an outback sheep farmer from outside Adelaide. He was in Campeche licking his wounds and celebrating his newfound freedom.

"Single life has its advantages...new Sheilas." Harry said, placing another blue-rimmed glass in front of Skip, "This one's on the house...Last Call," he added, loudly, looking expectantly at the middle-aged dentist from California sitting two stools away. The only thing keeping the man's head from crashing onto the mahogany bar was his fist propped under his chin.

"*No mas,*" he grunted, waving Harry off with his non-load-bearing hand.

"C'mon, one more for the road, partner," Skip said.

Being the only two customers at Harry's, they'd bonded. Archibald flew to Campeche two days every other month to volunteer at a clinic, which was two days every other month he escaped from Edith and her burnt pot roasts. After tipping their third shots, the dentist had promised a free root canal if he ever got to San Diego. "Well, hell, let's just do it now," Skip had suggested. They had been halfway to the cantina's doors when the dentist remembered he'd turned in his keys. "San Diego, then," Skip had said, slapping him on his back and guiding him back to their stools.

They polished off their last beers and stumbled out the door arm-in-arm, Archie hovering over the crazy, sidewalk steps, Skip saving him at the last second. He wasn't as intoxicated as he acted. The agency's first class had been on playing drunk while staying sober. More intel came from sharing liquor than punches. But tonight, it was more a release, a way of taking himself out of his own head.

"I'm going...that way," the dentist slobbered, bobbling in every direction like a hula dancer on a dashboard before selecting one. "Hotel Misíon is that way," he said, pointing opposite of where it was.

Skip ushered him across the cobblestoned street to their hotel lobby and got him started up the stairway. Moving hand-over-hand, he managed to hold onto the rail and navigate the red, sausalito-tiled steps to the first landing. Two seconds later, he reappeared, stumbling backward, nearly catapulting off the balcony. He reoriented himself, waved at his new buddy, and then successfully retackled Everest.

"*Borracho dentista...es* that way every night he's here," the desk clerk said, shaking his head. He had been watching the comedy from his office.

"*Mucho* novacaine," Skip joked. The clerk chuckled, "Too much tequila."

While playacting the snockered tourist, Skip had been chewing Wood Stephens over like a street tamale before swallowing. Lilac was only using *Woody* to spite him, but she had bought his story hook, line, and sinker. Before she left for the Petenes, he had chastised her for venturing into the jungle with a man she didn't know. As an ex-cop, she should have understood how badly that could end – and he should have known how the fiery redhead would take his criticism. The way Stephens had swooped in was too opportunistic. An archeologist appearing right after they discovered an ancient artifact was a bothersome coincidence – Skip didn't like coincidences. Maybe he was who he said he was, his credentials sounded solid – as *he* presented them - but Skip had had solid backgrounds of his own.

The Hotel Misíon had a small business center off the lobby for guest use. Skip tapped **Enter** on a computer and the home page of a porn site appeared. Centered on the screen was a video of two nude women, intimately situated, caressing a stainless-steel shaft. Midnight was a lonely hour for desk clerks. He closed the page, spent fifteen minutes searching Catherwood Stephens (not finding much), and then checked his Sedona Chi emails. It was 2:00 a.m. back home...*home*...

Sky, things are good here, weather's great, tamales are better, should be home tomorrow night. I need to ask a favor, a little research project. Lilac has met an archeologist down here. His name is Catherwood Stephens, on contract with the Smithsonian. Can you do your thing and see what you can find on him? I found several short posts, all pretty recent, not much else. Thanks, Skip.

Sky wasn't exactly on the government's list of most wanted hackers, but she was savvier about social media than he was. Maybe she could find something he had missed.

Skip closed his account and pulled the porn site back up. No sense alienating the desk clerk. This time it was two water buffalo, the male behind trying to keep his footing in the thick mud.

Lilac's new room was on the second floor, his on the third... *on the way*. He wasn't sure about Stephens, but knew he was in the same hotel. Another bothersome coincidence. Standing outside Lilac's room, he glanced up and down the hall. Knowing he shouldn't, he pressed an ear against the door anyway. *Relief* – no water buffalo noises. He considered knocking, but there was nothing they needed to fight about tonight that they couldn't beat each other up with in the morning. Deciding avoidance was the safer option, he walked back down the hall and up the stairway.

One step into his dark room, he knew something was wrong. Papers were strewn across the desk, trash was scattered, and the Spanish armoire doors were open. His clothes were piled on the floor. *Lilac...she had a key...Shit.* She had convinced herself he was hiding something and was fixated on finding what. No more waiting for the morning, they were going to settle things now. He turned and–

An elbow locked around his throat. *Not Lilac.* A punch landed in his lower back, crumpling his legs. Pain radiated around his waist, and he fell to his knees. Before he could recover, a pistol jabbed his temple.

"Don't move," a husky voice said, "Hands, behind your back."

"How about we..."

"Behind your back, wrists together."

Fuck! Skip knew what was coming but with a gun to his head he didn't have a choice. A zip tie cut into his wrists as soon as he brought them together. *Quick. That took practice.*

"Where's the formula?"

"What formula?" The man kneed him, aiming for the same spot in his back. Skip twisted just in time causing him to miss his mark. Another blow to his kidney would not have been good. The force still knocked him over. Lying on the floor, he saw Lilac's towels piled in the sink along with the spilled contents of his shaving bag. Mr. Zippy...a *masked* Mr. Zippy, had been ransacking his room.

The man grabbed the zip tie, wrenching Skip's shoulders, and yanked him onto his knees. "The Mayan vessel with the formula, asshole?"

"Thanks for the mess. They don't do housekeeping here. What vessel–" A hard jab landed in the soft spot between his shoulder blades.

"Get up – walk toward the door – open it. But don't go out."

Skip obeyed.

The man checked the hallway, then prodded Skip to go first, pushing him toward the stairs. "Sounding an alarm will just get someone killed," he warned.

"My girlfriend is across the hall. She sees the door open she'll check," Skip lied. If Mr. Zippy reached for the door, that might be his best chance. "She'll call the police if she sees this mess."

"I think we'll find her in a room downstairs," the man chuckled. "I'm betting your memory will improve when I begin *questioning* her," he laughed, reaching back for the door.

The gun momentarily moved off Skip...he had his chance. He violently threw himself into the man, and Mr. Zippy stumbled back into the room. Skip kicked the back of his knees before he could regain his balance,. With his hands still tied behind his back, he didn't like his odds, but he doubted the man was going to shoot – not here. He had to keep him from getting to Lilac.

Skip drove a knee, Karate Kid style, up toward his chin. The man dodged just in time and caught his foot, twisting his ankle and slamming him into the tiled floor. Without the use of his arms, Skip floundered like a fish in the bottom of a boat. Mr. Zippy had his gun on him again and stepped away, out of reach of Skip's feet, his back to the open door.

"You're not worth the trouble," the man hissed. "Your girlfriend will be easier."

Skip rolled onto a shoulder and swung his foot, but the man just stepped farther back.

"Your friends have left and your girlfriend...well, she's left you too," the man laughed, aiming his silenced pistol at his forehead. Skip kept swinging his feet, and the man started counting. He was having fun, "One...two...three–"

A noise behind the man...the door slammed shut. Someone else was there, but the man's body blocked his view. Mr. Chatty reacted too slowly, and Skip watched as the butt end of a Sig226 crashed against his skull. *Payback's a bitch.*

Zippy buckled but caught himself. The ski mask had cushioned the blow. Skip saw her now, moving to her left, her hand recoiling as the man spun around. Zippy chopped her wrist and the Sig swung away. He grabbed her arm, painfully torquing her wrist, snatching the gun with his other hand as it came free. She crouched, braced her feet, locked her arm, and drove her fist into his jewels. The man howled in agony but managed to grasp a fistful of long hair, pistol whipping her as he yanked her head down.

Her limp body fell on Skip; he remembered her smell.

Daria woke to a dull, constant pain pushing against the inside of her eyes. Unable to focus, it was a blur she saw moving toward her...a man. Flashes of memory returned, making her headache worse. Her hands searched for her Sig, finding only a blanket. She was lying in a bed. The blur approached her cautiously, offering something white.

"Here, put this on your head, there's no ice, but it's cold," Skip said, gently placing a cloth on her forehead. Her eyes swept the room looking for the other man.

"Tripp," she whispered.

"It's Skip Rhodes now."

His fingers lingered in her hair, caressing the damp strands as if he were remembering. He held the side of her face in his palm, absently tracing the outline of her ear and down the nape of her neck to her shoulder...as he had done so often in Singapore.

"They told me you were dead."

He started to remove his hand and Daria pressed it back against her face. His touch...again...it had been so long. She wanted to cry with happiness, but sadness slowly crept in as she saw the warmth in his eyes turn to anger. She had left him, the years apart, his new woman...so much had changed. She had hurt him.

"They told me *you* were dead," he answered, wiping a tear from her cheek. He rubbed her moisture between his thumb and forefinger, reconciling the fact she was real and not a vision.

"Tripp...I–"

"Not now. All of that happened a long time ago."

Daria composed herself. Yes, it had been a lifetime ago and what right did she have to expect forgiveness. That she had been given no other choice no longer mattered. "The man who I fought..."

Skip sat on the bed, facing her, "He decided to run. By the time I freed myself and got to the lobby he was gone. *I came back* to take care of you."

Daria ignored his rebuke. "Your woman, he threatened her?"

"She's okay, I checked. I didn't tell her what happened...or about you. She was mad as hell that I woke her up. We haven't been on the best of terms after your introduction at the fort."

"She is in a different room then?"

"For tonight."

Daria tried to rise, she could not stay here, not in his bed. Her head began spinning, and she sank back against the pillows. She closed her eyes waiting for it to stop. She had reacted by instinct when he was in danger, but now...now there were decisions to make. But the blow had jumbled her thinking, the cobwebs and his presence were mushing her thoughts.

Throughout the day, she had been torn, going back and forth in her mind between whether to confront him or avoid him. She settled on tracking him as he searched for her in the old town.

Seven years ago, following him had not been so easy. Tonight, she had watched him at the cantina and then hidden in a doorway outside his room. She had decided to see him; she owed him that. Then his door had opened and...

He had changed. His face was more wrinkled, his muscles were not as tight, and his hair was unkempt, but he seemed more at peace. His eyes were still, and he wasn't on edge. Even now, after the fight, there was an easiness, a softness that had not been there before. Letting the man get the jump on him underscored the change. In Singapore, he had been constantly on guard, nervous like a caged animal. Even making love had not quieted him.

"Why are you here, Daria? Are you after me?"

Seven years, seven long years since she had heard him say her name.

"Finding you was not what I expected either. I was also told you were dead," she said, trying to contain her emotions. Another tear formed in the corner of her eye, and she wiped it away.

Skip wondered...*Was she playing him?* He stood, looming over the side of the bed. "Again, why are you here? If it's not me, it's something else. Your assignment, Daria, what is it?"

"You are colder," she said, propping herself up, her head finally clearing.

"I'm wiser."

Daria neatly folded the washcloth, "Not wise enough to avoid the Guatemalans at *Uxmal*. In the old days, you would never have been caught so flat-footed. Without the lizards' intervention, you would have been captured."

"I had the situation under control." *So, she was following them. She stampeded the iguanas.*

Daria studied him. She had assumed he was sent by the United States. But she was having her doubts after following him for two days, watching him with the woman and the two dark-skinned

Natives. None of his companions were professionals. The red head at the fort…her relationship with Tripp had seemed personal…they had been sharing a room. Was she just a cover? He *had* spotted the Chinese team but had let them get away – unlike him – unless he was protecting his friends.

"You are not working?"

"I'm retired."

She took a deep breath and slowly let it out. The dizziness was gone, the pain subsiding, but she knew her reasoning had to be impacted by the blow to her head. She should not trust him, absence had made them strangers, but she needed him to trust her. "MOIS intercepted non-encrypted communications between your President and Hector Colon – you know who Colon is?"

Skip nodded, "That fool is not my President. I no longer work for the agency. You're saying that was a Guatemalan team at *Uxmal*?"

"And they are not the only ones."

"The Chinese and your country."

Daria arched her eyebrows and rolled her eyes. "Slow, but you are catching on. The chatter is the U.S. is illegally building a laboratory in Guatemala, with Colon's support, to develop biological weapons. They are creating a viral super-agent from indigenous flora. There is a formula on the vessel you were given: it is the key. The dead man you left behind stole it from a museum in *Palenque* before they could," she said, paying attention to his reaction. She was still unsure about how the Maya man had died. He had been alive until disappearing inside the temple with Tripp.

Skip shook his head, "Tell your Ayatollah it's a damn cup! An artifact, nothing more. Whatever the etchings around its rim say – they are not foretelling the next Armageddon. Surely, by now, your people know this U.S. President is a certified nut job!"

"Is not his instability part of the problem?"

Before Skip could answer, his phone jingled. *Lilac…she was paying him back for waking her up…wrong again…*

The number on the screen was Kuul's.

"Don't you have better things to do than–"

"THEY TOOK TONI KEMO!" Kuul yelled in a panic, "The Chinese, they kidnapped her – the man who threatened us at the cathedral – they want the virus! We told them we didn't have a virus – that we didn't know what they were talking about. He just laughed, Kemo! Then he said they will trade Toni for the Mayan vessel."

Skip exchanged glances with Daria, who was standing next to him, listening, "Kuul, where are you?"

"Progresso. It's a small town on the gulf. We were having dinner on the beach, beside the main street. Two Escalades pulled up, the Chinese jumped out and came after us. Same group that was at the market in Campeche. I TRIED KEMO! I TRIED! Toni held me back or they would have killed me. They forced her into one of the Cadillacs. All I could do was watch, but I got a plate number."

"Trade her when and where?" Skip asked. The license number wouldn't help. It would be diplomatic, and the police would only shoot it up the chain where it would be conveniently ignored. This wasn't his first rodeo in Mexico.

"Tomorrow, at the Merida Zoo, at noon."

17

ALIEN ENCOUNTER

SKY REGRETTED TAKING THEIR BOOKING. JOHANNA MOSBY, HER brother Jerry, and the Brooklyn Butcher wrestlers, Roid and Lloyd, showed up in a black Tahoe. Johanna insisted on taking their tank-sized SUV instead of Sky's van. No way would they get that thing parked in a tight Forest Service lot, and she could forget her membership in the *Green Minions* if her eco-conscious friends spotted her in the gas guzzling rig. She had spent six months patrolling Boynton Canyon vortex during full moons before they had let her even apply.

Huckabee Trail was her first choice, but on seeing the six thousand pound, V8, eight-seat monster she opted for Doe Mesa. Doe was farther away from town and the punishing uphill trail would be their penance. The pec-popping, beefy wrestlers would not fare well on the steep, switch-back grade. With any luck, by the time they reached the top, it would be just her, Johanna, and Jerry – the Brooklyn Butcher boys back at the car.

"We're going up there?" Lloyd complained from the parking lot. "Suck it up, bro," Roid said, punching his partner in the arm. "Screw this," Lloyd grumbled, before withering under Johanna's glare.

Sky and Jerry were at the back of the SUV unloading their packs and hiking poles. She had brought five avocado sandwiches, sun chips, a package of string cheese, snicker doodles she'd made last night, and two six packs of diet A&W. Eight, twenty-ounce bottles of water, two sparkling per Jerry's request, were in a soft-sided cooler with a shoulder strap. Thankfully, Johanna had passed on the yoga option, saving them from also toting mats, massage balls, and cork blocks.

"We have two mules," Johanna said, walking around the end of the vehicle and seeing Sky hefting the packs and cooler. Jerry was making no move to carry anything. "Take the packs and give the cooler to Bear Grylls," she ordered Roid, who had followed her. She shielded her eyes, staring up at the rim, "Looks like a hike?"

"Not as far as it looks," Sky answered, grabbing her backpack. Two hundred and twenty pounds of sweaty testosterone falling on her avocado and snicker doodle didn't sound appetizing. "I got this, bring the rest," she said, nodding at the smaller Greco-Roman.

"Cooler," Roid ordered Lloyd. "You carry it, water's heavy, man," Lloyd balked. Sky saw a headlock in the making and marched off toward the trailhead. She had her own water, her lightweight aluminum bottle attached to her shorts by a carabiner.

Both Brooklyn mules were lathered and panting after ten minutes, arguing the whole time, spending energy they didn't have to spare. Collapsing at a dead log past the second switchback, they chugged half their allowances of water.

"There's no more of that," Sky warned. Lloyd capped his bottle, but Roid smirked, taking another big gulp – Roid was going to be a problem.

Johanna listened to the exchange and barked, "No more until we're up top." Roid threw his bottle back in the cooler, zipped the lid, and tried handing it to his partner. "Your turn," she told him. Roid hoisted the chest, and he and Lloyd resumed their stumbling trek up the trail. Their boss followed, poking them with her hiking pole.

Sky and Jerry brought up the rear. "My guess is another ten minutes, either they give up or she sends them back," Johanna's brother whispered. Sky shrugged...*one could only hope.*

Right on time, the wrestlers' match with Doe Mesa ended. They had been stopping every ten steps, hands on their knees, gasping for air. "We're done," they both stammered, finally agreeing on something. Exhaustion, heat stroke, and dehydration had forged a bond between the bickering boys.

"There was an orange igloo with water at the trailhead," Sky suggested to Johanna.

"Fine," Johanna said, disgustedly, glaring at Roid and Lloyd. "You two can stay here or head back to the car, but the water goes with us. We'll be back when we're back." Johanna slung the cooler strap over her shoulder and stalked up the trail. Her brother shrugged and followed.

Sky stood over the tired wrestlers, assessing their odds. She felt sorry for them. Bloodshot eyes, labored breaths, no sweat – big muscles needed more fluid. Twenty minutes in the desert heat was all it had taken. Lloyd looked like he had crossed the Mojave and Roid wasn't much better. Good thing she had them all sign waivers. "It's downhill. Take your time and you'll be okay. Take these," she said, giving them their lunches and an extra bottle of water. "Sip it and it should last."

"Thanks," Lloyd mumbled. "For what?" Roid said, "She brought us up here, moron."

She caught up to the Mosbys past the next turn. The wrestlers' slower pace had made the first half of the climb easy. But without the stops, poor Jerry was puffing like George Burns on a cigar. Even Johanna was battling to catch her breath. The hard-charging pace she was setting was unsustainable. No amount of Peloton work in an air-conditioned gym prepared corporate types for hiking in thinner air at forty-five-hundred feet.

"Let's take five," Sky suggested.

"Sorry...about...the...boys," Johanna wheezed, holding two fingers against her wrist. "I should have...left them at our hotel. We were at a convention in Scottsdale. It was a busy week – manning a booth all day and then meetings and working dinners every night. Sedona was supposed to be to relax and detox – you know how conventions are."

"Not really, tour guides mostly get together at the nearest bar after putting their clients to bed."

"A lounge on this mesa top would be welcome," Jerry groaned.

"Sorry, but no such luck. What convention?"

"I am CEO of a boutique marketing firm for drug companies, *Pills4u*. Jerry is my Director of Sales. The two whiners are my security department; we oversee a lot of sensitive information for our customers."

"Well, if soaked shirts are any indication, your employees' detox is well underway. Don't know about relaxing, though."

"You think I'm too hard on them?"

"Tough and unforgiving," Jerry said, saving Sky from answering. "Don't forget we need them. They needed water."

"I gave them an extra bottle," Sky said. "It's hot today. Let's make sure we all get back safely."

"You're the guide," Johanna said, handing Jerry the cooler.

After another ten minutes of climbing through the sandstone rocks, they emerged onto a flat mesa top covered in acacia and brittle bush. Junipers grew low to the ground, the wind stunting their growth, their trunks twisted like wringed rags. Lonesome red buttes rose in the distance, with the brooding Mogollon Rim to the north and the Black Mountains to the south. Tiny Sedona sat below like a stage in a gigantic natural amphitheater.

Sky stepped to the rim of the mesa.

Even the Pills4U crew couldn't ruin the view. Gazing back down the trail, she saw Roid sitting at a picnic table by the parking lot, shaking the igloo cooler. *Whoops – maybe there was a cup or two left.* Lloyd stumbled out of a port-o-john and fell, then hopped toward his partner on one foot. At least they made it back. The required incident reports would have been endless if they had required evacuation.

"Hopefully, they have enough sense to sit in the shade," Sky mumbled to herself.

"Or to get in the Tahoe and turn the air on."

Sky turned and Jerry was behind her. He was laughing, jingling a set of keys. His sister was wandering away, leaving them alone. Normally, she appreciated her clients' humor, jokes made a tour fun, but dehydration was serious. Not an ounce of concern registered on his face...*maybe he just didn't know better*. Water wasn't a commodity city people thought to worry about.

Sky pointed at Johanna, "Your sister has found my favorite spot."

Johanna was a hundred yards away, standing on a ledge, overlooking Capitol Butte, Chimney Rock, and the winding stream of cars on Dry Creek Road heading to Sedona's most popular trails. But the traffic was hardly noticeable from five hundred feet above, and the theater-in-the-round view of Mother Nature's two-hundred-million-year-old creation was worth the hassle.

"She likes to get the lay of the land. Helps her stay in control," Jerry said.

"Control of what?"

Jerry shrugged.

From his body language, Sky guessed all things *Pills4u*...and her little brother. "We do yoga there when it's cool. Teaches *control* of our minds and bodies, opens the ignored pathways to our inner selves." Recognizing his amused look, she added, "Corporate types usually enjoy the release."

"The other night – that Big Bob fellow – he mentioned you were double-jointed, something about a trick with a nickel?"

"That's a different tour," Sky chuckled, filing away the abrupt segue from his sister. "Bob should have kept his mouth shut." It never failed, all kinds of fantasies popped into guys' heads when they learned of her hyper-mobility,.

"One trick, please," he said, offering her a nickel.

He had come prepared. She playfully grimaced at him and glanced toward Johanna, who was on her phone. "One, and no video."

She took Jerry's coin and laid it on the ground. She shrugged out of her backpack, then removed her boots and socks, wiggling her rainbow painted nails. A quick set of contortionist stretches kept his attention.

"This is interesting already."

Laying on her stomach, her nose pointing at Jefferson's head, with her shoulders pressed against the warm stone, she rolled her legs and feet backwards over her head.

"No way!" Jerry exclaimed, as Sky picked up the nickel with her toes. "Johanna has a friend who can do that kind of stuff. German gymnast."

Sky smiled and tossed him his coin. *And there it was...the look. Two hundred thousand years of human history and the male mind still went straight there.*

"You wouldn't be free for dinner tonight, would you?"

"Sorry, a raincheck? There's a project I have to do for my boss. He needs it done by tomorrow." Jerry was cute, but she was not a one-night fling and that's what he was after.

"Bosses...they don't respect the concept of time-off," Jerry said, nodding toward Johanna, trying to commiserate. "What kind of project?"

"He's in Mexico and asked me to research an archeologist he met. I think the guy's hitting on his girlfriend."

That was her bet, anyway. Lone Ranger had done or said something stupid again, and Lilac was teaching him a lesson. She should report that Catherwood Stephens was a rich, brilliant philanthropist with a long, tabloid record of seducing red heads – that would teach him.

"Rhodes doesn't sound like too great of an employer, mixing business and personal. How long have you worked for him?"

"A year...and you'd have to know him. We're a small company. How do you know his name – I didn't mention it?"

"From the brochure – Skip Rhodes. It's obvious he trusts you enough to leave the country and run things while he's gone. Does he do that often, travel that is? Johanna wouldn't leave us alone for an hour, afraid her whole enterprise would collapse. How long has he owned Sedona Chi Tours?"

Sky took her time tying her boots. *By her count, Jerry had rapid-fired five consecutive questions about Skip. She'd given a performance that should have left him drooling, not asking about a tour guide he had never met. And Johanna was still on her phone. Who could she be talking to and why now, of all places? Then there were the Brooklyn Butchers, they didn't strike her as the type of employees a CEO of a pharmaceutical marketing company would take to a convention...unless they were testimonials for a new steroid.*

"How long has your sister run *her* company?"

Jerry smiled. "Why don't you ask her, she loves to talk shop? But...uh, maybe later when we get back. Our employees are lacking direction," he said, pointing at the parking lot.

Roid was sitting on Lloyd's back, bending his sore knee, and twisting his foot. A van of elderly Road Scholars had pulled in. They had gathered and were shooting video. Their guide was doing a play-by-play of each wrestling move.

Chief Hoot Hooton of the Sedona Police Department ordered Officer Dickie to stay at the receptionist desk when he saw Big Bob out the window. The Chief fled to his office. It was well known that Baker was now doing Kempdinger's bidding. Two months ago, she had busted the Chief's balls over a hot air balloon sailing too close to Bell Rock; there wasn't much he could do since they had a permit, but that hadn't stopped her from filing a petition with the county commission. Three weeks ago, it had been a list of twenty-three jeeps parked illegally in Uptown.

"Kempdinger made me report it, Dickie! We witnessed another tourist taking a dump on Loose Trot Trail. Right in the middle of the path. It's the third time this month. Steel Calves says it's trending on Instagram; she even saw a video on TikTok. Loose Trot can't handle that much exposure. Pretty soon it will be as popular as Horseshoe Bend. She's threatening to have the Westerners send another letter to the Council if Hoot doesn't stop it."

"Mr. Baker, the Chief had me scour all five miles of Loose Trot the last time she complained, and I didn't find any human feces," Dickie whined, knowing Hoot would send him back again. This time, he thought, he'd bag some coyote scat from his backyard and call it a day.

"Just give me a note that says I was here," Bob begged. "A copy of the report too." Dickie threw up his hands and began scribbling on a pad.

Then the phone rang.

Dickie stared nervously at the flashing panel lit up like Christmas. *Damn!* Hoot had fired the civilian receptionist after her first day. The new phone system had more buttons than a double-breasted jacket for conjoined twins. He picked one of the blinking red buttons, there were three of them.

"Sedona Police Department, Officer Dickie." *Nothing.*

"The other one," Chief Hooton bellowed through the speaker. "That one's the intercom."

Big Bob pointed at the light in the middle.

"Officer Dickie, Sedona Police Department,. How can we help?"

"*Hola*, this *es Capitán* Urbano Nemuro *con el Ciudad del Campeche Policía* in Mexico. This is an international call, I need to... how do you say...speak to someone in charge. We have a murder involving persons of interest from Sedona."

Dickie covered the receiver with his hand, "It's Interpol...a murder. What do I do?"

"Send him to Hoot," Big Bob answered. He had leaned over the counter when the voice said *Policía* Mexico. God, he wished Steel Calves was here; she was bilingual.

Dickie nodded, his palm sweating from the prospect of transferring a call. The phone slipped from his hand, bouncing on the desk, and falling to the floor. He picked it up like it was a used condom found behind the high school, "Still there, Senior?"

"*Sí.*"

"Okay, *Capitán* Uno Numero...Me vamonosing to transfero you to mio Chief. Hold on." Dickie winked at Bob and got a thumbs up for his foreign language skills.

He stared at the phone, his finger spasming and shaking uncontrollably. Baker pointed to a button in the bottom right corner – Dickie pushed it, and the line went dead.

Big Bob shrugged, "Hoot should never have fired Maggie. Just because she brought a pet snake to work didn't make her a bad receptionist."

The phone rang and Dickie grabbed it, "Captain Numero?" Big Bob pointed to another button, but he ignored him. "Let me get him," he said, laying the receiver on the counter.

Chief Hooton jumped up when Officer Dickie ran through his door with Big Bob at his heels, "Listen Bob, you tell Kempdinger to stop writing letters or I'll arrest *her*! Now get the –"

Dickie interrupted him, "Chief, Interpol is on Line 2. They're saying someone interesting from here has been murdered in Mexico."

"I'll give Steel Calves your message," Big Bob smugly said.

Chief Hoot Hooton was at least six-ten and bald as a cucumber. He had taken to using Butch Wax to buff his dome and shape a wild, single strand of white hair sprouting from his crown. Unfortunately, with the short ceiling in his office and the warm, overhead, fluorescent lights, beads of moisture formed on his slick head that turned into yellowish globs of sludge.

But neither his dizzying height, shiny, polka dot dome, or Alfalfa crow's foot were his most distinguishing characteristic. That was his lazy eye, which bounced like a pinball on crack cocaine whenever he became agitated. Maggie had confided to Dickie she'd been so freaked she'd screamed during her interview. With the mention of Interpol, the frenzied orb began zinging around the room.

"INTERPOL!" Hoot thundered, his good eye on Dickie, the lazy one exploring water-stained ceiling tiles that looked like Mother Teresa, the items on his desk, and the 2019 wall calendar that Maggie had never bothered to replace, before alighting on Bob. "WELL, TRANSFER THEM!"

"I...I tried, Chief. We had a faulty connection."

The idiot had cut them off, it had been the mayor yesterday. Hoot's bad eye leapt toward his SWAT training certificate framed on the opposite wall, then moved to the second-place plaque for last year's chili cookoff on *Cinco de Mayo*. The good eye never left Dickie, who was shrinking beneath it.

"Line 2, Chief."

The good eye froze on the blinking red light, the other flickered between his deputy and Kempdinger's boyfriend. If only Maggie hadn't quit. Bob picked up the receiver, pushed Line 2, then the speaker button, and handed the phone to Hoot...

"Chief Hoot Hooton, Sedona PD. Who am I talking too?"

"*Capitán* Urbano Nemuro from Campeche, Mexico. A Skip Rhodes and Kukulkan Balthazar from your city met with one of my officers and reported a murder. I am calling to verify their identities."

Hoot glared at Dickie – *not Interpol and no one from Sedona murdered.* "We know them, Captain. What, exactly, happened?"

"Excuse me Chief Hooton, but when you say you 'know them?'"

"No criminal records. Rhodes owns a tour business. Balthazar is a plumber. He's fixed some pipes for Antonio Banderas. Cesar Romero made a movie here too," Hoot offered. *Mentioning two of Nemuro's famous compatriots would send a friendly signal.* The man probably had preconceived negative notions about north of the border law enforcement. "Kuul works for movie stars here with second homes. They like our town."

"Banderas is from Andalusia, Captain. Romero's parents were from *la Habana.*"

Different parts of Mexico, Big Bob mouthed to Hoot.

"It's Chief, and what did our boys get themselves into? They've been in the midst of a couple of past cases here, but never on the wrong side."

"We suspect they may be involved in the theft of a Mayan arti-fact...possibly the murder of an accomplice. Serious offenses. In Arizona, you have similar problems, I believe, with illegal trafficking in such antiquities?"

Bob broke in, "That's the last thing Kuul would be mixed up with."

"Yet Mr. Balthazar is Maya, no?"

Hoot brought both orbs to bear on Big Bob and empathically pointed at his door, punching the air. Baker crossed his arms and didn't move, so Hoot motioned Dickie to escort him out. Dickie looked like he had been told to relocate Monument Valley.

"Apologies for the interruption, Captain. My...uh... *deputy* knows both men. I do agree with him, though...Balthazar respects Native culture. He might live in our world, but he belongs to yours.

I've known him a long time, what you're talking about would be completely out of character."

"And Skip Rhodes?"

"Not as long. I don't know much about his background. Bit of a loner. Runs his tours and has a local girlfriend...what you're investigating doesn't sound like him either. He lives with an old showgirl from Vegas at her lodge."

There was no love lost between Hoot and Zula Ballsy. She was a bigger pain in his ass than Steel Calves Kempdinger. *Maybe this had something to do with those rumors about the money she used to buy the Sands – maybe it hadn't been her mob connections.* "Tell you what, Captain...I'll go check out his place and talk to his landlady. And you let me know if you learn anything else. We pride ourselves here on our multicultural relationships. You ever get to Arizona, stop by and visit."

"*Gracias, Señor.* I appreciate whatever you can do and look forward to hearing from you. *Adiós.*"

"OFFICER DICKIE!" Hoot yelled after hanging up. Dickie and Big Bob poked their heads around the doorway. "I could hear you both breathing on the other line...see if you can *manage* to call Zula. Ask her if she's heard from Rhodes and see if she plans on being around tomorrow."

GUATEMALAN CONUNDRUM

"**A**MERICAN COWBOYS, THEY ALL THINK WE ARE THE same," Hernando Gomez lectured his brother-in-law. "Remember that *Sargento Salamandor*."

"Advice I shall take to my grave, Hernando," Chuuy sardonically said. Listening to his 'advice' and orders all day was exhausting.

Hernando and Chuuy had followed the two Americanos to the Campeche Police Station. Hernando had ordered his men to stay at their hotel on the outskirts of the city, away from old town. Their screw-ups at *Palenque* and *Uxmal* had him in enough hot water. It had been Chuuy's idea to wait at a café outside the station where the real *Capitán* Nemuro took his lunch. Chuuy had asked about his routine from a friendly desk sergeant. Hernando, though, had insisted on being the one to call Sedona. What better way to find out who they were up against? Unless it was an elaborate cover, they did not appear to be government agents. Unfortunately, the subsequent call to *Coronel* Mancoros had not gone as well.

Mancoros was a man of violent emotions. Gomez had learned that after the American Vice President's mishap with the street dog – if only the woman had not tried to pet the vicious flea bag. He had been a second late in snatching her hand away. Because of her mistake, Hernando had been threatened with months of painful interrogation and execution if the incident was part of a wider plot to embarrass *Presidente* Colon. For all he knew, he might still be under investigation. Members of the Presidential Guard had disappeared in the middle of the night for far less.

The *Coronel* had given him forty-eight hours, not a minute more, to acquire the Mayan Queen's vessel. If he failed, he was ordered to return to Guatemala City with his team to face disciplinary charges. Perhaps this present mission was only a pretense, a justification to arrest him when he returned home.

"Mancoros said Colon is nervous. The trigger-happy American President has promised to bomb us back into the stone age if he does not get what he wants. He is a spoiled capitalist and thinks we are all racing across the U.S. border to rape their women and become dishwashers or fruit pickers. I do not know why Colon is so surprised. The man threatened Cuba with the same unless they buy Puerto Rico and annex Miami. *Sargento* Salamandor, gringos cannot be trusted, remember that."

"*Sí, Capitán*. But what do we do? The Americans have outsmarted you so far."

Gomez frowned. His brother-in-law might be a toadying idiot, but his sense of self-preservation, as was everyone's in the Presidential Guard, was finely tuned.

"Our new orders are to stake out the Merida Airport, they must fly home through there. Mancoros said to take the Mayan artifact if the opportunity presents itself. But only if there is no chance of causing an incident. What kind of order is that? *Que ardo en el infierno*, may he burn in hell. He is covering his *culo*."

"We have no choice but to get the vessel, Hernando. Returning to my beautiful sister and your ten children, even those that look like your cousin Fernando, depend on our success."

Gomez took a long sip of the lukewarm beer. Chuuy needed to take a good look at Lupe. *Beautiful*...maybe twenty years ago when her hair was still black, when her smile could melt butter, when she brought him lemonade on hot summer nights, when they made love to the sound of crickets and the enticing smell of her perfume, before her hips had grown wide from so many *niños*, before her words to him were all insults. *Return? Why?*

Challenging the Americans again was a damned-if-he-did and damned-if-he-didn't proposition, especially in a public setting like an airport. *What was Mancoros up to?* His doubts had grown since seeing the Mayan vessel in *Palenque*, he had expected something made of gold or silver. How could such a plain looking vessel be worth the attention of both his own government and the Americans? There had to be something else, something worth millions. *But what?* Colon already had countless Mayan artifacts stolen from his own country. Why would the corpulent dictator need another? It was time for Hernando to begin thinking about Hernando; he needed a retirement plan, one without Guatemala and without Lupe.

"We are the ones on the ground, Chuuy. Perhaps we need our own plan and to look for our own opportunities. With a valuable Mayan artifact, a man...or two men...could buy an island in Nicaragua and live like wealthy *capos*."

Gomez closely eyed his brother-in-law's reaction. *Sargento* Salamandor also stood to lose his job and the prestige of being a Presidential Guard because of Colon's foolishness, not to mention also being crushed under Mancoros's boot if they failed. *Couldn't he see that?*

"You mean we steal it and sell it ourselves? But what about Lupe, she would kill us both."

"We are just thinking out loud, Chuuy. That is all, *compadre*. It has been a long time since Lupe and the children, including those that are certainly not mine, visited your mother in Puertos Barrios. From there it's a simple boat ride to Belize and away from the *Coronel*."

Mancoros had said, "if the opportunity presents itself." Well, Gomez thought, their best opportunity just might be in the *Estados*

Unidos. If something went wrong, better to face the American sense of fair play than the hellhole of a Mexican prison, or worse, one of Mancoros's hidden torture chambers. He did have an invitation, after all...what had the Sedona Chief called it – *multicultural relationships – sí,* that was it, multicultural relationships.

19

Sonny O'Bryan Cabin

"I WOULDN'T," ZULA SAID. "YOU KEEP LETTING HIM TAKE ADVANTAGE of your relationship, which right now is employee and boss, and he'll keep doing it. Men need boundaries, Sky, even the good ones. Before we were married, if I told my late husband, Two-Balls, once, I told him a thousand times – just because I shake a leg at your floor show doesn't mean I shake your snake after hours."

"It's research, not a snake, and I haven't done it yet."

"Honey, it's always about the snake."

Sky and Zula had closed the book on their morning yoga and were chatting over herbal tea and black coffee on the front porch of the lodge. Spike, the javelina, was beside Zula's rocker, anticipating another handful of bacon bits to sprinkle the pine floor. The Sand's guests had all left for the day, except for a newlywed couple from Santa Barbara who had been holed up in a cabin since checking in seventy-two hours earlier. Zula had left omelets outside their door, but Spike had shown up later with egg on his face. She figured when they needed more fuel, they'd find it.

"I sent Skip an email this morning, telling him about the Mosbys. The trip to Montezuma Castle yesterday made me even more suspicious." She had told Zula about Jerry's game of twenty questions during their Lord of the Dance pose.

After the Doe Mesa hike, they had stopped for lunch in West Sedona at Oak Creek Brewery, the actual brewing site off Coffee Pot

Drive. Lloyd and Roid had perked up at the mention of cold beers and tamales. Sitting in the shady patio, Johanna had asked Sky to tour them to the nearby Sinagua ruins. Four adults on an easy, quarter mile, paved trail below the cliff castle wasn't a sale Sky felt she could turn down. She hadn't seen any harm in putting up with them for a few more hours.

It had been an embarrassing mistake. Below the castle, Roid had left the asphalt path, intent on climbing up to the fragile ruins after Sky had explained doing so was prohibited. He made the base of the limestone cliff before a volunteer interpreter had stopped him. Jerry laughed as the volunteer and two park rangers hauled him off to the visitor's center, sending Lloyd to keep an eye on them...like that was a plan. *The Park Service would no doubt be reconsidering Sedona Chi's discounted entrance fee.*

Johanna and Jerry had resumed the morning inquisition. Sky had tried her best to focus on the history, but Johanna, taking the baton from Jerry, continued the not-so-sly questioning about Skip Rhodes and his company. The woman had been pushier than her brother, picking at what Sky knew, or in most cases didn't know, about Skip's past. She had played dumb about where he was from or what he had done before tour guiding, which wasn't hard since she had no idea. Johanna's expression had all but called her a liar. The woman had become so frustrated that Sky finally told her she needed to talk to Lilac Williams, the woman he was involved with and had taken to Mexico.

"Not surprised about Montezuma, Honey...I didn't like the jib of those two bald peckerheads from the moment they walked into the SOB," Zula said, pouring another cup of coffee from the stainless-steel pot and crumbling a fourth strip of bacon for Spike.

Zula had taken a liking to the girl. Sky might believe aliens had bestowed her hypermobility during an intergalactic joy ride, but other than that, she had a good head on her shoulders. She saw things in people even Zula, with her worldly experience, missed. She had just needed a place to land, stability for once in her life, and a little dose of encouragement.

"Why don't you call him, honey?

"I wish *he* would call," Sky said. "The Mosbys are too interested in him. I don't know why; it doesn't make any sense. Something was wrong though; the woman all but insisted that I tell her his 'legal' name. She said "Skip" was an obvious nickname. I'm glad they left for Phoenix today to catch a flight home. I was afraid Johanna would ask for another tour. I'd had enough of the two wrestlers, and Jerry had kept hitting on me."

"You know, I've never thought to ask him about his name."

Sky had. He had deflected the question, joking that he didn't want it getting around. He'd explained his older brother had called him Skip, and it had stuck. She had tried questioning the use of a nickname in his legal correspondence and passport, but he had shut her down, changing the subject.

"Lilac is probably keeping him busy," she said, a little too meanly.

"Oh, Honey. He made his choice, give him time. I wasn't the first long-legged showgirl Two-Balls took a shine too."

Later that day, Zula decided to check on Skip's place, a responsibility she assumed when he was away. It was her property after all, she had a key. Isolated in the woods, an occasional limb was known to fall, wildlife was quick to learn people weren't around, shake shingles got blown loose – nature had a way of causing problems at an empty cabin -

Sky had passed, opting to tend bar at the SOB. Zula guessed the poor girl just didn't want to think about Skip anymore. Which was understandable, if Zula had been forty years younger when he had knocked on her screen door, holding her ad for the cabin...well, neither Lilac nor Sky would have stood a chance. The man was a throwback, undeniably attractive without knowing it. His mysterious persona, loner tendencies, and hint of past damage were right out of a Danielle Steele novel.

Spike was with her, trotting on and off the path, nosing around in weeds and sniffing coyote scat. He rooted out a crushed can of soda and flipped it to Zula with his snout. She always brought a bag for trash washed up from Oak Creek, but this can was clean. High-water junk was always caked in mud and covered with leaves. Unusual...*probably tourists*, this section of the path was part of a longer trail that led to Red Rock Crossing. She tossed the can in the bag thinking nothing more.

A big sycamore landmarked the turn from the main path to Skip's cabin, which was past a stand of cottonwoods on the far side of a small clearing. O'Bryan's homestead had been well hidden from outlaws, Indians, and curious, would-be visitors. Spike was up ahead, standing alert, behind a butterfly bush below Skip's porch. His hackled, stiff gray hair signaled something had spooked him.

Chief Hooton and Officer Dickie arrived at the Sands shortly after Zula left. Sky was on the porch of the lodge when the police cruiser's blue lights and siren erupted while coming down the lane. Dickie was driving and Hoot was yelling at him. The navy and black Bronco was new, and he pushed the wrong button after parking, not yet used to the electronic ignition.

The emergency quelled, Hoot exited the silenced cruiser and sauntered up the steps like John Wayne. Ascertaining the showgirl wasn't in, he asked Sky for a key to Skip's cabin and filled her in on the call from Captain Nemuro, omitting the part about a murder.

"How much farther?" Hoot asked ten minutes later, smacking a mosquito against his neck, the red smear making a baker's dozen.

Despite his objection that civilians were not permitted on official business, Sky insisted on tagging along…otherwise, no key.

Due to his height, the Chief exhaled more carbon dioxide than a normal human, attracting bugs in mass. Beating his head like a tom-tom, the crazy eye in a panic, he anxiously tracked the coordinated movements of a committed troop of blood suckers with stingers. Dickie, hoping for a service commendation, was on his tiptoes, brushing bugs off the back of his boss's scalp. The fog of skeeters formed around them both, launching a counterattack. Behind the vanguard of mosquitoes, flew reinforcements of moths and green flies.

"Not far!" Sky shouted, running farther up the trail, away from the swarm. "Once we leave the creek, they won't be so bad!"

"What do you hear, boy?" Zula whispered to Spike. The javelina was pawing the ground, acting like he was readying to charge a bobcat.

Zula heard glass break inside the cabin, someone had thrown a picture or plate against a wall. Sneaking onto the porch, she avoided the second step, which squeaked under the slightest pressure. Skip was supposed to have fixed it. *Damn male procrastination!* If the man wanted an alarm, Ace Hardware had a whole shelf of options. Spike stayed at the bottom of the stairs, scanning both directions, protecting her rear.

She heard voices…

"Nothing," a husky male baritone said, followed by a thud that sounded like furniture being flipped. "Fucking sofa's heavy, man. Maybe you can do something other than smash his beer glasses?"

"Look under the rug," a second male voice suggested.

Zula crept across the porch, pressing her back against the cabin's wall.

"Nada," the baritone answered.

She crawled below a window, raised her head slowly, and peeked into the room. *Damn...she should have brought her 12-gauge Beretta.*

The sofa was upside down, two of its legs broken, limp as Two Balls after his prostate surgery. Skip's recliner was in three pieces, and a man was ripping into the cushions. Every cabinet in the small kitchen, there were only two, was open, the doors hanging from their hinges. A second man was yanking out drawers, spilling their contents on the counter. The asshole had littered the linoleum floor with broken dishes. They were masked, but she had a pretty good idea...the peckerheads. A third man, or it could be the woman, Zula couldn't tell, came from the bedroom carrying a box.

"This was under the bed," a deep female voice said. *Answered that question.*

Zula started backing off the porch. Without the Beretta, this was beyond her investigative capabilities. Back in the trees, safe, she could call SPD. God help all of them if those boys got here in time. She heard a low snort behind her, and Spike charged up the stairs. *The second step...damn that pig!*

The woman from the bedroom heard the squeak and yelled an alarm. Zula turned to run, but a black plastic bag was pulled over her head, the drawstring tightening around her neck.

Officer Dickie reached the clearing first. Sky and the Chief were farther back. She had found a jar of Deet in her backpack and was spreading the gel over Hoot's exposed skin. His face looked like he had measles on top of a bad rash.

"*POLICE!*" Dickie shouted, seeing the scene on the porch. Zula Ballsy was on her knees with a bag over her head. A masked man, the size of a linebacker, was choking her. The old girl was putting up a fight, punching her attacker's balls. Spike, her pet javelina, had latched onto his calf.

Dickie pulled his service revolver, fired a shot in the air, and charged across the clearing, yelling, "POLICE! Hands in the air!"

One of Zula's blind punches landed. Instead of trying to hit him again, she grasped his crotch and tugged like she was in a July Fourth rope pulling contest. The man screamed and released her neck, chopping her wrist. With his other hand, he grabbed the skin behind Spike's ears and ripped him off, tossing the snarling pig over the railing.

Dickie was ten feet from the porch running flat out. The Chief and Sky were shouting from behind. An adrenalin rush equivalent to shooting a twenty-ounce can of Red Bull kept him from hearing what they were yelling. Suddenly, the screen door to the cabin flung open. Another masked man, even bigger, pointed a pistol and fired.

The shot went wide, and Dickie dropped and rolled beside the bottom stair, ending up against the latticework below the porch floor. Spike was under the steps with a *let's do this* look in his eyes. Dickie caught his breath and glanced back, the Chief and Sky were behind a pair of cottonwood trees. Hoot had his gun out, aiming! *Shit!* Dickie said three Hail Marys; his boss's shooting was on par with his eyesight. True to form, Hoot was sweeping the barrel side-to-side trying to settle on a target while hand-checking Sky, who was trying to take it away from him.

"Get the fuck back in here," a woman yelled from above him.

Dickie stuck his head above the porch floor; Zula was still struggling with the bag on her head. The thug had cinched it and tied the tabs. "Spike, attack boy! ATTACK!" she shouted, hearing her pet growling.

Spike sprung from his hiding spot, woofed, and charged up the stairs. A shot fired and Dickie heard a howl, then Zula screaming. A thud sounded against the cabin's wood siding, and he heard the echoing crack from a gun. It was Sky. She had Hoot's revolver and had shot at someone on the porch.

"Out the back," Dickie heard the woman order, this time from inside the cabin. He crouched, making himself a smaller target, and started up the stairs. Zula was laying on the floorboards, below the window, cradling the squirming javelina. She had torn her shirt and was wrapping Spike's hindquarter.

"Mrs. Ballsy, stay down," he whispered. Zula nodded.

He reached the porch and stood beside the open door, his finger on the trigger, his other hand cupping the butt of his pistol like Magnum, only in uniform. Sky and Hoot were almost to the stairs. The Chief had his weapon back, waving it somewhere in the vicinity of the door. *Jesus, please don't let him fire*, Dickie prayed. He counted to three and jumped through the open door, firing two shots as he dove behind an overturned sofa. *No return fire.* He peeked over the edge, expecting a volley of gunfire. *Nothing.* The back door banged close; they had fled through the woods.

Dickie checked behind the cabin before returning to the porch. Zula was free, her head poked through a hole in the garbage bag. She was cuddling Spike, who had just been grazed. Sky was stroking the fur behind his ears. The javelina seemed to be enjoying the attention. Hoot was on his phone, said, "Okay," and hung up.

"Mrs. Ballsy, did you recognize any of them?" Dickie asked, kneeling beside her.

"I have a pretty good idea," Zula and Sky chimed together.

Hoot reached to pet Spike, "That's one brave javelina, deserving of a civilian service award." The pig snapped at him. "We'll find them," he said, keeping his good eye on the snarling pig while wiping the gel oozing down his face. The gunk was stinging the red welts.

Zula chortled, "Hoot, you couldn't find your ass with both hands! That girl did your shooting for you. Why don't you go cite a tourist for puking in public." She leaned over and hugged Dickie. Spike licked his face. "Officer, we thank you for your bravery. Consider yourself permanently invited to our Tequila Moon parties. Your margaritas are free here."

20

Zoológico del Centenario

CHEN ZING DID NOT LIKE ANIMALS UNLESS THEY WERE PANDAS at the Beijing Zoo where he took his nieces. This small, dingy park in central Merida with metal cages, however, was where he would trade the Indian woman for the formula to a powerful, new biological weapon. A weapon being developed by the Americans according to the Chinese Ministry of State Security, MSS. What it had to do with an antique Mayan vessel had not been part of his briefing.

Double Dragon, the sophisticated cyber espionage program within MSS, had picked up rumors of an ancient virus being resurrected with the help of the Guatemalan dictator, Hector Colon. Zing's father, Chen Ling, Director of MSS, had ensured his son was given the honor of capturing the formula for the People's Republic.

Zing was a star within MSS. His father had shepherded the National Intelligence Law of 2017 that authorized MSS to employ counterintelligence and espionage programs both domestically and internationally. Zing, with his famous father's backing, had risen quickly in MSS's Second Bureau, responsible for foreign intelligence gathering. The handsome, unusually tall Chinese had conducted operations under diplomatic cover from Tokyo to Washington. His enemies, scattered throughout MSS's fourteen bureaus, found him arrogant and cocky. This current assignment, to a backwater corner of a backwater country, Mexico, had him pondering if his father's influence was waning in the Politburo.

Regardless of the Double Dragon hackers' insistence on the importance of the Mayan drinking vessel, Chen Zing found it hard to believe the Americans were using facilities anywhere in Central America. They were beyond primitive compared to the state-of-the-art research laboratories in Wuhan. That was particularly so for the impoverished, gang-riddled country of Guatemala. He had been there once and seen no reason for his ministry to bother with cultivating political relations. And now, he was supposed to accept they were capable of developing the world's next weapon of mass destruction? If Double Dragon wasn't the brainchild of Xi Jinping, no one would believe it. Not even his father dared to challenge him.

Zing was raised and trained to follow orders, to accept without questioning, but he had also been trained in counterintelligence. This chase after a virus had all the hallmarks of a hoax, a global American trick to distract the attention of the People's Republic and waste their cyber energies. Their two countries were in a cold, virtual war for world economic dominion, and this was how the ageless game of spying was now being played. Taking the Indian woman was only a first act, an attention getter, not the end itself.

In a complete reversal of roles, Skip was working hard to keep Kuul calm. Toni's kidnapping had been a body blow to the big man. He had assured him, over and over, that these trades were profession-ally executed, neither side wanted any blood spilled during the exchange. Violence was too unpredictable. Drama was a product of Hollywood, real life spy games had rules. The players – *and the Chinese leader was definitely a player* - just wanted to be done with it as smoothly as possible and leave, with both parties satisfied.

The sisal bag was dangling from Kuul's belt as they walked through pillars of faux-painted stone into the Merida Zoo. Lilac had insisted on coming, and Stephens was with her. The linguist, archeologist, biologist, *whatever the hell he was*, had been intent on helping protect the Mayan artifact. Lilac had extolled his numerous academic credentials and flawless breaststroke during their drive from Campeche, while Skip had inwardly fumed.

Their first tail intercepted them past a shady courtyard with a playground, gift shop, and restaurant. Happy, squealing children were racing through a dancing water feature, jets of water intermittently shooting into the warm, steamy air, while their parents laughed from the café's red, plastic chairs. Two men, both had been at the market in Campeche, were leaning against a tree pretending to watch the kids but more closely watching Skip and his group. The men dropped their cigarettes, rubbed the butts in the landscape chips, then followed them into the hippopotamus exhibit. The heavy herbivores were wading in a muddy pond - slimy, green mold grew from cracks in the concrete basin.

Skip waved at the men and led them down a cinder path with overgrowing, tropical foliage, past a rusty bird aviary. He turned at a sign for *The Meadow*, which shortly led to a fenced, dirt field with giraffes, zebras, and high-stepping ostriches. The second duo of Chinese accompanists was waiting there. This was becoming a parade.

Reaching a juncture in the path, three signs on a post pointed in three directions - the *African Prairie*, the *American Prairie*, and the *Eurasian Prairie* – apparently Merida was lacking mountain animals. Standing beneath the sign, Skip turned and shrugged to the growing collection of men in black suits. Like their leader had worn in Campeche, they all sported dark sunglasses, despite the manufactured, shady jungle setting. *No, not conspicuous at all.* One of them pointed left to the African Prairie.

Ten minutes later, past enclosure after enclosure of bored looking animals, they walked beneath a super-sized pair of plastic, painted tigers. Ahead were the cat cages. Boxes of chain-link fencing housed black jaguars, pumas, tawny-colored maned lions, leopards, and real striped tigers. Most were sleeping in patches of grass or cool hollows of dirt. A leopard stalked back and forth along the front of its fence, lazily tracking the circus gawkers outside its prison: its trail wore six inches into the dusty ground. A lone jaguar was poised on a concrete ledge, scored to look and feel like a mountain, guarding its mate lying half-in and half-out of an artificial cave. Past the jaguars, the path turned. It was the end of the park.

"I feel sorry for the animals, they don't belong here," Lilac said. "These exhibits are inadequate and filthy."

Stephens nodded, "very different from their native habitats. I wonder if they keep them drugged?"

Kuul snarled, "Not every country has the wealthy donors and budget of the National Zoo in Washington."

Skip rounded the turn, the jaguar menacingly peering down at him. Buried in its DNA was a marker urging it to hunt. They were brothers, the cat and he – the patience to stalk, the willingness to attack, the mental strength, *or lack of*, to coldly kill. They were both animals without a conscience. Weaker, less agile adversaries were food in their jungles. Kuul spoke soothingly to the cat, it jumped down joining its mate at the mouth of their den.

Skip spotted Toni before Kuul. She was by a bench fifty yards ahead, where the path turned back toward the entrance. The tall Chinese leader was standing beside her. She stepped toward them, but the man held her arm and pulled her back. A mottled, brown bruise along her jawline told him she had put up a fight. The Yavapai woman stoically nodded at him, letting him know she was ready for whatever happened. She signaled Kuul to stay calm, pressing her free palm forward like a horse whisperer training a wild stallion.

A high-pitched whistle tooted *Choo...Choo...Choo...*freezing all of them. A kiddie train with four open cars of boisterous children chaperoned by a handful of adults rounded the turn from behind.

"Be cool, follow my lead," Skip whispered to Kuul. He didn't need him to go off half-cocked. He could sense the tension increasing in the big man. The same anxiousness Toni had seen.

Skip glanced over his shoulder at Lilac and Stephens. They were facing off against the Chinese gang of four. There had to be two more somewhere.

The kids on the train were growling and roaring at the disinterested cats. Their teachers were paying little attention, most glued to their phones, fingers rapidly texting or scrolling the screen, glad to have their charges all aboard and corralled.

Kuul loosened the sisal bag and handed it to Skip, who motioned to the Chinese leader. The train slowed and stopped on the turn to allow pictures of the jaguar. The hunter had repositioned itself on the ledge again, sensing a kill and the possibility of leftovers. The conductor tooted the whistle and a lion several cages away roared; the children all screamed. Skip tossed the bag into a grassy area beside the pathway, about fifteen feet, halfway to the Chinese. The Chinese and Toni advanced like pieces in a game of chess. Kuul immediately started toward her, but Skip grabbed him. The Maya man glared at his friend, shaking his hand loose. Fury clouded his eyes.

"When she's beside the bag, she'll stop," Skip said to Kuul. "Don't move before I do."

Lilac and Stephens had backed up to them. "Just follow my lead for once. *Please*," Skip whispered to her. She was so close he could feel her pressed against his back. "This isn't the time for a display of feminine independence."

Lilac wanted to give him a piece of her feminine independence but held her tongue.

"When Toni stops, I'll walk toward her part way, and the man will do the same. Both of you stay put. If no one panics, we'll get out of this – with Toni," Skip said, exchanging a heartfelt glance with his friend. "Trust me."

The Chinese stopped fifteen feet from the bag, whispered to Toni, then sent her forward. She walked beside the bag and looked back, waiting for the Chinese leader's orders. Skip also stared at the Chinese. The damn sunglasses were on, so he got no read from his eyes. The man was a cool customer, however, smiling and waving at the kids on the train, the few who were watching him. His head swiveled back to Skip, nodded, and they both advanced; Toni began walking – slowly.

Skip reached Toni at the same time as the man reached the bag. They were ten feet apart. He reassuringly squeezed her elbow, while signaling her to remain still. The man glanced in the bag and then to Skip, taking off his glasses. Their eyes met. His expression was a mixture of curiosity and disgust.

"This is all?" Chen Zing asked.

"Yes."

"It does not look like much."

"What were you expecting?"

Chen Zing shrugged, "You know we must check you and your friends. To be sure."

Before Skip could say, *No Way* – the whistle blew and the kiddie train began moving, the metal wheels screeching against the metal track. The children were booing and roaring even louder as they pulled away. Skip looked back to Kuul, who looked like a bull being taunted by a red flag. Then at Lilac, the four Chinese were fanning out and advancing toward her and Stephens. Stephens was trying to push her behind him, but she brushed him away.

"Lilac, Kuul, *THE TRAIN!*" he yelled, suddenly darting from the path, and shoving Toni toward the tiny tracks.

The Chinese man just watched, smirking. There was nothing he or his men could do, not with so many witnesses. *"Jū!"* Zing barked, ordering them to hold back. Skip and Toni stepped onto the running board of the last car and grabbed its railing. Kuul ran and jumped beside Toni, wrapping her in one big arm. Lilac and Stevens followed suit on the next to last car.

"You don't think they'll follow us?" Kuul asked.

"Not here and not until they're sure they didn't get what they were after. With any luck, we'll be flying out of here before they do."

AEROPUERTO INTERNACIONAL DE MERIDA

CAPITÁN GOMEZ STATIONED HIS MEN THROUGHOUT MERIDA'S small airport, urging them to stay firm in their commitment and loyal to their commander – *Why did every international airport have cantinas and duty-free shops?* Merida's even had a tequila bar. Already, he had spied *Soldado* Perez sipping from a bottle hidden in his vest, insolently wearing an *I Love Mexico* ball cap. The fool had even proudly waved it at him. Gomez had made *Sargento* Salamandor confiscate it; the hat would make a nice gift for Lupe.

He and Chuuy sat at a table outside Hacienda Montejo, a restaurant on the second-floor gallery. *Aeropuerto Internacional de Merida Manuel Crecencio Réjon* only had one terminal, and from their perch they would see the Americans as they passed through security. Gomez had positioned a soldier outside to alert him when they arrived.

"You were right about their departing in the evening, Hernando."

Gomez nodded smugly. The cerveza here was cold and dark, much better than the swill in Campeche, though the Mexicans had taken to overcharging at their airports like their capitalist zealots north of their border. "*Sí.* That was my expert assessment. The Presidential Guard trains their elite commanders in the skillful analysis of targeted troublemakers. The quicker, direct flights to Los Angeles are at that time; the Americans are in a hurry. Someday, you may also learn these things."

"It was also helpful, no, that I noted the sticker on their rental car at *Uxmal* and bribed the rental agent here in Merida to get their drop off time?"

Hernando sneered. Two tickets to the *Estados Unidos* were in his pocket; taking his brother-in-law with him was not absolutely necessary. He could be sent home to Guatemala City with Perez and the other soldiers. Mancoros would be furious, but by the time he was informed of his lieutenant's absence, there would be nothing he could do. On U.S. soil, Hernando would be safely beyond his reach. Bringing Chuuy, however, would prevent him from singing like a canary to the *Coronel*. And who knew, he could yet prove useful. They would follow the Americans to Arizona, steal the artifact, and disappear. Chuuy's new *amigo*, the rental agent, had also given him their address. He would fly Lupe and his children, even Fernando's bastards, from Belize to wherever he settled...or so he had told her brother.

Once they had money, Chuuy could do whatever he wanted for Lupe. Gomez had bigger plans. With a private island in Nicaragua, he would send for his mistress, Gabriela. A singer at El Portalito, his favorite bar, she had seduced him with her sultry voice and songs *de amor*. God made her hips for a man to grasp and enjoy. He could picture her lying naked, beckoning him from a cushioned lounger by their own beach. A servant would bring them pisco sours after their lovemaking; she liked Hernando to use his finger to stir in a fine rum instead of the stronger Peruvian brandy. On special nights, she would tease him by separating the egg whites with her delicious tongue.

"What will you buy with your share, Chuuy?"

"A bigger trailer and television, connected to satellite. I would like to watch *Narcos* on cable. Also a microwave. But I am worried, Hernando."

"Worried?

"*Sí*. We do not know exactly what we are stealing."

Gomez frowned. Chuuy, idiot he was, had a point. But it was a detail they could sort out later. This was their opportunity, maybe his only one. Returning to Lupe and Mancoros was a nightmare – literally. Last night, he had dreamt of waking to find Fernando in his bed, spooning Lupe, when the *Coronel* burst into their room with his arrest warrant – his children suspended from the ceiling like puppets singing, *"There was something in the air that night..."*

No - Colon lived to fill his pockets with gold, of that, he was sure. "It is a valuable, ancient Mayan artifact. Worth millions of *quetzals*."

"*Sí*," Chuuy answered, rubbing his forehead, trying to think. He had seen many old cups, none of them valuable. *"Pero por qué es so valuable?* Mancoros has not told us. With the Americans chasing it, I am worried it *es peligroso*, dangerous. Do not take offense, my *Capitán*, but why did he select you? You who caused the American Vice President to catch rabies. What if it is Semtex, or worse, uranium, like in the movies!" Chuuy was shaking at the thought. "It could turn us green, and we would die vomiting poison!"

"It is an old Mexican relic, *Sargento*; you worry about too many things. That is why you live in the slum *La Limonada* in a polluted, crowded ravine, inside a metal box with a corrugated tin roof."

Daria Ahmadi was listening to the Guatemalans from the shadows of the tequila bar's fake palapa. *These two were the best that Hector Colon had to send?* In Tehran, they would be unemployed beggars pushing wheelbarrows of garbage. No wonder they had run from mindless iguanas.

Daria's mission parameters had changed since yesterday... since seeing *Skip. The simple name was so hard to use, the silly sound of it so different from the man she had known.* MOIS had ordered her *not* to get the virus: she was only to monitor the situation. Afshin Ghasemi, President of Iran, had decided acquiring the virus place too big of a target on their country. They were already enduring crippling Western sanctions due to fears surrounding their nuclear program. He and the Ayatollah had elected to step back and were debating how to proceed. Letting the erratic American President attain the virus was equally troubling, however, given his hatred of the followers of Islam. He had already severed the 2015 Joint Comprehensive POA negotiated between Iran and the world powers. With an election year on the horizon, his infecting and killing thousands of "raghead" Muslims wasn't out of the question.

A rogue Guatemalan Presidential Guard acquiring the formula and selling it to the highest bidder was not a good option either. She seriously doubted their ability to take it from the Americans, but trusting to chance, would leave the door wide open for the Chinese. Her former lover was a pragmatist and had made it clear he believed the *cup* was nothing more than a historical artifact, not a global tool of destruction. He would not risk much, certainly not the lives of his friends, to keep it out of the wrong hands.

Daria listened in disgust; *a mosquito infested island in the world's poorest country.* The man was a fool. If the Guatemalan knew the true value of the formula, he would be planning to buy an island off the coast of France.

Out of the corner of her eye, Daria saw *Skip* and the meddlesome red head, passing through security with the two Natives and a stranger – Who was he?

Rhodes, at least his last name fit, immediately began scanning the corridor. His search settled on the three teams of Guatemalans posted below. None of the teams had seen them yet; they might be good at standing outside a palace, but covert operations...*worse than worthless.* Still, it was only a matter of time. The red head and the Native woman studied a departure board, the latter pointing at the screen and speaking to the big Mayan. They headed toward their gate, the red head leading and Skip in the back.

Hernando – the other Guatemalan had said his name – finally saw them. One by one, his teams spotted them as well and glanced up to their leader. The American followed their gazes and nudged the red head; the Guatemalan leader was directing his men to follow and to wait on him. The Mayan man, his woman, and the stranger gathered around Rhodes, exchanging words. Then they passed out of Daria's view, below the edge of the far balcony.

Monitoring did not exclude interfering, Daria thought...as long as she made no attempt for the vessel and its formula.

"Here we have them outnumbered," Chuuy argued. "Why not take the cup now, while we have our men?"

"And what if they resist? Do you propose we fight them in a crowded *aeropuerto*? *Sargento*, have you not seen the Mexican police patrolling the concourse? Do you think they will ignore us if the Americans yell? No, Chuuy, we *make sure* they get on the plane, and then you and I follow. Patience, brother-in-law, patie –"

Gomez stopped mid-word.

Chuuy turned to his suddenly silent *Capitán*. Hernando was staring straight ahead, not down at their men who were awaiting his further instructions. His face was as still and pale as the virgin María statues during holy week. First one arm, then his second arm, awkwardly rose like a zombie in the *Walking Dead*, before he placed his hands flat on the table, his fingers trembling. A beautiful woman with a scarf partially covering her face had sat beside his brother-in-law. Her hand was under the table.

"Lupe would not be happy, *hermano*. You already have Gabriela."

"Fucking *idiota*! Are you blind? *Madre de dios!*" Gomez hissed, rolling his panicked eyes, "*Ella tiene un cuchillo* – a knife, imbecile – in my ribs."

Chuuy stupidly stared at the woman. Her arm moved, and Hernando twitched and moaned. Chuuy mimicked his brother-in-law, spreading his fingers on the table, "*El Capitán es* in charge, I know little," he whimpered.

Daria chuckled and whispered, "Signal your men to stand down –carefully." The captain did nothing and she pushed the tip of her blade into his jacket until he bucked, "Now...and send them back out the concourse."

Gomez wisely gestured to his men, using his index finger to make a circle that emphatically directed them back through the exit. *Soldado* Perez waved and whistled, seeing his captain's new pretty, dark-skinned *puta*. A *Federale* frowned at him and shook a finger at the men. Another Guatemalan grabbed Perez and pulled him toward the exit.

Daria smiled. Latin men and their blustery masculinity.

"In Iran, disrespecting women that way would cost your soldier and his superior their tongues. Do you know who I am?"

Hernando and the imbecile shook their heads, no.

"Have you heard of the Ministry of Intelligence Services for the Republic of Iran, MOIS?" The captain nodded, beads of sweat forming on his forehead. The imbecile's saucer-sized eyes began to water. Iran's counterinsurgency techniques had been a model for Central American death squads. "Do you believe I can have you imprisoned in Tehran within twenty-four hours? The guards are very unpleasant, sadistic even...and lonely." Daria heard dripping on the tile floor and the imbecile began to sob. A puddle was pooling near her feet.

"*Es the cerveza,*" Chuuy moaned.

"Keep your hands on this table. Do *not* follow me or them. I will be watching. You understand what will happen if you do."

"*El Capitán* gets fucked by a prison guard," Chuuy answered.

"*Tú también,*" Daria said, smiling as she turned and walked briskly away.

From the bottom of the escalator, she peered back at them. They were still in their chairs, and she suspected their hands were still on the table. An angry bartender was there, gesturing at the floor, berating the imbecile, and throwing rags at both men.

Daria exited the secured area. Outside, Hernando's men were milling around showing each other the trinkets they had purchased. She joined a line at the counter of an American airline. A first-class ticket for an early morning flight to Phoenix was still available. She wasn't ready to give Tripp up again so soon after discovering he was alive. She had a reason not too – a personal reason that even MOIS was unaware of. She needed to understand his life and what kind of man he had become. So far, she had been less than impressed.

Could he be trusted with their secret? A sweet, innocent, seven-year-old secret that as a mother she would die to protect?

WILY COYOTE RESORT AND SPA

THE NEARLY NAKED WOMAN MADE NO SECRET OF HER INTEN-tions. Her large breasts barely fit into her revealing bikini, and each time she twisted in her lounger to smile at Roid, a rosy button surrounded by dark areola winked at him. The swelling in his Speedo answered her titillating looks. He would have her to himself too; Lloyd was soaking his twisted ankle in the hot tub with his fourth Shirley Temple.

Roid glanced across the pool at his boss. A cool customer but too old for his taste. And the pock-marked face – well, that's why they made paper bags. Planet Fitness had sculpted one hell of a body, though, a monument to exercise and her adoration of chemistry. Her tattoo was a turn-on too, a red and black snake, stretching from her hip to knee, swallowing a fat rat. And tough. She was head of Bathsheba Cosmetic's security department and took absolutely no fucking prisoners. Screwing Johanna, if she swung that way – he had his doubts – would be like having sex with a lawnmower. She'd eat you alive and spit you out when she finished. The rose button chick disappearing into her private cabana was a much safer, better-looking choice.

"We may have to medicate your pit bull," Jerry Jessup, aka Mosby, snickered. He and Johanna had positioned themselves across the pool, beneath an umbrella, away from Roid and Lloyd. Unprotected from the sun, their Assistant Security Specialists were already resembling peeled radishes, their pale, white skin turning pink.

Johanna had given them all the afternoon off, but ordered they stay on property. Relaxing around the roadrunner shaped pool behind the Wily Coyote Resort and Spa had been their choice. They had time. Her counterpart, the *man* in charge, would be out of communication for hours. *Counterpart* – she had threatened to resign when Bathsheba's CEO had laid out the joint operation, informing her a longtime nemesis would be in charge. A notorious lone wolf within industrial espionage circles, an independent contractor who preferred operating in the dark. Who he was working for this time was above her pay grade, she had been told. The bonus promised her had overcome her reservations.

In the meantime, she didn't see any harm in letting the boys blow off a little steam, as long as they didn't bust any plumbing.

"She occupies him, we won't have to," Johanna scoffed. "A libido-blinded Romeo and a neanderthal that can't walk without falling. Neither was my choice."

"They were helpful in convincing the MIT chemist to accept Bathsheba's offer," Jerry said. With Roid and Lloyd, he had 'visited' the scientist who had developed a cream to treat chemical burn victims. It was also a remarkable wrinkle smoother. Even better, it contained a mild antihistamine and became addictive after prolonged use.

Johanna Molis, aka Mosby, had been with Bathsheba for five years. Jack Anderson, the company's CEO, had lured her away from Aphrodite GmbH, a German pharmaceutical firm, with a threefold increase in salary, Department Director and Vice-President titles, and the promise of a lifetime supply of anabolic steroids. Her deltoids had blown out two inches in four weeks. An informant in the Inspector General's Office of HHS had alerted her to a play by Stinckner Pharma for a secret weight loss formula being developed in the Mexican Yucatan. The information had been sketchy, but enough to take to Jack. Three days later, she'd been shocked when he told her they would be collaborating instead of competing with Orville Stinckner's company.

"Rhodes and his friends in Mexico...I don't read them as anything other than what our double-jointed ditz says they are," Jerry said.

Johanna recruited Jerry Jessup to Bathsheba eighteen months earlier. He had been with a small California startup that manufactured surfboard wax, sunscreen, and body paints. He also moonlighted, which is how she had first employed his talents. His babyface good looks, deep tan, and West Coast surfer persona hid darker ambitions and a complete lack of morals. Making him perfect for wrangling information from older, sexually aggressive female executives. He would do anything, at least anything she had assigned him, to get ahead and make a name for himself. The fact that the girl, Sky, had *read* his act was to her credit; unfortunately for her, that meant a different tact was necessary.

"Maybe," Johanna pondered, "It's suspicious that no one here seems to know anything about Skip Rhodes prior to five years ago. My counterpart was hoping we'd find out more – but that's his problem."

Speaking of the devil...a text appeared on her phone. "Americans leaving for Phoenix. Make contact soon," she read.

"Not too soon, I hope," Jerry laughed, nodding across the pool. Roid had joined the woman in her cabana, and she was closing the curtains. The strings to her bikini top were hanging down her shoulders, and she was holding her cups in place with her free arm. Roid's hands were wrapped around her from behind, his fingers slipped just under the waistband of her suit. "Let's hope she's here for a bachelorette party and not with her husband."

"Talk to him later, he's in your section. Tell him we'll have a better playmate for him tomorrow."

Jerry's eyebrows raised.

"That "double-jointed ditz" isn't as simple as you think. Be careful with her. There's more than just business between her and Rhodes. They have a history; my guess is she's in love with him. Unless he's a total dick – like you – that makes him vulnerable. Miss Sapphire Sky will be a nice insurance policy to have in our pocket."

"Leverage," Jerry matter-of-factly stated.

Johanna studied his cool demeanor. He was a cleverer strategist than she thought, more than a pretty boy. She needed to watch him. Rising up the corporate ladder was more about pulling someone else down than climbing.

The Aeromexico Boeing 737, little more than two-thirds full, leveled off at 32,000 feet. Skip was in an aisle seat, the middle seat empty, the window occupied by a college-aged kid who had been asleep since takeoff. Kuul and Toni were sitting together two rows up. Catherwood Stephens and Lilac were comfortably sipping champagne in first-class; thanks to, as *Woody* put it, his more than adequate per diem which compensated for poor academic pay. Skip had never heard of an expense account that covered an attractive woman, picked up abroad.

Seeing the Guatemalans at the airport had not been a surprise. Their pulling back had been until he spotted Daria and saw the Guatemalan Captain and a bartender hurling Latin curses on the balcony – she could definitely do that to a man. *What was her endgame?* Central America, China, Iran...he had half expected a cameo from Mossad and Russian Federation agents; they all needed to form a line and take tickets.

Questions – that's all he had. Couped up in a plane, he had at least four hours to think before landing back in the States. His mind drifted to Daria – the fort, his room, the airport – would he see her again? Did he want to? For a second time, she had entered his life and then left. Different story, same ending. Seven years ago, she had stripped his soul bare, broken through every defense he had built. He had been ready to share so much, for however long they could run. Had his instincts about her been that wrong? No, it had been his heart. Against all reason, he had convinced himself that they had a chance, and he had believed her. *That* was his mistake. If Iran wanted the damn cup so badly, he would see her again, and it wouldn't be another seven years this time. He would make her confess her reasons for leaving. They were good at confessions, not so good at what came later. Their bond had been a sham, a trick to build trust so she could escape. But why hadn't she ended their time together with a bullet to his brain? Questions, that's all he had.

What he was sure of was that Daria would follow him. He knew her, he could feel her, she was out there somewhere. She wasn't dead to him any longer.

He also knew that the incompetent Guatemalans and the more dangerous Chinese both wanted the formula. He doubted the latter, in particular, would give up the chase. Daria would have to battle more than just him for the cup. And who had he not seen. Who had not made their play yet? *This was supposed to have been a simple drop.* Once they were back in the U.S., whether Kuul agreed or not, they were dumping this shitstorm back in the laps of those that deserved it.

Hell, this kid next to him could be Russian or Venezuelan, or...or from any host of nations in the market for a new chemical weapon, which is what Daria was confident it was. His professional instincts had dulled from lack of use; he had made too many mistakes, too many errors in judgement. He could account for his slipping, but paranoia, once it got a foothold, was difficult to check. *No* - the kid was just a kid, returning from break, not a spy. His maroon and gold ASU cap hiding his face was real, not a cover. The pin on the bill was a souvenir, not a mike.

The captain turned the cabin lights off and Skip tried to relax. He regulated his breathing, counting the seconds used to inhale and exhale. Long, deep, even breaths. Sleep, something he hadn't gotten much of the past two days. Who knew what was waiting for them in Sedona? What better place to try than in a pressurized tube, without distractions or threats?

Three minutes later he was dreaming…*a smooth leg stretched atop a wet sheet – a ceiling fan, thump – thump – moans, his, whose, can't see – don't wake up, she will leave – pacing, pacing, pacing – a tanned face – softness - hair covering all but the corner of a shoulder – breathing, pacing, breathing – trying to wake up, struggling, confused – she needs to leave – NO, no good – cool breeze – window open, air moving – tinkling - door opening – chimes – whimpering, crying, sleeping, rolling over – gunfire, running, running – save her – the hair, still can't see – just let go, save her – his hands, holding her, crushing her, body against body – can't – break – free.*

His eyes fluttered inside their closed lids, and he vaguely sensed his conscious mind arousing. Coming awake was hard, and he wasn't ready. He floated back into his dream. He needed to finish…finish…with…*finish with…*

Air – warm air – blowing against his chest – sweet, stale, sweaty smell – don't let go, close yourself – trust, no trust, trust - No – no choice – stay, protect her – hide her from them, from him – run, now, run – strong arms, grasping him, begging him – future, what future, our future – where, how – a jeweled wrist, long slender fingers, gentle touch – hair – inhale, deep breaths – long hair, fingers sweeping back – soft smile, loving smile – strong arms - cuddling, cooing, soothing, assuring – we can, we will be – more hair – long hair – satisfied, resting, happy - strange senses, joined, devoted, understanding – it will be okay, rest – the morning - hair, covering his face – pressure, breath, pressure, breath – sweet taste, softness, lips – hair – hair – long red hair – White Flash…

Skip jolted awake. The cabin lights were back on. The Sun Devil beside him was latching his table in place. A flight attendant stood in the aisle, holding a plastic bag, smiling at him, "Trash?" He stuffed a napkin and nut wrapper in the cup on his tray and tossed it toward the bag. Missed. Sleep had not helped.

MAN WHO RUNS WITH THORN IN FOOT

"**W**E COULD HAVE TURNED IT IN," SKIP GRUMBLED. THE lack of sleep was catching up with all of them. Their plane had landed at Sky Harbor at midnight. By the time they reached Sedona it was two in the morning. They were at *Man who Runs with Thorn in Foot*, Kuul's old Winnebago motorhome. For his own safety, Lilac had talked the archeologist into accompanying them. Skip had wanted to leave him in Phoenix.

"Too much has happened, Kemo. Would turning the vessel in have made our situation better or worse? I don't think either of us can answer that. This is more than what you were told. Your *friends* have held back important bits of information. We're better off here until we find out what's going on."

"I can still make a call," Skip said, glancing surreptitiously at Stephens, sending Kuul a silent warning. He didn't want to share much with him listening. Nor for that matter, Lilac, or Toni.

Thorn, so named because of a chronically flat tire, was permanently docked amongst miles of scrub, overlooking a dry arroyo, past the end of a gravel Forest Service Road. The Minnie Winnie was Kuul's "small Sedona ranch." He also owned a hogan he had built outside Flagstaff as a short-term rental. The eight-sided hogan was popular with tourists thanks to its authentic Navajo design and a king-sized pillow-top. Conversely, *Thorn in Foot* had a four-inch foam mattress and a chemical toilet in a snap-together plastic shed the big man had bought at a garage sale. Staying at the remote, inoperable trailer was unendurable for anyone other than Kuul. Skip typically spread a sleeping bag on the roof and watched the stars.

Moonless nights at *Thorn in Foot* were very dark. Inky, black, can't see twenty feet dark. The only lights were operated by generator, if it had gas, which wasn't often. Tonight, the moon was off cycle and hidden behind overcast skies. An old-time kerosene lantern hung from the awning.

"Laying low and staying off the grid is our best bet," Skip answered. He didn't like it, but the low risk of their being tracked to a hidden campsite in the desert was acceptable...for now, anyway. Kuul's other questions about his *friends,* he'd get those answers later.

"You're thinking they'll follow us," Kuul said, stacking two logs tepee-fashion over the crackling campfire he'd built.

Skip sipped the coffee Toni had boiled, choosing the alertness from caffeine over rest. He swirled the cup, watching the crushed beans scatter and settle to the bottom. Coffee over an open fire always tasted better. There were warm beers in the fridge, but he needed a clear head, and to stay awake to keep an eye on Lilac. *Woody* was sitting hip-to-hip with her on a chunk of petrified wood that Kuul had hauled from Holbrook, his jacket wrapped around her shoulders. *Desert nights were chilly...but she always ran a little hot – why the hell did she need another layer*?

"The Chinese?" Kuul alluded.

Skip nodded, "and maybe the Guatemalans."

"Not the Chinese, why would they follow us?" Toni said, shaking her head. There were too many pieces of their conversation she couldn't fit together. The queasy feeling in the pit of her stomach was telling her something was wrong. "They have the Red Queen's vessel – don't they?"

Neither man said anything.

Kuul looked like a kid caught with his hand in the cookie jar. He glanced at Skip, who shrugged, indicating it was up to him to tell. "We substituted a souvenir cup. Once they realize they've been duped, well…"

"Where is it now – this Mayan vessel?" Stephens asked.

Skip glared at the archeologist. His arm around Lilac's back, his fingers tapping her hip like he was playing a goddamn piano. He wondered how much she had told him during their four hours in first class. Her eyes met his and she smiled sweetly. *Yeah, she was running a little hot.*

"Safe," Kuul replied, volunteering nothing further.

"Lock and key, or just protected by you two – better than I was?" Toni said sharply, poking at Kuul's tepee with a stick, and intentionally knocking it down. "What was the plan if they discovered your little trick before releasing me?"

"It was a very authentic looking substitute," Kuul weakly offered.

Sparks popped from the fire and rose in the cool air.

Lilac shifted so Wood's hand wasn't quite so intimately placed, "There are three foreign services after this artifact. It has to be important!"

"Three?" Stephens questioned. "Who besides the Chinese and Central Americans?"

Lilac stood and began futzing with the fire, using Toni's stick to arrange the logs she had knocked over onto the flames. She had not told Wood about Daria Ahmadi. Skip was shaking his head at her. Of course, he wouldn't want the others to know about his long-lost girlfriend, the secret agent from Iran. She doubted he had even told Kuul. He and Toni had the same questioning looks on their faces. They all deserved to know. She grimaced at Skip; his past life and whatever he had agreed to was impacting all of them.

"I meant two, the third was just a projection – the way these people keep popping out of the woodwork there has to be someone else."

Skip relaxed; unless it became necessary, he didn't want to scare them with Daria's presence, and by extension, Iran's interest. So far, she had been helping them, but he could not let her country acquire the cup, not if it was what she claimed. She was no different from the Chinese or Guatemalans. Like them, she wouldn't be far behind, and she wouldn't stop. With her actions at the Merida airport, the only question was the side she would choose if things came to a showdown.

Too many unanswered questions. And there would be more. He could see the anxiety on their faces. The others had not bought Lilac's retraction, particularly Toni with her special insights. He wouldn't.

"My assistant, Sapphire Sky," Skip said for Stephen's benefit, "has had an odd tour group here the past few days."

Lilac exaggeratingly exhaled, "You haven't involved her too?"

"I tried calling her when we landed, but she didn't answer. It *was* late," Skip noted, seeing the look of concern on Kuul's face, and ignoring Lilac's snarky question. "I mentioned them to Lilac, and given what happened in Mexico, we are both a little worried."

Another team gathering intelligence about his business and life was not farfetched. In fact, it was logical. He had given two professional teams the slip. Not checking his background would be incompetent. His guess was the Chinese, using a Caucasian team as cover. He had to also assume the Iranians knew he was involved; Daria would not keep that secret. Too many things were out of place, too much not adding up, too many coincidences.

He studied Catherwood Stephens. Was his joining them romantic bravado or something else? Hard to blame his anxious look. He had met a pretty red head on vacation and now found himself in the middle of an international conspiracy. How to bail gracefully had to be on his mind.

Lilac saw how Skip was eyeing Wood, "Let's take a walk."

Skip grinned at Stephens and started to stand.

"Not you," she said.

The moon had popped out from the clouds and was shining brightly in the black sky. In the distance, coyotes were yelping, and Lilac could hear the low, steady hum of a truck on 89a. Early morning delivery. She led Wood into a shallow arroyo that partially circled Kuul's camp. The dry wash made for easy walking, especially at night. Seasonal monsoons, still weeks away, kept the bottom mostly clear of catsclaw and other stickies. Every few steps, she kicked a small stone to alert any sidewinders that were out hunting.

"You're not afraid of getting lost?" Wood asked, looking back over his shoulder.

"The wash is easy to follow, and we'll see Kuul's lantern on the way back. He'll leave it on."

"Rhodes didn't like us leaving. He doesn't seem very trusting."

Lilac shrugged, "I choose who I walk with."

She pondered if there would be any future moonlight walks with Skip. Mexico was supposed to change how she was feeling. It had, but not for the better. Romantic walks along Oak Creek had once given her everything she wanted. She had not asked him for anything more. Sitting beside the rippling stream with the stars reflecting in the water, holding hands, making unspoken promises with their kisses, had been enough. But she needed more now after almost dying at the Grand Canyon and forcing him to open up about his past. What he had told her...she needed assurances. That awful night...she'd asked, begged, and his answer had been, "It doesn't matter." *Daria Ahmadi knew him better.*

"The pistol you picked up at your place, on the way here, doesn't play into your choosing somehow, does it?" joked Stephens, sensing her darkening mood. He was also curious about the extent of her armory. The size of the gun locker in her living room suggested a side to this woman he hadn't yet seen.

Lilac had made Skip stop at her home in West Sedona. She rented a small, one-bedroom condo past the library from a friend of a friend. It was all she could afford, thanks to the influx of digital nomads fleeing California. She hadn't shot anyone yet, but the time was coming.

"Only when necessary. I can show you my carry permit if you'd like."

Wood laughed and held up his hands, "Just want to understand the ground rules."

"Don't worry. I was a police officer in Tucson...still have a state PI license. But I've found teaching yoga and firearm training to tourists to be safer and more lucrative."

"Yoga and guns? At the same time?"

"You would be surprised how many wealthy, septuagenarian widows and divorcees enjoy blasting targets of their exes and meditating afterwards. For the tourists, it's a cowboy fantasy." She patted her belt, "This is a 9mm Glock43 – not the prettiest but perfect for conceal carry. Reliable. God made Adam and Eve, but it took Sam Colt to make us equal."

"You really think we'll need that?"

"Would have helped in Mexico. I take it you don't shoot?"

"It's frowned on at the Smithsonian. Machetes are more useful in a jungle, tools of the trade, along with a shovel and trowel. I do carry a Swiss army knife."

Lilac chuckled, "No blowgun?"

She liked this man; his humor and easygoing nature were a pleasant change of pace, and he didn't come across as too academic. He had the right stuff, a sexy mix of charm, intelligence, and humility. Most of the archeologists she had met were ancient themselves and loved nothing more than a scintillating conversation about carbon versus tree ring dating. And he hadn't left her at the first sign of trouble, not like someone else had months earlier at the Grand Canyon. On the other hand, she wondered how many of his female graduate assistants credited their *love* of the field to handsome Catherwood Stephens.

They stopped at a desert willow. Dainty, pink blossoms were emitting a soft, floral scent. The wispy trees loved arroyos and washes that held pools of rainwater long after spring storms. In the moonlight, their graceful branches and sweet-smelling pods created a private, intimate sanctuary. Songs had been written about sultry, desert nights such as these. Lilac gazed at Wood, inviting a first kiss, wishing she was shorter. She was confused, but not upset, when he took her hand.

"This is presumptuous, but I've been thinking about Mesa Verde – doing some research there. Toni's talk about the similarities between the ancients here and the Mayan world challenges me. I have connections at the Smithsonian's National Museum of the American Indian ...a field fellowship might be a possibility," Stephens cautiously said. He knew he was moving too fast.

Lilac wasn't sure what to say. Wood gently pulled her to him, wrapping his arms around her waist. Then he kissed her – not hard, his lips just brushing hers. She placed her palms on his chest, softly pushing him back – not far, but back. "Wood, I...I..."

"You're in a relationship," he said, stepping away. "I'm such an idiot."

"No, you're not. I like you, but he and I – it's complicated, he's complicated. We're working through our issues."

"And how is that going?"

"There is a connection between us I can't explain. He would not want me to explain."

"I don't understand."

Lilac sighed, "neither do I." She could see the hurt and confusion in his face. She owed him an explanation.

She had used him and led him on, which wasn't fair. But this wasn't all her fault, he was so damn attractive and attentive, and it wasn't just his sly Indiana Jones smile. Even rebuffed, after *she* had led him here, he was so patient and sensitive. With Catherwood, there would be no drama, no secrets. When he mentioned Mesa Verde, her heart had leapt, a relief that whatever had started between them wasn't ending. She would see him again. She could picture them exploring the ancient cliff castles. *But Skip...*

"He is struggling with who he is, his life has been..." She was searching for the right word. "Unusual. I love him, but that's not always enough."

"You were in Mexico together. You don't know who he is?"

Okay, maybe not so sensitive. Then again, her wishy-washiness had to be frustrating. "That's just it – I think we might have been there because of him. Because of his past." Wood started to ask a question, but Lilac put a fingertip to his lips and stepped back into his arms, letting him pull her close. "Let's not waste good moonlight."

Strolling into Kuul's camp, they sensed something was wrong. Skip was on his phone – at three-thirty in the morning. Kuul and Toni were huddled next to him, trying to hear what was being said. Kuul saw her and motioned them to stay quiet.

Skip stopped in mid-sentence and swore at his screen, spreading his arms in exasperation. "Son-of-a-bitch! They hung up."

"What happened?" Lilac and Wood asked at the same time.

"Sky and Zula. First Toni, now Zula and Sky. They have them and want the Mayan cup. I called bullshit and they tried putting Zula on. She yelled, "chicken shit asshole" at someone and a man screamed. I heard a slap, and then the call ended. This is fucking out of hand!" Skip exploded.

"They who?" Lilac asked. "The Chinese, they followed us already?"

"Not them. Not the Guatemalans. The caller was a woman."

Lilac scowled – *Daria Ahmadi.* That clinched it, Skip was up to his eyeballs in this mess. He had never left his agency like he had told her, this was another assignment. Yeah, this *was* out of hand. He had let it get out of hand. He had taken them to Mexico as cover and put them all in jeopardy. It wasn't enough that Toni could have been killed.

"Daria Ahmadi!" Lilac yelled at him. "You brought her here!"

"Who is Daria Ahmadi?" Kuul asked them both, sidling close to Lilac's gun hand, just in case. His friend's sullen mood...Lilac wandering off with Stephens...another woman; their cold war was starting to make sense.

Toni had moved off to the side, studying all three of them, Rhodes in particular. He threw his Stetson in the fire, grimacing, rubbing his forehead and the top of his head, increasing the pressure as if he wanted to crush his skull. Then he shouted at the sky, at his gods. Raw, undisguised anguish, tempered fury. He was blaming himself. She watched the dark spirits in him escape, dancing in the heat and sparks of the fire, preparing to battle his good heart. Kuul, Lilac, Stephens, herself – they were all trapped in the vacuum.

THE INDEPENDENT CONTRACTOR

OPTIONS, IT WAS ALWAYS GOOD TO HAVE OPTIONS, HE thought. Turning the formula over, once acquired, to the U.S. Secretary of Health and Human Services was one possibility. There were others. He had done jobs for Orville Stinckner before, the conclusion of which had always been lucrative for both parties. Stinckner was a businessman, and he understood the value of building long-term, trade relationships. He understood the billions his company stood to gain and the cost-benefit of using the contractor's independent services. As exceedingly generous as the remunerations were, the expense was still minor. But that was Stinckner dealing as CEO. of his family's pharmaceutical business. Now the man was head of a cumbersome, government bureaucracy kowtowing to a new POTUS, a nut job out only for himself.

The President had been a businessman as well. But without a Board of Directors checking his actions, he was a reckless, arrogant one with the IRS hounding every move he made. There was no long-term future benefit to working for him. Aside from a well-documented, litigious tendency to avoid payments, an election year was on the horizon, and the polls were not in the man's favor; CNN had just released a tape of the blowhard bragging about the harem he kept in Moscow. Even his Latvian born wife, a marriage arranged through a Russian matchmaking firm recommended by his 'good friend' Vladimir, had refused to say whether she planned to vote for him.

The unpredictability of the American electorate and the man's inherent weaknesses made acquiring the Mayan formula a one-and-done assignment for the contractor. And with those, the best deal was to find the buyer with the deepest pockets. Even if that meant screwing over a dependable client like Orville Stinckner.

Feelers had been put out to Koe and Klim. An all-natural, Native, weight loss program would fit right in with their branding. A commercial campaign featuring a tub full of chocolate and a line of cacao formulated sex toys was already in the works. Dr. Ooze was just as hot-to-trot; he was chomping at the bit to get started on social media promotions and his trademark, annoying ads on gaming apps. Yes, there were options.

The contractor had also reached out to his security contacts at Japanese industrial firms. If they bit, their pockets were infinitely deeper. Commercial conglomerates had no personal scruples against marketing and selling dubious food supplements, as long as they were legal, and liability was minimal. The Asian market promised a quick return and far fewer, if any, government regulations and standards – look at what powdered rhino horn was going for in Bangkok and Ho Chi Minh City...imagine the market for Royal Mayan, cacao derivatives.

The Chinese, however, were a problem. The newly rich Middle Kingdom was stretching its tentacles and muscles throughout the world's financial quarters. They had already dispatched a team and would have beaten the contractor to the punch, if not for the American outsmarting them. The fact they believed the formula was for a biological weapon was troubling. Geopolitically inexperienced, the U.S. President and his equally brain-numb counterpart in Guatemala had unintentionally set off an international arms race over a *weight-loss* product.

The contractor needed to make the acquisition before things got further out of hand.

"Stinky, I don't give a shit if he is my son or about the billion Twitter tweeples he has. DO NOT let him back in! Ground up tiger penis - I should have known better. The jiz almost killed me. You should have been here to stop the son-of-a-bitch!"

"Yes, Mr. President."

"That Bengal baby gravy made my shitting worse too. Doctors are insisting on keeping me four more days for observation. And these urges to hump Nurse Helga; little boy won't stay down when she changes the sheets. I will say, Stinky, the shit's better than a handful of blue pills. You should have your chemists check the stuff out."

Secretary Stinckner started to roll his eyes, caught himself, and rolled them back; his pounding headache worsening from the momentary dizziness. Fifteen minutes earlier, he had ended an unsettling phone call with his independent contractor. The update was not what he had hoped to hear. The man had been cagey, which in and of itself wasn't unusual for an industrial spy. He had not yet acquired the Mayan vessel or the formula but was getting close and had operatives "in place." *Whatever the hell that meant.*

Most bothersome, was his agent's suspicion that one of the Americans was in Mexico for more than a beach holiday. Skip Rhodes was his name, a guide from Arizona, and he apparently had skills other than touring elderly Floridians around the south-west. Stinckner had promised to have POTUS's Special Assistant on Domestic Disturbances, another entitled, unqualified, sneaky snit hired to run a subversive program for Herr Fuhrer, do a background check. Rhodes was a problem in multiple ways if he was also after the Mayan vessel. *Who had sent him?*

Stinckner knew that wrapping this up before POTUS was discharged was paramount. Once he started meddling with full access to White House resources, the inevitable rumors and leaks would start. They always did.

"Stinky, what have we heard from our Man in Havana?"

The Secretary groaned, yet another of the man's sophomoric quips to make him feel cleverer than his C.I.A. and F.B.I. chiefs. Stinckner fudged his answer, "His team has mobilized. I expect good news later today, tomorrow afternoon at the latest."

"Good. Make it so." POTUS was also a fan of Star Trek. Captain Kirk was a frequent dinner guest at the White House and technical adviser for the President's new Space Force.

"Live long and prosper, Mr. President."

"You just get me that chocolate, Stinky, and we'll do both."

Only the Lonely

"JOHANNA SHOULDN'T HAVE BROUGHT US BACK TO THIS cabin," Roid grumbled. "Christ, we barely escaped out the back door yesterday."

Skip Rhode's cabin would not have been Jerry Jessup's choice either. But Johanna was the boss. Transporting their two captives a shorter distance *had* meant less chance of being seen. And they had scored a twofer, getting both the young guide and the old woman, which gave them a spare. "Don't worry about it, we won't be here long. Those stupid cops would never guess we're back at the same place."

Both Sky and Zula Ballsy were currently locked in Rhode's bedroom. Taking them had been easy. They had finished a yoga set outside Ballsy's lodge and were sitting with their legs crossed and eyes closed. The Brooklyn Butchers had them tied and trussed in a matter of seconds; the only real resistance was a wild pig that had sunk its teeth into Lloyd's good leg. Jerry was fairly sure his shot had taken off an ear before the damn thing scampered into the woods.

"Shit, man, this is the first place I'd look when they turn up missing. I have no problem with snatching them, but holing up here? I don't know, man."

"You've seen how remote and empty this lodge is. It will be days before anyone realizes they're gone."

"Maybe, but Johanna's head's been busted since her demotion. And now she's left us – that doesn't bother you?"

Jerry was rummaging through an empty, old Norge refrigerator. Roid had been busting his ass complaining since Johanna had gone. "You know why she left. She'll be back – with company." There, stuck in the back of the freezer, where he remembered their being, a twelve-pack of Modelo Negras. "You believe the frost in this freezer? Few cold ones stuck in here, though – if you and Lloyd keep your cool."

"Don't know where you picked up those nicknames but eat shit."

Jessup chuckled, the girl in the bedroom had dubbed them after they'd been hauled off by the rangers at Montezuma Castle. He tossed Roid a beer and then sent Johanna a text – **bring food, wolves are hungry and need feeding.** She and the new boss, or partner as she preferred to call him, were supposed to arrive by midafternoon,

"Bring me some of the ice," the javelina-scarred Lloyd moaned from the sofa. "Rabies – I need to be tested."

"You've been stuck worse in a Jersey alley! Jesus fucking Christ, Jerry, can't you shut cry-baby up?" Roid yelled.

"Fuck you, bro...next time you wrestle the pig."

Roid had it up to his thick neck with his whining partner. At the resort, Lloyd had egged a pool boy with a bowl of fresh fruit into entering the hot chick's cabana. "Cumquats," the smartass teenager had smirked, watching them go at it. The horny kid had tried taking a selfie. Roid, with his speedo around his knees, had knocked him through the curtain.

"And if you hadn't hit the old bitch so hard, you wouldn't have had to carry her, dipsh–"

"*ASSHOLES!*" Zula Ballsy hollered from the bedroom, banging on the door. "THAT PIG'S HURT, YOU'RE GETTIN' A COLONOSCOPY WITH A YUCCA SPIKE!"

Jerry laughed...the old girl was awake and raring to go. No doubt she knew exactly how to administer a *yuka*. Whatever that was, it didn't sound like anything Lloyd would enjoy. He heard Sky whispering and the banging stopped.

"You boys hungry? I can rustle up some eggs," Ballsy cooed, calm as Nora Jones.

"SCREW YOU, YOU GERIATRIC SACK OF HARDENED ARTERIES," Roid hollered back.

The banging immediately started again, only this time harder, "YOU EVER HAD A BERETTA 12-GAUGE SHOVED AGAINST YOUR NUTS, ASSHOLE? THERE'S A BARREL FOR EACH SWEET PEA."

If only the twig had snapped two seconds sooner, Sky thought, things might have gone differently. She would have landed the mule kick on Roid's sweet peas. Instead, the wrestler had caught her ankle, twisting her leg until she'd ended up on her back like a helpless turtle. He had pinned her to the ground, rolled her over, wrenched her arms behind her back, and forced her hands into a zip tie. With Spike's fangs an inch into Lloyd's flesh, Zula had held her own...until the shot from Jerry. After shooting her pet, he'd pistol-whipped her, knocking her unconscious. The trip here had been one shove after another, all the way to Skip's cabin. Thankfully, Mosby had freed her hands before locking them in the room.

"Stop antagonizing them," Sky whispered for the second time. "There are three of them, five if we double-count the beefy wrestlers. I could outrun them if I get the chance, but not you. Threatening their manhood won't get us out of here."

"These dim-witted, sheep-herding sapsuckers aren't who they said they were. Marketing company my sagging ass!"

"The one named Jerry's not stupid, Zula. And absent Johanna, he'll be calling the shots. I don't think they'll hurt us, not yet anyway – unless you keep pissing them off."

"*Okay, fine...*what do you think they're after?

"With all their questions about Skip – best bet is this has something to do with him or his trip to Mexico. Dollar will get you twenty they took us for leverage. I wonder if the boys are back."

"Honey, things might get dicey when that East German shot-putter gets here. Olga doesn't strike me as a pacifist. If she didn't get the right answers before, she might insist this time."

"She can try. The others are scared of her. Our best chance to escape is before she returns."

Zula began searching for anything that might help, tossing the pile of laundry in the corner, pulling out drawers, unscrewing the incandescent bulb from a small lamp, "Might not stop all of 'em but jabbing broken glass in an eye will hurt like hell."

Sky took her cue and looked under the bed, finding a broken juniper stick, a shoebox of rocks – no slingshot...and a bag of embroidered fanny packs advertising Sedona Chi. *So, FedEx had delivered them.* She had ordered them six months ago and read the driver the riot act. Skip had sworn he hadn't seen them and warned her against ordering any more lollypop sticks.

"You'd think any self-respecting Arizonan would keep a gun in their nightstand," Zula griped.

"He's not from Arizona, and he doesn't have a nightstand," Sky said, showing her the two pieces of juniper, "best we got."

"Keep 'em," the retired showgirl smiled, holding up a nearly empty bottle of Don Julio Anejo. She'd found Skip's leftovers between the bed and outdoor stool that doubled as a nightstand. "Let's see if peckerhead's skull is as hard as it looks," she snickered, downing the last quarter inch.

"A broken stick and empty booze bottle aren't much."

"Don't forget the tiny light bulb."

"We still have to get out of this room," Sky said, pressing her ear against the door.

"I'm going out to the porch for a smoke," she heard Roid say. There was no answer from Jerry and only a grunt from Lloyd, who sounded closer, across the hall in Skip's cubbyhole latrine. "Jesus, what'd you eat?" Roid complained. "I'm outta here." The screen door to the cabin bounced shut.

Only two, with one injured and in intestinal distress – not good odds, but better.

"Just the two of us, this is nice. Thanks for the ride," Stephens said. "I would stay, but my sabbatical is ending, and classes are starting. I'm an adjunct at Georgetown and have an advanced seminar beginning on Pre-Classic Maya ballcourts and human sacrifice. Winning was an honor, but costly."

Despite Skip's bellicose objections, Lilac had left Kuul's camp with Wood. He needed to catch a flight home, which the jealous guide had been all for, even offering to drive the "archeologist" to his hotel, the Wile E. Coyote Resort and Spa. That was until Lilac said she was taking him. Then he had come up with a hundred and one reasons why they should stay. She ignored them all, telling him she'd be back in an hour...*unless Wood's room was ready*. Skip had furiously stormed off into the desert.

The room hadn't been ready, so they settled for a plush, turquoise sofa next to an unlit chimenea outside the hotel's Acme Lounge. Lilac was cuddled into a cushioned seat, her long legs propped on a rattan stool. Her boots and wool hiking socks, which she'd been wearing for twenty-four hours, airing on the outdoor rug. While Wood had been at the bar, she had finger-combed her hair, adjusted the girls, and slyly smelled her pits – *passable*. She'd decided to let things play out...what happened, happened.

"What time is your flight?" she asked, as Wood handed her a glass of white wine. She swirled the pale liquid, tipped the goblet, sniffed, and took a sip. "Mmm…light, cold, scent of pear, slightly bitter finish. God, that smooths the feathers after the past few days. There's more of this, right?"

Stephens grinned, "Definitely. Flight isn't until three…tomorrow." He bobbed the slice of lime skewered on a bamboo toothpick in his Bombay gin, "Cheers."

Their glasses clinked and Lilac asked, "Any plans tonight?"

"That's up to the lady," he said, smiling like a kid on Christmas morning.

"Let's start with a few more of these, right now. Maybe a shower when your room is –"

A woman appeared at the end of their sofa, wet from the pool, and wearing a one-piece black suit with a see-through coverup. "Oh, excuse me," she said. From the bar, Lilac had been invisible, slumped in the deep, oversized pillows. Wood's arm was stretched across her back, hiding her red hair.

"It's okay," Wood replied. "She was hard to see."

The woman smiled playfully at Stephens, barely acknowledging Lilac, her unexpected competition. She took a long sip from a short cocktail glass, packed with crushed ice, and topped with a sprig of mint. From the smell, Lilac guessed the drink was bourbon, straight up. A tough gal if the strong liquor and snake tattoo showing through the coverup were any indicators. Instead of gracefully venturing on, she boldly sat in a rocker across from Wood, "Mind if I join you?"

Lilac stiffened, but a waitress appeared with a bottle of Sauvignon Blanc before she could answer, *'Hell yes, this one's mine sweetheart.'* She poured a generous second glass then recorked the bottle, leaving it on the table.

"I told her to keep tabs on us," Wood said, mouthing 'I don't know her, do you?'

Lilac took two big sips, throwing eye darts at the unwelcome newcomer that shouted, *'Get the fuck out of here.'* She expected her to take the hint and move on.

The woman didn't.

Wood sat straighter, lowered his arm, and became fidgety, glancing around the open patio. Lilac wished she had accessorized with her Glock43. Five minutes passed that seemed like thirty. The woman had not said a word, sipped her bourbon, and occasionally looked up from her phone with no expression. Lilac had finished the second wine, gunned a third, and poured a fourth. She had a good idea what she was going to do with the empty bottle.

"Why don't we check if the room's ready," she finally said, brusquely rising and reaching for the bottle...*Whoa!...Wine rush!* The alcohol mixed with equal parts of incredulity and agitation had made her light-headed. Her knees wobbled and she balanced herself with a hand against the edge of the sofa.

"You okay?" Wood said, gripping her elbow before she fell.

"Just a bit dizzy." She glanced at the woman who was staring back. The ugly snake tattoo was slithering, and her face was stretching like in a circus mirror. "Why don't you walk me around the parking lot, I need some air."

"That would be a good idea," the woman said, smiling.

Lilac tried to follow the stepping-stones that led through a red-tipped, photinia hedge to the parking lot. Wood steadied her with his right hand, his left arm wrapped around her waist. Staggering more than walking, they finally got past the hedge to a sidewalk. Twice they had nearly done headers into the tight weave of sticks. Fighting to focus on putting one foot in front of the other, she could feel herself slipping away. She managed to turn in his arms and saw what she was afraid of...the woman was following them.

"Wood...I...I'm passing out...get us back...back inside. She's... she–"

"I've got you," she heard him say as her eyes closed. Sparkles lit the back of her eyelids, like her brain was misfiring, sparks shot across a black field. The last thing she felt was his catching her and lifting her in his arms.

TOE TO EAR

JERRY WAS SITTING IN A METAL CHAIR WITH A VINYL RED SEAT, remembering the same sixties style of kitchen set in his great-aunt's house in Queens. Aunt Gertrude and Uncle Ted Jessup had raised him. His mother had been a junkie with no idea who Jerry's father had been, the possibilities made too long of a list. The only good thing about his childhood had been watching the Mets, sitting at the foot of his uncle's lopsided Lazyboy, a sweating quart bottle of Schlitz beer on the tray beside him.

Whoever this Rhodes was, Aunt Gertrude had been an extravagant decorator by comparison. His empty fridge proved he wasn't a cook either, not a cracker, bag of ramen, or frozen dinner. Nothing except beer and purple prickly pear syrup. The furniture was secondhand – three owners ago. The whole place looked like the sorting section at the Goodwill warehouse where Jerry had worked as a teenager. If Rhodes had money, it was hard to see where he spent it. And the *west* coast of the Yucatan wasn't exactly an internationally renowned vacation hotspot. According to their reports, he had been staying in a sixty-dollar-a-night hotel.

The cabin was quiet, too damn quiet, a deafening, life-sucking quiet that would drive a normal man insane. But being in the middle of bumfuck nowhere worked for now. At least Bozo and Clarabell had stopped arguing. Roid, who he could see through a window, had left the porch and was emptying bird food from feeders, stomping the seeds into the dirt. Lloyd was propped on a black bear patterned microfiber couch with sandwich baggies of ice on each leg, wildly punching buttons on three different remotes. Some security assistants.

"Jerry...let's talk? Are you there...Jerry?" Sky demurely called from behind the bedroom door.

He had been expecting her to try something. Hoping actually, just to break the boredom. Acting nice had been his guess. She wasn't the type to just sit and pray for the best. She and Ballsy had seen their faces; they were smart enough to understand what that meant.

"Can we talk?" Sky called again.

He glanced at the clown he was marooned with. Lloyd had given up on the TV and was gingerly cleaning his bite with a towel from the bathroom. The moron was pouring beer over the wound. Roid was still draining the hummingbird feeders. *Stuck here for hours...with dumb and dumber...*

"What do you want to talk about?"

"Zula needs to use the bathroom. She's older. Can you tell me why you're doing this? Is it Johanna? You don't have to follow her orders...you can make up your own mind about what's right and what's wrong."

He heard Ballsy's angry voice followed by the younger woman's shushing. Using the older woman's age as an excuse to use the toilet didn't sit well.

"Tell her to find a trashcan," he said, chuckling.

"PECKERHEAD! I FIND A TRASHCAN – I'LL CAP YOUR GODDAMN HEAD WITH IT AND GO ALL RINGO STAR!"

Jerry laughed, this was much more entertaining than watching the hummingbirds attacking Roid, "Tell you what...I'll give her five minutes just to prove I'm more the easygoing, Paul McCartney type," he said, walking to the door. "Just remember, *Sweet Pea*, you don't have your Beretta, and I'm holding a Browning Black Label

380." He undid the bolt they had temporarily affixed to the door and pushed it open with his gun. *What the–*

Zula Ballsy was across the room, topless, swinging her breasts as if she were twirling tassels. Out of the corner of his eye he saw Sky cartwheeling toward him – *Fuck*. He jumped back as she launched herself with her hands, somersaulted in the air, and dove headfirst in front of him. She came up short, sliding along the floor.

Jerry pointed the Browning at her head, hesitating. Johanna would not be happy if he shot their leverage. Before he could act, Sky's legs swiveled from her hips like a Dyson vacuum, stretching up and over her back. One foot smacked his nose while the other snatched the gun. *Double-jointed freak*. She tossed it back toward Lady Godiva, but it landed short of Ballsy's outstretched arms. Jerry dove over top of Sky's prone body, lunging for the Browning laying on the floor between him and the old showgirl.

Lloyd charged into the room, grabbing Sky as she got to her feet. She popped both shoulders from their joints, letting them fall slack beside her. When his grip relaxed, she snapped back in place, driving the heels of her hands up into his chin, staggering him backwards. She leapt into the air, throwing her feet above her head.

Jerry was scrambling on the floor, stretching for the gun. "Have a shot of this, asshole!" Ballsy shouted, crashing the heavy tequila bottle against his temple.

Zula aimed Jerry's Browning at Lloyd, but the airborne contortionist was blocking her shot. The goon was crouched behind the girl, readying to catch her ankles and dangle her in front of his body as a shield. He snapped his fingers closed grasping – *nothing but air*. The girl had flexed her knees at the last instant, bending her legs at ridiculously impossible forty-five-degree angles. Her feet slammed his ears like a mousetrap.

Lloyd dropped to the floor, screaming, excruciating pain rocking his head, both eardrums burst from the change in pressure.

"Time to skedaddle, honey!" Zula yelled, pulling her blouse over her head. The bra could wait, the girls weren't going anywhere. She poked Lloyd's bleeding bitemark with the barrel of the Browning, grinding the gun into his wound. "This is for Spike. I'd shoot you if I weren't saving the bullets for the steroid-popping bouncer outside."

"Bitch," Lloyd moaned, his hands clawing at his ringing ears.

"Thanks for the compliment," Zula said, deciding she could spare a bullet. She fired a shot between his legs, inches from his peanuts. "You're lucky I don't want to start any bad habits – like shooting assholes. Now...any other names you can think to call me?"

Lloyd screamed, "CRAZY FUCKING BITCH!" He dropped his hands to protect his privates. Her shot had clipped off the ends of two middle fingers.

"Two appropriate adjectives, not bad," the showgirl chuckled.

"Zula, leave him alone...we need to get out of here," Sky said, running into the living room ahead of her.

Gun in hand, Roid flung open the front door as Sky entered the room. He had heard the shot...*where the hell were Jerry and Lloyd?* And how did she get out of the locked room – fucking Jerry had gotten bored and decided to have a taste, that's how.

Zula was seconds behind Sky and heard her gasp. The girl's back was to her, she was standing statue still, hands raised, staring at the front door. Zula charged out of the hall into the room wildly firing two shots. *Missed.* Seeing Ballsy with the Browning, Roid had ducked back outside.

"WE MAKE A STAND HERE!" Zula shouted, her blood boiling. "These yahoos tangled with the wrong damn innkeeper!"

"No – we're going out the back door!" Sky decided, rifling through a drawer in the kitchen and finding a butcher knife.

Zula saw Roid peek through the window and fired two more shots, one shattering the glass, the second through the open front door, thumping into a porch post. That should buy them time. She turned to follow the younger woman and bumped into her. Sky was frozen in her tracks.

The back door opened, and a new figure appeared...*Shit.*

Psychic Discovery

"**A** PSYCHIC READING ES LIKE OPENING ANOTHER DOOR, Chuuy, helping us make the right decision. *Es* like worshipping *Maximón, San Simón*, back home." The banners outside the Psychic Discovery Tea Shed, promising to tell their futures, had been too enticing.

Chuuy crossed himself. "*El santo negro*. Oh Hernando, *San Simón* tricks us with strong drink and good smokes. But at least he gives us something. This woman with her purple hair, colored beads, and glass ball, gives us nothing and charges one hundred *dólares*. That would feed your eleven children for six months."

"Ten, ten children!" Hernando Gomez snapped. The idiot needed to learn to count. They had followed the Americans and were in Sedona. Arguing in front of Madame Butterfinger was bad karma, according to the sign on the wall.

Chuuy snickered, "When did you last speak to Lupe, my brother-in-law?"

Captain Hernando Gomez of the Guatemalan Presidential Guard moaned; he should have chosen Private Perez and his private label bottle of tequila instead of Chuuy. Boarding the flight to the *Estados Unidos* had represented a commitment to their plan to steal the Mayan artifact, their plan to start new lives. His brother-in-law, simpleton that he was, had agreed. Gabriela was already packing her vibra honeybunny and extra batteries. No...there would be no going back, no matter how many of the scoundrel Fernando's *niños* sprang from his sister's womb.

Madame Butterfinger's Tea Shed was one half of a stone duplex located just inside the city limits, two blocks off Highway 179 where rents were cheaper. She'd been priced out of Frisco thirty years earlier. Jackson Browne, an old 'acquaintance' had suggested Sedona during a far-out trip to Tijuana. Now, she was only three months and twenty-one days from Social Security and once the first check arrived – back to the Grape State of weed and feed. She wasn't about to let these two suckers slip through her fingers.

"Okay, okay. Seventy-five dollars and I'll also see who on the *other side* I can put you in touch with," Madame offered. "I'd throw in free parking, but public works put in meters last month. The bastards are in cahoots with Tlaquepaque Mall, trying to drive me out of business.

"See Chuuy, not only will she tell our futures, but you can revisit your blessed mother," Gomez said. "I will go next."

Dragged by the plum-haired medium wearing a pink, paisley bathrobe, through a beaded curtain with broken chips of soda bottles, his reluctant brother-in-law disappeared into a back room. Chuuy sorrowfully glanced back, looking like she was leading him to a rotting cell in the notorious *Escuintla Prisión*.

Hernando stepped outside into the bright Arizona sunshine to enjoy an American *cigarillo*. *Magnifico*, he thought in wonderment, gazing at the red rock formations. *That one*, he said to himself, pointing his smoldering Marlboro at a series of smooth humps – it looked like the cartoon dog, Snoopy, that his favorite *niña*, María, watched on their flickering black-and-white Motorola. Maybe he would find a way to pry her away from Lupe – she had so many *bambinos*, what could one less mouth matter?

The temperature was hot but pleasant, the smells clean and fresh, absent the suffocating humidity and stink of Guatemala City.

This would be a fine place to bring Gabriela, María could stay with their Nicaraguan maid. Here a man did not have to worry about being shot, stabbed in the back, or having their limbs hacked off by sadists like *Coronel* Mancoros. Hernando filled his lungs with the last sweet breath of tobacco and blew rings into the sky, adjusting his head until they framed the excellent view. He flicked the *cigarillo* butt to the ground, crushing it with the sneaker he had purchased at Phoenix City.

Two persons were entering the shop in the other half of the duplex, a tall, unhappy looking man with a stomach the size of two *futballs* and a fit, older woman with blue, spiderweb veins crisscrossing her taut legs. The sign above the door read Nutty Emporium. The *gringo* had his head down and the *gringa* was poking his backside with a pole.

The woman stopped and glared at Gomez's boot, pointing at the butt with her stick. He quickly picked it up and she smugly nodded, pushing her companion through the door.

Chuuy should never have listened to Hernando. As *Capitán*, his brother-in-law should have gone first. Leaders do not follow. Madame Butterfinger had led him into a dark closet with two rickety folding chairs. On the table between rested a shiny ball with three holes in the shape of a triangle, each hole held a glow stick. Below the holes was the word Brunswick, which he imagined to be a *gringo* spirit.

"Hold those sticks," the priestess said, pointing at two that were glowing. "Close your eyes and stay very still, do not be scared if you feel the table wobble."

"*Madre de dios, protégeme,*" he muttered, praying for protection.

Squinting, he watched Lady Butterfinger grasp the other unlit stick. Her eyes were shut, and her head began to roll, left then right then left. Suddenly it plummeted to her chin and began bouncing up and down against her chest. Her lips cracked and white, bubbly foam that smelled of *naranjes* and baking soda spilled from her mouth. Chuuy felt his bladder weakening.

"Pepsi – Pepsi – Pepsi," she moaned repeatedly, wiping her chin, and spitting into a cup. He needed to pee badly but was too afraid to move. *Madre de dios*, he privately pleaded, don't let me soil her shag carpet.

"Pepsi – Peepisi – Peeeepsiiii," she continued moaning, her chant growing louder and longer.

Chuuy glanced around the room searching for a cooler or refrigerator. The crazy priestess must be thirsty. He preferred Coca-Cola, but Americans were different...quite different.

"Do you need refreshment," he squeaked.

"Ssssh – Not, Not, Not Pepsi – it's Pepita – Pepita..." Her glow stick flickered on and off, the priestess seemed to be squeezing it. She sighed and dislodged it from its hole shaking it violently until it stayed on. "PEPITA IS HERE," she finally said, replacing the stick.

Chuuy released his sticks in shock, furiously making the sign of the cross over and over. He began to cry. Pepita was his dead mother; God rest her sainted soul. She had raised him and Lupe by herself in the barrio, their deadbeat father never showing his face, never bringing so much as a loaf of stale bread.

"I have something to tell you, my son. Important to our *familia*," Butterfinger whispered in a strange, higher-pitched voice. It was his mother's voice, she had learned *Inglés*.

"*Mamá*," Chuuy wailed, the first uncontrollable dribble starting down his leg. "*Mamá, qué...qué es Mamá?*"

Butterfinger snuck a peak at the crying man. This was too easy. "This is your *Mamá*. My precious *niño*, I need you to listen. Your father, Chuuy...*tu padre es* Colombian...a priest from Medellin...he defiled me in a pew...cursed you at birth."

"Oh, *Mamá,* I am to burn in hell," Chuuy cried, the new American-brand jeans Hernando had bought him soaking in urine, "I am cursed by God's servant."

Madame Butterfinger was on a roll. One more little push and his boss's wallet would open up like a ripe peach, "And your girlfriend, my darling son...pregnant by a Venezuelan Narco."

Chuuy shook with emotion, "*Mamá, Mamá* – the Narco's name, his name *Mamá.* I will – I will..."

Wait. What girlfriend? He did not have a girlfriend. How could *Mamá* be wrong, she was in heaven with Jesus and the angels? No, this was wrong, this was not his mother...but how did Madame Butterfinger know her name, Pepita. How did she know his mother's name? Chuuy trembled...this woman was the devil *Maximón!*

"*DIABLO, Tú Eres El DIABLO!*" Chuuy screamed, rising from his chair.

"It's what I saw Pedro!" Madame Butterfinger said, exiting the closet quickly. Who knew the little fucker wouldn't have a *chica* back home.

Chuuy followed her, shrieking, "*DIABLO, DIABLO, DIABLO.*"

"CALL 911, BOB! BUTTERFINGER'S IN TROUBLE!" Kempdinger yelled, jumping into action, dropping the gallon jug of niacin supplements. "I've told her she attracts too many crazies with those past life regression ads in the Red Rock News. Whoever is yelling, "Devil," sounds possessed...and that fire bug standing outside... damnit Bob, don't just stand there, do something!"

Big Bob and Steel Calves had been chatting with Becky Hazelnut when the screaming started. He'd been holding three recyclable bamboo bags of chia seed, cholla flour, raw yucca root, pine nuts, and an assortment of almonds, toasted, roasted, basted, and broiled, along with a large bottle of distilled canola oil with a squeezable flip top – good for assorted purposes. All beneficial for lowering his cholesterol. What he really needed was a shot of cortisone. Nights with Kempdinger left his legs as weak as Jell-O left on the hood of an overheated Buick.

By the time he handed the bags to Hazelnut, fished through five pockets for his cell, and thumbed 9, Steel Calves had run out the door, shouting, "Citizen's arrest...Citizen's arrest..."

Big Bob charged out the nut shop door. Becky's and Butterfinger's Tea Shed shared one long porch separated by a three-foot-high railing. Through a window, he could see Madame Butterfinger throwing miniature, souvenir crystal balls at a man hiding behind a cabinet stacked with jeweled, Aries spiritual wands. The man was bobbing up between whizzing spears, crying, *"Diablo, Diablo, Diablo!"* Kempdinger was pummeling the careless smoker with her hiking pole. The woman was a storm trooper when it came to the foul, carcinogenic smell of tobacco; as Steel Calves had put it when he'd tried lighting a stogie with Mustang, "Your choice Bob, blown or blow."

One stride, two strides...*Steel Calves was in deep shit*, the asshole had snatched her stick! He timed his third stride to jump over the barrier. *Shit*, a poorly placed dog bowl for Becky's customers furry friends...

Bob's size fifteen boot fit perfectly in the bowl. Stumbling into the railing, he smashed through the wood spindles like a bowling ball and rolled to a stop below the window. Kempdinger was again screaming Barney Fife's famous mantra. He rose on all fours, shaking his captured foot, preparing to dive shoulder first through the glass, but the nicotine crusader had regained the upper hand. She was fighting the smoker off by throwing boxes of aphrodisiac Vitamin E packets. He recognized the phallic shaped pills spilling on the floor, same as she kept in her nightstand.

A whooping siren and strobing blue lights saved Butterfinger's window. An unmarked SUV screeched to a halt, feet from the building. Chief Hooton's bald head popped out the passenger side window, one eye on each half of the duplex. Clubfoot Bob gestured, pointing to Butterfinger's shop, "Inside! Butterfinger's under attack!"

Hoot opened the SUV door, heard the commotion coming from Butterfinger's shop, and ran up the walk, booming in a foghorn-leghorn voice, *"ASTROCHILE, WHAT IN THE VORTEX SAM HELL IS GOING ON!"* Astrochile was Butterfinger's first name.

"Making a citizen's arrest, and they're resisting," Steel Calves shouted, through the open door. A nervous truce had been called inside once they realized the police had arrived. "Madame *Diablo* took our money," a male, Hispanic accented voice yelled back.

Officer Dickie, pistol drawn, joined Hooton as he stomped up the porch steps.

"Put that damn thing away, Dickie."

Big Bob fell in behind as they marched inside.

"Whose money?" Hoot growled, surveying the scene. Astrochile Butterfinger had a small, male suspect in a headlock, and Kempdinger and a larger man were facing off like a pair of sumo wrestlers searching for an opening.

"Mine," the little man chirped, trying to twist his head from Butterfinger's hold. "She disrespected my saintly mother." Astrochile grabbed his ear and twisted until he screamed.

"Let go of him for God's sake," Hoot ordered, "Before he charges you with assault as well as theft." The madame was clearly up to her old tricks, which had gotten her banned from the Chamber of Commerce. Not an easy task to accomplish short of not paying dues.

"He and his buddy are disrupting the peace," she retorted. Hoot rolled his eyes.

Kempdinger was furious, "And what about this one...*Chief*? He attacked me when I entered the studio. A brazen assault in broad daylight. This rampant crime wave has to STOP! Your coddling unknown assailants instead of assisting honest Sedona residents is going to cost you in the next election. You're soft on crime, Hoot!"

Steel Calves owed Astrochile for the reading that had led her to Big Bob. The medium had seen an extra-large cooker at Walmart in her future; the next day Kempdinger had met Bob buying a deep fryer in Housewares. Close enough. He was a man with all his parts functioning, a rare bird in Sedona's retirement crowd.

Hoot stared at Chuuy and Gomez, his good eye fixed on the bigger of the two, his lazy eye bouncing between Chuuy's scratched face, wet pants, and the money in his hand. Without a doubt, Butterfinger tried scamming these boys and got caught. But Kempdinger had a point – the same point the mayor had made at their last sit down.

Astrochile saw the Chief looking at the money, "Hoot, he snatched it from my poor, arthritic hands, the little sneak."

Hoot sighed, "Officer Dickie, escort these men to our patrol car. We'll sort this out at the station. And write Butterfinger a receipt for the money, it's evidence for now."

"Escort!" Kempdinger huffed. "You're not arresting them?"

"It's a voluntary interview. *Which could change*," he emphasized, the loose orb swiveling between Gomez and Chuuy, who both nodded in agreement. "Bob, I suggest you calm your lady down."

Big Bob groaned. He had successfully shrunk against the back wall, out-of-sight-out-of-mind, behind the displays of archangel amulets, soy-based votive candles, and pocket Totem spirit boards. Steel Calves found him and glared; she'd have a lot to prove thanks to Hooton's misogynistic comment.

LINGUISTIC CONFUSION

DARIA AHMADI HAD CAUGHT THE NEXT DIRECT FLIGHT FROM Merida to Phoenix. She had found the sedan MOIS had parked at the terminal and was in Sedona by noon. From the friendly and chatty ambassador at the small town's Chamber of Commerce, she'd learned of "Skip Rhode's" company, Sedona Chi, and its business address at a remote lodge outside the city's limits.

Two guests were sitting in rocking chairs on the porch of the lodge; neither knew Rhodes. There was no one else, not even a manager in the hotel's rustic lobby. Debating her options, she spied a woman on a path coming from the woods. Her tough face and rough demeanor aroused Daria's sixth sense. The woman could be just a serious hiker, but she had seen that alert, focused look in too many back alleys in too many countries. Daria hadn't survived by ignoring the signs. She ducked into the shadows, watching her leave. Five minutes later Daria was on the path following a small creek.

She wondered if the blabbering city marketer could be wrong. She claimed to know Rhodes and that he lived at Zula Ballsy's Sands Retreat and Lodge; she was friends with Sapphire Sky who worked there. Perhaps it was just his business address, Daria thought. Ten minutes later she found the cabin and the sentry stationed outside.

Concealed behind a thorny bush, she watched the sentry. Clearly he did not belong here. His collared sport shirt with a pattern of anchors, his black oxford shoes, his grinding the seeds in the earth, nothing about him fit the outdoors. He was as out of place here as she. Believing Tripp Street, the man she had fought and loved in Singapore, was living in a cabin in the woods like a hermit, with birdfeeders, required a stretch of her imagination. As a hide-out maybe, as a home unlikely. Nothing superficial linked the cabin to Tripp. Yet this is where his trail had led.

A switch camouflaged on the mottled trunk of a large white tree was her verification. She followed the nearly invisible cable up the tree to where it branched in both directions into clusters of leaves. He had wired the entire perimeter of the clearing with explosive charges. Enough to make an ear-shattering, disorienting, shock-and-awe show as the American press called it. Non-lethal unless you were unlucky enough to be standing in the wrong spot as limbs crashed to the ground. A distraction. What tricks did he have in the cabin?

And who was this man who hated birds? He looked like a gangster in an American movie. A heavy, not the boss. More interested in tormenting animals than keeping look-out. A Tehran schoolgirl could sneak up behind him. A gun negligently tucked in his belt suggested a lack of professionalism – not the kind of associate she would expect for Street. Was he alone or were there others in the cabin? Was Tripp there?

She half-hoped he was, half-hoped he wasn't. The surprised look in his eyes in Mexico, how he had gently touched her hair and cheek in his room, had rekindled her buried feelings – and then his cold glare as he remembered how she had left him. He had to hate her. If only he knew. No, that time had passed, passed in a different world when they were both different people.

MOIS had found her, making contact in a market their last day in Singapore. They had given her two choices, kill him that night or they would kill them both. In return for her renewed devotion and leaving, they had acquiesced on his death. Daria had convinced them he no longer represented a threat; she knew when he woke and found her gone, he would be as good as dead. Five years ago, when she learned he had died, the hopes she still harbored in her dreams died with him.

For an hour, she observed his cabin, contemplating a closer reconnaissance. There were more people inside. How many she couldn't be sure. She had seen two different men through the window but sensed there were more. Then the situation changed. She heard human voices coming from the trail by the creek. Sliding farther into the shadow of the bush, she scanned the woods around the clearing. There...on the path, the woman she had seen leave the lodge earlier.

"His place is just ahead," the woman said.

Daria had no idea how many others might be with her. Whoever she had brought didn't respond...there wasn't time – *a gunshot sounded from inside the cabin, and a man screamed*. The sentry charged up the steps to the cabin and flung open the door, immediately diving away – the front window shattered, and three shots came from inside.

"ARE RHODES AND HIS GROUP STILL AT THE INDIAN'S CAMPER?" the woman on the path yelled behind her. Running into the clearing, she motioned at the sentry pressed against the wall of the cabin. "STAY PUT!"

Daria considered taking them out, but there were three problems. One, MOIS's reaction to an unapproved assassination on U.S. soil, which is how they would see it. Two, the other person or persons she had not yet spotted. Three, she was in the dark about what was happening in the cabin. She had been trained to use deadly force only when the outcome was assured. Which was far from the case here.

"NOT SURE. THEY WERE!" an unseen man yelled from the woods across the clearing.

Daria spotted him in the trees running toward the rear of the cabin. He burst into the open as he reached its far side and disappeared around the back corner. She recognized him. *Another unexpected piece to this strange puzzle.*

Sky dropped her knife. The sandy-haired stranger at the back door was holding an automatic pistol, a type she had seen Lilac Williams carry. She knew it was capable of firing multiple rounds in seconds.

"Drop your gun or I shoot her," he said to Zula.

"How about you drop yours, and I don't shoot you!" Zula wasn't giving up the only protection they had. "Don't know you from didley squat, mister, but we already took out your goon squad – laid 'em out in the other room."

The stranger grinned. Zula heard the floor squeak behind her, but before she could react, a hand grabbed her gun, and she was sucker punched in the side. Fucking Eva Braun, Johanna Mosby, had kicked her in the back. The wrestler twisted her wrist and threw her hard to the floor. She managed to get off a shot, splintering a ceiling beam, before Roid wrenched the Browning from her fingers. *Bushwhacked!*

Taking advantage of the distraction, Sky attempted the same move she had used on Lloyd. This stranger was quicker and saw it coming, stepping back just in time. She landed in a crouching-tiger-hidden-dragon pose; one knee down and one foot planted on the floor, her mind racing. The man still had his gun on her but with an amused look.

Zula was squirming under the wrestler's boot, scratching, and trying to bite his ankle. Roid laughed. "I'll find your pig after I finish you," he said, grinding his foot on her neck.

"DON'T! We may need them," the new man ordered.. "A lesson might be in order, however. Care to do the honors?" he said, nodding at Johanna, seeming to mock her. Zula tried tripping Mosby as she advanced on Sky. The woman kicked her in the side of her head ending her fight.

Sky leapt toward Johanna, but she caught her like an annoying child, locking her powerful arms around Sky's neck and shoulders, clasping her hands together in a vise grip. Sky tried to pop her shoulders loose, but the stronger woman's hold was too tight. She wildly swung her arms, trying to grab a hunk of hair. Johanna lifted her parallel to the floor and released her midair, flattening her hands against Sky's shoulder blade and the small of her back, slamming her down next to Zula, who had just begun to stir. Sky turned her face at the last second, saving her nose from being the point of impact.

Roid was chuckling like a senior watching the initiation of a freshman. Sky's left arm was paralyzed from the pain. This is the point, she thought, when Dick the Bruiser typically tagged in, climbed the ropes, and did a reverse cannonball on his opponent. But this butcher just kept laughing.

Johanna moved in for the kill, grasping her left leg around the ankle.

"*ENOUGH!*" the stranger commanded. "Lock them up and go check on the rest of your crack team."

Johanna glared at him, her eyes on fire, torn between the adrenalin rush of inflicting a *coup de grâce* and accepting an order from a superior she didn't respect. She forced herself to decompress, but not before violently throwing Sky's foot against the wood floor.

Roid's disappointed expression looked like the television screen had gone dark at the climax of a Netflix thriller. "Lock them back up," Johanna ordered him.

"I didn't tell him, I told you," the stranger said, coldly. Johanna stared at his Sig P220, pointing at her now. He smiled wickedly, slowly lowering the pistol to his side. "He has another job – getting our package from the trunk of the car. Unless you want to lug it all the way here?"

Daria Ahmadi silently slipped over the railing of the porch to follow the sentry to their package. Her guess – they had acquired the vessel with the formula. At their car, she discovered something different. A tangled mass of red hair spilled from the tarp that Roid pulled from the trunk. The package was not the Mayan Queen's vessel. And rescuing collateral was not her assignment. She needed to find Tripp.

CHIEF BIGFOOT

"**T**HIS CHIEF, HOOTON, HIS EVIL EYE, *ES LOCO, ES EL OJO DEL diablo*," Chuuy whispered to his *Capitán*, still spooked by the strange woman summoning forth his blessed, dead mother. "*El pueblo está loco*, the whole town my brother-in-law. We should never have left our beautiful Guatemala.

"You speak as a fool, Corporal."

"*Y muy caliente, mis testículos es* rotting, Hernando. The seer was the witch, *La Tatuana*. I saw her tattoos. She tried to steal my soul and did this to me. And this cell, this mattress stinks of vomit and bad tequila. What have you gotten us into? *Es–*"

Hernando slapped his whining brother-in-law, but in doing so their handcuffed hands smacked his own jaw as well. "See, you have made me flagellate myself, Corporal – that is where your peasant fears and superstitions have gotten us. Idiot. This is not a mattress, it is a soiled sofa, and we are not locked in a cell, this is an interrogation room. We will explain ourselves to Chief Hooton and be rewarded. Have faith in your commander, Chuuy."

"Corporal?"

"Our titles no longer matter, brother-in-law," Gomez sighed. "We have no valuable vessel to sell, no country, no future...no Gabriela," he groaned. "There is no going home either. Mancoros would have us both shot for dereliction of duty. Now, we have only information. We must be wise, wiser than we have been, in how we use it. This American Chief will soon speak to us, wanting to know why we are here. We must disclose just enough information to worry him. And the trick, Chuuy...the trick...will be to not disclose too much too soon. Then, he will wash his hands and turn us over to those above him, who will give us new identities and house us like kings in Las Vegas. Our wits are our best tool...remember that brother-in-law."

"Your wisdom, Hernando, will be remembered by generations of Lupe and Fernando's offspring."

Chief Hooton and Officer Dickie had been listening through the intercom system. The Guatemalans had ignored the phone's beeps and red flashing lights as Dickie worked his way through the buttons. Hoot, accustomed to his looks scaring the wits out of stoned tourists from California, had smiled at *"ojo diablo."* Disturbing his town was a capital offense...or should be. *Loco* was easy with inebriated visitors withering beneath his dysfunctional eye; two revolutions and they puked all over themselves. "Might as well put a disability to good use," is what Sedona's Human Resources Manager had told him during his orientation. That was after he'd asked if the Northern Arizona Healthcare Plan would pay for corrective surgery.

"I've requisitioned a new couch," Dickie said. "What's your take on these two, Chief? Sounds like they're running from their *patrone*. This guy Mancoros sounds bad – maybe the gang cartels the President talks about?"

"Probably MSG222, real tough outfit...you should read the bulletins once in a while. We'll have to loop Border Patrol in for sure. But let's talk to them first." Hoot snickered, "House them like kings." Those boys will either be deported, locked up in a detention facility, or have their asses shipped to Guantanamo."

"Gitmo's closed, Chief."

"That's just what they want us to think, Officer."

"We should ask them about the vessel they planned to sell. Sounds like they were counting on a big score," Dickie said, stroking his chin. "I wonder...that call we got from Interpol about antiquity trafficking and Skip Rhodes – coincidence?"

Hoot's tuft of white hair stiffened, and his eye bounced around the picture of the department's softball team, the photographer had cut off his head in the shot. Dickie had a good point – the Federales, *not Interpol*, calling from Mexico, the attack on Ballsy at Rhode's cabin, and now two suspicious, gang affiliated characters from Central America. The last "coincidence" in Sedona had been when the Ocean's Eleven star and Laura Croft, Tomb Raider showed up on separate vacations. It had taken three officers and very nearly the jaws of life to get her off that Friends star.

"You're learning Officer Dickie; I was wondering the same thing. Seems that Criminal Investigative Seminar in Prescott is paying off."

Chief Hooton ducked below the doorway to the repurposed copy room. Dickie was covering his six. Giving his *loco* orb free rein to explore, Hoot trained his good eye on the gang leader before settling it in a bug-eyed gaze at the one called Chuuy, *"NOW, WHAT DRUG DEAL ARE YOU TWO BORDER BANGERS TRYING TO SET UP IN MY TOWN!"* he boomed, using his best John Wayne, pilgrim voice, while explosively kicking the sofa with his size eighteen Laredo square-toed cowboy boots, lifting the two Guatemalans a foot off the floor.

Chuuy cracked on landing, whimpering, *"Es* uranium, *Capitán Diablo*, or...or Semtex. Please, I beg you, leave me my soul." He covered his face, fearing the worst. The huge, black boots were covering the devil's hooves...and the man's eyes...oh, those horrible glowing, different colored eyes...tinged red with fire like the Guatemalan spirit *El Cadejo*, like the ends of two lit *cigarillos*. "*Baño, baño,*" he screamed, feeling the weakening in his groin.

Dickie whistled. "Uranium! Semtex! Holy Shit, Chief!"

Gomez yanked their handcuffed wrists, "*Silencio, Sargento! Silencio, lo es* too soon. You will ruin our mission!

"MISSION? SERGEANT?" Hoot hollered, fumbling with the flap on his holster. "These two are military, Dickie! This is serious, boys, very serious."

Roid, breathing hard from carrying the package, threw the tarp onto the cabin floor at Johanna's feet.

He had been halfway to the car before realizing he didn't have the keys. Asshole Jerry had kept them on purpose. Ever since getting to this shithole town, Johanna had been killing him with one fucking trek after another. Now with Lloyd out of action, he was at the bottom of the pecking order. When he left, his partner had been mumbling his words and picking splinters from his nuts with his eight remaining fingers.

Jerry had recovered and was wearing a tube sock tied around his head, bandaging the gash from his own gun. The sock kept slipping, and he finally ripped it off, throwing it at Johanna, "Thanks for the first aid, the damn thing stinks."

"Was she awake?" Johanna asked, kicking the tarp.

Roid leaned over and grabbed a bunch of auburn hair, spinning the tarp for fun – a low moan came from inside.

"Did anyone see you?" the new man asked. He was in the kitchen, holding a plastic cup. A bottle of Bombay blue gin rested on the table.

Roid didn't know this dick from Adam, just his reputation. He looked at Johanna, who nodded that it was okay to answer. "No, but when my back was turned, that damn ugly pig tried taking a bite of my ass." he answered.

Banging began again against the locked bedroom door, "*THAT UGLY PIG HAS A LONG MEMORY, DICK-FOR-BRAINS!*" Zula yelled.

"Our guests would like some company...*Dick*," the new man laughed, pointing with his gin bottle at the red hair spilling from the tarp on the floor. "Before she wakes up."

DESERT SEEP

SKIP, INSUFFERABLY BOORISH AFTER LILAC'S DEPARTURE, WAS nervously waiting inside Thorn in Foot, for the follow-up call from Sky and Zula's kidnappers.

There was nothing any of them could do until the next contact; they had ruled out calling the police, at least until they had more information. "A kidnapping would automatically trigger notification of the Feds," Skip had argued. "Their playbook would begin with poking into all of our lives to eliminate us as suspects. We would lose control and time." Surprisingly, Kuul had neither countered his ridiculous points nor backed Toni when she tried.

Walking in the high desert, Toni decided, was preferable to sitting and listening to Skip's angry threats and continued harangue against the linguist. "He needs to be alone," she said to Kuul after they were away from his camp. "I enjoy your company. In Mexico, you showed me a new side to your spirit."

"But...not here," Kuul answered slowly, seeing in Toni Wathetewa's dark eyes that she had more on her mind.

Kuul strayed from the main trail, the same dry, gravelly path Lilac and Stephens had been on hours earlier. He led Toni up a small arroyo, its banks a cascading series of sandstone ledges and slides of loose rocks where acacias and desert sage flourished in patches of trapped sediment. As the arroyo narrowed, the tumbled sandstone changed to chunkier, charcoal-gray basalt, the remnants of an ancient lava flow. Ahead, the foliage became denser with soft tamarisk, tall grasses, and wild lilac scenting the arid air with their purple blossoms. The path ended at a ten-foot-high, rounded wall of black lava stacked on a layer of sandstone; the underlying red rock undercut like a riverbank, creating a natural alcove. In the rainy season, stormwater, draining from the surrounding hills, rushed over the lip. But now, water trickled from out of the wall into a small bowl where the overflow had hollowed out a depression in the rock. The temperature was cooler than along the trail. A natural bench of sandstone, its edges worn smooth, rested in the deep shade.

Toni reverently touched the timeless seat.

"It's a seep," Kuul said. Toni nodded. "This water has been filtering through the rocks for thousands of years. It might have fallen on your ancestors as rain," he said, dipping a hand in the pool and watching the liquid run through his fingers. "They sat on that rock, resting."

"You continue to surprise," Toni said, wistfully. "The water is why you live out here, isn't it?"

Kuul shrugged, "That and the land. They are both part of my mother's blood, her People were molded from this clay, same as yours...and the Forest Service doesn't charge rent."

Toni smiled and sat where her fathers had. Kuul sat beside her.

"Why do you trust him? Why follow with so few questions?"

Kuul tossed a pebble into the pool, studying the ringed vortex that spread outward. "His spirit is recovering, and I am part of that journey. At first, I wasn't, but one night, we were laying atop Thorn, talking about the stars, the heavens, our places in life."

"You were both drunk you mean."

"Only a little. Skip was in a strange mood; you know how he gets. He shared his story...part of it. He has travelled a long way,

Toni. When men share their stories, they either become enemies or brothers. No one, not even Lilac, knows his full history, how he came to be here and who he was or is becoming. The things we do always stay with us, they never completely leave us. They make us who we are."

"And those things have made you trust him?"

"More than any man I know."

Toni looked in his eyes, seeing sincerity and purpose. Kuul was indeed a deeper soul than she had appreciated. He was a better man than Rhodes, maybe that was his point. Had he been chosen to lead his friend away from a dark path, toward whatever light he might find? Was that *his* journey, *his* inner quest? Their bond was strong, unbroken. Was there space for her – if she chose him?

"These things that have been happening to us, the man in Mexico, the Red Queen's vessel, my kidnapping and now Zula and Sky's...they are not random incidents of bad luck. His journey has led us here, hasn't it?

"Our journey," Kuul answered.

Skip stared at the phone on the foldaway dinette. *Ring damnit!* Despite his friend's example, patience was never going to be one of his virtues. Especially with the three women in his life in trouble and all of it his fault. Correction, four women. Regardless of how tenuous the connection, Daria was alive.

If Sky and Zula's captors didn't call soon, he would be forced to take other actions; the start of a chain that would lead down holes he didn't want to go. And Lilac, what the hell was she thinking? *Catherwood Stephens*, a compound of Frederick Catherwood and John Stephens, the two men responsible for the modern era rediscovery of the Maya civilization in the mid 1800's. Woody's story had been so full of holes, he could have driven a truck through them.

For Lilac's sake he should have, but the mission protocol covered a simple drop, nothing more, no directives about handling external complications. His old handler had assured him, "Tripp, an hour out of your vacation and the favor is repaid."

The phone refused to ring, but it did begin vibrating across the table. Skip grabbed it – **Unknown Caller**. He put it on speaker and listened.

"Rhodes?" a woman's voice asked in a bossy Germanic accent. She paused, waiting for him to speak. He didn't. "Take us off speaker," she demanded, hearing the echoey sound of her words.

Skip did, cooly saying, "Proof of life."

"Not now." The woman laughed, "They don't behave themselves when let loose."

"You know who I am?" he growled threateningly. If she had hurt them, she would be paying with her life. "If you hurt them, I will find you and you will pay. And just so I'm clear, I'm rather clumsy at collecting payment. It can take days."

"And you think your ineptness scares me?"

"If I don't get a call from them within an hour, you will find out just how *inept* I can be."

The woman snorted, "You are someone who will bring us the Mayan vessel...that's who you are. If not, you will be too busy *collecting* pieces of your three friends."

Three friends, not two, Skip noted. Either Greta couldn't count, or they also had someone else – Who? "You're boring me, tell me how the exchange will work? Where and when?"

"First, we want a photo of the vessel. There is an inscription, include that too." She chuckled, "Neither of us are very trusting... are we? Text the picture to this number and don't bother running a trace. That would just be a waste of both of our time."

Johanna's disgust had been palpable after her partner admitted he'd never seen the vessel. The Indian travelling with Rhodes had kept it in a sack tied around his belt, he had told her. Even the Butcher boys had sensed the tension between them, moving to the opposite side of the cabin. They could be chasing the man's loose change or spare arrowheads...one more reason she should have been in charge of the operation.

Men...testosterone fucked up everything – Jack Anderson, Bathsheba's patronizing, skirt-chasing, CEO – her *partner*, the contractor heading this team, smirking at her from across the table – and Skip Rhodes, mystery man, thinking he could bully her. They shouldn't even be allowed on the bus, let alone be driving.

"Where and when?" Skip repeated. "I'm not a goddamn photographer."

"I told you, the pictures first. Then we will talk. And don't take too long, your friends do not have a lot of time."

Call Ended appeared on the screen. Skip slammed his fist on the tabletop, frustrated that he knew no more than when the call began.

No, that wasn't true. He had learned something. There was a third captive, and the woman wanted a picture, which meant she wasn't sure he had the cup. But how did she know about the...the trailer's metal stairs creaked, and he felt the camper shift slightly... *someone was outside*. The doorknob turned and stopped. He pulled the old school, government model Colt 45 he'd taken from Lilac's apartment, aiming it dead center.

CHEN ZING

CHEN ZING STUDIED THE DILAPIDATED TRAILER THROUGH MILI-tary grade Ziyouhu rangefinder binoculars. Four hundred meters. The non-reflective coated lenses and desert camouflage color matched the QBU bullpup rifle the sniper lying beside him had trained on the door. He assumed the man inside was armed. The way he had handled himself and directed the others at the Merida Zoo was not the work of an amateur. He didn't plan on underestimating him again, especially on his home turf.

Too many of his fellow intelligence officers at the Ministry of State Security, MSS, showed a lack of respect for American capabilities. They dismissed as unenlightened any cultures as new as those in the west. The morally corrupt, upstart Americans being the worst. Zing knew better, he had lived with them and studied their systems, their capitalist business practices, their republican government, their strengths as well as their weaknesses. Barbarians had conquered Rome, had they not?

Barbarians they might be, but America's agents were clever, and to the man, streetfighters. Unpredictable. What they lacked in subtlety they made up for with brute force. And in the field, violence, and the willingness to use it, won more often than not. He had seen the same steely attributes in Skip Rhodes's eyes at the zoo. Poised to aggressively act, he had been smart enough to find an easier solution. An adversary worth being careful with.

Zing remained under orders to obtain the Mayan vessel and formula – the next generation biological weapon. The idea of a deadly, infectious, chemical formula scratched onto an artifact over a thousand years ago and buried in the jungle, still seemed incredulous. To possibly sacrifice members of his QRF, quick response force, over the acquisition angered him. Stuck in their Beijing chambers, the Politburo and MSS Bureau heads were too locked into a battle where counter-punching the Americans was an objective unto itself.

They were too worried about the mad U.S. President weaponizing a new contagion as payback for the recent pandemic; Double Dragon had intercepted the man's personal cell phone calls to Kim Jong Un urging him to send anthrax-infected cattle across the border to Mongolia. The latest fear was that recent Washington envoys to Taipei were negotiating formal diplomatic ties for missile bases. Global idiocy, Zing thought, all based on the rantings of a deranged autocrat and his friend, the sycophant dictator in backwater Central America. Where would it end?

No one at MSS, including his father, had listened when Zing had questioned why America, China's most sophisticated, technically shrewd adversary, would send a team of agents so unprepared and acting so cavalier about a virus capable of wiping out whole populations? Using a fake Mayan vessel at the zoo had been clever, and Rhodes had been with the train of schoolchildren, but an Indian carrying the formula to the world's most lethal weapon in a burlap sack? Even the Americans would not be that stupid. Dismayed by MSS's arrogance, Zing had stopped pushing, accepting that his job was to complete the mission, not question his superiors.

His Chinese QRF team had been positioned since early morning, surrounding the trailer and reconning the Americans' activities. They had observed two of the Americans, a woman and man, leave in the morning. The Indian called Kuul had stayed, the bag still attached to his belt.

Later, he and his woman had gone into the desert, leaving Rhodes alone. Unfortunately, he had not taken the bag, preventing Zing from ending the mission with two silenced kills from the Bullpup.

The Americans' splitting their team had tactically dictated delaying the assault. A cautious leader, Zing had sent a scout team to scope out the camp for boobytraps and an assessment of their firepower. Taking the trailer and dispatching one man would be a simple exercise but was complicated by the unknown location of the formula...he could not allow Rhodes time to render it useless. He had considered greenlighting the sniper, but what if the vessel wasn't there? What if the Americans had hidden it somewhere in this barren landscape?

Zing's comtac crackled, "Subjects returning. Five minutes." Two of his men had been following the Indians. Now was the time, he thought. Or wait, wait until the situation *might* be more advantageous.

Zing made up his mind, "All teams, on my...*BÙ! ZHŌNGSHI!!* HOLD, HOLD, CONFIRM HOLD."

On the verge of giving the GO order, he had spotted another person, a quarter mile away. A woman with black hair and olive skin was stealthily moving toward the camp, concealing herself behind scraggly pines and thick groundcover.

"Repeat – hold position," Zing commanded.

Skip leveled the Colt at the door. The knob stopped turning, and he heard light footsteps quickly retreating to the back of the trailer. Seconds passed and heavier steps advanced across the campsite. The metal step creaked again.

"He must still be inside," Toni Wathetewa said, opening the door and stepping into the camper. Seeing Skip's gun, she froze and raised her hands, "Don't shoot, Whiteman. We come in peace," she said, mockingly, putting her hands down. She went to the tiny fridge for water, tossing a bottle to Kuul, who had been behind her.

"Little jumpy, Kemo."

"Shut the door," Skip whispered. "We have company."

Toni glanced to the back of the Winnebago expecting to see Lilac. At least they were rid of the linguist. Her return was a good sign. Maybe Rhodes would calm down and think better.

"Company," Skip repeated, his expression emphasizing his seriousness.

Kuul closed the front door and stepped away from the window, "Lilac?" he whispered, hoping he had misread his friend.

Skip shook his head and pointed toward the rear of the camper, "Someone is outside."

"Only one way to find out," Kuul said, reaching into a cabinet for a boning knife and sliding a black-handled cleaver along the counter to Toni. "You first, Kemo. You have the gun."

"Might be a bigger one waiting for us."

"There's the roof hatch," Kuul said, remembering the other opening.

Toni counted four empty Modelo bottles on the table. A cleaver...what was she supposed to do, cut a chop? "It was probably a nosy rabbit, a hiker that changed his mind, or Lilac at the last moment wisely deciding against a reunion. Maybe the wind, the breeze has picked up. With the temperature cooling this tin can might have just popped from the change in pressure."

"The kidnappers called too. I suppose I imagined that as well," Skip answered. "I know what I heard. You want the roof or the door," he said to Kuul.

"How about the Colt, and you choose your exit?"

Toni wanted to brain them both. They were in the middle of the desert, off the beaten path, and she and Kuul had just walked across the immediate area. There had been no vehicles, other than their own, nothing out of place, and no lurking strangers. "You two are more likely to shoot yourselves or step through a water-rotted seam in Thorn's roof," she said, stepping around Kuul and pushing the door open, while glaring back at Butch and Sundance. "See, nothing, just bare desert. And it will be more of the same from up top, down below, around the ends, and from wherever else you look."

Kuul pointed out the open door…a woman in brown khakis stood on the metal step, her gaze alternating between Toni and the wash. Her dark complexion and long straight hair looked Native, but the eyes were cat shaped. She was carrying a short-barreled pistol. He yanked Toni behind him, making short, back-off thrusts with his boning knife. A firm hand from behind gripped his bicep.

"It's okay," Skip said quietly.

"Who–"

"Daria Ahmadi," Toni interrupted, putting two and two together. The woman's name Lilac had yelled at Skip earlier. The woman he had shrugged off as an old acquaintance he'd run into in Merida. The fire in Lilac's eyes had told her there was more to the story.

"Let her in," Skip said.

Daria scanned the desert before entering the trailer. Tripp had released his friend's arm, but he was still shielding the Native woman. Without a word, she brushed past him to the bedroom in the back and then opened the curtain to the bathroom. *Clear*, but not clean.

"Yours?" she asked Tripp.

"Mine," Kuul answered.

Daria nodded, meeting her former lover's eyes, "*Skip Rhode's* cabin is far more interesting and crowded."

She had tracked him, Skip realized. If she could find his cabin in a matter of hours, then so could others. There was only one reason she would risk operating here. The United States was a very unfriendly country for Iranians, even those fleeing religious repression, seeking asylum, hoping for the promise of a freer life. Daria

Ahmadi, MOIS agent, had been expecting to find the cup at Zula's lodge. *Crowded? Sky and Zula?*

"If you've hurt them–"

"The feisty old woman and the young, pretty blond?"

"You found them? At my cabin? You're playing games, Daria, and I'm not a piece you want to mess with."

Daria could see how much the two women meant to him. Her eyes softened and she gently rested a hand on his arm. He was trembling; she didn't know whether it was from anger or fear. "They are at your cabin, being held by four men and a woman. They were both beaten in a fight. Not badly." This wasn't the time to mention the red head, unconscious and perhaps more severely injured. His eyes were anxious enough, a sign of empathy he would have kept hidden in his dark days.

"Who are they? Tell us what you know!"

"Not a team I recognized. Poorly trained, but not amateurs. Certainly not a sanctioned government operation. They are American, except for a woman."

Daria hesitated and Skip could tell she was holding back.

"What else?"

"One of the men, he arrived later – the man from Mexico who accompanied you."

Daria watched as his body tightened. His anxieties were dissolving into a steely recognition of a job to do. Their eyes met. She knew he wanted to ask about the red head but was afraid. She simply nodded and his transformation was complete. The frenzied fears were checked, giving rein to the icy, emotionless killer she'd trailed to Singapore.

"They have Lilac," Tripp Street, no longer the tour guide from Sedona, said to his friend. "We have to go."

Daria blocked his exit, "One more thing before you charge to her rescue – you have guests outside. Very formidable, Chinese guests."

BLISTERING BUD SPUDS

"**T**HE PRESIDENTIAL BUD SPUDS ARE CHARTREUSE AND PINK with a stripe of green, Stinky! I'm going to hang that kid for treason!"

POTUS had taken an unexpected turn for the worse. He was flat on his back, buck naked from waist to toe, his large butt and legs hoisted in traction with his feet spread apart. An unknown infection had candy-striped his privates, wracking him in pain with the slightest contact.

"It's time for your bath," Nurse Helga said, entering the room and waving a loofa as the fat man groaned. "The dead skin has to go," she gleefully added.

"Let Stinky do it, he's not an underpaid sadist," POTUS moaned.

"Better him than me," Helga said, smiling sickly at the suddenly panic-stricken Secretary Stinckner, "as long as the tissue is vigorously debrided."

POTUS muttered "bitch" under his breath, his orange cheeks turning red, tiny blue capillaries appearing as spidering green lines beneath the tinted tanning goop.

"Fine, then I'll do it," Nurse Helga grinned, wedging a wood block with rubber ends between POTUS's thighs and pushing it in place. "My son, Hannibal, made this in shop class. Piece of work, isn't it."

"Do your worst, Ratchett," POTUS bravely hissed. "You'll be treating frostbite at Zebra Station One in Antarctica when I get out of here."

"You mean the Arctic, Mr. President. The pole to the north... not the south," Stinckner said, immediately regretting his contradiction. Helga saved him, slapping an icy cold, alcohol compress on the two inflamed bud spuds. The howling could be heard in the first-floor lobby.

"Give me the latest from our spy in *Mỹ Lai*," POTUS ordered. Helga was gone, but Hannibal's contraption remained between his legs, and a fan covered with a damp filter was blowing moist air up the President's ass. A direction of flow Stinckner found preferable.

The twenty-four hours Orville Stinckner had promised results within had come and gone. Thanks to Helga's heroic actions, spurred by a five-figure deposit to an account of her choice, and POTUS's son wanting to continue playing President, the big man had been distracted and not asked for an update. If only Rachel Ray hadn't been broadcasting an infomercial for chocolate-covered, avocado tacos on FOX while hearings on the President's trumped up travel budget were making news on CNN.

Despite his desperate hourly calls and messages, Stinckner had heard squat from his contractor.

The Special Assistant on Domestic Disturbances, a twenty-six-year-old theology graduate from Liberty University, had proven equally inept, failing to uncover any background on a Skip Rhodes. The first name was innocuous, he'd claimed, not short for anything, usually a reference to someone named after their maternal grandfather. As far as the Skip Rhodes in Sedona, the most interesting fact was the lack of information. Social Security said the number belonged to a Howard Rhodes from Warrensburg, Illinois, born

February 11, 1980. Oddly, there was no work record, nor did the IRS have any record of Howard ever being claimed as a dependent. No driver's license, passport, or voter registration card for Howard broadened the mystery, which was capped by a fire in the Macon County Recorder's Office selectively destroying only the relevant filing cabinets.

"Our man is close...imminent is the word he used this morning," Secretary Stinckner lied. "The American tourists have proven less than cooperative. Seems one of them is of Mayan ancestry and feels the vessel should be turned over to the appropriate Mexican authorities. He has also reported there is foreign alien activity in Arizona, which has caused some minor complications."

"ALIENS!" POTUS roared. "OUTERSPACE GREEN BASTARDS! Get Kirk on the line, Stinky...no by God, wait...let's get Carl Sagan on this. He has a direct connection with the sons-of-bitches."

"Sagan is dead, Mr. President."

"STINKY! We have to get on top of this, we're facing intergalactic competition, those fuckers get around. Call that pinko Grassy fellow.

"JESUS H. CHRIST! GET IT OFF ME, STINKY!" POTUS howled, wildly gesticulating. One end of Hannibal's thigh brace had slipped and was thumping against his raw sores.

"Not extra-terrestrials, sir, foreign nationals," Stinckner corrected, trying to dislodge the brace that was now stuck below the President. "I meant Guatemalans, President Colon's team. Two of them had an altercation with local police and are in custody. Hector claims they went rogue."

POTUS satisfyingly sighed, "That's better Stinky, a little to the left. Ah, right there, that's it."

Stinckner continued tugging the brace; given the next bit of news it was best to have the man in a good mood. "Ezekial, your head of Domestic Disturbances, has been making calls...according to the Sedona Chamber of Commerce...there was a middle eastern woman inquiring about one of the Americans. We don't want to jump to conclusions, but –"

"A-RABS! Those head-bandaged camel herders are going after Hoover Dam again, Stinckner!"

"CIA, NSA, military intelligence, and the White House Terrorism Council have no indication of that, sir. They are still assessing; she could be just another of the five million, foreign tourists that stop there on their way to the Grand Canyon."

"*Oooh*, sorry about that Stinky, just a little gas. Move it to the other side...better...but she asked about the American, the unpatriotic fellow?"

"He operates a tour company. According to the Chamber, it is not that unusual for visitors to ask for recommendations. Again, sir, we are checking it out. However –" Stinckner hesitated. "The boys at Langley intercepted a communique between MSS and a team in Arizona."

POTUS appeared puzzled, "What the hell does Social Services have to do with anything?"

"MSS is China's Ministry of State Security, Mr. President."

"Hmmm. Beijing Benny is after the formula, Stinky. Xi figures that chocolate will keep him kicking through the year of the jackass. Get the Joint Chiefs and don't listen to their pontificating bullshit...I've promised them that hundred billion and they'll get it when I damn well want to give it to them. Tell them we need Chuck and Delta One on standby, there's an extra healthy bomber in it for them.

"Stealth, sir."

Give an idiot enough rope and knot a loop, Orville Stinckner thought.

FAMILIAR TERRITORY

THORN IN FOOT'S FRONT WINDOW EXPLODED, GLASS SHATTERING, shards flying through the air.

"It's a warning!" Daria yelled, hitting the floor.

"A damn effective one!" Toni yelled, laying prone beside the oven. Kuul was beside her, blocking her body from the open window.

Skip was sitting on the floor beside the banquette, back pressed against the wall. "Is that Sig your only weapon?" he asked Daria, peeking around the edge of the seat through the window, trying to spot a shooter in the maze of scrub outside. The cabinet above his head splintered, a second shot echoing from the hills surrounding the camp.

"Unfortunately, I didn't fully appreciate your popularity," she quipped.

"Mags?"

"Three, two of them in my car. You?"

"Only what's locked and loaded. Kuul, get Toni in the bed–"

Another shot suddenly blew in the horizontal window above the bed. "MAKE IT THE BATHROOM!" he yelled.

Before they could move, two simultaneous, concussive blasts rocked the trailer, knocking it from its rear leveling jacks, causing them all to roll backwards. Shrapnel peppered Thorn's outer skin. Skip fell onto Daria, who was wedged in the stairwell by the door. Kuul and Toni were jammed in the narrow passageway to the bedroom.

"FRAG GRENADES, ANYBODY HIT?" Skip yelled, raising his gun hand and seeing blood splatter. He checked his arm and shoulder but didn't see or feel anything.

"Just a scratch," Daria said from beneath him. A bloody line angled across her neck. A piece of shrapnel had pierced the door. She was lucky. "If those had been placed underneath or lobbed through the windows – we'd all be dead. They are warning us. They want the formula."

"Kemo, it's not looking good, brother. Toni's leg is bleeding, there's a tiny hole in her calf." He had crawled forward, yanked a towel from the stove handle and was tying it around her wound.

"I'm okay, I can still move."

"Thorn's not an armored tank, Kemo. A second wave and we're toast. You two have any ideas? Even one would be good right now."

Chen Zing had let the olive-skinned woman approach the camper. He hadn't been sure what was going to happen; maybe she would do the dirty work. It had surprised him when the door opened, and she disappeared inside. His other option had been to let the sniper take her out. He hadn't liked allowing another gun in the trailer, especially one that bespoke a professional owner, but until he understood her role, he had decided to keep her alive – keep all of them alive. All he wanted was the formula, preferably without casualties and a full-out assault on American soil that would be difficult for MSS to explain. Careers ended and agents disappeared over sloppy, foreign entanglements.

From their higher ground, with the Ziyouhu binocs, Zing could see the American leader and the late arriving woman crouched by the door, the two Indians farther back. The shots had been warnings; the handheld, T86 internal rocket-launched nutcrackers to confirm their helpless situation. Sixteen hundred metal bearings had done the trick...almost too well; he could see bloody smears on both women. They were shouting at each other, arguing over their next move.

Maybe he could help make up their minds.

"Spot the Indian woman, but don't fire," he told the sniper. "Wait...spot the other woman, the one their leader is attending to." Through his headset he ordered the rest of his men to close to twenty-five meters, staying in the cover of the swale and a small hill.

Skip watched the team repositioning outside Thorn in Foot. Kuul was right, they couldn't survive another assault. The firepower differential was overwhelming, not to mention being outnumbered, by how many he couldn't tell – more than enough to get the job done. Daria and Toni were both injured, and sundown wasn't for another ninety minutes, total blackout an hour after that. Even then, their chances of slipping out were slim, but trying it now was tantamount to suicide. The second they stuck their heads out of the Winnebago they'd be shot down. That left negotiating. *Simple favor my ass!* The Chinese wanted the damn, *wish-he'd-never-seen-it, if-I-get-out-of-this-alive-I'm-coming-for-you-and-your-fucking agency, CUP!*

Kuul had crawled into the bathroom and come back with a rusty, tin box, a red cross painted on its top. He rustled through the contents and found a bandage, then tossed the box to his friend. At least there were moist alcohol wipes.

Skip began ministering the cut on Daria's neck. A red dot appeared on her forehead. *SHIT – Not Now!!* Shoving her beneath him, he covered her head and body with his torso, pushing her away to create a pocket of dead air space. Maybe the bullet wouldn't pass through him and kill her as well. "Daria, I..."

The impact shredded a plywood panel inches above their heads. "Barcelona...our love...he's with my sister," she cried amidst the deafening explosion, praying one of them might survive.

"Now, the same, placed above the Indians," Zing coolly ordered. The sniper targeted the dot on the other woman, adjusted his sights slightly higher, and fired.

Zing casually walked toward the trailer to join his men. He had no fear of the Americans returning fire; they understood the consequences. The man inside was a professional, negotiating was his only remaining option...while stalling and staying alert to any opportunity for escape. Zing would let him talk; escaping would be totally up to their turning over the vessel and formula.

Confidently, he strolled to the charred campfire with a man on both sides, one pointing a bullpup assault rifle, the other a hand-held, grenade launcher. He turned a chair to face the door of the pockmarked trailer and sat, reaching into a breast pocket. Calmly, he stirred the ashes. Not finding a red ember, he lit his cigarette with a lighter, blowing smoke rings into the late afternoon sky.

"WE MEET AGAIN," he spoke loudly in an even voice.

Zing waited for a response and grinned to himself when none came. To use an expression he had been fond of in Washington, *these people were hard nuts, but the shells crack easily.* In this case, the stressed fiberglass was barely holding their 'fortress' together.

"There is no cavalry coming. Must I provide another demonstration? As I requested in Mexico, we only want the formula...the Mayan vessel. Let our governments work this out, it is not worth dying over."

"WHAT IF I TOLD YOU WE DON'T HAVE THE FUCKING THING!" the man's voice yelled from inside.

Zing nodded at his man holding the bullpup and gestured above the door, moving his index finger horizontally, the smoke from his cig leaving a trail in the air, "There." The man fired a burst above the door, leaving a string of punctures ten feet long.

"I am afraid I wouldn't believe you. Throw your weapons and the Indian's bag outside. We have no intention of killing any of you unless you make us."

Zing heard whispering and angry grunts from inside the trailer and called loudly, "WOULD A PLEASE HELP?" He nodded at his man and another burst ripped two feet below the last. "The formula and your guns...neither will be of use to you much longer."

Two automatic pistols flew out the broken front window.

Zing smiled, "And the formula."

The door to the trailer slowly opened, and the American stepped out, his hands raised.

"We have a lot to discuss," Skip said, tossing the sisal bag to the Chinese.

"Unlikely," the leader said, followed by an order in Mandarin to Red Ryder Boy who aimed his rifle at Skip's chest, no doubt imagining the pattern of a Chinese character.

The Chinese looked inside the bag – not what he had hoped. His expression unchanged, he re-cinched the leather string, twirling it around his finger and then back off like a yoyo, thinking.

"What is your name?"

"Skip Rhodes."

The Chinese snorted, "A very inane moniker. It suits your games, however. Now, before I bring your women out here and begin asking them...not as nicely as I have asked you...where is the formula?" he said, tossing the bag of black beans back to Skip.

"Look Mao, as should have been clear to you in Mexico, you can shoot me, shoot them, it won't matter. *We – Don't – Have – It! Understand?* Search us, search the trailer, tear this place apart, the only cup you will find says Sedona and has a picture of those red rocks," Skip half-yelled, pointing toward a distant formation.

"We will, and if you are telling the truth...well, then, you are of no use to us." Zing coolly responded. Americans were so excitable, so quick to call names; emotion accomplished little and only resulted in more problems. This man's anger seemed personal, and in Zing's experience that kind of anger was mostly factual. Rhode's eyes had been locked with his as he spoke. The man never blinked, showing no signs of nervousness over his lies being discovered. Intuitively, Zing knew he was telling the truth. Why would he lie, he had nothing to gain and everything to lose? The cowboy was buying time. A commodity which he currently had no control over.

"But – I do know who does," Skip said. "How about we discuss a mutually beneficial deal?"

SLOPPY HOUSEKEEPING

LILAC HAD NO RECOLLECTION OF HOW SHE ENDED UP IN SKIP'S bed, but she knew that's where she was, even before opening her eyes. Wrapping herself in the warm, Pendleton blanket with the familiar, wool scent and falling back to sleep was all she wanted. Isolated in his rustic cabin, she always felt safe and cushioned from the baying outside world. It wasn't until she lazily reached for him that her mind registered something was wrong.

She awoke with Zula and Sky prying loose a zip tie binding her wrists. "Not often you find yourself tied up here, huh?" Sky said.

"See if you can slip your thumb through," Zula said, seeing Lilac's eyes open. She gave Sky a stern look, "And you keep trying to stretch the tie. I'll do the same."

Lilac blinked and began glancing around the room...Skip's room. The last she remembered she was walking through the Wile E. Coyote's parking lot with...*Wood*...where was he? She twisted, searching the room. Just Zula and Sky.

"Hold still," Sky said. Lilac's twisting had tightened the tie around her thumb.

"Where is he?" Lilac asked anxiously. "He was with me."

"We haven't seen him, Honey. He was in Mexico with you." Zula studied her eyes; they were cloudy and her pupils a little dilated. Damn, she thought, Skip wouldn't have left her alone like this unless something had happened to him and Kuul. "Let's just get you loose, and then we can talk about how you got here. Skip Rhodes can take care of himself."

Lilac nodded absently.

Sky could tell Lilac was half out of it. She was searching for someone, mentally struggling, trying to piece together what was happening. She wondered if Lilac had been with Skip – or maybe Catherwood Stephens, the man he had emailed her about? The man the fiery red head had been chumming around the Yucatan with. Sky'd forgotten about the archeologist and hadn't checked his background. Now she wished she had. If it was Stephens that Lilac was concerned about, where was he? Where was Skip? Had something happened to them?

"You're cutting my wrists," Lilac grumbled, managing to slip a thumb from the tie, which allowed her to slip her fingers out. The white, plastic tie was left dangling around her other wrist. She tried sitting up, but a wave of dizziness and nausea made her slip back down.

"Take it easy for a minute," Zula cautioned, handing her a bottle of water their captors had left. She was guessing peckerhead or one of his goons had drugged her – about the only way they'd get her here trussed up like a Thanksgiving turkey. The girl was a fighter. "Trust me, we're not going anywhere."

Lilac raised her head. The door was closed, which didn't make sense. She looked at Zula and got a shrug in return.

"Let's get your feet under you first, then we can explain," Zula said. "Drink as much of that water as you can stomach. It will dilute whatever they gave you."

Lilac guzzled half its contents.

Ten minutes later, she was sitting up, pillows propped behind her, feeling better. She had filled Zula and Sky in on the Mayan vessel, the attacks in Mexico, and that the others were at Kuul's trailer. Sky had told her about the Mosbys, Roid and Lloyd, and their escape from the room and how the stranger had recaptured them. Lilac could see from the marks and bruises on their faces that they had not given up easily.

"Your trouble in Mexico and our scrape here are too big of a coincidence," Sky said, thinking. She was even more curious about the archeologist after hearing Lilac's story. Lilac was worried about him, but Sky wasn't so sure. His appearance in Campeche seemed too convenient...and his returning to Sedona with them. When coincidences started piling up, they stopped being coincidences.

Sky asked, "What does your archeologist look like?"

Lilac gave her a hard look, "He's not mine, and I didn't say he was an archeologist. He's an ethnological linguist from the Smithsonian."

"Did he give you his card and vitae?" Sky asked, smartly. She didn't see any reason to tell her about Skip's request.

Sky was too smart for her own good, Lilac thought, which annoyed the crap out of her. She wasn't just another flirty girl who had caught Skip's eye. Even if he was honest, and their relationship was innocent, she kept hanging around. It wasn't that she didn't like the girl, she was just a little too close.

Lilac turned to Zula, "Wood's tall, maybe six-one, six-two, sandy hair, light blue eyes, wide chin, dresses like a cleaned-up version of Indiana Jones." The cop in her could have drawn a picture if she'd had a sketch pad.

Zula kept glancing at Sky with each description, height, hair, good looks, dress. "Sounds like our bushwhacker, the sidewinder that stopped us and unleashed Johanna Mosby on you."

Sky nodded, "To the tee. He doesn't sound like a librarian."

Zula agreed, "Might not be a professor, but he's smarter than the others, that's for sure. The two with Johanna and her brother are dumber than a pair of lizards sunning themselves on a Sedona roundabout. He acted like their boss. Johanna, or whatever her name is, would not have deferred to him otherwise. She's too aggressive and mean, too used to ordering others around. The more I think about it, there might be a wedge there we can pick at...and I'm a world-class picker."

"If they are the same man, it means this is well organized, and extends across borders. If governments are after that Mayan vessel, your boyfriend is likely working for one, Lilac," Sky stated. As she talked, she began fitting the pieces together. "Johanna has an accent, but the others are clearly American. That's why Stephens let Skip and Kuul bring the vessel here – where he had backup, and we could serve as bait."

"Well bankrolled too," Lilac said irritably, unsure whether her anger was more about being fooled by Wood or Sky's pointing it out. But there was still a possibility that Wood wasn't the same man. He could be hurt, locked up like her, or worse. She desperately needed to get a look at the man on the other side of the bedroom door. The strange woman at the lounge, was she Sky's Johanna Mosby?

Skip opened the door to Thorn in the Foot, yanking it hard before it popped loose. The bullets from the Chinese bullpup had shattered its alignment. Zing Hu was behind him, his men outside surrounding the trailer. At least they wouldn't be launching an aerial assault with their leader inside. Daria was at the top of the steps, poised to strike; Kuul was three feet behind her, blocking Toni. Not much of a defense against the vanguard of the world's biggest army.

"It's okay," Skip said on entering, seeing Daria's attack posture. "We've reached a working agreement. This is Zing Hu, they're standing down."

"For the moment," Zing said.

Daria saw his gun was still out, though pointed at the ground. His men, however, still surrounded the trailer, every weapon trained on the door. *Working agreement*...surrender was what it smelled like. But trusting Tripp was the only viable option left; she had thrown her Sig out the window.

"I think it's time we compare notes," Skip said.

Daria backed away slowly. Kuul was in the area fronting the tiny kitchen. Toni was back on her feet, leaning out of the bathroom. Zing cautiously stepped into the trailer, keeping himself shielded by Skip's body. He had no way of knowing if they had tossed all their weapons out or not.

"Maybe we start with a round of introductions," Skip said, trying to keep WWIII from breaking out, which he and his friends would quickly lose. Even if they overpowered Zing, they would only have his weapon. Kuul had been watching him for any kind of signal indicating a plan. "Toni's right, this is Daria Ahmadi, an old friend – from before."

Kuul's eyes widened slightly, he knew enough about his friend's "before" to guess the woman was probably an agent. And probably NOT one of theirs.

"We ran into each other in Campeche."

"We seem to have run into a lot of interesting people in Mexico," Kuul said, glancing at the Chinese man holding the only gun in the small space.

Skip continued with the strained introductions, "Zing Hu, Chinese..." He paused, searching for the right word–

"Diplomat," Zing offered.

"Diplomat," Skip repeated. "He's been sent to collect the Mayan vessel, which contains an inscription for a formula his government would like to have. I've explained we no longer have what we were told was a sacred cup belonging to a Mayan queen, but that we know who does."

"The vessel is a sacred relic," Kuul answered. "According to the museum in Merida, the etching is just a formula for royal cacao

– *not* tea." Whether his friend was just stalling or actually had a plan, he wasn't sure. They both knew where the vessel was and no one else. At some point, the Chinese would realize they had been lied to. Skip's plans always spelled trouble.

"Is it what you are after as well?" Toni asked Daria, not expecting an answer.

Daria nodded. "And the Guatemalans that attacked you at *Uxmal*. Their president and your president have secretly developed a deadly viral agent. It is easily transmittable, and there is no antidote or vaccine. Your president is planning to weaponize it against my people. The Islamic Republic of Iran does not find that acceptable. Your friend, Skip, had you in the wrong place at the wrong time, as usual."

Toni wondered – Daria Ahmadi's last line dripped with sarcasm. *Wrong place, wrong time*...this woman was mocking him. Maybe Skip had them at the right place at the right time but hadn't been expecting company, not Ahmadi anyway. There was something deeper between them, something personal. Why else was she here alone? And her hushed words to him moments earlier...Barcelona, our love, my sister? There was hurt in her voice.

"And to threaten my country as well," Zing Hu said. "The Maya's understanding of mathematics and chemistry was very advanced. It is only the western world that considers any pre-European culture to be primitive. Our scientists believe the virus is the original SARS, even more potent, and that the jungles of the Mayan world were its zoonotic origin. The vessel you have contains its formula."

"*Had*," Skip said, still not revealing the location of the cup.

Skip laid out his plan to Daria and Zing, telling them about the taking of his Sedona friends. Four kidnappers against him and Kuul weren't good odds, especially when the four were holding two aces, Zula and Sky. He needed help, and they had the experience and training. If their governments wanted the cup, they were going to have to deal.

"There's another team and another player you don't know about," Skip continued. "An archeologist, calling himself Catherwood Stephens, wormed his way into our group in Mexico. Catherwood Stephens is an alias, and I believe our friends' captors are working with him. That's why he came back with us." *Now for the hook and lie,* "Stephens left here with another of our friends, Lilac Williams, who you met in Mexico," he said to Daria. "The Mayan vessel went missing after they left. We are convinced Stephens stole it and were deciding our next steps when you blew up our trailer," he said, switching his focus to Zing. "Your *vessel* is in another team's hands."

Daria had listened intently to Skip's story. And that was what it was – a story. She didn't believe for a second that Stephens had been able to steal anything from her old lover. Not unless he had let him. But what he might have done was give it to Williams. Another team having the vessel was a fabrication. He was co-opting his adversaries into allies, attempting to redefine their missions.

Since she was also under Zing's guns, it suited Daria's purposes to play along. But what Tripp did not know was that his girlfriend was with his other Sedona friends. If Williams or Stephens had the vessel, and she was betting on the woman, she needed to get back to the cabin.

"Zing, I came here from Rhodes's cabin. He is telling the truth," Daria said. "That is where they are holding their people. Stephens is not who he claims to be. He is there, heading an American team sent to stop us." She turned to Tripp, "And he has your woman. She was bound and unconscious."

Kuul watched his friend change. No one else noticed, except the Iranian who was also closely watching him. Skip had been calm, in his element, throughout the Chinese attack. The shots into Thorn in the Foot, the grenade blast, even Toni and Ahmadi being wounded hadn't shaken him. The more dangerous things became, the cooler he got. He had seemed relaxed leaving the trailer to meet Zing. But now, now that Lilac was in trouble, his shoulders fell, and fear replaced the cold, calculating stare Kuul had seen while he told his lies.

Daria felt sorry for him, she had pulled the rug from beneath his feet. His face became the same torture mask of pain she had seen seven years ago, when he had capitulated and handed her his gun, telling her to end it however she wanted. It was clear he loved the red head. There would be no recapturing what they'd had, that time had passed.

"We need to go. Now! How long ago did this happen?" Skip hissed, anger flaring his nostrils. "Why did you wait to tell me? How long, Daria!"

"We go nowhere before we search this trailer," Zing said, pointing his gun at Rhodes who was becoming more agitated by the second. "If you are not lying about having the vessel, then we'll talk." He motioned to two of his men, and they entered the trailer, pushing past Kuul and Toni.

"Knock yourself out," Kuul said as they flipped the mattress in the bedroom.

"There's no time for this, Zing!" Skip yelled. Kuul grabbed his friend to keep him from attacking the Chinese.

He is scared, Daria realized. She understood his pain, but fear, panic? Not reactions she ever imagined seeing from him. Had he acted like this in Singapore after waking and finding her gone? She had always pictured him as angry and self-reproaching that morning, cursing her and himself for his mistakes. Was he doing the same now for putting Williams in danger? She gently placed a hand on his shoulder, and he immediately shrugged it off.

"Tripp...let them finish, it is a small space and will not take long. You will lose all of them if we charge in without a plan."

"If you are not lying, we will take you to your cabin," Zing said. The play between the Iranian and Rhodes was puzzling, but his men were finding nothing. "Doing so serves our purpose. The People's Republic will take the vessel," he said, staring at Daria.

Zing would hit his cabin the same way he had tactically attacked Kuul's trailer, Skip thought – with overwhelming firepower. The Chinese only wanted the cup, any hostages were expendable. "No! This can't be a heavy-handed, military-style assault. There cannot be collateral damage."

"Our friends would be in the crosshairs," Kuul added. "If you want the vessel, you do this our way."

"I can just take it," Zing countered. "We can do this operation without you."

"That's if you're sure they have the vessel and that you can find it. We're the only ones who have actually seen it," Kuul said, insinuating the Chinese leader didn't yet have all the facts he needed. "The vessel could have been one of those pottery pieces your men just smashed on my floor."

"We need each other," Skip said. "Your men attacking a U.S. citizen's home is a one-way ticket to a work camp in Uyghur for you."

Zing snarled, "China treats the peasants in Uyghur well. America should be concerned with their own reservations."

"Stand your squad down, Zing. Or better yet, send them home," Daria calmly suggested. "Making this an international incident would be a loss for all of us. We are shadow warriors. Not soldiers or politicians. We can discuss what to do with the formula when we have it. The main objective here is to keep it from the American madman."

Zing's men had finished tossing the trailer and found nothing. Hu wasn't a fool; the Indian could have hidden the vessel with its formula anywhere in this godforsaken desert. This was a big country and finding a small cup, as Rhodes kept calling it, would be impossible. He didn't like trusting the American cowboy and the Iranian woman. There was no operational confirmation of there being another team – an archeologist yes, he'd seen him, but that was it. The Americans were good at lying and misdirection. But the Iranian was right, using his men would be messy. Dead Americans on U.S. soil would lead to consequences even his father wouldn't be able to fix.

"My squad will stay here," Zing compromised. "The vessel and formula go back with me to China," he said, icily.

Skip's patience had worn thin, "ARE YOU ALL INSANE! IT'S NOT A FORMULA FOR A FUCKING VIRUS! Is the world this mad? Do either of you really think the Maya, without running water, modern sewers, or antibiotics, developed a devastating germ and scribbled its recipe on a cup? They would have killed themselves. Zing, your people couldn't control COVID in sophisticated twenty-first century labs."

"Kemo," Kuul said, quietly, "We need their help rescuing our friends."

"All of you need help," Toni Wathetewa muttered under her breath.

35

SMART COOKIE AND KEVLAR

STEPHENS BACKED LILAC UP WITH A RUGER LCP PISTOL POINTED AT her head. Leave it to the backstabbing son-of-a-bitch to carry a six shot, baby, pocket pistol. "You're alive because of the leverage you give us," he sneered.

Lilac had been speechless when he entered Skip's bedroom. But a few words slowly came to mind – stupid, shocked, ridiculous, disappointed, disillusioned, furious, and mad-as-hell-and-ready-to-shoot. She had her suspicions from Sky and Zula's description, but she wasn't prepared for the emotional wallop the truth brought. She had been a fool. A giddy, pie-eyed schoolgirl fawning over the popular boy. Skip had been right, but she had been too jealous and too pissed-off over Daria Ahmadi to see it.

"Not the smart cookie you think you are," Stephens said, laughing at the look on her face.

"And you're not an archeologist," Sky chimed in.

He hadn't planned to reveal himself, but William's non-stop badgering through the locked door had worn him down. The other option had been to let Johanna deal with her, but, the satisfaction of seeing her realize how well he had fooled her and her meddling boyfriend won out. Identifying him wasn't going to change her fate or her friends' – those were sealed.

He had learned enough about her and the tour guide's combative yet romantic relationship to know what Rhodes would do if she were threatened. He wouldn't be able to get here with the vessel fast enough. Thanks to Johanna, he also knew 'Skip Rhodes' wouldn't be going to the authorities for help. It would just be him and his lackey Mayan pal. And if he was lucky, the Indian woman, otherwise he could have Johanna deal with her later. With the three of them and Lilac Williams, he'd have the formula and everyone he needed to silence in one place.

"Who are you?" Lilac demanded, regaining her composure. She was out of her restraints. The red welts around her wrists indicated it had not been easy. The fire in her eyes showed she would have sawed off a hand to get at him.

"He's another sidewinder that needs branding and a new coat of pitch and feathers," Zula said.

Stephens chuckled – a few hot irons had no doubt poked the old cow in her day. The younger woman, Sky, was standing quietly off to the side. Based on her game fight against the bigger and stronger Johanna, she warranted keeping an eye on.

"I've been threatened with worse and by better opponents," Stephens smugly replied. "*Who am I?* I'm the man that played your boyfriend, and all the well trained, well informed, government agents sent after the formula. I've also fooled the most powerful man in the world, the President of the United States, though he doesn't know it yet. But none of them were as easy as you."

"You're making a lot of enemies," Lilac said calmly, refusing to take his bait. He had read her like a book. He wanted her irrationally mad, going off half-cocked, instead of thinking.

"It won't matter once I have the Mayan vessel. A weight-loss recipe based on chocolate is worth billions to competing pharmaceutical corporations. Tens of millions for me in ongoing royalties. Imagine how much the public will pay for a Cadbury Egg that actually burns calories. That kind of money will keep me safe enough."

Weight loss? Lilac didn't believe him. According to Kuul, the etching on the vessel was a recipe for chocolate. Could he be wrong, could it be for something else? Ahmadi and her Iranian bosses, the Chinese, the bumbling Guatemalans...would they go to all this trouble to make a new diet pill. Could they all be wrong?

And Skip – they might be arguing, but in her heart, she knew he wouldn't knowingly put her, Kuul, and Toni in danger. But had his old agency roped him into a simple assignment that had somehow gotten out-of-hand? If he believed he was just picking up a new weight-loss ingredient, it would be just like him to treat their trip as a vacation. They had a lot to talk about if Skip was their bag man, regardless of how innocently he viewed the job. But first, she needed to get herself, Zula, and Sky out of their current fix.

Sky was also putting the pieces together. Skip and Lilac had gotten themselves mixed up in something in Mexico. Something big. She was guessing that the stranger holding the gun was the archeologist Lilac had hooked up with. The same man Skip had emailed her about. He kidnapped them to lure Skip and Kuul to the cabin, where they had no idea what they would be walking into – Johanna, her brother, their two henchmen, and any others she hadn't seen. She, Zula, and now Lilac, were the bait. And nothing good ever happened to bait.

"The only part I can't figure," Stephens mused, "is why the Chinese and Iranians are so desperate to attain the formula? The Iranians keep their women sealed in bulky, oversized burkas. They aren't interested in commercial secrets pertaining to the cosmetic and weight-loss industries. The Chinese, on-the-other-hand, would steal a new recipe for baby food, but they wouldn't stage a military operation to do it. Neither of them would risk international sanctions over this, which would be how POTUS and Congress would retaliate."

Stephens wondered if the blowhard in the White House had been running his mouth about the *big deal* he and his good friend in Guatemala were cooking up. There had to be a leak somewhere. The information had been misinterpreted. That was the only explanation that made sense. He smiled, thinking about the growing international interest in the formula. *Why* didn't really matter. His Japanese suitors had money, but not like China. China was the new economic lion. They would pay a premium just to beat everyone else.

"Regardless of why they want the vessel, their interest means a larger payday," he said, thinking aloud.

Zula Ballsy chuckled, "Peckerhead, you better hope those Chinese and Iranian boys negotiate in dollars and not lead. And that's after you deal with my tenant, who can be one sour cuss when he's upset."

"Shut up! Just remember who has the guns to your heads," Stephens snapped, hearing a nervousness in his voice that hadn't been there before. The old flapper was right, this might not be as easy as he had planned.

He backed out the doorway and slammed the door. Lilac heard the bolt slide, locking them in.

Hoot had been stewing for over an hour. What was he supposed to do with the Guatemalans, Gomez and Salamandor? With their service weapons drawn, shouting orders in pidgin Spanish, he and Officer Dickie had marched both men into a holding cell after discovering their military background. Dickie had searched for the key while Hoot had kept their hands pressed against the concrete blocks. The little one screaming about uranium and Semtex the entire time; his boss cursing him in Spanish. They hadn't broken any laws, but this had all the makings of a terrorist plot.

"Officer Dickie!" Chief Hooton bellowed from his office, his bad eye twirling like the baton of a Scorpion High majorette. Guatemalans, Mexican Federales, Arabs...his stomach had joined his eye on its circuitous journey. The beans from his lunch burrito were jumping inside like a bag of Orville Redenbacher popcorn in a microwave. What else could go wrong?

Dickie ran into his Chief's office, notepad in hand. International conspiracies were complicated. "Right here, Chief. I've got the number for Border Patrol," he said, shuffling the papers. "Whoops, must be back at my desk."

"Don't bother. Sounds like those boys are set to bomb something. That's outside Border's jurisdiction."

"CIA, Chief?"

Hoot snorted, which led to coughing and spitting up a spoonful of undigested beans in his half-empty coffee cup. Just the thought of being interviewed by government spooks gave him heartburn. If this was some secret shit, he and Dickie could end up locked in the basement of Langley staring at a light bulb.

"Another cup of coffee, Chief?"

The tiny bell above the door to the station began jingling and didn't stop. "Jesus H.," Hoot moaned, "Sounds like a goddamn parade. Go see who it is, Dickie. And it better not be Big Bob and Steel Calves with reinforcements complaining about tourists defecating on the trails again. If it is, turn them around and march them right out of the office. Sedona PD is not doing any more poop patrols because of Kempdinger. That woman's one step away from my arresting her for harassment. You tell her just that, word for word."

Before Dickie was out of his chair, three men with mirrored sunglasses, dark blue windbreakers, and navy ball caps emblazoned with FBI stormed into the Chief's office. The lead agent threw a thick stack of paperwork in front of Hoot, "You the Chief?"

Hoot nodded.

"These are warrants from the U.S. Attorney General authorizing the confiscation of your computers, files, and the temporary sealing of your offices."

"Hoot, maybe it's anthrax instead of uranium," Dickie said.

The federal agent ignored him. "There are also warrants for your two prisoners, Hernando Gomez and Chuuy Salamandor. We are taking them into federal custody," J. Edgar said matter-of-factly, throwing more paperwork on the Chief's desk. "Both warrants are issued by Executive Order from the Office of the White House." The agent glanced at Hoot's bald head and smiled, "We should be out of your hair within an hour. Questions?"

Hoot opened his mouth–

"Outstanding work, Chief. We appreciate your cooperation," the agent said, motioning for his men carrying packing boxes to begin with Hoot's laptop and printer. "The key to your holding cell," he finished, holding out his palm.

Dickie fished in his pocket, pulling out a set of keys attached to a copper cutout of Snoopy Rock. He looked at Hoot for permission. The agent didn't wait, plucking the dangling gaggle of keys from his hand.

Ten minutes later, Hoot and Dickie watched as eight agents, three with moving dollies, carted the department's computers, phones, and boxes of files to three idling, unmarked cargo vans. J. Edgar and another agent led Gomez and Salamandor, handcuffed, to an unmarked sedan. The last words they heard were Chuuy's, "I beg you *señor*, *por favor*, do not waterboard me, *mi* bladder *está* weak. Lupe and your *niños*, cousin, what about..." Their heads bent by the agents, both Guatemalans were shoved into the rear seat. J. Edgar walked back and handed Hoot a receipt in the parking lot, then got in the sedan and drove away.

"If I live to be a hundred!" Dickie exclaimed, back in Hoot's office. "They should be working for Mayflower."

Hoot had a bottle of Cuervo Classic on his empty desk and was pouring double shots into plastic coffee cups. They had taken the Keurig and ceramic mugs; the tequila he'd hidden in his spare boots. Ingesting alcoholic substances on duty was against policy, and it was unprofessional to drink with his officers, but right now he didn't give a root tootin' fart about procedure.

"That will be seventy years after the mayor fires me. Right after the emergency city council meeting authorizing my termination. Yours too, I'm sure. What the *hell* just happened?"

"The FB–" Dickie began, quickly shutting his mouth as Hoot's bulging eyes bore into him. Dickie cleared his throat, summoning his courage, "Chief...uhhh...they took all the files...*all* of them."

Hoot's bad eye shot toward his file cabinet, both drawers were open, even the metal dividing bands were gone. They had taken everything, including his personal files containing several sensitive records – investigations on secret developer agreements with councilmembers, squashed D.U.I reports on important citizens, including the mayor, hookers at a Chamber mixer, a record of arrest for indecent exposure by...that one he really hoped didn't get out. Those files had saved his ass more than a few times. Who knew what the feds would do with them, probably turn them over to the State Bureau of Investigation. That's all he needed. Hoot knew he had to do something, but what...*the Mexican feds had implicated Skip Rhodes in this mess.*

"What are we going to do, Chief?" Dickie knew what was in the files.

Hoot answered, "We're going to start with Zula Ballsy and check out the Sands. We need to find Rhodes and Kuul, see if they're back from their trip. They seem to be in the middle of this shitfest, which wouldn't be the first time. Break out the Kevlar...for the Semtex...God knows what those boys are mixed up with. Good thing they were in the trunk, the fuckers emptied out our storeroom and locker."

36

POSITIONING

IT WAS KUUL WHO SUGGESTED THEY GO THE BACK WAY TO SKIP'S CABIN. After crossing the creek, he led them through the woods, paralleling an established trail by a hundred yards. No sense announcing their arrival. Avoiding the path from Zula's lodge might not make a difference, but it seemed safer than charging into a fight like a bull into a bullring. And his friend was in a very bullish mood.

The merry gang of rescuers numbered four: Kuul, Skip, Daria Ahmadi, and Zing Hu. Kuul insisted on first taking Toni to the walk-in clinic in Sedona. He had cleaned and dressed her wound at the trailer, pressing a washcloth over the small hole and wrapping it tight with two straps from a backpack. Not ideal, but good enough for a short time. The bleeding had stopped, and the next step was removing the shrapnel. Toni hadn't asked him to stay. She understood his commitment to a friend, and that asking him to choose would only make his going harder. It was a lousy way to end their trip and he hoped their journey could continue. That would be up to her.

After the clinic, they stopped at Lilac's apartment. Skip made that decision – firepower from the ex-cop and firearms trainer's gun locker. Zing had reluctantly returned Skip and Daria's pistols but refused to loan them any heavier weapons. The Chinese agent was not happy about the Beretta 12-gauge tactical shotgun Skip had chosen to go with his Colt. Ahmadi picked a customized SIG P210 with a two-tone black and chrome finish, saying it was pretty. She also strapped on a double holster hanging in the cabinet, Lilac's SIG on her left and her old dependable on her right. Sam Peckinpah would have been proud; they were a wild bunch.

While at Lilac's, Ahmadi and Zing developed a plan of attack. Skip had been a ball of tension raring to go, arguing for an in-their-face, break-the-door-down, bust-their-head approach. Kuul had let them talk, knowing things rarely went as planned when his friend was involved. A clever, strategic, well-choreographed battle plan wasn't his style when threatened. There would not be any negotiating, Kuul knew that much.

The final plan was for Skip to approach his cabin alone, with Zing and Ahmadi tactically situated to cover the front door and porch. Kuul was to cover the rear. Skip was to broker a deal, negotiate terms, and scout the number, position, and strength of Stephen's team. He would be playing a high stakes game of poker without the vessel, bluffing with an empty hand against Stephen's three queens. Skip had unconvincingly nodded in agreement at each point. The Iranian woman had studied him closely but had not pushed.

Kuul knew better. His friend had his own plan; make them adapt to his way in the field amidst the chaos. Zing and Ahmadi were both professionals. That was worrisome. Zing had his own agenda and saving their friends was secondary. They were expendable as long as he acquired the formula. Ahmadi's motives were cloudier. His friends weren't her first priority either, but might she be torn between her duty and Skip? How strong was their connection? Kuul knew there had been a woman in his past, but that was the past. Could she be counted on today?

"We need to be ready!" Zula said, lowering her voice. "The boys will find us, and they'll need our help."

After Stephens locked the door, the three women had blankly stared at each other hoping one of them had some kind of an idea. Stuck in the room, their options weren't good. Sky wandered to the window. They could break it; it was a small opening, but they could squeeze through. She and Zula had discussed it before, deciding the risk was too great. The noise would alert their guards, and Roid had been in the front yard and would have seen them before they hit the ground.

Sky could see into the woods, but not far. The sun had dropped below the tops of the trees and shadows made everything black farther in. Rays of filtered sunlight lit the ground in places like a spotlight on a stage. If they could make the shadows – maybe she or Lilac should try the window now? Roid was back inside, she could hear him arguing with Lloyd.

"What if all three of us ram the door at the same time?" Zula suggested.

"And then what?" Lilac said, shaking her head. "You're right about Skip and Kuul, though. They will find us. We need to get out of this room, but we need to *stay* out. Getting into a fight we'll lose won't help. What if we–"

"Bathroom?" Sky said, guessing what she was thinking. "We tried that. They won't fall for it again."

"Not what I was thinking. That would just get one of us out and not for long." Lilac had another idea. "He wants a Mayan vessel… let's give it to him. Or at least convince him that we can."

Sky wanted another shot at Johanna Mosby…woman on woman. She had a feel for her now. Mosby was a predictable mauler who relied on overpowering her foe. With maulers, you use their strength against them. The woman telegraphed her moves, relying on brute force and the weight of her momentum. She was addicted to her own power. The next time they tangled, and they would, Sky would be ready. It would end differently.

Sky continued gazing out the window, planning how she would finesse Johanna, given another chance. She'd start with a cartwheel move off the wall and...*movement...entering a sunlit spot...bodies... Kuul, and Skip was right behind him!* Kuul saw her in the window and motioned toward the back of the cabin. He held up two fingers, pointing at himself and Skip.

Sky whispered to Lilac, "If you know a way out of here...now would be a good time. The boys are here...outside. I think they plan on coming in the back."

Lilac and Zula crowded her at the window. Kuul repeated his motions, this time ending with five fingers in the air – five minutes. Lilac raised her hands and spread her fingers, emphatically pumping her palms, the universal sign to hold.

Stephens was tired of waiting, especially with his present company. Sitting around and just letting things happen went against his nature. There was no better way to lose control than to give others the time to grab it. In this isolated cabin, he was lacking eyes and ears on the outside. That was his mistake. Beginning in Mexico, he should have deployed additional assets to back him up, to keep tabs of Rhodes and his team when he couldn't. He was giving the guide too much time. Why hadn't he sent the pictures of the Mayan vessel? Johanna was clear about the cost if he didn't. His growing uneasiness was a warning.

"Get Lloyd off the couch and post him out front, on the porch," he ordered Roid, who had found a bag of stale potato chips. He had emptied them into a bowl and was fishing for those with a crunch. Roid looked at him with contempt, spitting what he didn't like into a metal pan.

"There's nothing but deer and skunks out there. Why bother?"

"Because I said so!" Stephens barked. The idiot was an obstinate child. You cannot ask them; you have to tell them. He didn't need to explain himself.

"Why not Jerry?" Roid grumbled, wiping his hands on his pants. His wrestling buddy, Lloyd, could use a break. "Send him, he can use the fresh air."

Jerry was in the living room with an aching head, nursing his battered nose. Ballsy had done a number on him. "I can't even breathe," he moaned, throwing a blood-soaked rag at Roid.

"Now! And you just volunteered," Johanna said to Roid. She had heard Stephen's order and came into the kitchen. Bored, she would like nothing better than for Roid to keep arguing. Not finishing things with Sky had left her unfulfilled. One less hostage wouldn't make a difference. Stephens had just been letting her know who was in control. "And go to the backyard instead of the porch, in those trees where you are out of sight. We can keep an eye out front."

Roid threw the pan in the sink, "Can't be any worse than in here. These chips suck. One of you generals should have thought about food."

Johanna stared at Stephens, noting the cloud of booze as he stared back. The Bombay gin bottle was half empty. The junk had made him run his mouth. Playing peacock to their captives earlier had served no purpose. He had always been too cocky. Now he was making mistakes. It had been a mistake to leave Rhodes alone, a mistake to not get rid of the redhead, a mistake to hide out in this cabin, and a mistake to not secure their perimeter. When this was over, she would make sure he didn't make any more. She had overheard his bragging to Williams. Getting the vessel was the key. Once she had that...well, she had never needed men.

Johanna also thought it was a mistake keeping the women locked in the bedroom. Rhodes and his Indian friend were not following instructions. With each minute that passed, they were more likely to show up unannounced. This was Rhode's place; they were in his playground. If that happened, having the hostages close could dissuade him from any rash moves.

"Rhodes should have contacted us by now," Johanna said, standing over Stephens. Roid had disappeared out back, and the other two babies were busy nursing their wounds.

Stephens knew Johanna resented his lead. Hell, she resented men. She was smart and aggressive. He knew she was just biding her time. But right now, she was a tool he needed. He could have tried buying her off, making her a partner in his deal. She was no more loyal to her employer than he was. But sharing wasn't what wolves did, and they were both wolves.

"We need to bring the women out," Johanna said, "to keep them close. If he shows up, it will be better having them between us."

"He doesn't know we're here."

"This is his place, eventually he'll show up. We should have held them somewhere else."

And so it begins, Stephens thought. The challenge. One lone wolf turning against another. He wondered when she would make her play. *Power*, that is what she wanted – he understood her all too well. He thought it over, sipping his gin. He slid a glass toward her, but she scoffed at it, turned it over, and slid it back to him. Not yet, he thought...not yet. Jerry was standing in the archway between the living room and kitchen, behind his boss. Could he count on him? He doubted it, none of them were honorable people.

"Whatever you want," Stephens said. "You two let them out but tie all three. The young one's a fighter, Williams is an ex-cop, and that old bitch is crazy as hell. They are your responsibility."

Johanna kept her eyes on Stephens. "Jerry, send Lloyd to the porch, then bring the women out here, and keep them together."

LEMON AND EUCALYPTUS OILS

SKIP WAS TIRED OF THE SIGNALING. WHY THE HELL DID LILAC want them to wait? All systems were *GO*. Daria and Zing were in position, covering the front and sides of the cabin. He was going in the back – alone, which he hadn't yet told Kuul. They needed to go now before the kidnappers spotted them. Waiting would only multiply what could go wrong.

He ended the gesturing by emphatically holding up ten fingers – ten minutes – *get ready, I'm coming in ten minutes*. Lilac nodded and all three women disappeared into the room.

Lilac's plan was to tell Stephens that she knew where the Mayan vessel was hidden. It was a ruse to get them out of the locked room. But before she called out, the door opened. A grimacing new face with a swollen nose and golf ball sized lump on his head held a Browning automatic pointed at her midsection.

"His name's Jerry," Sky said from behind her, "a real snake."

Skip and Kuul had crept farther back into the shadows, moving inside the tree line until they could see the back door. They were expecting to spot a sentry on the landing, but the coast was clear.

"Okay Kemo, what are you planning?" Kuul knew it would be different from what Ahmadi had outlined.

Skip was holding the Beretta shotgun, barrel down, the Colt tucked in the back of his khakis. He had a plan, sort of, in his head. There were at least five marks inside the cabin – if they hadn't been reinforced – the four Daria had seen and Stephens. Given his limited intel and mission prep, he decided on a direct approach. The less complicated the better – he liked uncomplicated. He was reasonably certain they wouldn't shoot him on sight –they wanted the cup. If they did shoot first and he made it inside, he calculated his chances at fifty-fifty. He'd played this game with worse.

He answered Kuul without taking his eyes off the cabin, "With any luck they won't see me coming. I'm planning to walk across the yard and knock. Then we will talk. They are probably sitting in there waiting for the pictures we were supposed to send. Anybody spots me and shoots, I go in hot and do what I've done before," he said, coldly.

"What about the girls? If you start blasting that scattergun…"

"They're locked in the bedroom. They would not have been signaling us from the window if there was a guard with them. Once I'm inside, no one is getting to that door."

Kuul saw too many ways this could go badly, for his friend and the girls. Skip could be shot in the yard. Or Stephens might not even open the door – he wouldn't. Or there could be an armed guard just outside the bedroom door who would reach the girls before his friend. Or Kemo could miss; all it would take was one of the captors left alive. Daria and Zing offered no help from their positions. All they could do was catch anyone fleeing out the front – *after-the-fact*. There were too many variables, too much risk.

"I'm going with you," Kuul said.

"I need you back here in case something goes wrong. In case I go down. We cannot trust Zing or Daria with protecting the girls."

"I'm going with you," Kuul said, forcefully. "They are my friends too. You will need me inside backing you up."

Skip stared at his friend for a moment and knew his mind was set. There was no arguing with him nor time to do so. Any second, Stephens or his team could get lucky and spot them or Zing or Daria. Surprise was all he had – and the pump action Beretta.

"Here, take this," Skip said, handing Kuul the Colt. He had refused to arm himself from Lilac's locker. His friend did not like guns; he had never seen him use one. The men and woman inside would not be similarly conflicted.

"You know holding a gun makes you far more likely to be shot," Kuul said, eyeing the weapon.

"Tell that to Stephens and his gang, I'm sure they'll hold their fire."

Kuul took the gun, tucking it behind his belt.

"You ready?"

Kuul nodded. They left the protection of the tree line. Fifty feet of open space stretched ahead of them. The clearing had been made by the old ranch foreman who built the cabin. Skip had added another ten feet and a dozen butterfly bushes to attract humming-birds, but nothing that would stop a bullet. His friend held his shot-gun level, shoulder high, targeted on the back door. Kuul, the Colt still safely tucked away, focused on the window.

Ten feet – seconds to the door. Kuul pulled the Colt and held it low. He had never felt so exposed or faced a longer journey. He doubted his friend planned on knocking. No faces had appeared in the door glass or window. So far, so good...

They both heard the distinctive click of a pistol from behind. *Shit!*

The buzzing around Hoot's head had been non-stop. The path along the creek to Rhode's cabin was infested with mosquitoes, wasps, biting green flies, gnats, and every other police hating insect known to man. They had been waiting for him.. He thought he had pre-pared appropriately, spreading a homemade concoction of lemon and eucalyptus oils over his bare skin. Instead, he smelled like an Australian pound cake, which sweat bees were finding irresistible.

Spike, Zula Ballsy's javelina, was also following them. Dickie was giving it Skittles from a bag stashed in his belt, where his radio should have been. He tossed a green candy to the pig, who let it land on his snout and then flipped it into the air catching it in his mouth. "It could be worse," he said, trying to console his boss, "At least there aren't koalas here." The Chief looked like a cartoon of Winnie the Pooh after he had poked a hive. Yellow and black bees were swarming him like coyotes on a wounded cat.

Hoot had hoped to find Rhodes at Zula's. That's where the guide spent most of his time when he wasn't leading a tour. And wherever Rhodes laid his hat, there was a good chance of finding Balthazar. If their Mexican escapade had caused the FBI raid, he intended on getting some answers. He needed facts and a good explanation before meeting with the mayor.

Ballsy's Sands Retreat had been a ghost town. Not finding the old showgirl or Sky minding the store was unusual. He had been counting on avoiding the gauntlet of insects to Rhode's cabin, but no such luck.

"Chief, what's the plan if Skip and Kuul are at his cabin?"

Officer Dickie wished they had brought sack lunches from Basha's. For his money, this was one of the prettiest sections of Oak Creek. The sycamores were thicker, and the ranchers had built a series of check dams to pool the water. Time had collapsed the dams, but the stones had created a series of small waterfalls. And if you waded out into the middle, which was easy to do, there was a postcard view of the backside of Cathedral Rock. The same view every hotel in town had hanging over their front desk.

"Just follow my lead this time," Hoot said, swatting a dozen bees and a persistent wasp off his hat while picking up his step, hoping the little bastards would give up the chase after they turned away from the water. "No more heroics like our last visit. I haven't forgotten that you allowed the perps to get away. If you'd followed procedure, we might have had some answers by now. They are still out there somewhere."

"You thinking they are involved somehow?"

"Let's don't put the cart before the horse, but there could be a connection. Too many odd things are going on. Stay alert and don't get ahead of me."

"10-4 Hoot. Maybe we should have brought back-up?"

Hoot had mulled that over when no one was home at the Sands, he didn't like how quiet it had been. But with the Mountain Bike Jamboree, Hummingbird Festival, the premiere of the new Nicolas Cage movie at the art theater, and California schools on break, it would have meant authorizing overtime. He had already authorized double shifts this month for the Wine Festival, Spiritual Healing Gathering, and Cinco de Mayo. He had enough troubles with the mayor and council without a blown department budget halfway through the fiscal year.

"Just keep your eyes open, Dickie. We just want to ask the boys what they know about the murder in Mexico. We're not planning on arresting anyone."

Officer Dickie spied their turn ahead. A large sycamore marked a side trail that led to a worn set of railroad steps. From there, it was no more than ten minutes to Rhodes's cabin. Compliments of the water, the sycamores and cottonwoods grew farther away from the creek than in most areas. Scrub oak, manzanita, and low-growing junipers filled in the gaps. A hundred yards farther, he could see the late afternoon sun shining into a grove where the cabin rested. The spot couldn't be more peaceful, Dickie thought.

Spike trotted ahead, seeking his human friend and whatever treats might be waiting.

BABY RATTLES

THE CLICK SKIP HEARD WAS THE SOUND OF AN AUTOMATIC pistol. His trainers had taught him to recognize the cocking of a weapon, even in a busy street setting. His final exam had been in a jammed souk in Marrakesh with dozens of shouting merchants luring clueless tourists with gold jewelry and indigo blue bolts of silk. There, it had been a tiny, metallic tick that was out of place. Here, in the woods, it sounded like a metal hitch dropped on a trailer ball.

His mind put the pieces together in a millisecond. Stephens had a lookout in the woods. He had been too focused on the cabin to hear someone coming from behind. His front is where he expected the threat to materialize. He had grown lazy. Acting on instinct, he shoved Kuul to his right and dove left, bringing the Beretta in front and below him as he fell. Red dust puffed between them, then the crack of the man from behind's pistol. Skip pumped his gun and fired. The man was big, but the impact to his chest knocked him off his feet. He fell backwards and didn't move after hitting the ground.

"This part of your plan?" Kuul yelled.

"Unexpected," Skip answered, jumping up and charging the back door.

He covered the last few steps in seconds. Kuul was right behind him with his Colt drawn. It was his door, and he knew what it was capable of withstanding. The hinges and lock he'd reinforced, but the door itself he'd left unchanged. Holding the Beretta tightly in both hands, he didn't slow down, throwing his left shoulder hard into the old wood. It splintered into pieces, and he rolled into the kitchen.

Daria had worked her way closer to the front porch of the cabin. Zing, across the clearing, concealed amongst the low-growing, wild shrubs, was also edging closer. She was sure Tripp wouldn't follow their plan; he had barely listened. He was a cowboy, and she knew that. He did not trust her or the Chinese. When the time came, he would do this his way. All she could do was put herself in place to cover his moves...and to capture the Mayan vessel. She prayed she wouldn't be faced with choosing between the two.

Daria also knew better than to trust Zing. The Chinese agent could have lied about calling off his team. In these thick woods, his men could be trailing behind, waiting for his signal. Zing Hu was a patriot, a patriot charged with protecting his country from their enemies; in that, they were no different. But unlike Daria, he had no *personal* reasons to keep any of them, inside or outside the cabin, alive. He would not face any crisis of conscience in doing whatever he had to do or killing whoever he had to kill. He was dangerous, more so than the team inside, a wolf hiding amid the lambs. She would not hesitate to eliminate the threat if necessary.

Stephens had stationed a lookout on the porch. Daria hoped Tripp had slowed down enough to look for another out back. The man was limping, pacing the porch, stupidly watching the clearing instead of the woods, which is how anyone with half a brain would scout the cabin. Putting him down would be easy but would sound the alarm. With Tripp approaching the back door, she could not risk alerting those inside. She hoped Zing was thinking the same, but doubted he cared.

Daria crept closer, using the red-blooming bushes to move from one tree to another. Their perfumed scent contrasted with the bitter taste of nerves in her mouth. Once Tripp made his move, she needed to get to the cabin fast. Zing was already less than ten feet from his end of the porch. If he took out the guard and crashed inside, she needed to be with him. He would not discriminate with his shooting.

Daria crawled the last few feet. Scanning beneath the porch floor, she saw Zing crouched in the front, beside the stairs. She knew she needed to make the first move. The guard was just above her now. She waited for him to turn and walk away, planning to scale the short railing while his back was turned...

She didn't get the chance – *a pistol shot rang from behind the cabin, followed by a blast from Tripp's shotgun.*

Daria fought the impulse to charge around back. The next thing she heard was a loud crash, and then shouting from inside. A man and unknown woman began yelling, and the red head, whose voice she recognized, screamed, "NO!" The guard on the porch ran toward the door. Zing had risen and was racing around the steps.

Daria had no choice now, she stepped onto the edge of the porch floor and vaulted over the railing. The guard saw her and fired a wild shot, his bullet harmlessly flying into the woods behind her. Daria crouched behind a metal glider, leveling her gun, aiming center mass...

Lilac watched in slow motion horror as Skip rolled into the kitchen, a Beretta pump action pointing in front of him...her Beretta! The man Sky called Jerry was standing next to her and froze. But the woman, Johanna, had her gun out, sweeping it toward Skip.

"NO!" Lilac and Sky both screamed at the same time.

Stephens jumped behind the woman, his back to hers, pulling his Ruger pocket pistol. His eyes met Lilac's, his surprised look quickly turning into a smirk. He pointed the snub barrel at her and shouted back over his shoulder.

"RHODES, YOU FIRE AND SHE GOES DOWN! COUNT ON IT!"

Skip didn't fire.

"Where's the Indian?" Stephens said, gathering himself. "Johanna, shoot the asshole if he moves a finger!"

Lilac knew Kuul couldn't be far behind. Was there anyone else with them? Jerry recovered his senses and grasped her arm, wrenching her elbow behind her back as he moved behind her. He shoved his Browning into her side, jabbing the barrel into her ribs.

"Keep her covered," Stephens ordered. "If he shoots, kill the other two."

Zula took a step toward Jerry, "Screw you and your tequila swilling, loose-legged, whore of a momma!" she spat. Sky grabbed her and was struggling to hold her back.

Stephens laughed, "We need somebody alive to lead us to the vessel...but it doesn't have to be you." He turned to Rhodes, who still had his shotgun pointed at Johanna. A twitch from either and they would both fire. "Put it down, Rhodes. You might get her, but you and at least two of your friends will be dead before she hits the floor."

Skip didn't respond.

"PUT THE GUN DOWN!" Stephens repeated, using an irritatingly reasonable tone of voice.

"You first," Kuul said, stepping into the kitchen with his Colt pointing at the archeologist. "Or add yourself to your body count."

Daria could not allow the guard to get inside the cabin. The window was open, and she could hear enough from inside to understand there was a standoff, any more firepower on one side could prove critical. *She* needed to swing the pendulum, not the guard.

Lloyd had his hand on the door but turned as he had heard Zing's foot hit the squeaky second step. The Chinese agent brought his pistol up to fire, but Daria beat him to it. She saw the guard's bandaged leg and shot him in the same spot, expecting him to collapse. The man surprised her and stumbled into the cabin. She leapt in after him, a Sig in each hand, shifting left and ducking behind a ragged sofa. Zing was behind her and moved to the right, tipping over a flimsy desk.

With Tripp lying prone on the floor, his shotgun on the female captor, and Kuul covering Stephens, Daria aimed her guns at the man holding the red head. Zing was coldly surveying the situation, his pistol moving between the bodies in the room, including Tripp and his Indian friend. He was clearly still calculating who he would target, if shooting started.

The cabin was deathly still, except for the big guard sprawled on the floor moaning, his leg bleeding, pleading with the woman for help. No one had the upper hand. The centers of attention were Tripp and Stephens. Everyone else had a bit part in the scene. How this played out was in their hands. Daria did not like it, but it was what it was.

Without letting go of his toy gun, Stephens raised his hands in a calming gesture, "We need to hold up a minute and talk. A shootout in the corral isn't to anyone's advantage. There's a deal to be made."

"The deal is you turn over the Mayan vessel and formula to the Chinese government," Zing hissed. "America isn't to be trusted, not with the crazy warlord sitting in your White House." Zing aimed his pistol at Stephens, "The People's Republic insists."

"Is the People's Republic prepared to pay for it?"

"That's not going to happen," Skip growled from the floor, speaking for the first time. "Zing, don't make this situation worse than it is," he threatened. "We told you what the formula is – you don't need it."

"Unfortunately, you Americans, especially your leader, have a well-documented history of lying. The People's Republic isn't in a position to blindly believe your version of the story...*that's* not going to happen. We made a deal. If you're backing out, maybe I should deal with this man," Zing said, indicating Stephens.

Daria was leery of the turn this was taking. China's acquiring the formula to a new biological weapon was only slightly better than it being in the hands of the Americans. She would be facing a hard decision if the Chinese agent turned on Tripp and his friends,. The end game for Iran was making sure neither of them held the keys to Armageddon. But she was getting the sense that Stephens was in it for himself, not his country. He seemed more than willing to sell the vessel to the highest bidder if he could get it. MOIS had not briefed her on that possibility. There were an endless number of bad players in the world with money. Maybe the Chinese were the best of only bad options.

Daria stared at Tripp. His blood ran through their son. He needed her help, and her heart told her she could not sacrifice him now.

"Zing!" Daria barked, pointing the red head's borrowed Sig at him. "This man doesn't have the vessel to sell you, and Rhodes isn't willingly turning it over to anyone. Choose whose side you are on, and let's get on with this. Our two countries can settle matters later...if one or the other of us are no longer available."

Sky was confused. She realized that she and Zula were afterthoughts to what was happening. She didn't care. While the representatives of the world's governments were bickering, she had been edging closer to Johanna, who was focused on Skip's shotgun. Zula was the only one who noticed. Stephens and the olive-skinned woman were paying closer attention to the Chinese man. And Jerry was keeping his eye on Lilac. Something bad was going down soon, and she wanted to get to Johanna. She had a score to settle.

"ENOUGH WITH THIS BULLSHIT!" Skip shouted, rising from his prone position.

Johanna glanced at Stephens for direction, questioning whether to shoot the guide. His having a shotgun aimed at her was not part of her plan. Everyone else, including herself, held pistols. In close quarter firefights, adrenalin pumping, combatants didn't always act as expected. Under stress, handguns weren't as accurate as in the movies. The blast radius from a shotgun, however...

Stephens shook his head at her. Rhodes could be the one person who knew the location of the vessel. Killing him could be a problem. Johanna was a wild card, though. She always had been, there was no telling whether she would obey him or not. If she didn't, all hell was about to break loose.

With everyone focused on Rhodes, Stephens silently shuffled behind Lilac. Jerry still had his gun against her ribs. It was a shame, Stephens thought, that she hadn't succumbed to his charms back in Mexico. He wouldn't be in this situation if he had gotten the vessel there. He still couldn't understand why the Chinese and Iranians cared about a formula for the next generation of fen-phen? Going to this extreme didn't make sense...*unless*...unless he had been played by POTUS and Stinckner. Was that possible? The vessel might be worth more than he thought.

Skip cautiously entered his living room, moving parallel to Johanna, putting the woman between him and Zing. He reached a small flatscreen television sitting atop a two-shelf bookcase and stopped, holding the Beretta low, not yet ready for a confrontation.

Stephens slid farther behind Lilac and grabbed the old show-girl who was to his right, shoving his gun in her back and pulling her beside him as additional cover. "Rhodes, you have to the count of five."

Skip was holding the remote to his television and glanced at Kuul who nodded.

"The vessel! NOW!" Stephens shouted. "Your girlfriend will be next!"

"Which one?" Lilac defiantly jeered.

"Shut up," Jerry nervously hissed, jabbing his gun in her side.

"NOW RHODES!" Stephens yelled again, louder.

"Kemo, I'm giving them the vessel, our friends are more important," Kuul said, untying the rawhide prayer bag attached to his belt. "Whatever it is, it is not worth dying over, brother. This needs to end."

Kuul tossed the bag at the archeologist's feet. Stephens nudged Jerry, who eased his gun off Lilac to pick it up and hand it to him. They were both holding the rawhide when it shook...*then it rattled.*

"Goddamn Indian!" Jerry cried as a four-foot diamondback fell from the prayer bag, coiling on the wooden floor, its ringtail stiff and clattering. The snake's triangular-shaped head was poised to strike.

Except for Skip and Kuul, every eye in the room was riveted on the rattlesnake. Skip tapped 6385▸▸234Play on the remote – the code for the C4 explosives he had placed in the trees around the perimeter of his cabin....

39

BOOM!

CHIEF HOOTON AND OFFICER DICKIE HAD MADE THEIR WAY TO Rhode's cabin. There was little doubt this was a wild goose chase. Hoot didn't even know for sure if Rhodes and Kuul were back in Sedona. They could still be in Cancun with Williams and Wathetewa, soaking up the sun and slurping frothy margaritas. At least the bees had backed off. Next time, Hoot thought, he would remember to bring a fogger. That would teach the buggers.

"His cabin is up these railroad ties and through that clearing. I don't see anyone around, maybe they are inside. No smoke or noise." Officer Dickie stated. He was studying the setting like he was Kit Carson scouting a Navajo rancheria. Their last visit was still fresh in his mind.

If Dickie started talking about tracks and put his ear to the ground, he might shoot him, Hoot swore to himself, swatting a fat, green fly intent on biting a patch of unclaimed flesh.

"We'll find out when we knock on his door," Hoot said, sarcastically. "I'll follow you...Sieber." Al Sieber was another famous Chief of Scouts during the Apache Wars. Hopefully, the flies would choose a new victim if Dickie led the way.

The path led them through a thick stand of low growing junipers. Hoot spotted a spider web, the setting sun highlighting the silver threads. A fellow blue blood, he thought, taking satisfaction at the yellow and green suckers captured in its trap. Hopefully, a SWAT team of bats were dispatching the other creepy–

Hoot's head jerked and his bad eye spun out of control at the pop and boom of two guns. *Target practice? With a shotgun?* Rhodes better have his license handy...

"Shots fired!" Dickie yelled and began running toward the gunfire.

Young hotshot officers, Hoot cursed under his breath, he needed to brush up their training regimen. But he had no choice other than to follow. They entered the clearing in time to see a woman with long black hair and a man charge through the front door. The man looked Asian.

"Hold your position!" Hoot hollered. "Those two are armed!"

His good eye locked on the door expecting...well, he didn't know what to expect. His bad eye was bouncing like a cow stuck on an electric fence. The rest of the clearing looked clear, no bogies, bad customers, no Rhodes or Kuul either, no swarms of heat-seeking insects. But that could change in a hurry. The gunshots...the way the two unknowns had charged the cabin...something was happening inside. The boys had not been shooting at June bugs.

"Officer Dickie, get your ass behind one of those bigger cottonwoods and call for back up," Hoot ordered, finding his own tree. "We are not crossing that clearing until we know what's going–"

For a brief instant, the sycamore Hoot was behind trembled... before it exploded thirty feet over his head. His lazy eye stared upward as a ball of fire erupted, and the trunk cracked. The top third of the old tree seemed to disappear in bright blue flame and smoke, the trunk hesitating like a wobbling bowling pin, before crashing into the opening. A series of treetop explosions occurred in sequence, Hoot counted eight, dominoing along the periphery of the clearing from both sides. He stared at Dickie, the gun in his hand shaking; his tree was still standing but a large cottonwood ten feet to his left had suffered the same fate as Hoot's sycamore.

"The Semtex," Dickie hollered through the din of concussions.

In less than ten seconds, the clearing was ablaze with burning, toppled trees, and dark smoke. Surprisingly, Hoot thought he smelled almonds, the same odor he remembered in his mother's crescent-shaped Christmas cookies.

"Call for backup! Now!"

"No signal, Chief!"

Hoot cursed – if Dickie had left the radio back in the squad car...he would be spending the rest of his brief law enforcement career patrolling backcountry trails by unicycle.

The only good news was the fires weren't growing, the flames from the downed trees were not spreading and the first of them were already dying out. There didn't seem to be much chance of their setting the woods on fire. The smoke, on the other hand, was doing just the opposite. The clearing resembled a dark, foggy battlefield from an old black-and-white war movie. Hoot could no longer see the door to the cabin; he could barely make out the edge of the porch.

Ballsy's javelina, Spike, poked its nose from a hollow spot in the ground, woofed, and charged into the smoldering fray. Stupid pig! Hoot's weak eye pivoted between Spike and the tops of trees still standing, half anticipating more explosions. During one rotation, he caught sight of Dickie Braveheart running out to back up the pig – he could forget the unicycle, he'd be on foot lugging a sixty-pound search-and-rescue pack. Nonetheless, Dickie and the pig had made his decision for him.

Hoot lumbered into the clearing, leaping over the trunk of the downed sycamore, trying to recall his training about assaulting positions in hostage situations. He was sure deploying a javelina wasn't standard operating procedure. He caught up to Dickie twenty feet from the porch and shouted, "Let the pig go in first!"

Skip had calculated the blast radius of the C4 and the best height to place the charges for maximum effect. His aim wasn't to blow up every living thing in the immediate surroundings. The noise and fireworks had been to instill shock and create a distraction. He had hoped deploying the loud and destructive pyrotechnics would never be necessary but had planned as if they were. With his past, he could never be sure who might come calling. Retribution for old sins could be a bitch.

With the shudder of the first explosion, every head in the room except Skip's, Kuul's, and the diamondback rattler's spun to the front window as the burning trees kept falling.

Stephens was backing away from the snake before the explosion. A rattlesnake's normal striking distance is half its body length, but this highly agitated, cornered snake didn't know that. He was turning back from the window when the diamondback struck, lunging, and releasing venom from its retractable fangs into the underside of his gun arm. Screaming, he dropped his baby Rutger and grabbed the snake below its head, ripping it from his punctured skin and throwing it on the floor.

Kuul rushed Jerry. The man's attention was split between the explosions outside and the snake on the floor. He saw him at the last second and raised his Browning, aiming at the charging Indian. Lilac chopped his arm from behind, kneeing him hard between his legs. The bullet hit the wood floor, splintering the soft pine wood – nothing a rug couldn't cover. Kuul punched him in the solar plexus which left him gasping for air, the gun flying from his hand.

Out the corner of her eye, Daria saw Zing readying to shoot. Tripp had made his move toward the woman called Johanna, but from Zing's angle it looked like he was attacking him. She levelled her Sig and fired, intentionally missing the Chinese man's nose by inches, the slug lodging into the fireplace mantle beside him. He dropped to a knee, swiveling toward her, and found himself facing her weapons. Neither of them fired. Daria shook her head – *not if you want to live.*

Zing lowered his gun. Now was not the time. Their score could be settled later, in another place. The Iranian's chilling stare said she understood and accepted a temporary truce.

Sky was closer to Johanna than Skip. *"She's mine,"* she mouthed to him. The bigger woman had been ignoring her. Like Jerry, the explosions and Arizona's favorite reptile had distracted her. Sky guessed she had written her off, having already beaten her once. She had choreographed her attack in her head...putting Johanna on the ground would neutralize her lower body strength. On the floor, she had a chance against the stronger woman.

Sky launched herself feet-first at the back of her knees. Johanna buckled, a shot from her gun hitting the ceiling as she crumpled. The woman threw a wayward punch around her side, hitting only air. Sky crouched behind her and jabbed her ribs as hard as she could. Johanna hunched over and fell to her knees. Ramming both elbows into her back, Sky used her weight and momentum to drive the larger woman to the ground. Grasping her gun hand, she violently yanked her muscled arm across her back until it popped. Not done, she grabbed the woman's braid, pulled her head up and slammed it against the pine floor. Johanna grunted. Sky could hear her labored breathing and the whistling coming from her fractured nose.

Sky was sitting on top of her, Johanna's belly against the floor. She felt her spinning a fraction of a second too late. The woman twisted and spun beneath her, punching the heel of her free hand into Sky's chin. The pain shocked her, but Johanna had lacked the elbow space to land a crippling blow. Sky shook it off, blocking her follow-up. But the woman's hands were free, and she crunched

Sky's arms, pinning them against her body – the woman bucked, lifting Sky off her enough to wiggle partially free.

With Johanna squirming underneath, Sky's hands came free. She began hammering the larger woman's face with negligible effect – like punching a concrete block. She knew the contest was over if the more powerful Johanna got loose, but it seemed inevitable.

"Here, try this, Honey!" Zula Ballsy said, slapping Jerry's Browning into her palm.

Sky grinned while Zula stomped on the woman's wrist, the butt of the pistol thudding against Johanna's temple. The bigger woman stopped struggling.

"You should have shot her steroid-fueled brain," Zula said, sounding a bit disappointed.

"There's duct tape in a kitchen drawer," Sky answered.

Kuul surveyed the quickly deteriorating situation. Things were happening fast. The rattlesnake had landed next to the guard who had stumbled through the door. The idiot had tried grabbing it and been bitten twice. The snake and guard were both coiled now, the snake preparing to strike again, the idiot curled into a ball and whimpering like a baby. The man with the bandaged head had bolted toward the open front door. Ahmadi and Zing were performing some kind of evil eye dance. And Stephens had run out the back door with the prayer bag, Lilac six steps behind in hot pursuit. Skip had raced after them.

DEALER'S CHOICE

HOOT WAS TAKING THE PORCH STEPS TWO AT A TIME TO KEEP UP with Ballsy's javelina. The pig was snorting and woofing and not slowing down. He had heard the old showgirl shouting from inside and was charging up San Juan Hill to the rescue. Straight into trouble.

Hoot's boot hit the porch just as an unknown, unarmed perp ran out the door, looking back over his shoulder. The man turned his bandaged head at the last second, seeing the super-sized police chief but overlooking the snarling javelina at his feet. Spike recognized him though, the same human that had shot at him. Spike jumped, jaw open, aiming for the man's balls – they weren't bacon, but meat was meat.

Jerry saw the javelina in time and hurtled over it...crashing into the giant in uniform, who had lowered his shoulder. Hoot swept him off like one of the testy gnats circling his bald dome; his hat had flown off in the blast. All it took was a shrug at the moment of impact to send the man crashing down the stairs.

"Cuff him, Dickie!" he yelled. "I'm going in! Standard procedure – remember your training! I go left, you go right and cover me! NO HERO STUFF!" Hoot stepped beside the open door, back to the wall, and checked his service weapon.

"10-4 Chief," Dickie yelled back. He'd wrapped his cuffs through the railing post and secured the perp, who was only half conscious from his fall. Racing up the stairs, he took his position to the right of the door, waiting for Hoot's next move.

Dickie stared at Hoot waiting for the signal. The Chief's good eye locked with his. Then, the bad orb began bouncing between him and the doorway. Hoot must have changed his mind, Dickie thought – he was motioning him to *GO*. He took a deep breath and charged into the room, moving to his right as instructed.

Kuul was making sure Sky and Zula had the woman secured. She was out cold but had seemed the most dangerous of the kidnappers. Lilac had run after the archeologist unarmed, but Skip had followed with the Beretta.

Ahmadi and Zing had settled their immediate differences and ran out the back door after them and the Mayan vessel. That made three guns against Stephens, including one angry, pushed-past-his-limits, former assassin turned tour guide. Kuul guessed Daria Ahmadi and Zing Hu met the same occupational profile, except for being *former*. Skip could handle Stephens; he had seen him in action. The biggest danger facing his friend was getting shot in a crossfire.

Zing was the problem. He had seen him aiming at Skip...if Ahmadi had not stopped him...

"GO! We've got Olga taken care of," Zula shouted at him. "Beijing Charlie didn't look too friendly!"

Kuul nodded, but Officer Dickie stopped him, charging into the room, dropping to a knee, and shouting, "FREEZE! SEDONA PD!" His service weapon grasped firmly in both hands, he swept the room, "ALL CLEAR!" he yelled over his shoulder.

"We're safe now, Barney," Zula said sarcastically. "HOOT, are you hiding your cowardly ass out on the porch?"

"They left through the back door," Sky said as Dickie lowered his gun. "This one's not going anywhere, but one of them ran out the front–"

"The Chief threw him down the steps," Officer Dickie said, covering for his boss...who hadn't followed him inside. He must have decided against facing the wrath of Zula Ballsy.

"For the last time – *GO!*" Zula ordered Kuul. "Dickie, go find your lost boss."

Kuul cautiously peeked out the back door. No sense recklessly running into trigger happy gunmen. The coast was clear, and he jumped down the stairs. Coming from the side of the cabin, out of sight, he heard threatening voices. The loudest was Stephens, "PUT THE GUNS DOWN OR I KILL HER RIGHT NOW! He sounded shaky and scared, the snake's venom was making him sick. A cornered animal, Kuul thought.

He hugged the back wall of the cabin, edging his way to the corner. Lilac's Colt was still in his belt. He prayed he could keep it there. All life was sacred, even bad lives. Taking life, even an enemy's life, marked and haunted the killer with the evil spirit of the dead. His Mayan ancestors with their sacrificial practices had ignored that, which helped lead to their downfall. His troubled friend, in danger around the corner, had long ignored threats to his soul.

A pistol shot shattered his hopes...nothing from a shotgun... then two screams...

The trick with the snake had been genius, and the C4 distraction had turned the tide, but neither had stopped Stephens from scooping up the bag and escaping. Skip had yelled at her to wait, but Lilac had run after him. Letting the man get away was not an option. Not in Tripp Street's world anyway.

He had raced after her, watching her and the archeologist disappear around the corner of his cabin. She wasn't thinking straight. She had charged, unarmed, after the archeologist. Skip had seen the look in her eyes. She was mad as hell, hurt, confused, and, he guessed, feeling foolish about being duped. Anyone of those affected judgement. Emotion always pushed aside reason. Even if she had stopped or hit the ground he could not have taken a shot – not with a shotgun. The spray would hit her as well. The Beretta was worthless as long as she was close, and Stephens had seen him, realizing his advantage.

Skip rounded the corner and pulled up...Stephens had his partner's Browning on Lilac. She was standing five feet from him, her back turned to Skip. Stephen's eyes were on fire from nerves, pain, and fear. Skip had seen the look before in poorly trained operatives and paper jockeys playing spook who realized too late that they were in over their heads.

"Drop the gun," Stephens tensely barked.

Lilac glanced back at Skip. Her brown eyes apologizing, telling him she was sorry, she had messed up. Whether it was for not trusting him in Mexico or for getting caught, he wasn't sure. Her will to fight was still there, but so was resignation. He didn't have a choice and laid the Beretta on the ground.

"Move away from the gun, slowly." Stephens said, motioning with his Browning for Skip to move to Lilac's right. She took a quick step toward him before he corrected, aiming at her again. "I have plenty of bullets."

The back door banged against the cabin interrupting their glares. Seconds later Daria and Zing eased around the corner, guns drawn, spreading apart as they assessed the standoff. "What do you want?" Daria said, like they were two businesspersons in a conference room negotiating a deal.

She understood the situation and that Stephens was desperate. He was becoming unhinged, and Tripp had stupidly relinquished his weapon. The Indian's bag was in Stephen's free hand. Though the man did not realize it yet, he had already lost the Mayan vessel. There was no way he was leaving with it or the formula.

But he could make acquiring it costly. Tripp and Williams were right in front of him. Daria knew who he would shoot first... the bigger threat...and men always assumed that was another man. Their being so stupid had saved her many times in the past.

"All I want is to disappear...with the vessel," Stephens answered. "It's not what you've been told. There is an inscription on the rim for a nutritional supplement – to lose weight. THAT'S ALL IT IS! If your governments think otherwise, you've been tricked by the conman in the White House. *IT'S NOT A FUCKING WEAPON! NO ONE NEEDS TO DIE TODAY!*" Stephens screamed, his panic taking control.

"Do you believe we are fools?" Zing warned him, moving slowly to his right. "You are not leaving here alive with the formula."

Skip was closer and noticed the change in Stephen's expression. The archeologist's eyelids narrowed, and a blank stare replaced the scared look...his finger was tightening against the Browning's trigger. The man had made up his mind.

"Zing," Skip yelled, but too late. The Chinese man had misread the archeologist, expecting him to back down. Stephens closed his finger instead.

Zing had a surprised look on his face as he dropped to his knees, his pistol falling from his fingers as he clutched his side where the bullet had entered. In all his service, in all the lousy, dangerous places he had operated, he had never been shot. Was this how he was to die, he wondered, growing lightheaded – in the American woods, from the hands of a...a...a nobody. It was the Iranian he had been worried about, not this nervous capitalist pig. *What would they tell his father?* MSS would not even claim his body, denying it was even him. Zing felt himself fading – they would tell his father nothing of course. Zing's eyes closed and he fainted.

Daria had been as surprised as Zing. She had misread Stephens as well. This was not how the situation had played out in her mind. Stunned, she had watched Hu collapse and been slow to react.

Stephens swung his Browning toward her, shouting, "DROP IT!"

Daria's instincts were to shoot now while she could. She had faced worse and survived. But if she lost...she knew where his next bullet would go. Tripp, her child's...

"Daria," Skip whispered, "He's too close."

Daria dropped both Sigs, never taking her eyes off Stephens. She regretted it instantly. It was an impetuous, emotional decision. Her odds of living to see her son become a man were far less now than seconds ago. Tripp no longer loved her, what they had was dead; she had killed it on their last morning in Singapore. Her heart had now made her a fool, waiting helplessly for what would happen next.

"Move beside them," Stephens ordered, again motioning with his gun.

Daria moved next to Skip. She, Tripp, and Lilac were standing in line, facing an unpredictable shooter, ten feet away, holding a gun on them.

"You can't get all three of us. One, two at the most," Skip growled.

Stephens laughed, "Bang, bang, bang," he repeated rapidly. "That's how quick it will be. Care to guess who will be–"

"*POLICE! DROP YOUR WEAPON!*" Chief Hoot Hooton bellowed from the front corner of the cabin; his service pistol fixed on Stephens.

Stephens reflexively swung his weapon toward Hoot. Lilac and Daria seized the same opportunity, springing toward him, but they had too much ground to cover.

Skip doubted Hooton would shoot. Sedona police did not have shootouts with armed kidnappers; he had been here four years, and all he'd heard of was their shooting a rabid bobcat. Deliberately killing a man was different. Things went through your head the first time. Processing them took more time than the Chief had. The quick actions of the two women also complicated his decision. Hitting Stephens and missing them would take a good shot. Unless the archeologist panicked, he had enough time to shoot Hoot before turning on Lilac and Daria.

Stephens didn't panic, sliding sideways, putting Daria between himself and the chief. Daria froze as he fired over her shoulder at Hooton, hitting him square in the chest. The big man fell over backwards. The Browning swung back toward Lilac and Daria, wavering between the two.

Skip had a split second to act before the archeologist chose his next target. His gun wavered back and forth, pointing at Lilac, then Daria, back toward Lilac, before finally stopping between the two. Stephens eyes narrowed again, his nostrils flaring along with his eyes...his finger began closing again...

"SKIP!" Lilac screamed.

Tripp Street dove in front of Daria Ahmadi as Stephens gun fired.

OLD LOVE. NEW LOVE

KUUL REACHED THE BACK CORNER OF THE CABIN AS ZING COL-lapsed. Crossing the open ground between there and his friends was impossible without meeting the same fate. He had the Colt in hand now, but there was too much traffic, too great of a chance of hitting Skip or the women. Approaching Stephens from the rear, through the woods, was a safer option, but time wasn't on his side.

He moved swiftly through the undergrowth of junipers, acacia, and red-branched manzanita. The downed cottonwoods and sycamores from the explosions provided a thick screen of cover but made the going slow.

The sun was now far below the treetops, mottling the woods with shadows. This was the time of day when he and his friend would normally be relaxing on the porch – Skip with his pink margarita and him with a cold beer. They would be listening to the soothing sights and sounds of twilight, after the afternoon winds settled. Birds flocking to the feeders, deer rustling in the underbrush, an occasional doe or buck crossing the clearing. The melodic hum of water rushing over the polished stones lining the banks of Oak Creek. Overhead, the hawks and turkey vultures would be floating in the warm spring air searching for their dinners. Hopefully, the vultures won't buffet here tonight, Kuul thought.

He crept to within a hundred feet of Stephens. His chances of ambushing him in time increasing with each carefully placed step. Stephens had all three of them under his gun. Ahmadi had dropped her pistols, and Zing was on the ground, passed out or dead. If he had to, he could shoot the archeologist in the back, but that went against his grain.

He weaved through the branches of a still smoldering cottonwood that was propped against a smaller pinon. To get within striking distance, he had to negotiate a tangle of broken limbs higher than his head. It was like passing through a cornfield after a bad storm. Snapping a branch or brushing the blackened leaves would alert Stephens.

The last section of limbs was the hardest. The farther he went, the more tangled the smaller branches became, imitating a poorly maintained thicket. Good cover, but he would have to crash through the last ten feet. He would be exposed, but the distraction would give Skip an opportunity.

Chief Hooton ruined his plan. He appeared from the front of the cabin, bellowing at Stephens. When the archeologist shot him, Kuul had no choice. He began barreling through the last of the branches, watching helplessly as Stephens turned his gun on Lilac and the Iranian woman. Kuul reached for the Colt, but it was gone, snagged by the cottonwood when he started running.

He saw an opening in the thick mess of limbs ahead. He was only steps from Stephens now. With the shouting and gunfire, he'd gone unnoticed. He dove through the opening, the prickly tips and broken nubs of the blackened tree grabbing at him, hitting Stephens in the back as he fired point-blank at Skip.

The archeologist went down hard but didn't lose hold of his gun. Kuul rolled past him.

"Fucking Indian!" Stephens yelled, rising on a knee. "This is all your fault. This vessel...this old *cup*...is going to cost you and your friends their lives!" he screamed, still holding the bag, and shaking it at Kuul.

Kuul stared at his friend. Ahmadi was holding him. He was limp in her arms. Her hands were bloody from pressing the wound in his head,. Lilac was behind Stephens inching toward him; he'd forgotten her in the heat of the moment. Kuul just needed to buy a few precious seconds.

"You have nothing but a tin camp cup," Kuul sneered.

Stephens glared at him. In the cabin, he hadn't taken the time to look inside the bag. He had felt the shape of the drinking vessel and just assumed. Truth be told, he had been afraid of there being another snake or scorpion or other wild Indian trick.

"Where is it?"

"You just shot the one person who knew."

Stephens swore, pointing the Browning, "Then it's your turn."

A foot scuffled in the dirt behind him. He twisted to fire and met Lilac William's size ten, Avenger Breaker hiking boot with reinforced toe square in the face. Inside his head it was too dark to even see stars.

"Is he alive?" Lilac asked. Her heart was breaking, Skip wasn't moving, and Daria was pressing a hole an inch above and to the right of his right eye. Blood was oozing down her hand. She feared the worst, but her mind couldn't yet imagine his being gone.

Daria looked up at her, tears trailing down the beautiful Iranian woman's cinnamon-colored cheeks. "His heart beats, but it is weak."

"He saved you."

"Stephens was going to shoot me," Daria whispered, nodding at the unconscious archeologist. She wasn't sure that was true, none of them could be. The way the man had swung his weapon back and forth, he could have been planning to first shoot the red head.

"He chose you," Lilac said. Like Daria, she was uncertain who Wood was going to shoot. But it was certain who Skip had chosen to protect. And now she might never know if he had seen something they hadn't. Had he seen Wood glance at the last second toward Daria, and then chosen her, or had he been as uncertain as them and acted out of instinct...out of love.

"I'm a mother," Daria said, not sure why, except that her son was on her mind as she wiped the blood from Tripp's face.

Lilac didn't need a genealogy chart to tell her who the father was, but the question came out anyway, "His?"

Daria was going to answer, but another police officer began calling for help. He was assisting the Chief who Stephens had shot. The big man was on his knees, breathing hard, unstrapping a vest covering his midsection.

"We've called in a medivac...twenty minutes...can he make it?" the young officer called out.

"He won't die...not now," Kuul answered.

42

SCORPION HOT

"**T**ELL ME THE SON-OF-A-BITCH IS DEAD," POTUS WHINED, from his bed in the Oval Office.

The Commander in Chief had forced his release from Walter Reed. The First Lady had absolutely refused to allow the unstylish hospital bed in the presidential apartment – it was too big and smelled; the same reasoning she used to expel POTUS from her own private suite. His one simple request was that she apply the steroid cream to his chafed groin; she'd pulled back the sheet, screamed, and flown off to Palm Beach in a huff claiming she needed five weeks in a spa to recover.

"The guide is still unconscious. The doctors are saying he will recover," the pretty, nubile HHS Special Assistant to the Director timidly answered. POTUS had fired Stinky and appointed her as his interim replacement because she looked like a seasoned ointment applicator.

"He knows too goddamned much. Don't we have someone in Arizona who can pull a plug or stick a cocktail in an IV? What about that ass-kisser I endorsed who's running for the Senate? He sure as hell owes me a favor."

"They just arrested him. He shoplifted a pint of Tequila, and the Scottsdale police caught him polishing it off outside an elementary school with an underage prostitute."

"A pint? What was the moron thinking?"

The HHS Special Assistant to the Director opened a desk drawer, taking out a tube of cortisone and a pair of surgical gloves from a half-empty carton. She'd already submitted her resume to every law firm in town and a dozen Wall Street firms. A few more weeks – surely, she could hold on for a few more weeks. The last thing she needed was to search for a job while unemployed. She'd been counting on Secretary Stinckner's recommendation, but he was busy fighting off a growing list of congressional subpoenas.

An exposé in Sedona's Red Rock News had blown the lid off POTUS's latest grift, detailing how he and Stinky were colluding with the Guatemalan dictator. The only thing keeping the HHS Special Assistant to the Director from quitting was the satisfaction of mixing Tabasco Extra Hot Scorpion Sauce with the cortisone. *And the idiot couldn't figure out why he kept getting redder.*

"Besides," the HHS Special Assistant to the Director said, snapping her gloves around her thin wrist and squeezing out an extra-large goop of cortisone and squirt of tabasco, "According to the local PD, the guide didn't have your cacao weight loss recipe. They had no idea what our investigator was even talking about. They did have enough C4, however, to wage war against Canada."

"Hell, every survival nut in Montana has a van full of that stuff. I tell you though, what pisses me off is the damn CIA losing track of the Iranian and Chinese agents. When you're done here..." POTUS smiled, lasciviously winking, "Prepare me a list of names to be the next Spook Director. I'm firing that son-of-a-bitch too."

"Why don't you use the same list we prepared for the HUD Secretary?" the HHS Special Assistant to the Director suggested – *heck, he was firing a secretary every other week now, what difference did qualifications make?* She pulled back the sheet covering the President of the United States...yup, he was ready.

"Torpedo boy's rash seems to be getting worse," POTUS grinned, anticipating her soft, gentle grip.

The HHS Special Assistant to the Director squeezed another glop of scorpion, extra-hot, tabasco-tainted ointment on her glove, grasped the presidential joystick and started the treatment. The asshole had it coming!

43

ONE MONTH LATER – FLAGSTAFF MEDICAL CENTER

AN ETERNITY OF MENTAL EXERCISING FINALLY LED SKIP TO believe the coal-black void he had been studying was the inside of his eyelids. Blackness surrounded him, but he felt comforted by his semi-consciousness. The same feeling as when he lingered in bed after a good sleep, trying to steal another hour of rest. His grandmother had appeared to him, not as a dream, but as a figure beside him, holding his hand, forgiving him for all he had done, for what he had been. His grandfather was beside her, saying he had only done what was necessary. They assured him his soul was safe. The fires of hell were for truly evil men. Both ancestors had sat patiently, promising him he would be accepted. Other people he recognized from old family photos hovered behind them. The only thing telling him he wasn't dead were the female voices coming from somewhere outside the darkness. At first, they had just been background noise, like the interminable clicking of a clock nagging him in the middle of the night.

"...against his training...operative's life...always more important...sacrifice," he heard a woman's voice say through the fog. Who was she? Not his grandmother. The lilt, the sweet but cool timber of her sound, it was familiar, but he couldn't focus.

"There is a child?" the second voice asked. The tension, twinge of anger – he knew those sounds too.

Skip slipped back into the blackness, fighting with his mind and body to regain control. The fog would lift and then slide back over him, noises from the other world sliding away with the mist. He tried focusing on his hands and then his feet, trying to move a finger or wiggle a toe, but his brain stubbornly refused any connections. Every part of his body seemed unattached. And, strangely, he didn't care. He felt no personal stake in whether his limbs responded or not. There was no will to move.

"...Barcelona...safe with–" the first voice said softly, stopping suddenly.

Skip sensed a release of pressure as if something had let go of him, left him. Was it in his hand? Had he moved a finger...or had someone or something squeezed him and then let go? With that thought, with the understanding that something from outside had crossed into his closed world, he realized his brain was awakening from its sleep. *The woman, the voice...*

"He moved, I felt him move," the soft voice said.

Who was she?

"I must go, I cannot be here when he wakes."

NO, don't leave! Skip's recovering brain screamed.

"He would make you stay," the second voice said. *There was more warmth to her tone than before.*

Daria didn't answer right away. Daria, the name had come to him slowly, the scrambled letters floating through the lifting fog. Skip had watched them in his mind as they formed a name – Daria. Was she the first woman? He tried searching his memory, but it was hazy and refused to clear. The memory of her was right before him, tantalizingly close but out of reach.

"He loves you," the second voice said, sadly.

"He belongs here now, with you. What we had was a brief reprieve from reality. It wasn't genuine. Keep him safe...please," Daria said.

The pressure on his hand released. Whoever Daria was, she had let him go. He desperately wanted to open his eyes, but the blackness refused to give up its hold. He fought harder but failed...again – failed, again – failed. Mentally, he collapsed, the exhaustion and futility of trying to move, to wake up, to think, sent him down again. His mind shut down. He fell asleep.

Lilac was there when he awoke. She was sleeping in an uncomfortable chair pulled close to his bed. His memories had flooded back. His thoughts, however, came hard and slow like they had crossed through chicken wire and needed piecing back together. It took time, but he remembered and sequenced everything – Mexico, the dying man, the damn cup, the fight with the Guatemalans at Uxmal – Zing, the zoo, the attack at Kuul's trailer, Catherwood Stephens, his cabin – Zula, Sky, he knew they were okay. And Daria. He remembered all of it, right up to his being shot. He glanced at the IV stand and the fluids feeding into his arm. He was in a hospital. His head felt like a tow truck winching a semi, grinding as it worked. How long, how long had he been out?

The clock above the door told him an hour had passed when Lilac stirred. She had been sleeping soundly. The rhythm of her breathing, the gentle rise and fall of her breasts had almost lulled him back asleep. She was wearing a sleeveless top, and her neck and the muscles in her shoulders smoothly rotated as her tanned, lean arms stretched. Her hands absently ran through her red hair before locking beneath the base of her skull. Her eyes finally opened and met his. She smiled unguardedly for a brief moment, before realizing they were both awake.

"Welcome back," she said, seizing his hand and leaning close, studying his eyes. They were dull from the medications but clear.

"How long?" His voice sounded raspy, and the sudden vibration of his vocal cords scratched and hurt.

"The doctors removed the tube a week ago after you were out of danger, and there was no fear of you not breathing on your own. You are going to be okay but getting better will take time."

Skip nodded. He heard a rustling on the other side of his bed. He had been watching Lilac so intently he hadn't looked that way. *Kuul* – another uncomfortable chair.

"A month, Kemo. You have been in an induced coma. Do you remember being shot?"

"By Stephens."

Kuul smiled, at least his memory was intact. "The doctors said it was a one in a billion shot, anything different would have killed you outright. Too many things went right...too many to be luck. The bullet came from a handgun, lower velocity, it passed through only one hemisphere, missing what the doc called "high-value real estate." It missed your major blood vessels, and it passed all the way through the right side."

"You were lucky," Lilac said, releasing him and leaning back in her chair, "Maybe it fixed a few parts,"

Kuul placed his hand on his friend's. "Not luck," he said, staring at Lilac. "If any one of those things had been different, he'd be with his ancestors, either dead or as a vegetable. His ancestors and his spirit kept him safe for a reason. That is what I believe."

Lilac rose and backed away toward the door. She wasn't the hugs and kisses type, Skip knew that. But he was alive, some kind of emotional reaction would be nice. She coolly slipped her loose hair into a ponytail, staring at him. It wasn't a look that said, 'Thank God, I almost lost him.' It was an oddly cold, serious assessment.

"I should get the nurses," she said. She started to leave, but turned back, lightly touching his bandaged skull, looking deep in his eyes, "Love never ends, does it?" With that, she walked out to the nurse's station.

Skip was confused by her sudden change, but he had been shot through the brain. Processing words was challenging enough. Reading emotions would have to come later.

"We have much to talk about, Kemo. When you are better."

"Chief Hooton?" Skip asked, the image of the police chief going down had entered his head. *At least that part was working.*

Kuul grinned, "He was wearing a vest. He's fine. Everybody is fine." Kuul paused, wondering if his friend was going to ask about the Iranian woman, but he didn't. "The President is awarding Hoot and Dickie Congressional Medals of Honor. We are both invited to the ceremony. The military services are up in arms, though. The award's reserved for acts of valor while engaged in military action. Civilians, even police, aren't eligible. POTUS is arguing they kept the nation safe from foreign agents – he says that's close enough. It's a shitstorm in D.C., Kemo."

"I'll hate missing the ceremony."

Kuul beamed, it was good having his friend back. "Humor's good for the soul, brother. Glad you still have both."

"Zing?"

"Chinese are smart – smart enough to not get shot in the head – like someone we all know. He survived. I haven't been able to verify it, but the rumor is he defected. He was in the room across the hall for one day, guarded by two blue suits, and was gone the next morning."

Kuul was still waiting for him to ask about Ahmadi. He didn't. Two nurses came into the room, the younger one radiating joy at their patient's recovery, the older one checking the monitors connected to Skip. Lilac wasn't with them.

The younger nurse, a squat, twenty-something with bright blue streaks in her blond hair and a tattoo on her arm of a bear claw, asked, "Why did Lilac leave? She's been here round-the-clock since you were airlifted in."

"Check his vitals," the older nurse instructed. "You're a lucky man, Skip Rhodes, very lucky."

Five Months Later – Uxmal. Mexico

"**S**OME THEORIZE THE MAYA BELIEVED IN REINCARNATION," Kuul Balthazar said.

Toni Wathetewa was walking close beside him, beneath the great Pyramid of the Magician. They stopped in front of the Temple of the Jaguars with its intricate carvings and colonnaded façade. The same temple where, months earlier, they had prepared to stand and fight the team of Guatemalan Presidential Guards.

Skip lagged behind. He had traded his cane for a hiking pole – it fit him better and was less conspicuous. Another few months of physical therapy and he would not need it. He had done everything but begged Lilac to join them. None of her litany of excuses for why she couldn't had held water, but she had stuck to her guns, even when asked by Toni.

"The *Popul Vuh*, our bible in a way, tells the story of the Maize God," Kuul said, speaking to his friend. "He dies and descends into the dark underworld and battles monsters for nine days. He then comes back to this world and is reborn. Reborn as a King with more powers. Your monsters are many my friend, it took you a month."

"I don't recall any monsters." Skip said. He hadn't told Kuul about the visions of his grandparents, or of his great-grandfather who had explained his own set of rules born in the trenches of WWI France.

Kuul smiled, "You wouldn't."

Skip wasn't sure what his friend meant. Did he mean he was incapable of understanding his past? Or had he battled his demons in another realm of consciousness, wrestling with them under a cloud of drugs and induced sleep, before experiencing a reawakening like the Maize God. Unlikely. He tended to agree with Lilac – he was impossibly lucky.

Kuul spoke again, sounding priestly, "Maya believe the soul and body are joined at birth. With bad sickness or injury, the two are torn apart. The soul passes to the afterlife on its way to death. During that journey, it communicates with and learns from its ancestors. If the person survives, the soul returns, and they keep those lessons in their heart."

Toni thought Kuul was wasting his time teaching Rhodes. He would have to see the dance of his ancestors and follow them in his own way. Educating him about his Spirit Being wasn't why she had returned to Mexico. She pointed toward the seminal point in their story, the House of the Turtles, where they had encountered Gabor Cocom.

"It's in there?"

"It never left," Skip answered.

They made their way through the ball court and crossed the field of grass to the House of the Turtles. The sun was high overhead, and the room was darker than they remembered. Before, rays of sunlight flooded through openings, spotlighting dancing dust mites. Now, the room was full of shadows, hiding the niches and cracks in the ancient stones. Except for one circle of light shining through a hole in the roof.

They gathered around the space where Kuul had held the Mayan man as he died. Where Gabor, with his last breath, had seen Kuul's soul and trusted him with the Mayan secret.

"Be with the gods, Brave Man Who Listens," Kuul said reverently.

"Maya people acknowledge seven dimensions," he said, his voice deepened by the sacred surroundings. "East, North, West, South, but also Above, Below, and Center. The Center is our personal being, our inner world. They have a prayer to signify new beginnings, new life. Some say we are praying *to* the directions for their help – others believe we are calling *ourselves* to the directions:

"From the East, House of Light
May wisdom dawn in us
So we may see all things in clarity.

From the North, House of the Night
May wisdom ripen in us
So we may know all from within.

From the West, House of Change
May wisdom be transformed into right action
So we may do what must be done.

From the South, House of the Sun
May right action reap the harvest
So we may enjoy the fruits of planetary being.

From Above, House of Heaven
Where star people and ancestors gather
May their blessings come to us now.

From Below, House of Earth
May the heartbeat of the crystal core
Bless us with harmony to end our fight.

From the Center, our inner world
Which is everywhere at once

> May everything be known
> As the light of mutual love.
>
> *Yum Hunab Ku Evam Maya E Ma Ho*
> Hail the harmony of mind and nature."

"The prayer is familiar," Toni said, recognizing parts of the chant. "Similar versions are used during Medicine Wheel and Circle of Life ceremonies."

Kuul smiled, prayers honoring the heavens and the earth were universal among Native Peoples. His Mayan ancestors weren't the first nor would they be the last to believe man was a part of nature, a part of an all-encompassing whole, no different no less than the wind, the stars, and the waters. Everyone had a role. Everything had a place.

Skip stepped into a dark corner, tracing his hand over the far wall of the room, feeling for the loose stone he had stuck in place months earlier. He found the sliver of wood he had wedged in the crack and left as a marker. A marker only he would be able to find. He wiggled the wood loose and removed the stone. Behind was a dead space, the Mayan vessel Gabor Cocom had died protecting was inside. It had been waiting patiently in the House of the Turtles to be found again...the Red Queen's cup had never made the trip to Merida or Sedona. It had never left the homeland of the Maya.

"You and I will return it to Palenque to *Tz'aakb'u*," Kuul said to Toni. "One queen to another."

"Another of your journeys," she laughed.

"But not before we copy the chocolate recipe," Skip added.

Epilogue: Viva! Las Vegas!

HERNANDO GOMEZ MARVELED AT THE BRIGHT LIGHTS, SHINY yellow Lamborghinis, and beautiful showgirls parading outside the Venetian Palace. The Vegas Strip! The glamour, the money, the opportunities, the freedom.

"I told you Chuuy! Did I not tell you this would happen? We should ride that golden gondola and give thanks to the FBI. This is a place where men such as us, Chuuy, can spread our wings. America is the land of milk and honey, and we are here to drink it all," Gomez exclaimed, slapping his old Sergeant on the back.

"I did not care for the thirty-dollar pancakes," Chuuy grumbled. He missed his corrugated metal home in Guatemala City. The tiny television in the crummy hotel room where they were staying didn't even have Netflix. He didn't know what was happening to the Narcos in Mexico.

Gomez and his grumpy brother-in-law had spent the past few months in an FBI safe house in Fredericksburg, Maryland, spilling their guts. The CIA had been excited over the firsthand intelligence on Colon, his regime, its paramilitary capacity, and their secret Russian advisers. The DEA had interviewed them, convinced of the role of Guatemalan gangs in transporting drugs and criminals across the U.S. southern border. A Treasury agent had questioned them for days about their knowledge of Colon's laundering activities. Chuuy had sworn it was done in huge vats by street women. But it was the FBI and Justice Department lawyers who spent the most time with them, poking at the connections between Colon and their own bombastic Commander in Chief. The well-dressed, well-groomed agents had taken copious notes, smiling at every revelation about the presidents' illegal attempts to acquire the Mayan vessel. In the end, they had released both men in Vegas – Hernando's choice – and given them each *five thousand* American dollars.

"Do not worry about the lousy pancakes, Chuuy! You think too small. We can soon turn our American windfall into enough money for me to bring Gabriella here and for you to find your own woman. In Las Vegas, the fools give fortunes away – money pours from machines with pictures of wild bulls and juicy cherries. We have found the promised land, brother-in-law – I promise you."

"I have a surprise for you, Hernando," Chuuy grinned.

"For me, Chuuy?"

"*Sí*. I used our payments from the FBI."

A chorus of "Papa, Papa, Papa," erupted from behind the two men. Chuuy was smiling from ear-to-ear. "It is Lupe and your *niños*," Chuuy clapped, jumping with joy. "Even those who look like Fernando. And he is here, with Lupe, who wanted him to accompany her on their travels."

"Ohhhh, Chuuy," Gomez groaned.

AUTHOR NOTES

MAYAN HISTORY, ASTRONOMY, COSMOLOGY, AND RELIGION ARE presented as accurately as possible. Because of their obscurity and the fact that new discoveries are being made every year, there are often competing theories and interpretations of what the ancient Maya believed and practiced. I encourage the reader to visit their land and to further explore their remarkable civilization. *Chichén Itza* and *Uxmál*, place settings in the book, are also presented as accurately as possible. The structures mentioned and discussed can be visited today. Literary license may have been exercised with a step here or there, or a detailed description of a room.

A note on the tone of this book. It is meant to be a farce, the plot providing context for what is in essence a story of personal relationships and growth of Sedona Chi characters.

My apologies to any readers who may think they recognize POTUS. He is a fictional character and not meant to suggest any past, present, living, or dead President. Any similarities are purely coincidental. That any such character could be elected is, of course, beyond belief. The American electorate is far too wise.

TO RECEIVE NOTICE OF FUTURE RELEASES AND AUTHOR EVENTS
SUBSCRIBE TO MY WEBSITE AND BLOG AT:

www.SedonaChi.com

There are links to the first two books in the Sedona Chi Mystery series, *Tale of the Broken Spoke* and *Whitewater Honeymoon*. In Broken Spoke, Skip, Kuul, and Lilac solve the cold case murder of a mountain biker and get tangled up in the shadowy world of antiquity trafficking. In Whitewater, they find themselves escorting a wealthy woman and her scandalous movie star daughter while retracing the steps of a 1928 honeymoon couple who rafted the Colorado River. And be on the lookout for the next Sedona Chi Mystery. Word on the street has it Skip may be visiting Barcelona, Spain while an older story unfolds here in Arizona.

Most importantly, I enjoy feedback from my readers. You can contact me through my author website, www.SedonaChi.com.

AND PLEASE LEAVE A REVIEW ONLINE AT WHEREVER YOU PURCHASE.